Alex Connor writes conspiracy thrillers set in the art world. She is a working artist, art historian and FRSA.

Also by Alex Connor

Isle of the Dead
Memory of Bones
Legacy of Blood
The Rembrandt Secret

THE CARAVAGGIO CONSPIRACY

ALEX CONNOR

Quercus

First published in Great Britain in 2014 by

Quercus Editions Ltd
55 Baker Street
7th Floor, South Block
London W1U 8EW

A CIP catalogue record for this book is available from the British Library

PB ISBN 978 1 78206 504 3
EBOOK ISBN 978 1 78206 505 0

10 9 8 7 6 5 4 3 2

Printed and bound in Great Britain by Clays Ltd, St Ives plc

Typeset by Ellipsis Digital Limited, Glasgow

Michelangelo Merisi da Caravaggio
was expelled from the Order of the Knights
of St John, Malta, August, 1608.

His crime was never recorded, but he was
referred to as a 'rotten and fetid limb'.

So began his life on the run.

His great Sicilian altarpieces isolate
their shadowy, pitifully poor figures in
vast areas of darkness . . .

Langdon, Helen, *Caravaggio: A Life*

'PORTRAIT OF CARAVAGGIO'
Copied by the author from a contemporary sketch

'DAVID WITH THE HEAD OF GOLIATH' BY CARAVAGGIO

Copied by the author from the original painting

'LUCA MERISS WITH CARAVAGGIO'S STOLEN "NATIVITY"'

Original painting by the author. Oil on Canvas

Prologue

Naples, Italy
Early 1610

Silence.

Hold your breath.

Listen.

He is shrinking back into the shadow of the doorway, out of the spread of the torchlight as his pursuer stands at the mouth of the alley, holding the light aloft.

He can't have lost him.

He hit him. Surely.

He could feel the knife judder against the man's jawbone.

He hit him.

But how badly?

Enough to kill?

Cautiously, the attacker moves forward on the uneven street as his victim flattens himself against the door, pressing his body into the shadow of the porch. Scarcely breathing, he watches as the light comes closer, and then pauses only yards away. He can smell the smoke, see the shimmer of illumination rise and fall as his attacker lifts and lowers his light. And then he takes another step forward – and stops.

Listening.

There are only yards between them. In the doorway, Michelangelo Merisi, known as the painter Caravaggio, is hiding, wounded. Reaching up, he can feel the violence of the attack, the slashing of flesh from the outer corner of his eye, down his cheek to his jawbone. But missing the artery.

He breathes in. So softly, hardly making a sound in his own lungs. If he can escape, he can survive. Disfigured, but alive. He can feel the blood running into his shirt, the night air burning into the open wound.

His attacker is pausing, only twelve feet away.

Rigid, Caravaggio realises that one breath, one twitch, one muscle flicker will give him away. The silence is so complete, so absolute, that any noise will betray him as readily as cannon fire. And then he feels it. The first trickle of blood running from his jawline, down his chest, towards his arm. He tenses. The blood, sticky and treacherous, slides down to his wrist, then crosses his palm. For an inexplicable instant it seems to pause, lingering at the tips of his fingers for an eternity before, finally, losing its hold.

And dripping, loud as a pistol shot, onto the ground at his feet.

Monday

One

Cork Street, London
January 2014, 8.36 a.m.

The police had cordoned off the area with yellow tape, closed both ends of the street to prevent any traffic entering or leaving. An ambulance, its siren muted, was parked at the entrance of The Weir Gallery and two police officers stood guard at the door.

It was seven thirty on a winter's morning. Sleet was making the capital's streets unwelcoming, a mordant sky promising a fitful, chilly, January day. But inside the gallery, where the heating had been turned up to the maximum, over a hundred degrees, a distraught man was sitting with his head in his hands by the stairs that led to the downstairs gallery.

'Jacob?'

Hearing his name, he looked up. 'Gil. Thanks for coming.'

He stared at the thickset man standing in front of him. Wiry dark hair, nose broken from a fight in his teens, stevedore's hands. Not the kind of man anyone would expect to see in an art gallery.

'You were the only person I could turn to . . .' His eyes moved towards the back of the main gallery, where a partition screen had been pulled across. 'I was going to call the police straight after I'd phoned you – but Oscar beat me to it.'

The name resonated in Gil's head. Relax, he thought. There are a lot of men called Oscar. But he knew before asking which Oscar this would be.

'He was here until a few minutes ago. You just missed him. I need you to help me. I need you to take on the case.' When Gil didn't reply, Jacob hurried on. 'The police won't let me leave. Surely they can't think I had anything to do with it?'

'They want to talk to you because you found the bodies,' Gil said, sitting on the steps next to the dealer. 'They just want to ask some questions.' He felt in his inside pocket and then remembered that he didn't smoke any more. Hadn't smoked for over seven years. Since Berlin. 'How did Oscar find out what had happened?'

'I don't know. He didn't say. You know Oscar, always in on everything.'

As he talked, Gil noticed the smell of alcohol on Jacob's breath. At 8.45 in the morning? Jacob Levens had been a heavy drinker for a long time, but the previous year ill health had forced him to give up. Supposedly.

'Why were you here, Jacob?'

'We had a breakfast meeting at eight. I was early, but the

door was unlocked and so I walked in. The lights were on, so was the heating–'

'You're not kidding. It must be over a hundred degrees in here. Why doesn't someone lower the thermostat?'

'I was going to, but we can't touch anything.'

Gil watched the tableau that was taking shape at the end of the gallery. Old memories, unpleasant and unwanted, forced themselves on him.

'I haven't been here for a long time.'

'I'm surprised the police let you in–'

Gil shrugged. 'I know the officer on duty.'

'Still got influence?'

'I hope not.'

He glanced at Jacob – the man who had hired him many times, and over the years had become a friend. The man who had stood by him after the death of his first wife and introduced him to his second. The man Gil liked, admired, even though his weaknesses were common knowledge. But friendship only went so far. Now Jacob Levens was calling Gil back to the world he had rejected. And if it had been anyone other than Jacob he would have refused.

'I'll be back in a minute,' Gil told him, as he moved towards the partition.

The officer who had let him into the gallery was talking to a detective, another man familiar to Gil. Detective Phil Simmons, around forty, with bags under his eyes and an angry rash running from his neck up to his forehead. Seeing Gil, Simmons gestured for him to approach.

Gil hesitated.

No, he thought. If I walk behind this screen, I'm involved. I'm back where I used to be, investigating the art world, down in the midden with the crooks and the grandees who pose as honest men. Among the money men who manipulate them all. If I go behind the screen I go back to my other life. Before I met Bette. Do I really want to risk the future by revisiting a past I despised?

Well, do I?

'I thought you'd given all of this up,' Simmons said, again beckoning for Gil to come forward. 'Seem to remember that you swore off the investigating work.' He scratched at his blotchy skin. 'Heard you were a researcher now.'

'I am.'

'So why are you here?'

'Jacob called me in. He's a friend.'

Simmons glanced over his shoulder towards the dealer. 'He found the bodies.'

'Yeah. He said.'

'You know you've put on weight?' Simmons remarked, grinning.

'I got married again.'

'She can obviously cook.'

'We're having a baby.'

'Are you carrying it?'

To his surprise, Gil laughed, slipping back into the old informality.

'You ready?' Simmons asked, jerking his head to indicate that Gil could walk behind the partition.

And *still* he hesitated.

'Come on!' Simmons barked. 'I haven't got all bloody day.'

The Weir brothers were obviously dead. Sitting, stripped naked, back to back, their necks bound together with picture wire. Their legs had been bent into the yoga lotus position, their genitals exposed, their scrotums bloodied, punctured by deep, lacerating wounds.

'Nail gun,' Simmons said, pointing to the discarded tool lying only inches from Sebastian Weir's left foot. 'Tortured. Both of them.'

Gil stared at the brothers, at the twins who had been preeminent on the London art scene for over a decade. Two successful dealers, skin white as coconut milk, hair bleached blond. Vicious and generous by turns. Never seen apart. Not even dead.

'Oh, shit,' Simmons said suddenly, leaning down towards the brothers and staring into their bloated faces. He glanced over to the pathologist who was examining the bodies. 'Is that what I think it is?'

Dunning paused. 'I don't know. What d'you think it is?'

'Around the mouth. Is that–'

'Rabbit size glue,' Gil interrupted.

'Thank God. I thought it was semen,' Simmons replied. 'What's "rabbit size glue"?'

'A mixture used to prepare canvases. It goes on first, before the canvas is primed.'

'So why put it in their mouths?'

'Search me,' Gil replied, still staring at the corpses,

wondering when Dunning – or Simmons – would notice what he had seen at once. What he hadn't wanted to see, because he knew what it meant.

'Come on,' Simmons urged the pathologist. 'What killed them?'

Dunning looked like a kid in a man's suit. Ignoring the detective, he reached out his gloved hand and touched the bloodied head of Benjamin Weir, then frowned as the scalp moved, slipping forward over the victim's face, exposing the skull.

Gil took in a breath and Simmons glanced at him.

'What? You want to say something. What is it?'

'Sebastian will have been scalped too.'

The pathologist touched the head of the second corpse, and then nodded.

Curious, Simmons glanced back to Gil. 'How did you know?'

'I've seen it before.'

'Anything else you want to tell me?'

'Only that the killer will have swapped the scalps. Benjamin will have Sebastian's scalp, and Sebastian, Benjamin's.'

Two

He was back in the past without realising it. Back in time seven years to a case he had been working on. Not in London – this time it was Berlin. An eminent art dealer, Terrill Huber, had been found in a storage facility naked, bound with picture wire, his genitals mutilated with a nail gun, rabbit skin glue in his mouth. And he had been scalped. An hour later his wife, Alma, was found naked and bound in their gallery on the Friedrichstrasse, also scalped. Her breasts were spotted by wounds from a nail gun and rabbit skin glue had been poured into her mouth after death.

What had given the events a hideous comedic slant was that fact that the husband was wearing his wife's scalp and she was wearing his. The sight of a pot-bellied, ageing man lying disfigured and bloodied had been made ridiculous by the topping of his wife's dyed hair. It had added a cruel, morbidly vicious touch. As for the wife, she had been slumped against the gallery's inner office door, her husband's bloodied bald pate crowning her beautiful face.

The image had never left Gil. It had remained lodged in

his psyche. And for all his investigations – and those of the Berlin police – the killer was never found.

Two months later Gil's own wife was dead.

Grieving, he had given up his investigative work. Had gone into research instead, hired by writers to help with their books. The subjects varied: crime, the art world, even sport. But that suited Gil. He snuggled down into words, took comfort in a lullaby of facts, all the time knowing that it had been an accident, a fluke which had killed Holly. A set of traffic lights malfunctioning. Sticking on green when they should have changed to red. So that the car coming towards her didn't expect Holly's vehicle – and couldn't avoid it in time.

'Were they gay?'

Drawn back to the present, Gil shook his head and glanced over to Simmons. 'No.'

'You sure?'

'Yeah. They were asexual. Advertised the fact. They'd been celibate for years.'

Both men watched as the corpses were lifted into body bags, put onto stretchers, and wheeled out. A group of onlookers had already gathered around the gallery entrance, the slam of the ambulance doors echoing in the dead morning.

'You said you'd seen something like this before.' Simmons glanced over to Gil. 'Where?'

'Berlin. I was called in on the case, but I had no luck. Neither did the police. I thought I was close to him once, but didn't get him.'

'When was this?'

'2007.'

Preoccupied, Simmons scratched at his neck, Gil watching him.

'How d'you get that rash?'

'I won it in a raffle,' Simmons replied drily. 'The doctor said it was something I ate. I've tried three different creams, but nothing works.' Still raking at his neck with his nails, he turned back to Gil. 'Were there other similarities, apart from the scalping?'

'The other victims were naked too. And the man's genitals had been mutilated.'

'*The man's?*'

'Last time it was a man and a woman,' Gil explained. 'Husband and wife. The woman's breasts were mutilated.'

'What about the rabbit shit?'

'Rabbit skin glue. There was some in both of the victim's mouths.'

Simmons raised his eyebrows. 'And the scalps were swapped?'

'Yes. Their bodies were found in different locations. The killer took the husband's scalp all the way across Berlin.'

'Where he then stuck it on the wife's head? *After* he'd scalped her?'

Gil nodded.

'And then he crossed Berlin again *with her scalp* to put it on her husband's head?' Simmons paused. 'So he killed the husband first?'

'Yes.'

'Why did he scalp them?'

'We never found out, because we never found him.'

'And now the Weir brothers have been murdered the same way. Same killer?'

'Maybe.' Gil shrugged. 'I don't know what's been going on for the last seven years. I'm out of touch. Perhaps there have been other murders like this–'

'Not in London.'

'Well, maybe you should check out what's been going on in Germany. And everywhere else, if it comes to that.' Gil sighed. 'Look, it was a long time ago, when I used to do this for a living.'

'You're doing it now–'

'No. I only came because Jacob called me. I'm not directly involved.'

'But you know I've got to ask you about Berlin, don't you?'

Gil nodded. 'Yes. But if I help you, you have to help me. Give me access to the pathologist, to your witness statements – the usual. I'm discreet, you know that. You can trust me.'

Simmons put his head on one side. 'So you *are* taking the case?'

'I'll have a quick look at it for Jacob. But I'm not getting caught up again. I'm retired, remember?'

'Oh, I remember,' Simmons replied, pointing across the gallery to where Jacob Levens was still sitting. 'Question is, does he?'

Three

Berlin, Germany
9.30 a.m.

He was using straighteners, because he hated the way his hair crinkled up. Liked it to look groomed. Not like coarse, peasant hair. Still, he thought with pleasure, it was a luscious head of hair for a man over forty. Leaning towards the mirror Luca then studied his teeth, checking there was no plaque, no irritating reminder of a rushed lunch.

The only part of his face he truly liked were his eyes. Dark brown, but not welcoming. Hard. Compelling. At times inviting, at other times cold. Rough trade eyes . . . His gaze moved down to the waiter's uniform he was wearing. An outfit soaked in resentment, sticky with humiliation. Everything that a customer thought was in their eyes: words were irrelevant. Their expression said it all as they looked at him: *man nudging middle age, waiting on tables. Trying to be pleasant and obsequious instead. An outsider, with his slicked-down Mediterranean hair and rent boy lips. Overblown, slipping out of his good looks and youth . . .*

Yes, Luca thought. I know how you see me.

But not for much longer.

Breathing in, he relaxed. Everything was in place at last. Within hours he would launch himself on the internet. He would also contact the papers, magazines, radio and television, and begin his blog. Facebook and Twitter were poised like greyhounds in the slips, ready to run.

He had the name, after all. A name that was famous and, more importantly, infamous. The name of a painter who was also a murderer. Of course Luca knew that people might not believe him. Might never accept that he was a descendant of Caravaggio and the notorious Roman prostitute Fillide Melandroni. But he was prepared for that. Prepared for people to scoff and think him a madman.

He knew better. He knew his bloodline, and what it meant. How it carried a secret. How he was the only man alive who knew the whereabouts of Fillide Melandroni's portrait, long thought destroyed. But that wasn't all. Luca also knew the hiding place of the most famous missing painting in the art world – *The Nativity with St Lawrence and St Francis*, stolen from Palermo, Sicily, in 1969. Allegedly by the Mafia.

The portrait of Fillide was believed to have been destroyed in Germany in 1945. *The Nativity* had been missing since 1969. Although both works were valuable, *The Nativity* was a legend. Too famous to be sold on, too valuable to be destroyed.

In hiding.

As he had been.

Waiting.

Of course when he went public Luca Meriss knew that he would be setting himself up as a target, and not just for abuse. Revealing the portrait would be a coup. Its history was extraordinary, likely to catch the interest of the world. Luca wanted that. Fillide Melandroni was his ancestor: a beautiful, violent whore whose image shimmered out of many of Caravaggio's paintings. Who wouldn't want to own it? But *The Nativity* would stagger the art world. A painting valued at more than £60,000,000 would incite interest and greed across the globe. Every collector, gallery, connoisseur – and villain – would want it.

But only *he* knew its whereabouts. Only Luca Meriss. Anyone who wanted it had to come to him. And if anything happened to him? It would be lost forever.

As guarantees went, it was irrefutable.

Four

London

Bette had been watching her husband from the doorway for several minutes. Knew the look. The same look Gil had worn when he told her about the death of his first wife – the clever, enigmatic Holly, of whom she was still jealous. The same look he had before when he was talking about his previous life and work. When he had mentioned the murder case in Berlin.

Sensing her presence, Gil looked up. 'Did I wake you?'

'No.' She glanced at the clock. 'Where were you? I woke up and you were gone.'

'Jacob Levens called me. He had a problem.'

'What kind of problem?'

He didn't want to tell her – not now, when she was only weeks from giving birth.

'What happened, Gil?'

'There's been a double murder. The Weir twins. Jacob found the bodies.'

'Jesus.'

'He's in a bad way.'

Bette sat down at the table, thinking of Jacob Levens. It had been summer a few years earlier and Bette had been working in the fashion business. A business in which she had failed dismally. On an impulsive gesture she had fled Milan and come to London, staying with her divorced mother. Which was something else Bette failed at. Two strong characters, they had clashed and before long Bette had been desperate to get a job and rent her own flat.

At the same time Jacob Levens had been deserted by his long-time receptionist and, with an exhibition imminent, was frantic to fill the post. So when Bette applied to work at Jacob's gallery, he took her on. Stylish, intelligent and a quick learner, she was exactly what he needed. The bonus was that she found a father figure, and Jacob a surrogate daughter. She was sparky enough to keep him on his toes, his irritation flagging in the face of her indifference. And when he drank, it was Bette who moved the bottles that Jacob thought he had hidden so furtively.

She had looked after him because he had no one else. And Jacob had returned the favour by introducing her to Gil Eckhart.

'You have to help him,' Bette said, putting her hand over her husband's. 'He needs you.'

'I'm not doing investigations any more. I swore off it, you know that.'

Pausing, Gil wondered how much to confide. He had told

Bette that the Weir brothers had been murdered, nothing else. And he hadn't mentioned the similarities between their killings and the ones in Berlin seven years earlier. He didn't want to tell her that. Didn't want to put it into words, shake it loose again.

She stared at Gil curiously. 'The police don't suspect Jacob, do they?'

'No. But it would have been a hell of a shock for him to find them like that.' Gil was lying, trying to avoid giving her any more information. 'Maybe Jacob overreacted. Maybe he doesn't really need me. The police can handle it.'

'I'm pregnant, not stupid!' Bette snapped. 'I hate it when you keep things from me.'

'I'm not keeping anything from you.'

'You are, Gil! Tell me what's going on.'

He hesitated.

'Gil, what is it?'

'You remember the case in Berlin I told you about? The murders of Alma and Terrill Huber?'

She was beginning to understand. 'Yes, I remember.'

'The Weir brothers were killed in the same way.' He stared at her, held her gaze. '*Don't* ask me for details.'

She wasn't about to. 'So the police will want to talk to you about the Berlin murders?'

'They already have. The detective in charge – Phil Simmons – was at The Weir Gallery when I got there. We talked and then he called me back. He'd been looking into the Berlin case and wanted to go over some details.'

'Does Simmons think it's the same killer?'

Gil didn't reply.

'The killer no one caught?'

'Let it drop, Bette. I'll sort it out. It'll all be over by this afternoon.'

She wasn't about to be brushed off. 'But if it *was* the same man, where's he been for seven years?'

'Abroad. In prison. Hospitalised. Who knows?'

In that instant Bette realised that their life might be threatened, shuddering under some sudden malignant force.

Immediately Gil picked up on her anxiety. 'Look, the police will just ask me some more questions and that'll be it.'

He smiled at her, but she didn't respond. Instead she huddled into herself, folding her arms across her pregnant stomach. She could feel the baby moving inside her, restless, unnerved. Like she was. There were only a few weeks left of her pregnancy. Why couldn't Jacob Levens have called in someone else? Why Gil? She owed the dealer her happiness, Bette knew that, but she was suddenly afraid. She didn't want the stink of torture and murder coming into her home. Didn't want her husband back in the life he had hated. She wanted Gil to be painting the nursery with her, counting down the last weeks of her pregnancy with her. Not travelling, not mixing with criminals, not talking to the police, not reliving the past. Not going back to Berlin. To his old life. To the memory of his first wife.

'You're retired. Jacob knows that.' She paused, staring at

her husband. 'Anyway, why you? Why does Jacob want *you* to investigate?'

He was trying to dodge the questions, to field the truth. 'I've worked for him before, on other cases.'

'That was years ago.'

'Maybe so, but Jacob knows me, trusts me.'

She shook her head.

'No, there's more to it. Like you said, he just found the bodies. So why the need to drag you in?' She paused, holding her husband's gaze. '*Why do these murders matter so much to Jacob Levens?*'

'I don't know.'

'Yes, you do! Tell me.'

He paused, then answered her. 'Alma Huber was his sister.'

Five

New York
3.30 a.m.

'Hello? Hello? Is there anyone down there?'

Catrina Hoyt paused, listening. It was still dark, dawn slow to show its face. Always a bad sleeper, she had woken to some sound she couldn't place. Certainly loud enough to permeate the double-glazed windows. Turning over, she had listened for a moment. But apart from the endless siren and cab horns that embroider every New Yorker's sleep, there had been nothing unusual.

Then she heard another sound coming from inside the building, and jumped out of bed. Groping in the drawer of the bedside table, she pulled out a hand gun, gripping it tightly as she moved downstairs. The apartment steps were separate from the main building and ran behind the alarmed gallery area. Catrina made for the basement door.

Flicking the safety catch off her gun, she opened the door and pushed it back with her foot. But when she turned on the light switch, nothing happened. Then she heard another noise coming from the basement. A noise that seemed as though someone intended to be heard. Spooked, Catrina put out her left hand, took the torch from the back of the cellar door, and shone its light down into the darkness.

Silence.

She wasn't afraid.

She could handle herself.

Besides, Catrina was five foot eleven, muscular and naturally aggressive. If someone had broken into her gallery, she was going to take them on. It wasn't the first break-in she had had. Slowly, purposefully, she descended the first few steps.

A noise.

A shuffling.

She paused halfway down the steps, shining the torchlight around the cellar below. Packing crates were stacked against the walls, some propped up like coffins, others gaping open like the mouths of timber giants. Scanning the area, the torch beam picked out the workbenches on which the paintings were packed for shipment, and, next to them, the other benches where the pictures were unpacked, ready for exhibition.

In the furthest corner, the solemn red eye of an alarm sensor blinked. *Someone had walked past it.* Catrina swung the torch, but whoever had tripped the sensor had moved out of its orbit again. Unnerved, she moved the light around, trying to catch sight of whatever was down there.

The red light flicked on again.

And off.

She could hear movement, only yards to her right.

She swung the torch round.

Nothing there.

Then the noise moved to her left.

Again, she swung the light in its direction.

Again, nothing.

Then she heard the unmistakable sound of footsteps just behind her.

Six

Hampstead, London
1.00 p.m.

Jacob Levens was in the sitting room of his flat, staring apologetically at Gil.

'I shouldn't have called you. Not this morning, and not just now. I don't know why. I didn't think. I'm sorry.'

Jacob shrugged. He was nursing a whisky, making no attempt to hide it. And it obviously wasn't his first drink either. He was, as ever, immaculate. Portly, yes, but carrying his excess weight as though he had paid good money for it.

He gestured to the chaos around him. 'Someone broke in. Wrecked the place.'

'Have you called the police?'

'No.'

'You have to call them, Jacob–'

'You think this is related to the Weir murders?'

'Maybe. Have you touched anything?'

'No.'

He looked at Gil, reassured by his calmness. If truth were told, he had missed him. Like everyone else, Jacob could understand Gil Eckhart's exile and his grief over the terrible and unexpected death of his first wife – but he had still missed him.

Life had gone on for both of them – phone calls exchanged a few times a year, a note in a card at Christmas, but no meetings. Widowed for many years, Jacob's whole focus had become centred on the gallery. He enjoyed the company of other dealers, but mistrust abounded in a business that relied on competition and luck. On the finding of a *sleeper* – an unknown masterpiece – or the successful bidding for an important lot at auction. It was a cultured environment but it had a venomous heart, and Gil Eckhart had known that.

They had met when Jacob had hired him to investigate a theft at the gallery years earlier. His appearance had come as a surprise to Jacob, who had not expected to find a cultured intelligence inside a bruiser's body. Physically strong, Gil had honed his fitness in sports, running every day wherever he happened to be. It was, he told Jacob once, the best way to get to know a city. But Gil was less forthcoming on how he had become an investigator. He said only that he had been in the police force briefly, and then worked in security in the Far East. Jacob's best guess was as a bodyguard, but Gil never confirmed it, and surprised his friend again when he let slip mention of a degree in Fine Art.

Such a conundrum, Jacob thought, relieved that Gil was back in his life again.

'Why would someone do this?'

Jacob shrugged.

'Anything missing?'

'Not that I can see. I don't have anything expensive in the flat anyway. The valuable stuff's in the gallery. There's nothing worth taking here.'

'Is the gallery OK?'

'It must be. The alarm hasn't gone off or the police would have contacted me.' Jacob paused, nervy. 'I was out for lunch, but I could have been home when this happened.'

'No, I don't think they were after you. Just giving you a scare,' Gil remarked, looking at the man he had known for over fifteen years. 'I had to tell Bette the truth,' he added, 'otherwise she wouldn't understand why I agreed to help you.'

'You didn't tell her everything?'

Gil gave him a steady look.

'She's heavily pregnant. There's only so much I want her to know. I left some things out, but I told her you were connected to the murders in Berlin seven years ago. Told her that Alma Huber was your sister.' He paused, watching the words take effect. 'But not the rest. Not the details of *how* Alma was murdered.'

Jacob was fiddling with his shirt cuffs, trying to hold on to himself.

'I was *supposed* to find the Weir brothers, wasn't I?'

'I don't know, Jacob. Were you?'

He nodded. 'It was set up for me to find them. For me to

see them, to know it was the same person who'd killed my sister. I'll never forget seeing her body in the morgue. Never forget what was done to her.' He paused, repeating the words emphatically. '*I was supposed to find the Weir brothers*.'

'Why?'

'I don't know.'

Gil kept staring at the dealer.

'Nothing was taken from your sister's gallery seven years ago. Apparently nothing was stolen from The Weir Gallery this morning. And now this.' He looked around at the mess. 'Again nothing taken. So if it wasn't robbery, what was the motive?'

Jacob shrugged.

'When you arrived for your meeting with the Weirs, did you notice anything unusual? Was there anyone hanging around the gallery? Any cars parked nearby?'

'I don't think so. I didn't notice anything out of the ordinary, but then I wasn't looking for anything out of the ordinary,' Jacob replied testily. 'I'm not good in the mornings.'

'Not when you drink, you're not.'

He took the comment full on, flushing. 'I've been under a lot of pressure lately—'

'Were you hungover?'

'No. Yes, a bit,' Jacob admitted. 'I phoned them to cry off the meeting, but they didn't answer and I had to go.'

'When did you call them?' Gil asked.

'About seven.'

'Did you leave a message?'

'I couldn't. There was no voicemail.'

'Really?' Gil said. 'That's unusual for a business. Or did you call them on their private line?'

'I don't have their private line number. I called the gallery phone.'

Gil nodded. 'So when you couldn't get hold of them you had to keep the appointment. What time did you arrive?'

'I've told you, just before eight.'

'Was the door locked?'

Jacob was getting flustered. 'Open, or I couldn't have got in, could I?'

'You went in by the front door?'

'Yes.'

'Was the lock forced?'

Jacob thought for a moment. 'No. It was just unlocked, like it is in the daytime. The buzzer sounded when I walked in and I called out to them, but no one answered. It was so hot in there—'

'What was the meeting about?'

'Some Guercino drawings. Sebastian had bought a couple in Japan and wanted to know what I thought of them.'

'At eight o clock in the morning?'

'They were early risers, liked to have meetings before they opened the gallery for the day.'

'What about the flat over the gallery? How long had they lived there?'

'Twenty years,' Jacob replied. 'They were a unit. They

lived and worked in the same building, entertained their clients there, had had the same staff for years.'

'The police have already checked out the staff – they all had alibis.'

'*Of course they did!*' Jacob snapped. 'Whoever did this was a lunatic. The same lunatic that killed my sister.'

'Did Alma know the Weir brothers?'

Jacob paused. His hands were agitated, his mouth dry, aching for a drink.

'She dealt with them on and off. But mostly we knew different people. Alma lived in Berlin all her life. I married an English girl and hardly ever went back to Germany. Only to visit. I don't know how much Alma dealt with the Weir twins.'

'But *if* the same man killed them then they must have had some connection,' Gil persisted. 'Both the Weirs and your sister dealt in Italian art?'

Jacob nodded. 'Yes, but Alma preferred the Baroque period to the Renaissance. She always wanted to handle the big names. She once bid for a Gentileschi painting, but she didn't get it.'

'What was she dealing in when she died?'

'*We went through this seven years ago.*'

'And we have to go through it again,' Gil replied firmly. 'What was Alma handling when she died?'

'Nothing important. Still life, mostly. Her husband had had a heart attack and they were taking it easy. I don't know if she had any new exhibitions planned. I don't remember–'

'Concentrate.'

'It was seven years ago!'

Gil's irritation was obvious.

'You asked for my help and I'm helping. But you have to help me. You don't want to go back seven years? Well, neither do I. You lost your sister back then. I lost my wife. I've spent seven years building my life back up and you're asking me to risk it all again?' He leaned towards him. 'Well, I will, Jacob, because I owe you.'

'You don't owe me anything.'

'We both know that's not true,' Gil replied dismissively. 'I *do* owe you and we *are* friends. But you have to work with me, you hear? Because this isn't just your past we're talking about. And it sure as hell isn't just your future.'

Seven

New York
7.00 a.m.

Shaking, Catrina sat down at her desk. Not that she would have admitted it to anyone, but she was rattled. The bastard who had broken into her basement had escaped, but not before he had touched her on the shoulder. Mocking her. Showing her that he was smarter, quicker. That he could have stabbed her as easily as he had touched her.

Suddenly her mobile rang. 'We should talk.'

She could tell at once that the voice was distorted. The caller was using a device to disguise himself.

'Was it you in my fucking basement?'

'I was having a look around. I was surprised you came down on your own, but then you're pretty tough, aren't you? You look tough.'

Her voice was contemptuous. 'I had a gun. I could have blown your fucking head off.'

'You couldn't even see me!'

They both knew that was true.

'I've called the police.'

'Ms Hoyt, you're lying,' the voice said gently. 'You could hardly risk calling the police in. I mean, not before you had a chance to clear out the drugs. You're still a user, I see. Cocaine. And all those anabolic steroids. How is the body-building going?'

Now she was really listening.

'OK, you've made your point,' she said. 'This morning you disarmed the alarm system, broke into my gallery, but took nothing. What d'you want?'

There was a pause, almost a slip of confidence.

'To do business.'

'So why the pantomime? Why not just come into the gallery to talk?'

He ignored the comment.

'I've got something interesting for you. A missing Caravaggio painting.'

Exasperated, Catrina hung up.

She was wondering how the caller had got her number when he rang again.

'Ms Hoyt.'

'How did you get my private number?'

'Why did you ring off?'

'Because I'm not interested in a fucking hoax—'

'But what if I told you it *wasn't* a hoax?'

Her voice was dismissive. 'I get crank calls weekly, and they're all hoaxes. So I reckon yours would be the same.'

'I went to a lot of trouble to show you how serious I was,' the caller went on. 'I could have hurt you this morning. I know what you are and what you do. I could expose you.'

'Like hell!'

'But that's not what I want. I need you as a dealer, Ms Hoyt. I need your seal of approval.'

'On some fake?'

'This is no fake. I've got proof. I know where two missing Caravaggio paintings are.'

She still wasn't taking him seriously. 'And you know this how?'

'I have insider knowledge.'

'Of course you do.'

'I've got information no one has.'

'Yeah? Well, I've got work to do.'

'Don't hang up!'

But she did.

Eight

London

Coughing up a gob of phlegm, Bernard Lowe wiped his mouth and then relaxed into his seat in the back in the car. Next to his feet stood a portable oxygen cylinder, a standby for when his emphysema worsened with a build-up in his lungs. For a moment he was tempted to use it, then he opened his mouth wide instead, dragging in a thin breath as he lowered the window six inches.

From the front seat, his driver watched him. Wondered how someone so sick could still be such a bastard. Only that morning Lowe had denied him time off. Gary Rimmer snatched another look in the rear-view mirror. Lowe was banging his chest like an ape, trying to loosen more catarrh, to unwedge the shit inside his lungs. Any minute now, Rimmer thought, he'll cough up again.

Today was a bad day. For both of them. Rimmer hadn't got his time off, and Bernard Lowe was gasping like a sick goat. And wearing the shit toupee he always wore, Rimmer thought, glancing at his employer in the mirror again. Salt-and-pepper hair: supposed to look real, but made the old man look like he'd had his head thatched. Moron, Rimmer thought. How could he think it convinced anyone?

The car phone rang in the back and Lowe picked up, his northern accent pronounced, the vowels hard.

'Hello? Who's this? Harvey Crammer! Haven't heard from you in weeks . . .' Suddenly Lowe's gaze met his driver's, and without waiting to be told Rimmer slid the partition closed.

What Lowe didn't know was that his driver had left a gap just wide enough for someone with sharp hearing to catch the gist of the conversation.

'Catrina Hoyt, that big-jawed slut. You're mixing with a rough one there.' Lowe coughed again, spat, then leaned back. The traffic lights had turned red and Rimmer could hear the conversation clearly now that the engine was merely ticking over. 'I don't believe anything that transvestite says. What? *I know she's a woman!* She just looks like a man in drag.' Lowe sat up in his seat, his nicotined fingers gripping the phone as he listened. 'She told you this? *Caravaggio!* Two missing paintings!' He laughed, rocking backwards and forwards like a shifty clown. 'Christ! If you believe that, you'll believe anything!'

But Bernard Lowe was listening carefully, Rimmer could see that. Something had caught the old bastard's attention. And the name Harvey Crammer rang a bell. Rimmer stared at the red traffic light, then remembered the Canadian, well over six feet tall, forehead broad as a playing field, a drooping nose topping a frog's mouth. A relentless traveller, with a reputation for sniffing out sleepers.

That Harvey Crammer.

The lights back to green, Rimmer slid the car forward, disappointed as Lowe finished his call. In the years he had worked for Bernard Lowe, Rimmer had managed two things: one, a growing hatred of his employer; and two, an accumulation of facts about the art world. Facts he was sure he could either barter or sell. As he drove Lowe around the art centres of Europe, Rimmer had assuaged his boredom by eavesdropping. And gradually random names and facts had created a medley of character studies, insights and rumours.

It hadn't taken Rimmer long to piece together the facts with the relevant person, or the rumour with the rumour-monger. He knew about Catrina Hoyt, with her size eleven feet and butcher's hands. Knew about Jacob Levens, the dapper ex-alcoholic. And he knew about Harvey Crammer, charming as a silver bullet to a werewolf. It was all fascinating, but what Rimmer had just heard was electrifying.

Bernard Lowe had mentioned *Caravaggio*.

Rimmer knew about the Italian painter. Well, he knew how much his pictures were worth and how they never came up for sale. He glanced in the rear-view mirror again. If Harvey Crammer was talking about it to the bastard Lowe, there must be something in it. Puzzled, Rimmer frowned. They were rivals, two avaricious collectors butting heads at all the big sales. So why would the Canadian deliberately tip his competitor off? What advantage could there possibly be for Crammer?

Thoughtful, Rimmer studied his employer as they stopped at another set of traffic lights on Baker Street. Bernard Lowe had finished his call and was reading a magazine about oriental ceramics. But Rimmer knew better. Lowe might feign indifference to what he had just heard, but it wasn't working.

Instead he had the twitchy look of a man in a betting shop picking out a winner for the third race.

Nine

Standing in the doorway of the nursery, Bette looked at the new cot and the magnolia walls. They needed painting, a job Gil had promised to do, but now it would be delayed. He was working for Jacob instead. Sighing, Bette reassured herself that the case might not take long. After all, wasn't that what Gil had said?

Moving away from the nursery, she gazed around the flat. In one of Battersea's town houses, it had high ceilings and wood floors, a Victorian fireplace and a window seat. A bargain, the estate agent had said when they bought it. Cramming in the clashing styles of Gil's ultra modern furniture with Bette's rustic chic had resulted in a mishmash, but the house was inviting, the kitchen looking out onto a long narrow garden and a shed where Gil kept his motorbike.

He seldom used the bike, but Bette had heard him leaving on it earlier. Easy in the traffic, he had said. I can get around quickly . . . Back to the old bike. The old life. The old wife . . . Bette had never met the mercurial Holly, only inherited her echo; that constant presence second wives feel around the breathing marriage to the widower.

In all fairness, Gil had not made an idol of Holly. In fact, his reticence on the subject managed to excite more interest. If he had referred to her often – *Holly liked this. Holly used to say that. Holly loved to visit that place, read that book, watch that film* – it would have been easier. But he didn't.

So Bette created her own personality for Holly. She took the bare, wire hanger of what she knew and hung a full character on it. A photograph on Holly's old website provided her with the image of a brunette with a long, narrow face and deep-set eyes, unusual, but attractive. Her intelligence was obvious; this much Bette could read from the photograph. The rest she guessed: that Holly was sexually confident, proud rather than self-conscious about her gangly legs and arms. That her work in computer science was indecipherable to most, but merely challenging to her.

That she was a force of nature.

Dead, but still deadly powerful.

And Bette hated her.

Hated that she had shared the reckless portion of Gil's life. That it had been Holly who had known him, made love to him, lived those dangerous, exhilarating years with him. She would have relished the thefts and murders Gil had investigated. She would have discussed his cases with him. She would never have told him to be careful. Because she wasn't careful herself.

Bette paused, ashamed of her hatred of a dead woman.

She had no reason to feel threatened. She was carrying Gil's child. Holly had never done that. She had made him a new life. She had won. With her, Gil Eckhart was a researcher, working from a home office, living in libraries, over the phone, or on the internet. *She* looked after him, made him laugh. He was a lifetime away from the art world and its machinations. He was safe. He was hers. And yet . . .

Before she married Gil, Bette had asked Jacob about Holly Eckhart. He had known her, and yet he had always been elusive about her.

'She was unusual,' Jacob had said, when pressed. 'People were attracted to her. She had a force about her.'

'A force? What d'you mean?'

Jacob had hesitated. 'She was always travelling, always busy. Always on the hunt.'

'What for?'

'For everything. For experiences, work, people. Holly didn't rest much.'

'Where did Gil meet her?'

'I don't know,' Jacob had replied. 'He never said, and I never asked. He met her, he married her, he lost her. But now he has you. And that's all you should think about. Holly's gone.'

Or at least she had been. Until Jacob Levens had made the phone call that had changed everything. The phone call that threatened to take Gil back to the past – and back to Holly.

Ten

St Thomas's Hospital, London
4.15 p.m.

Having been given access to Dr Dunning, Gil stood by the mortuary table with his arms folded, watching the pathologist. It was the same man who had been at The Weir Gallery, now looking even younger in his greens and his white cap.

'Detective Simmons is delayed,' the pathologist offered, 'but he said I could talk to you. I know you two have spoken already and that you've seen my reports—'

Gil interrupted him.

'Actually, the police were late sending them over to me. I haven't finished them yet.'

'So what d'you want to know?' Dunning asked. He was defensive, intimidated by the burly man on his turf. 'The Weir brothers died from strangulation. They were tied together with picture wire that extended around both of their necks. It was used as a garrotte – someone tightened it by winding it around a piece of wood at the side of Sebastian Weir's neck.'

'What about the torture?'

Dunning paused. 'It wouldn't have killed them.'

'How long would it have lasted?'

'About an hour, maybe a bit longer.'

'So the killer must have been in the gallery around six, if not earlier.'

'How d'you work that out?'

'He would have had to get in, overpower the brothers and tie them up. Then torture them. That would have taken time. Jacob Levens didn't get there until just after eight and they were dead then.'

Or were they? Gil wondered. He only had Jacob's word for that. Perhaps they were still alive when the dealer had got there. He might not have murdered them, but perhaps he had *refused* to save them. After all, it was a hell of a coincidence that Jacob Levens had found the bodies, considering his connection to the original crime in Berlin. It was true that there had been no obvious blood on Jacob's clothes, but how much blood *would* have got onto a man who had not taken part, just watched the Weir brothers die? In the past Jacob had been a nasty drunk, prone to blackouts. Hospitalised more than once. And now he was drinking again.

Gil baulked at how quickly he had returned to his old life. At how easily he suspected everyone. Even a friend. It was one of the reasons he had left detective work. Not just because of the murders in Berlin or the death of Holly, but because he feared the change in him – the return of a man he had grown to despise.

'How difficult is it to scalp someone?' he asked, turning back to the pathologist.

'Depends. In this case, the killer knew exactly what to do.'

Nodding, Gil glanced around at the newly modernised surroundings, with their even lighting, pristine tiled floor and sterile metal worktops. More Ikea kitchen than NHS morgue. Then he moved over to the far wall and studied the banks of drawers lined up. One drawer for each body. Neat. Hygienic. Uncomfortably familiar.

'It doesn't make sense,' he said, talking more to himself than the pathologist. 'How could one man overpower two men? Tie them up, torture them, and then kill them . . .' He glanced back to Dunning. 'Were there any drugs in the bodies?'

'No.'

'And no defence wounds? Nothing to suggest that they struggled?'

'Like I said in my report,' Dunning remarked officiously, 'I found no defence marks.'

'And that didn't strike you as odd?'

'Maybe they knew their killer.'

'And let him tie them up?'

'They were naked. Maybe it was sexual,' Dunning offered tentatively.

'And then they just sat there while someone fired nails into their balls?' Gil asked, moving over to the far wall and reading the labels on the cadaver drawers. 'May I look at the bodies?'

The pathologist nodded. 'Detective Simmons said I was to give you any help you required.'

Gil pulled out the drawer named SEBASTIAN WEIR and drew back the sheet which covered the corpse. He could see the Y-shaped autopsy incision and the lacerating garrotte wound to the throat. He then studied Sebastian's body, from the head downwards, staring at the vicious mutilation of the genitals.

'How much blood would they have lost from the torture?'

'Post or peri mortem?'

Gil turned. 'Some injuries were inflicted *after* death?'

'Yes, quite a few.'

'Same amount of wounds on both brothers?'

'Yes. Exactly.'

'How many?'

'Eight.'

Taking in a breath, Gil nodded. Seven years earlier, in Berlin, Terrill Huber had had nails driven into his scrotum. Eight of them. And Alma Huber had had nails fired into her breasts. Eight again. No one had known what it meant then. Gil didn't know what it meant now.

He turned back to the pathologist.

'How *could* a single man incapacitate two men? And even if the killer managed to persuade them to strip and be bound together, how did he torture them without them fighting back?' Gil paused. 'The Weir brothers were celibate. Never any rumours – and the art world gossips, believe me. People would have known if they had any sexual quirks.'

'But people hide things like that.'

'One man might, but *two* brothers?' Gil shook his head. 'No, I doubt it.'

He thought back to Berlin and *knew* that the same killer was active again. The murderer was spelling it out for him. Drawing the participants of the earlier case back into his sphere. Jacob Levens, brother of Alma Huber, conveniently finding the Weir twins. Gil Eckhart, the investigator on the Berlin case, called in to work on the Weir murders. Who else? Gil wondered, thinking back. Who else had been involved in Germany?

And then he remembered Harvey Crammer.

Eleven

New York
10.00 a.m.

Rubbing her cropped hair dry, Catrina walked back into the sitting room in the apartment over her gallery in the meat-packing area of Manhattan. She had inherited the residence and business from her late father, Frank Hoyt, a place he had used for laundering money from his casino in Las Vegas. And for housing a slutty string of mistresses.

Catrina's childhood had been punctuated by overblown, simpering seventeenth-century French art, and a slew of overblown, simpering unsuitable women. When Catrina reached the age of twelve her mother ran away, exhausted by Frank's infidelity and violence. Left in the care of an incompetent nanny, Catrina had skipped school. She grew tall and athletic, with a natural gift for sports. Which she ignored. Instead, by the time she was fifteen she had fallen in with a street gang, proving her worth in fights and taking on all comers.

She was pretty. And aggressive. No boy ever got close to Catrina unless she wanted him to. Restless in New York, she began to travel, ending up in Miami. But her explosive temper, unchannelled and uncurbed, resulted in a charge for assault at the age of eighteen. She had used a knife. The police then discovered that she had a gun in her possession.

When Frank heard about the charge, he left Vegas and confronted Catrina in Miami, dragging her back to New York and playing – too late – the heavy father figure. He said he wanted to become a bigger part of her life. That he was sorry for not being around much in her childhood. That the way she had turned out was probably his fault.

Catrina laughed in his face. Embarrassed and angry, he struck her. And she struck back, cutting him with the kitchen knife she had been holding. Frank never threatened his daughter again. Instead he hired a lawyer to arrange for the victim to be pacified, to drop the charge and settle out of court. Catrina didn't thank him. She was too angry, too bitter about her past to let him off the hook.

Unable to communicate with his daughter, Frank Hoyt went back to Vegas. When he talked about Catrina to his cohorts, he always bragged about her. But in truth, she scared the shit out of him.

When he died Catrina was thirty. She had changed over the years. At nineteen she had left the street gang and taken up sports. Her body, lithe and muscular, became her personal weapon. She was strong enough to fell a man, sexual enough to seduce him. Rumours began to circulate that she was a lesbian. She was, for a short time. Rumours also circulated that she was a whore. Which was true. Then she inherited the gallery.

Once hers, she tipped out the French nudes and took a trip round Europe, buying the art she was drawn to. Her taste was laughable. She lost money. Worst, she lost face. An affair with an English dealer was no accident. Catrina had hand-picked him, choosing the man who could teach her the most. Six months later, she knew about Italian art and he knew about bondage. Catrina thought it was a fair swap. Her progress continued. If she could seduce knowledge out of someone, she would. If not, she would buy it from them. She didn't believe in love or affection. She didn't believe in any god or any devil. She was predatory, courageous and ruthless.

And now Catrina Hoyt was standing in front of her laptop, intrigued as she looked at an email that had just come through. Someone had written:

> Dear Ms Hoyt,
> This email is from Mr Luca Meriss.
> Mr Meriss is in possession of some valuable information about 'Portrait of Fillide Melandroni', missing since 1945.

So some nutter – or some partner of the nutter who had broken into her basement – was now trying to contact her by email?

She read on:

> Mr Meriss knows that you are interested in the Italian's works. He also wishes to make clear that this is no stunt. Mr Meriss is a descendant of the artist Caravaggio. He has proof. He also has proof of the whereabouts of the portrait – and another famous work long missing.
>
> Mr Meriss has just released a statement to the press and on his website.
>
> Please reply.
> www.meriss.icon.com
> Cell phone: 0 . . . .

Curious, Catrina clicked on the website link. A photograph appeared immediately. The face was fleshy, soft-skinned, handsome but overblown, the lips pomegranate red. A piazza boy outgrown his trade, she thought.

Luca Meriss claimed to be the descendant of Caravaggio and the notorious Roman prostitute, Fillide Melandroni. There was a photograph of her portrait too: slyly erotic, hair a black aura round her impious head. Catrina glanced at the drawing of the artist placed next to Fillide, the well-known features of Caravaggio scowling from the page.

Fucking idiot, she thought. Could this Meriss man *really* believe he was a descendant of the painter? In every biography she had read – and she had read them all – there had never been mention of Caravaggio having sired any offspring. Indeed, the twentieth century had made him into a gay icon, until another authority suggested that his fight with Ranuccio Tomassoni was actually Caravaggio's attempt to castrate the man with whom he was sharing Melandroni. Jealous rage had provoked the final, fatal attack, an event that had sent the fugitive Caravaggio fleeing Rome for Naples.

Catrina read on, amused. Well, if someone was going to claim an ancestor, why not pick the most notorious painter who had ever lived? She thought back to the break-in and the phone call which had followed.

I need you as a dealer. I need your seal of approval.

Maybe it wasn't a hoax . . .

Catrina thought about her public admiration of Caravaggio, her writings on the Italian artist. The art world might try to dismiss her as a tyro, a freak, but there was no one more determined to prove them wrong. The knowledge she had built up about the artist was phenomenal. His violent nature was familiar to her, the street-smart contempt with which he had treated his contemporaries understandable. She could identify with him as gang-runner and yob. Wilful, hysterical and self-destructive. Doomed to die young. Lucky fuck, she thought.

As for his paintings, some forty or so survived but a number had been lost. And much as the art world might keep trying to claim pastiches or clodhopping copies as original works, a true Caravaggio spewed out its genius from the frame. Catrina knew, because she had travelled the world studying them. Standing for hours peering into the yielding flesh and the murky backgrounds. And her haphazard education hadn't held her back. She had developed a passion, and become besotted.

Glancing back at the painting of Fillide Melandroni, Catrina thought about what she knew of the Roman's portrait. Most of the art world believed that the likeness had been destroyed long ago. Throwing aside the towel she was holding, Catrina picked up her laptop and walked into her office. There she reached for a catalogue and found the entry she was looking for.

Portrait of Fillide Melandroni.
Creator: Caravaggio, Michelangelo Merisi da, 1573–1610
Date: ca. 1597
Date destroyed or lost: 1945
Nationality: Italian
Medium: oil on canvas
Object dimensions: 66 x 53 cm
Former repository: Gemäldegalerie (Berlin, Germany)
Former inventory number: Inv. Nr. 356
World War, 1939–1945 – Destruction and pillage – Germany
World War, 1939–1945 – Art and the war

Catrina stared at the entry, then glanced back at the email. She had dismissed him – this Mr Meriss – but now she was wondering if she should have listened to what he had to say. His choice of name amused her. How obvious to pick Meriss – aka Merisi, the town where Caravaggio was born. It was all so clumsy, so gauche. But then again, a professional fraudster would have been more polished. Perhaps the naivety of this approach made Mr Meriss seem all the more genuine?

She looked back at the email again.

> Mr Meriss has proof of the whereabouts of the painting and possibly another, larger, work . . .

She felt her skin flush and a frisson of excitement. He couldn't mean the missing *Nativity*, could he? The most famous missing painting of all? *The Nativity with St Lawrence and St Francis*? Number 1 on the FBI's Missing Works of Art, no less. The sacred cow of the art world that had had people chasing their tails for decades.

God knows how many times Catrina had heard rumours about a collector hiring someone to investigate its whereabouts. A month or a year later, the result was always the same. Nothing. But then an unexpected, and remarkable, solution to the mystery had presented itself. In 1996, at a trial in Italy, a Mafia cohort, Marino Mannola, said that *he* had stolen the picture in 1969. Along with the help of other men, he had used a knife to cut the painting out of its frame over the main altar of the Oratory of San Lorenzo, Palermo, then rolled it up. Unfortunately, in doing so the canvas had been ruined.

Apparently, when the anonymous man for whom he had stolen the work saw the masterpiece he had wept.

It made him cry, Marino Mannola explained. *It was not . . . in a usable condition any more.*

Some doubted Mannola's story. But he was considered a reliable witness and had no reason to lie. Besides, it fitted nicely with the theory that *The Nativity* had been stolen by the Sicilian Mafia. The mystery was solved . . . for some. Others believed that the painting had met another end. Some adopted the rumour that amateurs had stolen the work and, finding it too notorious to sell on, had had to destroy it. Whichever theory a person favoured, the painting remained lost.

But there were a number of dealers, collectors, conspiracy theorists and optimists who believed that one of Caravaggio's greatest masterpieces was still out there, hidden away. Maybe in Italy, maybe in the Far East, maybe in someone's bank vault. But not destroyed.

Her mobile rang suddenly and Catrina picked it up. 'Who's this?'

'Are you at your computer?'

She was surprised to hear a voice she hadn't heard for months.

'What the hell! I've nothing to say to you.'

It was the early hours of the morning in London, but Bernard Lowe hadn't gone to bed. Instead he'd been busy and his northern vowels were now reverberating over the Atlantic.

'This isn't a social call – I can't stand you any more than you can stand me. But you should hear me out, Catrina. Just look at your computer.'

She turned back to the screen. 'What am I supposed to be looking at?'

'Go to www.meriss.icon.com and see what just gone up on line. See it?' She couldn't tell if he was coughing or laughing. 'Now read it, and weep.'

Twelve

Berlin
5.00 p.m.

He had prepared himself for the event, straightening his hair and applying a little – very little – foundation to his skin. It evened out the tone that time had mottled, and gave his sallowness a youthful warmth. Any minute now, Luca told himself, the phone would start ringing. He had posted the information online and declared his blood tie to Caravaggio. It wasn't his fault that Catrina Hoyt hadn't responded. He had been scrupulous in going to her first, but it was her choice whether or not she contacted him. If not her, there would be many others.

He glanced at the list by his hand. The New York dealer Catrina Hoyt; the British contingent: Jacob Levens, dealer, and Bernard Lowe, importer and collector; the German dealer Oscar Schultz; and the Canadian collector Harvey Crammer. All devotees of the Italian Baroque. All devotees of Caravaggio's work.

Luca felt a shudder of anticipation. The art world wouldn't be able to resist him. Or his story. Or his knowledge of the missing portrait. And the hint that he knew more. About another, even more important work.

One thing at a time, Luca told himself. He had planned it for so long there was no need to rush. Let out the information slowly. Drip-feed the public. Let people cajole him, flatter him into confidences. Let himself be courted.

He had done his years of begging for scraps. He was at the head table now, the denizens of the art world below the salt. Fame was only seconds away. Money, recognition, status within a heartbeat.

And he was ready for it.

Whatever happened now.

He was ready.

He wasn't.

The first reply came online. In response to Luca's posting on his blog someone had sent a photograph. Excited, Luca fumbled with his keyboard, desperate to open the file and see what it contained. An old computer, it was slow to download. Then finally the photograph emerged – blurred, then focused, filling the screen.

At first he didn't know what he was seeing. Then leaned back, repelled.

He was looking at a tabletop. On it were two bloodied scalps, lying side by side.

Thirteen

London
5.30 p.m.

At any other time Gil would have confided in his wife. But Bette was heavily pregnant, with only weeks to go. Not the time to frighten her. Because it *would* frighten her. He knew that much. So instead he stood in the entrance of a block of flats on Wimpole Street and rang the bell for the third time. A moment later, a voice came over the intercom.

'Who's there?'

'My name's Gil Eckhart–'

'I'm busy!'

'Hear me out, Mr Crammer. I need to talk to you. We have a mutual friend. Jacob Levens.'

The door was buzzed open for Gil to enter and a man appeared at the head of the first flight of stairs. He was in his fifties, very tall and round-shouldered, his mouth wide, frog-like.

'Come up, please.'

He waited until Gil drew level, then gestured to the open front door of his flat and followed his visitor in.

Harvey Crammer had obviously just returned from a trip: an unpacked suitcase lay on the coffee table in his sitting room, a crumpled overcoat was thrown over the back of an armchair.

'Been travelling?'

'I'm always travelling.' Crammer's wide mouth broadened into a smile, his fleshy nose casting a shadow over his top lip. Not so much the Ugly American as the Ugly Canadian. 'And I'm sorry I have to hurry you, but I'm due to give a speech tonight and I'm running late.'

'I just wanted to ask you a few questions.'

'Questions? About what?'

'A murder.'

Crammer put his head to one side, scrutinising his visitor. 'I think I know you, Mr Eckhart. I think our paths have crossed before.' He moved over to a side table. 'Drink?'

'Thanks.'

He passed a whisky to Gil, motioning for him to sit down before taking the window seat. The winter afternoon had long gone, lamps were switched on in Crammer's apartment and shone out from the windows of the houses across the street. In the distance a burglar alarm sounded.

'I *do* know you, don't I? You see, I don't suffer from that common failing of not remembering faces. Faces are only another language. And I have a facility for languages.'

'We have met before.'

'I thought so.' Crammer sipped his drink. A stuffed deer's

head hung on the wall above him, and beside it, a couple of antique maps of Europe. 'Where was it? I travel a lot – put me out of my misery.' He was Canadian, but there was no trace of his native accent left. 'You said we had a mutual friend in Jacob Levens?'

Gil nodded. 'Yes.'

'How is he?'

'Not too well at the moment. He's had a shock.'

Gil could see the flicker of interest in Crammer's eyes.

'What kind of shock?'

'He found two bodies. The Weir twins were murdered this morning.'

'I know. I saw the news.'

'Where?'

'On my laptop.'

'I mean, where were you when you found out?' Gil pushed him.

'About three thousand feet above the Atlantic, on a flight back to Heathrow.' Crammer paused, head on one side. 'Did we meet in New York?'

'No.'

In fact Gil had come across him seven years earlier, in Berlin. Crammer had been visiting the city to see an exhibition of Barocci's works at the Huber Gallery. Ostensibly he had wanted to buy some drawings. But he had made no purchases, just disappeared – vaporised into nothingness – straight after the murders of Alma and Terrill Huber.

'Rome?'

Gil shook his head.

'Perhaps Berlin?'

He had known all along, Gil realised. Just playing with him.

'Yes, I remember now. You were investigating the Huber murders.'

'Which happened just before you left Germany,' Gil replied. 'And here you are, back in London – just after the Weir murders. Strange, isn't it?'

'No. What *is* strange is your being here asking me questions. Almost – dare I say it – interrogating me. Why is that, Mr Eckhart? The police haven't contacted me, so why are you here?' He paused, then carried on when Gil didn't reply. 'The Huber murders were grotesque. I remember the fallout from those killings. No one felt safe for a long time. And they never caught the murderer, did they? Neither the police, nor you.'

'No, we never caught him.'

Crammer was thoughtful. 'You said that Jacob Levens found the bodies of the Weir twins?'

'Yes.'

'And of course you know that his sister – Alma Huber – was one of the Berlin victims.'

'Of course I do. I was involved in that case,' Gil replied shortly. 'In fact, three of the people who were around at the time of the Berlin killings are now involved again. You, Jacob Levens and myself. But now it's London.'

Crammer's tone hardened. 'I have nothing to do with the Weir murders. Or, if it comes to it, the Huber deaths.'

'But that's not true, is it, Mr Crammer?' Gil said evenly. 'After all, Alma Huber was your ex-wife.'

Fourteen

Berlin
6.00 p.m.

Luca was still shaking when his mobile rang. For a moment he was tempted to ignore it, but then he answered tentatively. 'Hello?'

'Luca Meriss?'

'Who's this?'

'Catrina Hoyt. You've just emailed me.' She paused, surprised by his lack of response. 'You wanted to talk, so talk.' Frowning, she continued. 'For God's sake, you've been pestering me enough! You even broke into my gallery—'

'What?' Luca replied, taking a seat in front of the laptop and slamming down the lid to obliterate the image online. 'I never came to your gallery!'

'But you called me.'

'No, I didn't! I just contacted you by email. How could I come to your gallery? I'm in Berlin.'

Surprised, Catrina thought for a moment.

'Aren't you pretending to be Caravaggio's descendant?'

'I *am* his descendant,' Luca replied. 'I have proof.'

'And you said that you knew about the Fillide Melandroni portrait?'

'Yes.'

'And another very important Caravaggio work – a famous missing work?'

'Yes, yes,' he agreed. 'That was me.'

'So who the hell broke into my gallery?' Catrina asked, thinking quickly. 'This story of yours–'

'It's no story! It's all true.'

'OK, whatever. Who else knows about it?'

'No one.'

'Someone must,' she said drily. 'I don't like to be the one to break it to you, Mr Meriss, but I think someone's trying to steal your thunder.'

'*But no one else knows!* I've only just put it up on the internet–'

He stopped short. 'What's the matter?' Catrina asked, alert.

'Nothing.'

'Don't mess me about! You were going to say something. What was it? Has someone contacted you already?' She could sense she had hit a nerve. '*What?*'

'Why would they send it?'

'Send what?'

'The photograph. Someone sent me a photograph–'

She took charge at once. Afterwards she would ask herself why. Was it just because she wanted to know about the missing paintings? Cut out her rivals? Thumb her nose at the art world who had sneered at her for so long? Or was it because she wanted to know who had broken into her gallery? Who had had the gall to trick her and make a fool out of her?

'Forward it.'

'What?'

'Forward the photograph to me.'

'I can't–'

'Do it!' she snapped.

A couple of moments later Catrina Hoyt was staring at an image she hadn't expected. An image she hadn't wanted to see. But she had invited the image into her life – and could never delete it.

Fifteen

London

After leaving Harvey Crammer's flat, Gil made his way into the centre of the capital, to the sluggish heart of the art district. The protracted recession had buckled the business; trading was still continuing, but in a limited, cautious way. The Russians and the Chinese were now buying, bringing their cash into the British capital in the same way the Arabs had in the 1970s.

Walking up New Bond Street, past Asprey, Chanel and Versace, Gil took a turning towards Cork Street. Some of the galleries had closed for the night. Some had changed and were now under different names or different management, but many of the old stalwarts remained. The same genre scenes and Dutch still lifes groaned from their gilded frames, the same smattering of Elizabethan portrait heads smirked out of doily ruffs, and the same brittle German nudes glowered out into the winter dusk.

Gil was staring at one when someone called out to him.

'Gil, is that you?'

He turned, trying to make out the figure that was silhouetted against a street lamp, finally recognising Oscar Schultz. Of course, Gil thought. Who else? The tom-toms had been working overtime. He had only been in the area for minutes and had already been spotted.

'Are you working on the Weir case? I hope so – we need you. Everyone's really scared.' He looped his arm around Gil's shoulder, apparently impervious to his resistance. 'It's good to see you. How long has it been? Five years?'

'Seven.'

Oscar nodded, giving Gil a quick hug and then releasing him. He didn't appear to notice the animosity coming from the other man. Or maybe he did, and was just deliberately ignoring it. Just as he made the deliberate mistake of saying *five* years instead of seven.

'Jacob's in shock. In fact, I think he's drinking again, and that's not good. Not good for him at all,' Oscar went on. 'The police are talking to all of us, interviewing everyone, but no one knows anything. I mean, why would they?' He dropped his voice. 'Jacob said they'd been tortured.'

'Yes, they were.'

'But I heard that nothing was stolen. Is that true?'

'I don't know.'

'But if you're working on the case you should know—'

'*Should* I, Oscar?'

He could feel his blood rising, his anger veering out of control as he faced the dealer. This was the man he hated, the man he blamed for ruining his life. And much as Gil might hope his feelings had faded, they had not. Instead they had seemed to flourish during the intervening years.

The German's boyish face flushed. 'I see there's a little bad feeling between us.'

'Not a little, Oscar – a *lot* of bad feeling,' Gil countered, staring at the man who had killed his first wife.

Oscar Schultz had driven into the side of Holly's car in Berlin seven years earlier. He had been travelling at speed and the impact had crushed the vehicle, trapping her in the wreckage. It had taken over an hour for Holly to be cut free. Sixty minutes, while the paramedics struggled to stop the bleeding. Sixty minutes, while they tried to resuscitate her. For a short time it seemed that she might survive, but Holly Eckhart died in hospital later that night.

Everyone said it had been an accident. That the traffic lights had been faulty and that Oscar Schultz wasn't to blame. But he escaped from the crash with trivial injuries and Holly died. And now, meeting up with her widower, Oscar Schultz couldn't – or *wouldn't* – even remember the year it had happened.

'I'm sorry you feel that way,' Oscar went on, his tone injured. 'I've found it as hard to live with as you have—'

'I doubt that,' Gil said, moving off.

Embarrassed, Oscar followed him.

'*Are* you taking the Weir case? Jacob said that they were killed the same way those dealers were—'

'*The Hubers*. Their names were Alma and Terrill Huber.

You know that well enough.' Gil paused, looking the man up and down. 'I see you and all I can think of is that time in Berlin. The art colony was panicking then too, just like they are now. Everyone terrified that the killer would come after them. *You* were terrified, Oscar. Scared shitless. But not scared enough to miss a PR opportunity. I remember you giving interviews to the press in Berlin, and on the television. You were even thinking about going into politics, weren't you? But then you killed Holly. So I suppose the political career didn't come off?'

'*It was an accident!*'

'Yeah, that's what you say. That's what everyone says. But you know something? I don't believe it. I didn't believe it then, and I don't believe it now.'

Oscar snorted with outrage.

'*You think I deliberately killed your wife?* Are you bloody crazy? What reason would I have?'

'I don't know. But you were in Berlin when the Hubers died. You'd done business with them for years, but suddenly you'd become enemies. There was a rumour that you'd had an argument about a painting–'

'Dealers argue about paintings all the time! It's the business.'

'Maybe. But you'd been close friends. You weren't just dealers; your families socialised. And now here you are, in London, and the Weirs have just been killed–'

'I came over for an auction!'

'Did you buy anything?'

'No,' Oscar said, his tone incredulous. *'You think I had something to do with the murders?'*

'Which ones? The ones in Berlin or the ones in London?'

Oscar folded his arms, suddenly arrogant.

'You suspect me of being involved with the Weir killings because I was around when the *Hubers* were killed? That's coincidence, not motive.' He paused, taunting Gil. 'But then you never found out what the motive was, did you? Neither did the police. To all intents and purposes it might just have been some lunatic. A drug addict looking for easy money.'

'Nothing was stolen from the Huber Gallery. Not even the petty cash,' Gil responded. 'And the Hubers were tortured. *So what were they hiding?* Eventually I came to the conclusion that they must have told their attacker what he wanted to hear, otherwise there would have been more murders.' Gil paused. 'But that can't be the case now. Not when the Weirs have been killed in exactly the same way. So I'm back to square one. What did – *does* – the killer want?'

'How the hell would I know?'

'You wouldn't. Unless you were the killer.'

Oscar Schultz's smooth features softened into an unexpected smile.

'You've no other suspects? What about Jacob Levens? Alma Huber was his sister. And then there's Harvey Crammer. I distinctly remember the Canadian being in Berlin seven years ago. And he *was* married to Alma Huber once.'

Gil watched him pull out names like corks from a row of bottles. He was guilty of something, but Gil wasn't sure if it was murder. All he knew was that an innocent man wouldn't have been so prepared. Oscar Schultz was prepped.

'Frankly, Eckhart, you're clutching at straws suspecting me.' The winter evening was curling in, a cold wind shuffling up Cork Street towards the two angry men. 'You've nothing to go on.'

'You're a liar and a thief – that's a start.'

Oscar Schultz flinched.

'And what are you? A bruiser with a history of picking fights.'

'I never pick fights. I never start anything. I just retaliate.'

'Is that supposed to scare me?'

'No,' Gil replied coldly. 'But this is – if I find out that you killed my wife on purpose I *will* kill you.'

Sixteen

New York
11.30 a.m.

Unnerved, Catrina stared at the grisly image Luca Meriss had sent her. She could tell that the scalps were human, the blood fresh, and her stomach heaved.

Finally she picked up the phone again. 'You've no address, no name, to tell you who posted this?'

'Nothing,' Luca replied, locking the door of his flat in Berlin. His hands were damp, trembling as he clung to the phone. 'I'd just launched my website, announcing who I was.'

'I know, I saw it,' Catrina replied, trying to gather her thoughts. Bernard Lowe had seen it too, which meant that by now most of the London art world knew. And then it would spread to the rest of the business, in cities around the world. She stared at the image on the screen. 'Did this photograph come through straight away?'

'Almost immediately.'

'Who knew about the website? That it was up and running today?'

'No one. Only you.'

'Well, I didn't send it,' Catrina replied drily. 'Have you checked your emails since?'

There was a pause; she could hear Luca's fingers tapping on the computer keys, then a surprised intake of breath. 'I've got over fifty messages!'

'OK. Look down the list. Is there one from Bernard Lowe?'

He checked. 'Yes.'

'Read it to me.'

'. . . *I'd like more information, Mr Meriss. Also would like to talk about your ancestor. If, of course, you can prove it's your ancestor. Please reply and we can correspond.*'

Luca paused. 'That's it. Nothing else. No attachments or photographs.'

The phone line was becoming indistinct and Catrina raised her voice over the static.

'OK, now read me the names of the others who've sent you messages.'

'You think one of them sent me that photograph?'

'Just read the names!' Catrina snapped, concentrating as Luca read down the list. Suddenly she stopped him. 'Did you say Harvey Crammer?'

'Yes,' Luca replied, reading out the message the Canadian had sent. '. . . *Please contact Mr Crammer by email. He would like to talk. . .*'

The long-distance phone connection was poor, worsening by the second.

'Go on,' Catrina urged him. 'Keep reading out the names.'

'Goldstone, A. F. Holdings, The Fine Dealers Limited.'

She kept listening, then flinched and sat bolt upright.

'Say that again!' Catrina snapped. 'What was the name?'

But there was no answer.

Only a long, dead humming down the line.

Seventeen

London

Moving over to a far table at the back of The Wolseley, Oscar Schultz ordered a coffee and a salad. No meat. He was a vegetarian. A non-drinking vegetarian, who had never smoked and never taken drugs. A healthy specimen, his body athletic, toned, his face sculpted. Listlessly he picked at the watercress on his plate, then jabbed at it with his fork. Fucking Gil Eckhart. Fucking, fucking Gil Eckhart!

His head down, he thought of Eckhart's threat and his hatred. Schultz *had* killed Holly, that much was true, but it had been an accident and the world had moved on. Gil Eckhart had moved on too, or so it seemed. Married again, apparently got over Holly easily enough. Oscar frowned, brooding. They had run into one another a number of times while Gil had been working in the art world. He had seemed to come from nowhere, arriving as unexpectedly as a yob at an opera. But not quite the yob he seemed – that much was soon apparent. To the surprise of the artistic elite, Gil Eckhart had an extensive knowledge of the arts. No one expected a bruiser to be able to tell a Fra Angelico from a Fra Filippo Lippi.

A broken nose, meat-packer's hands and a serious weight-training habit didn't gel with the denizens of the art world. Neither did the fact that Eckhart had a reputation for using his fists when provoked. In short, he didn't fit in. But then again, he hadn't wanted to. His speciality was investigating crimes and solving them; his knowledge gave him the entrée, his bulk the clout.

Oscar stared at the watercress on his plate, looking up when someone slid into the chair next to his.

'What's the matter?'

'Nothing to do with you!' Oscar snapped, glancing over to the woman beside him. She was fair-haired, around twenty-five, with an accent that he could place only too easily.

'I didn't mean to pry.'

Oscar reached out, taking her hand. 'Sorry for shouting at you. So, how's my little nurse today?'

Frieda dimpled back at him. 'Thank you for finding me the job. I really needed it.'

'No problem.'

'I was struggling, and you helped me out. I'll never forget that.'

He had no intention of letting her.

'It was just a favour, nothing at all. And your patient – how's he?'

'Old, bad-tempered.' She shrugged. The pay was good

enough to compensate for the drawbacks of working for a sick man like Bernard Lowe. 'I've had worse.'

'I bet you have,' Oscar replied, temporarily putting Gil Eckhart out of his mind. 'You remember what we agreed?'

She nodded, but looked a little anxious. 'I just wondered why.'

'*Why?*' he repeated, smiling as though he was amused. 'It's business, libeling – that's all. The art world's a cut-throat place – you have to take any advantage you can. And besides, what's the harm in it? You just have to listen to what's going on and pass what you hear on to me.'

Her reservations were fading; she was too anxious to please the glossy Oscar Schultz.

'I heard him talking about the murders. You know – the brothers, the dealers.'

Oscar nodded. This was going to work very well. Very well indeed.

'I know about that, but I want you to tell me what else he talks about – and to whom. I want to know who visits him, when, and why.' He stroked the inside of her arm sensuously. 'There will be a bonus in it for you, of course. A little extra reward.'

She ran her tongue over her lower lip. 'I can do it.'

'I know you can,' Oscar replied, his hand sliding further up her arm. 'You're a quick learner. Anyone can see that.'

Tuesday

Naples, Italy
1610

He was still bleeding when he reached the house, pushing open the door with his shoulder and stumbling in. A woman, her face covered in sores, glanced up from the table where she was sitting with two men, and then looked away. Face averted, Caravaggio, the most famous painter in Italy and now its most infamous fugitive, slunk into the space under the stairs. Once there he leaned back against the straw, his focus blurring as he slipped in and out of consciousness.

He had held all of Italy in his hands; Malta had once idolised him; Sicily had worshipped him. Notables had come from abroad to view his works and the Church made him a temporal saint in Rome. From his early whoring days he had clambered out of the shit into the Roman sun. From selling himself, and posing for cardinals' titillation, he had painted his way out of the midden. Rewards had been opulent, plentiful. He had been courted, wooed like a virgin, Italy thrilling to the talent of her brightest son.

The sun goes out. Night comes readily, and the long dense shadows of cities draw back their wandering child.

Sleeping, his mouth falling open, Caravaggio's hand rested against his knife, the short-blade sword always with him. Fame had not changed him. There was always a fight, some altercation he couldn't avoid, some insult he couldn't resist. Some provocation prepared, some friend insulted, some peer mocked. He swaggered like a greasy little tug amongst a fleet of shining vessels, bearing no colours but his own.

Down, down, down into the dark, into the burnt umbers and blacks of paints, into the tinted aspic of his works. And as his fame increased, so did his temper. Beaten out of shape by struggle.

Caravaggio turned over and pressed his face against the straw, dribbling from his cut mouth. He would sleep a little and then eat something, get back on his feet. His pardon was due, on its way from Rome, from the Pope, friends working their magic on the Pontiff to excuse a murderer.

He had never denied it. He had attacked Ranuccio Tomassoni. Not in an argument over a tennis game – as many first believed – but because of Fillide Melandroni. Jealous, believing that Tomassoni was her pimp, Caravaggio had cornered him. It was tradition, the machismo settling of scores. In one stroke Caravaggio had severed his rival's femoral artery. The blood came pumping out under the sun, no shadows then, exposed in the daylight. Tomassoni clutching at his groin, shocked, the screaming cut off. Caravaggio standing, confused, the sword in his hand, his shadow like a tree stump, dark and blasted.

He had meant to castrate him, tradition for a jealous Italian. He had wanted Tomassoni neutered, never to make love to Fillide again. She was Caravaggio's whore. She was Rome's whore: beautiful and violent, dirty at times, at other times shining, glossy with massage and oils. Her face had forced itself into Caravaggio's mind first, then his paintings. His Madonna, his St Catherine, his Judith cutting off the head of her lover Holofernes. Placid in paint and calmly, rigidly beautiful on canvas.

On the street, a whore. From the notables, the rich, Fillide slid at night into the bar brawls, the street fights. She could use a knife, was a match for anyone. Caravaggio was alternately stimulated and awed by her. She made a mouse of him, then a bull. She was uncontrollable, capricious, a liar without remorse. Afraid of nothing.

Oh, but she was, and Caravaggio knew it. Knew that she heard the seasons passing, and with them the terrifying power of her appeal. She would age. The fights, the drinking, the whoring – all would age her. If she lived until she was thirty, Fillide Melandroni would die foul.

Caravaggio shifted his position. The blood had dried, beginning to knit together the wound. And he knew he would live. That he wouldn't bleed out. Wouldn't be found stiff as a stuck pig on a pile of straw . . . His eyes flickered under his closed lids as he remembered Fillide – his idol, his vicious muse, the woman who had brought him to his knees.

All of Rome had come to see his paintings, and her. Gazing at the woman who aped a saint. Pretending goodness were there was none. A damned soul mimicking salvation.

But I would do it again, Caravaggio thought. Every day, every fight, every insult, every whore. Every drop of blood drawn by me or from me. His spirit flared like a damp match, struggling against itself. A fugitive he might be, shamed, hunted, but not for long. He would return and be the same again.

Everyone might pardon me, Caravaggio thought, the Pope might wipe my sins away as if they were little more than mud, but I would do it again.

I would do it all again.

Eighteen

Belgravia, London
9.15 a.m.

Summoned to the home of Bernard Lowe, Gil found himself directed into an uncomfortable drawing room overlooking a garden which was in the process of being landscaped. The house, in Eaton Square, had the usual grand façade, but inside the furniture was a mêlée of Italian antiques and hideous gilded reproductions. A variety of small chairs hugged the peripheries of the room like wallflowers at a school prom, and a high-backed sofa stood, obese and overstuffed, facing the bay window.

Gil hadn't known that Bernard Lowe was in the room and was surprised when the old man peered round the side of the sofa.

'Mr Eckhart, good to meet you,' he said, pulling a portable oxygen cylinder closer to him as he made room for Gil to sit down. 'You got my message?'

'Loud and clear.'

'So you'll work for me?'

'Not a chance,' Gil replied, sitting down and trying to get comfortable on the unyielding seat. 'I've already been hired by Jacob Levens.'

'But you can work for me now.'

'Like I said, I'm hired.'

Bernard Lowe wheezed. He had the look of a man who was undernourished and over-medicated, his wig badly fitted. 'So why waste my bloody time coming over here?'

'I want to pick your brains, just like you want to pick mine.'

Lowe smiled, showing over-large false teeth. 'You speak your mind, don't you?'

'Always.'

'I like that,' Lowe replied. 'I've just had the house redone – garden's being landscaped now. Buggers rob you for a few bleeding plants. Cost a lot of money, alterations do. And furniture. But then again, all good things cost money. Like paintings.' He wheezed again, coughing like a goat, then composed himself. 'You've seen the website, I take it? Mr Luca Meriss trumpeting his lineage and dropping hints everywhere like rabbit shit?'

'I've seen it, but I can't get hold of him.'

'You think the wrong kind of people might be after him?'

'Don't act naive, Mr Lowe. You know the business. For every respectable Cork Street dealer there's a villain. For every rarefied collector there's an underling hired to grub around for the prize.'

Lowe feigned ignorance. 'Meriss might be in danger?'

'If he knows the whereabouts of those paintings, yes. And if not now, he will be soon.'

Lowe coughed, then thumped his chest like a scrawny ape. 'You have to find him. Find out what he knows. That's your business, isn't it? Finding things out.'

'Not any more. This is a one-off. I'm just doing a favour for Jacob Levens. But I'm guessing you already know that. News travels at the speed of light in the art world.'

The old man ignored the comment.

'Want a drink? Or some coffee?' Lowe's hand wiggled in the direction of the refreshments, an incongruous plastic coffee pot sitting alongside bottles of Johnny Walker Black Label. 'Jacob's back on the sauce, you know. He was gibbering like an ass on the phone earlier.'

Gil sighed. It had happened sooner than he had anticipated, Jacob losing his nerve and talking. He always talked too much when he was drunk, always showed his hand. Sober, he was courteous and judicious; inebriated, he was a fool.

'What did he tell you?'

'That he'd found the bodies of the Weir twins and hired you to find their killer. A little bit of prodding got it out of him that it looks like the same killer who topped the Hubers in Berlin all those years ago.' Lowe paused, his hands fiddling with the plastic tubing that ran from the oxygen cylinder to the mask on his lap. 'You know what I'm up to, don't you?'

'You want to know about the Caravaggios. About the Fillide Melandroni portrait – and the other work Luca Meriss was hinting about. And if that turns out to be the Palermo *Nativity*,' he paused for effect, 'what wouldn't you do to get your hands on that?'

'But you said Mr Luca Meriss had gone quiet. Perhaps he's missing? Or is he in hiding?' Lowe asked artfully. 'Of course if he *does* know where the paintings are, killing him would be pointless. The secret would die with him. Unless someone got it out of him first. With a nail gun in the bollocks.'

'You think Luca Meriss is connected to the Weir killings?'

'Now who's being naive?' Lowe replied deftly. 'Think about it – Meriss bursts onto the scene announcing that he knows about the Caravaggios just after the Weirs have been killed.'

'Coincidence.'

'Nah!' Lowe pooh-poohed him. 'The Hubers were dealers like the Weirs. The killer's after a painting – he has to be.'

Gil thought about the rumour he had heard about the Hubers having fallen out with Oscar Schultz over a picture. But he said nothing, just let Lowe run on.

'There must have been a painting in the mix in Berlin. Someone knows about it. And I'm wondering if it's anything to do with the Caravaggios – which have, so conveniently, got back into the news just after the Weirs have been killed. Now, tell me, don't you find that just a bit bloody strange?'

Inwardly Gil agreed, but he wasn't about to admit it

and changed tack. 'What *is* your business, Mr Lowe? Oh, I remember – shipping. You must save on costs when you buy abroad. Shipping paintings is usually so expensive. Shipping artefacts isn't cheap either.'

The intimation hit home. There had been rumours about smuggling dribbling around the art world for some time.

'You're on thin ice, Mr Eckhart,' the old man warned him. 'You want to mind what you say. People might take offence. Or perhaps you just like poking tigers to see if they'll turn round and bite you on the arse.' Lowe put the mask over his face and inhaled some oxygen; his lips were bluish. After a couple of moments, he took the mask off again and stared at Gil. 'I'm not the enemy. Not this time anyway. You've got Oscar Schultz and Harvey Crammer to worry about. Bloody Schultz! Comes over so friendly, but he's dangerous. In – and out – of a car.' Lowe could see that he had struck a nerve. 'I bet that's another reason you want in on these murders, hey? Get close to Schultz again.' When Gil didn't take the bait, he pressed on. 'Maybe you should have a look at Jacob Levens too?'

'I've just remembered what I missed about the art world,' Gil said wryly. 'How loyal you are to one another.'

Unmoved, Lowe continued. 'And there's Catrina Hoyt in New York. Well, mind your step there. She knows about Luca Meriss.'

'By chance? Or because you told her?'

'I told her. And I'm telling you all this for one reason and one reason only – *I want the Caravaggio paintings*. That's why

I'm helping you, Mr Eckhart. You see, there's one thing no one knows but me.' He turned off the oxygen, one hand resting on the metal cylinder, staring at it pensively. 'If you smoke around one of these you can blow yourself up. Did you know that? Blow your bloody head off. How's that for short of breath?'

Gil kept his patience. 'You want to tell me something, Mr Lowe. What is it?'

'You couldn't catch the killer in Berlin, and you won't catch him in London, *because you don't know what his motive is.*'

'No, I don't.' Gil's pulse rate speeded up. 'Do you?'

'Well, that depends. Can you get those paintings for me? If this Luca Meriss is genuine, can you get the pictures from him? I'll pay him, I'll pay you. But I want them – no collector, no dealer's to get them.' Lowe paused, distracted by a knock on the sitting-room door. 'I've a meeting now, Mr Eckhart. Come back later, around six.'

'Why can't you tell me now?'

Lowe grinned. 'I don't do business like that, Mr Eckhart. I like to do things my own way, in my own time. Besides, I've a few jobs to do before we talk again.' He heaved himself to his feet laboriously. 'I want those pictures, you hear me?'

'I hear you.'

'I'll give you the motive in return for the paintings. Fair swap, I'd say.'

Nineteen

Berlin
11.00 a.m.

Luca Meriss reached for his phone and pressed the redial.

It was answered almost immediately.

'What happened to you?' Catrina asked, sitting bolt upright on the side of her bed. They had been cut off mid-conversation, just as Luca was about to tell her the name of one of his email correspondents.

'Someone attacked me.'

She thought of her own break-in and flinched. '*What did you say?*'

'Someone broke into my flat. The whole place has been trashed. I was knocked out and I've just come to. They cut the phone line – I'm using my mobile.'

'Who broke in?'

'I don't know! Some man,' Luca said, almost in a wail. 'He came up behind me, tried to strangle me. I told you, I blacked out.'

'Was anything taken?'

'Nothing. It's all messed up, but nothing's gone.'

She was baffled, trying to gather her thoughts. 'What did he say?'

'Nothing!'

'He must have said something! Didn't he ask you anything?'

'No! I've told you, he knocked me out. He must have just wanted to search the place.' Luca was almost hysterical. 'I can't stay here! I have to get away.'

Catrina was silent, thinking. Thinking that Luca Meriss was in trouble. That his naive grasp at fame had triggered a reaction he had never expected. He might be mocked for his claim to be related to Caravaggio, but the danger was not in his hubris but in his supposed knowledge.

'*Do* you know where the Fillide Melandroni portrait is?'

After a pause, Luca replied in a low voice. 'Yes.'

Catrina felt a thrill shoot through her. 'And the other painting – the one you hinted at – do you know where that is?'

'Yes.'

'You have proof?'

'Yes.'

Her voice took on a suspicious tone. 'So why didn't your attacker ask you for it?'

'*I blacked out!*' Luca wailed. 'How could he? Maybe he was in a hurry, maybe he was scared of getting caught, maybe something scared him off. *How do I know?*' he went on plaintively. 'What if he comes back? What if–'

'Is the proof with you?'

'Of course not! I'm not *that* big a fool! Jesus, what the hell's going on?'

'Calm down!' she snapped, thinking back to their interrupted conversation. 'You were reading out the names of the people who'd emailed you. What was the last name you mentioned?'

His mind was a sudden blank. 'I dunno, I can't remember–'

'Think!'

'It was . . . it was . . . The London Galleries Limited.'

The name jangled inside her. It was familiar, but as more of a rumour than a fact. Where had she heard it? Where?

'I'm leaving,' Luca said suddenly, looking around him. 'I have to get out of here! I have to leave Germany. I'll be in touch.'

'Where are you going?' Catrina shouted, desperate not to lose track of the man who could lead her to the Caravaggios.

'I don't know. I just have to get away from here.'

'Have you got any family?'

'My father. He lives in Palermo.'

Palermo, Sicily – the place from which Caravaggio's *Nativity of St Lawrence and St Francis* was stolen decades earlier. A coincidence? Catrina thought not. In fact she was beginning to believe Luca Meriss's story, incredible as it sounded. And then she realised that the attacker was not the only one who knew about Luca's claims. Bernard Lowe would have spread the news in the art market, and Luca's postings on the internet would have already reached every nosy cranny of the art world. When he put up his first post Luca Meriss had all but painted a target on his forehead.

Catrina took her second gamble in two days. 'Come to New York–'

'*What?*'

'I'll pay for the ticket. Just get here. I'll text you the details on your cell, and my address. You *do* have a passport, don't you?'

'Of course I do. I've worked all over the world.'

'And another thing, Mr Meriss,' she said silkily. 'That *proof* you were talking about . . .'

'About the paintings or about who I am?'

'Both. Bring it with you. Don't leave anything behind. Don't contact anyone. Don't tell anyone where you're going – just leave Berlin.'

He paused. 'Why are you helping me? I can never repay you for this.'

'Oh, but you will,' Catrina replied drily. 'One way or another, you will.'

Twenty

St Bartholomew's Hospital, London
12.00 noon

Pushing open the doors, Gil hurried towards the ICU, heading for a cubicle cordoned off with curtains. Seeing him enter, a nurse moved over.

'You're not supposed to be in here, sir.'

'My wife's just been admitted. An emergency.' He gestured to the screened-off area. 'Is that her? Is that Bette Eckhart?'

'The doctor's seeing to her now.'

'What happened?' Gil asked, running his hands through his hair, out of breath from hurrying. 'What happened?'

'If you'd just take a seat.'

Without answering, Gil moved past her, arriving at the curtained area just as the doctor came out. He was startled, but regained his composure fast.

'Can I help you?'

Gil glanced over his shoulder, catching sight of Bette in the bed beyond.

'That's my wife,' he said, pointing at her. 'Is she OK? Is the baby OK?'

'Your wife had a fall. She was bleeding.'

'I know, she left me a message, but I've only just picked it up.'

The doctor nodded sympathetically. 'As I say, she was haemorrhaging, but we've managed to stop the bleeding and she's stable.'

'The baby?'

'Is doing fine.' The doctor smiled. 'We have to keep your wife hospitalised though. She's too near term to risk anything.'

Nodding, Gil thanked him and moved towards Bette. She hadn't seen him, that much was obvious, and her face was pinched, taut with anxiety.

Gently he touched her arm, then bent down and kissed her. Relieved, Bette buried her head in his shoulder. 'I thought I was going to lose the baby.'

'No way. He's tough.'

'Like his father,' she murmured as Gil took a chair and sat beside the bed. 'You look tired.'

'I love you,' he said by way of reply. 'How did you fall?'

'I was on the back steps. I lost my footing.'

'That's what happens when you can't see your feet.' He teased her. 'You just fell?'

'Isn't that enough?' Bette replied, laughing. 'I was so worried that you'd pick up my message too late. You know, that the baby . . .'

He touched her stomach. 'He's still in there. Safe and sound.'

'What about you? Are you safe and sound? How's the case going?'

'It's not. I packed it in.'

The lie was out of his mouth before he had time to think about it. But it was what intended to do. In less than two days Gil had seen enough to worry him, and Bette's fall had done the rest. He should have been with her . . . The thought sickened him. Why was he risking everything? For Jacob? No friendship was worth that. And besides, the killer was now active in London. Too close to home. Way too close to *his* home.

'Why are you dropping the case?' Bette asked. 'You can't. You've given your word.'

'I gave my word to you when I married you. I didn't marry Jacob Levens.'

'He'd make someone a great wife.'

'Only if he stays off the booze,' Gil teased her, then became serious again. 'It's not worth it. I want to be with you for the next couple of weeks. When the baby's born, I'll go back to it,' he lied again, glancing away from her because he knew she could read his thoughts. 'I've lost the appetite for detective work.'

'No, you haven't,' she said briskly. 'Relax, Gil. I'm here, being looked after twenty-four hours a day. Me and the baby are fine. Safe as houses. Nothing can happen to us here. So what's the point in giving up? You want to take this case, I know you do.'

'I don't.'

'*You do*, because it's unfinished business.' She sighed. 'I've been thinking while I was lying here. About us. About Berlin, and now the killings in London. I won't lie, I didn't want you to get involved – but that was selfish. You *are* involved. Because this didn't start yesterday, it started seven years ago.'

Gil said nothing.

'You said that you thought it was the same man. Same killer. And then I got to thinking about Holly,' Gil held her gaze, 'and how her death happened at the same time as the murders in Berlin. And how you'll now have to talk to the man who killed her. And all the other dealers and collectors that were around seven years ago. And how it will open up all those old wounds. Theirs and yours.' She sighed, shifting her position in bed. 'And you can't run away. And *I* can't, not from Holly.'

He frowned. '*Holly*? She's no threat to you.'

'But I've made her one. And I've only just realised it. I'm having your child, we're making a family, that's what counts now. Only that. I don't want to risk losing it – and I don't want any darkness left over from the past.' She touched his cheek. 'You can't run away.'

'I'm not running away.'

'You are if you give up this case.' She held his gaze. 'I want you to solve it, Gil. Not just because I want you to catch the killer, but because I think it'll lay the past to rest. *Your* past.' Her voice was urgent. 'Do it, please. If not for yourself, if not for me, then do it for our child.'

Twenty-One

Alaknanda, South Delhi, India
5.30 p.m.

Moving his position on the sofa, Naresh Joshi touched his sleeping lover, feeling the warm flesh of her lower arm and the drowsy pulse at her wrist. She murmured in her sleep, but didn't wake as Naresh rose and moved into the bathroom. They had made love earlier that afternoon and dozed off, the evening sliding in around them.

Naresh stepped into the shower. He wasn't thinking about his lover, but about an event which had taken place years earlier. What a fool he had been, he thought, letting the cool water run over his shoulders. Why hadn't he followed it up? He had liked Luca Meriss when he had met him in Italy but had not taken him seriously; had thought that the excitable Italian had been deluded, a fantasist. If Luca Meriss had been more circumspect, more subdued, Naresh would have listened, but he had been garrulous and obsequious by turns and easy to dismiss.

Naresh tilted his head back, feeling the water run over his face. The Indian art market was expanding, dealers and connoisseurs looking further afield to amass collections. Recent developments and openings of galleries in Delhi had caused excitement, Naresh's own writings perpetuating the interest.

Educated at Cambridge, Naresh Joshi had worked for the Courtauld Institute in London and then moved to the USA, where he had researched some of the Getty Collection in California. Highly articulate, with a profound knowledge of the Italian Baroque, Naresh had not settled in the USA and moved back to London, before finally returning home to India. Modest to the point of shyness, he played down his knowledge and appeared unassuming, certainly not the intellectual powerhouse he was. In fact, with his bland features and cultivated voice, Naresh resembled an accountant, some backroom player, content in the shadows of brighter, more flamboyant men.

Stepping out of the shower, Naresh dried himself. He had missed such a chance! he thought. Why hadn't he listened to Luca Meriss's claims? He had wasted years and now here he was, running behind, while everyone else was grabbing a seat on the bandwagon. Meriss had gone public, trumpeting his claims worldwide. Claims he had shared years earlier. Claims Naresh had dismissed.

It had happened in Rome. Naresh had been giving a speech on Caravaggio and the new attributions which were causing a furore in the art world, and afterwards Meriss had come up to him. Asking for five minutes of the historian's time, they had gone to the bar and Meriss had confided his knowledge of the missing Caravaggio portrait of Fillide Melandroni.

'I'm going public when I'm ready,' he had said, 'but you're a living authority on Caravaggio and I wanted to talk to you.'

Naresh had been cautious. There had been a few people – eager for prestige – who had pretended a blood tie to a famous painter. Luca Meriss hadn't been the first.

'I have proof about two of his missing paintings. The portrait of Fillide Melandroni—'

'—was destroyed,' Naresh had said kindly. 'There were 417 works of art housed in the Kaiser Friedrich Museum.'

'Which were moved to the Friedrichshain flak tower for safety during the Second World War,' Meriss had added, nodding. 'I know.'

'And the Flakturm, the tower, was burned down in May 1945. All the paintings were destroyed, including the Fillide Melandroni portrait.'

'They weren't *all* destroyed. The portrait was saved.'

Despite his doubts, Naresh had been intrigued. 'How d'you know?'

'During the fall of Berlin the towers were places of sanctuary. Hitler had four of them built, and the Flakturm – like the others – formed its own community. Thirty thousand Berliners took refuge there.'

Naresh had heard of the Flakturm and had known of its

destruction, but this information about people living in it was fresh and had surprised him. He had thought of them as temporarily occupied, not established communities.

'The towers only surrendered to the Russians when the supplies ran out. Then the occupants were forced to leave.' Meriss had sipped at his glass of wine before continuing. 'The Flakturm was burned, but not entirely. And although many of the works of art *were* destroyed, one was saved.'

Naresh had stared at him. It was incredible! What an addition to the Caravaggio oeuvre. He would write about it, add it to his lecture tour. One more intellectual diadem he could share. A triumph for India, a jab at the pompous European and American dealers. Dealers, Naresh knew, who viewed him with contempt. An untouchable, rejected from the upper artistic echelons.

'*You can prove this?*'

Luca had nodded. 'Someone cut the Fillide Melandroni painting out of its frame, and took it with them on the run.'

Hardly breathing, Naresh had struggled with the information. Could it be true? Could a lost masterpiece really have survived the Second World War? *Could* it have been saved? As he talked on, Naresh had studied the Italian. Luca Meriss seemed coherent, well informed. But then again, a dip into Google could reveal what had happened to the Flakturm.

But not what had happened to the portrait.

'Who took it?'

'I can't tell you that. Not yet.'

'Where is it?'

'I can't tell you that either. Not yet.'

'You said you knew about *two* missing Caravaggio paintings. Was the other in the Flakturm too?'

'No . . . It was in Palermo.'

Naresh had been barely able to speak. '*The Nativity with St Lawrence and St Francis*?'

'Yes, the most famous missing painting in the world.' Meriss had glanced around him cautiously. 'I can't tell you any more.'

'Why not?'

'I need to know that you're committed to this. That you believe what I say. I know you're an honest man, Mr Joshi – your reputation is beyond doubt. But I have to be assured that what I tell you will not be bastardised, or mocked. You must use the knowledge wisely. This is very important to me.'

Naresh had nodded. 'Yes, I can see that.'

'Both of the paintings are important, but the portrait matters most.' Meriss had finished his drink and, unblinking, had held Naresh's gaze. 'You see, Fillide Melandroni was my ancestor. She had a child with Caravaggio–'

'*What?*'

'I'm Caravaggio's descendant.'

Naresh had suppressed a disappointed sigh. So the Italian was a fame hunter, he thought. Some jumped-up art groupie.

In that instant Naresh Joshi had dismissed Luca Meriss.

And now the historian was sitting on the edge of his bath and realising that he had missed an opportunity the like of which he would never see again.

Twenty-Two

London
1.00 p.m.

'I thought you'd gone off me,' Simmons said, recognising Gil's number as he picked up his mobile. 'Was it something I said?'

'It's *everything* you've ever said,' Gil replied, smiling as he walked away from the hospital towards his car. 'You wanted to talk?'

'The case in Berlin. The German police are being very cagey about it. Won't let me have anything but the basic details. I've got the case file, but it's not complete. At least, it doesn't tally with what you told me.'

'What's missing?'

Simmons reached for his notes.

'No witnesses, no suspicious people in the area. According to the file, no one saw anything. Until the bodies were found by the Hubers' daughter, Greta. She called the police.'

Gil unlocked his car door and slid into the driving seat.

'That's odd. I remember someone mentioning a man who'd been hanging around. He'd been seen on Friedrichstrasse days before the murders, close to the gallery.' Gil thought back. 'They said he was tall, scruffy, looked like he'd been sleeping rough.'

'Who told you about him?'

'Greta.'

'But there's nothing about him in the police file.'

'Have you got a list of the people they interviewed?'

'I can't tell you that!' Simmons said with mock outrage. 'You've supposed to be helping *me*.'

'To solve the case. Yeah, I know. And as both of us want this over and done with as soon as possible we might as well pool our resources. If you try to get into the art world without my help you'll have no chance. They'll close up tighter than a bear's arse.'

'OK, OK.' Resigned, Simmons began to read out the names: 'Hans Oppenheim, the janitor.'

'He's dead now.'

'So you don't think he killed the Weir brothers?' Simmons asked mockingly, before continuing. 'Lena Hertz – she was the accountant at the gallery – and Anton Hadstadt. He worked with her. They were cleared . . .' Simmons read down the list. 'All these people were cleared, alibis checked out. No one was suspected. The German police couldn't find anyone to charge. No one with a motive, no one with a grudge.' He paused. 'They looked at the daughter—'

'That was just routine. Greta had nothing to do with her

parents' death. She was with friends that day, and besides, she had no motive.'

'She inherited the gallery and her parents' house.'

'You haven't met her,' Gil explained. 'She's tiny, nervy, very academic. Teaches English in Berlin, or at least she did. Greta was shattered by the death of her parents. She had to have psychiatric help to get over it.'

'How d'you know?'

'I kept in touch with her for a while after the killings. But I haven't spoken to her for a few years now.'

Simmons took in a weary breath. 'So – off the record – who did you suspect?'

Normally Gil would have refused to answer. But he wanted the case finished. He wanted the killer caught before he could get to his family, or get into his head. He wanted Bette safe, along with his unborn child. He wanted – above all – for the echo of Berlin from seven years earlier to be expunged. And he was prepared to take any help he could to make that happen.

'I investigated Oscar Schultz,' Gil began. 'He's a German dealer in Berlin and often visits London. There are rumours that he hires runners to undercut dealers – he's even been suspected of getting his men to steal to order. Nothing proved. Had one conviction for fraud in his twenties, but thinks no one knows about it.'

'You think he might be the killer?'

'Honestly? I don't know. Schultz is a wriggler. Can't get a grip on him. Deals in Italian and French art, always on the periphery though. Never quite been accepted by the old guard. Handsome, but a bit of the car salesman about him. Hides his background.' Gil paused, thinking of the man who had once shattered his life. 'He seems friendly and open, but he's a coward at heart. I wouldn't put anything past him if he thought he was under threat.'

He left out the part Oscar Schultz had played in Holly's death.

'I investigated Harvey Crammer too.'

'What's he like?'

'Clever, brilliant mind, very learned. Knows the art world better than anyone and keeps what he knows to himself. Big man – has gravitas, presence. A powerful man with powerful friends, some of them in American politics. He's no stranger to European royalty either. Comes from a medical family, parents were both surgeons, well respected.'

On the other end of the phone, Simmons was juggling with his notes, finally getting them in order and reading out his last entries.

'I've got some other names I want to run by you. Jacob Levens.'

Gil flinched. 'He's harmless.'

'You sure?'

'Yeah, I'm sure.'

Was he? Gil wondered. Was he really *that* sure about Jacob Levens?

'What about Bernard Lowe?'

Surprised, Gil wondered if he had been watched as he visited the old man earlier.

'Lowe's on his last legs. He couldn't murder a bacon sandwich.'

'Just one more name for you,' Simmons went on. 'Catrina Hoyt.'

'Based in New York. I don't know her personally, only by reputation. It's said that she barbecues kittens, but it's only a rumour. Look, if you're asking me if she's a killer I don't know, but frankly, I wouldn't think so.'

'Why?'

'Catrina Hoyt's certainly capable of murder. She's easily as strong as a man. But she's a fighter – you know what I mean by that? In your face, no backing down, street hard.'

'So?'

'This killer's not like that. This killer's sly. He's been waiting seven years. *Seven years* – that takes persistence. You need restraint to wait so long. And it takes a certain temperament to torture people slowly, making it last. The person who killed the Hubers and the Weirs is controlled, disciplined. Patient. I reckon he's got a grudge, something that's needled him for a long time. He's unusual in another way too.'

'Which is?'

'He tortures men *and* women. That's rare. Not many killers torture both sexes in the same way.' Gil paused. 'But I've been thinking about it and I realise that there *was* a difference. He used the nail gun on the men's genitals, but he mutilated Alma Huber's breasts, not her genitals.'

'So?'

'Why?'

Phil Simmons was mystified. 'Why what?'

'Why would he do that?' Gil asked. 'Why not stick to the pattern? Torture them all by mutilating their sexual organs? But he didn't. For some reason he didn't go that far with Alma. It was too personal, too private.'

'He killed her, for fuck's sake.'

'Yes, he killed her. But it wasn't sexual.'

'He mutilated her breasts!'

'That's different,' Gil insisted. 'That's like he's playing at it. He didn't rape her, or assault her, and she was still a very beautiful woman. He murdered her – but her torture was post mortem. Alma Huber died quickly, from a heart attack, so it was over then. But he didn't leave. He carried on with the torture to give us a signature. So we would know it was the same killer. I think it was window dressing, done to match the man's injuries.'

Simmons urged Gil to continue. 'So, go on, what's the bottom line?'

'The killer had limits with Alma Huber. And that made me wonder.'

'Would you like to share?'

'Maybe he knew her.'

The suggestion swung between them, Simmons the first to speak.

'Which would point to someone in the art world?'

'Maybe.'

'It's strange that both Crammer and Schultz are in London now, just like they were in Berlin when the Hubers were murdered.' Simmons paused, thinking aloud. 'Between you and me – if you had to guess the killer – who's your money on?'

'Crammer's never put a foot wrong academically or socially,' Gil replied. 'But he's a loner.'

'A murderer?'

'If Crammer's a murderer you'll only know it when he sticks the knife in your ribs.'

Twenty-Three

London
12.45 p.m.

Disgruntled after his meeting, Bernard Lowe slumped into his seat in the back of the car and glowered at his driver through the mirror.

'Jacob Levens' gallery, Cork Street,' he snapped, then rang his secretary from his car phone. No mobile phones for Bernard Lowe, no texting. 'Any messages?'

'Nothing, sir.'

'Not heard from Gil Eckhart?' When the answer was negative, Lowe put down the phone. A few minutes later they arrived outside Jacob Levens' gallery and Lowe clambered out, brushing aside the help of his driver as he clutched onto his portable oxygen tank.

Having spotted his visitor, a surprised Jacob hurried towards the front entrance of the gallery and unlocked the door. Since the Weirs had been killed the previous day, the open-house atmosphere of the London galleries had changed. Porters who normally worked in the basements on packing or repairs had been pressed into action as surrogate doormen, and bouncers and receptionists greeted unfamiliar visitors nervously. No one was working late. No one left alone. No one trusted anyone. Even colleagues.

The atmosphere was brooding. Everyone had heard about the murders. Everyone was gossiping about the torture the Weir brothers had suffered. Some remembered the Huber killings and discussed the connection furtively as titbits of rumour and gossip surfaced. Everyone was terrified.

Showing the old man into his office, Jacob smiled diffidently. There was a faint whiff of whisky in the air, hardly obliterated by the pungent aroma of peppermint.

'Good to see you, Bernard. What can I do for you?'

'Come off it,' the old man snapped. 'This is you and me talking and I don't have time to piss about.' He sat down at the desk, facing Jacob as he took his seat. 'It can't have escaped your attention that the murdered dealers were all connected to each other. The Hubers to the Weirs, *and all of them to us.*'

Jacob glanced over to the door, to check that it was closed and that they couldn't be overheard.

'I never told anyone about our association with *Der Kreis der Acht*–'

'The Circle of Eight!' Bernard snorted. 'I always thought it was a fucking stupid name. It's none too accurate either, not now that four of us have been killed.'

'It was just a business arrangement,' Jacob said heatedly.

'People form groups all the time. You know the art world – we all believed we'd do better if we combined forces. And we did.'

'We *think* we did,' Lowe contradicted him. 'But how do we know? You think Oscar Schultz and Harvey Crammer have been telling us everything? And you, Jacob? Have you been an open book?'

'If it comes to that, what about you?'

'Yes, *what* about me?' Lowe replied. 'We made money trading with the Hubers and the Weirs. We had Europe covered, and the USA controlled by Harvey Crammer, and we were right to keep quiet about it. Why tip off the competitors? Nothing against the law in combining forces.'

Jacob was watching him nervously.

'But?'

'When Terrill and Alma Huber were murdered in Berlin I thought it was a one-off. Some nutter. Just one of those things. Until now. Now the Weirs have been killed and that's not a coincidence.'

'And I found them.'

'I know,' Bernard said, nodding. 'I think you were meant to. I also think we're in trouble, Jacob. Someone's picking off the members of *Der Kreis der Acht*.'

'We did nothing wrong!'

'We cheated a few people, but it was business. Business *is* competitive. Hardly worth killing us for.' Lowe sighed, exasperated, and pointed to the waste bin. 'For Christ's sake, Jacob, you're not fooling anyone! Get yourself another drink.' He watched as the dealer poured himself a double whisky. 'I can't say I blame you. It must have been nasty, finding the Weirs like that. Must have brought back a lot of old memories. About your sister—'

'I know who you mean!'

'Alma was a handsome woman,' Lowe said admiringly. 'I remember when she was married to Harvey Crammer. I was surprised that marriage didn't last – they seemed suited.'

'Crammer wasn't a homebody. He liked travelling too much. Alma loved Berlin, the gallery. She didn't want to spend her life in hotel rooms. She wanted a family. When she married Terrill and had their daughter she was happy.'

'How *is* Greta?'

'I don't know,' Jacob shrugged. 'I haven't seen her for a long time. I know she's my niece, but Greta's very independent, always was. Last I heard, she went to India to teach English. She wasn't fond of Berlin, certainly not after her parents died.'

Lowe was watching the distracted dealer, trying to force something out of him. 'What do you know that I don't?'

His eyes widened. 'I don't know anything!'

'You can't even guess at a motive?'

'No.'

'Well, whoever killed the Hubers didn't get what they wanted. Maybe they didn't get it from the Weirs either. Which will leave the rest of us in trouble . . . Oscar Schultz is terrified, Harvey Crammer implacable as ever. You? Well, it's clear you're not sleeping.'

Jacob took a long drink of his whisky.

'Who's to say we'll get targeted? It might be over! It might all be finished—'

'You believed that?' Lowe asked sardonically. 'I don't. I think someone wants to kill us all. I just don't know why. We made money, I smuggled some paintings. Don't act surprised, Jacob – you knew all about it. You just didn't ask for details. But that doesn't stop you being involved. The Weirs made a killing with that Murillo painting, but that was just luck. There has to be a *real* motive, a reason to kill.'

'I don't know what it is,' Jacob said brokenly. 'Ask the others.'

'I intend to,' Lowe replied, adding, 'Of course it could be someone in *Der Kreis der Acht*—'

Jacob's head shot up. 'It can't be!'

'Can't it? Harvey Crammer's a hard man. Oscar Schultz, who knows? Even you're beginning to look a bit suspect—'

'You're a member too—'

'I'm dead on my feet!' Lowe replied, laughing drily. The only thing I can kill is time. Nah, it's not me.' He changed tack. 'You've hired Gil Eckhart – that's good. I wanted him to work for me, but he refused. The killer's got to be caught this time.' Lowe reached into his pocket and slid a note across the desk to Jacob.

He picked it up and read:

WATCH OUT, OLD MAN, SEE YOU LATER.

Stunned, Jacob stared at his visitor.

'God Almighty.'

'Won't help me now,' Lowe replied. 'Where's Eckhart? I can't reach him on his mobile phone or at his home. Have you got another number?'

Jacob shook his head. 'No . . . What d'you want Gil for?'

'I need his help – and I need to tell him something. I *have* to tell him something important.'

'This note's serious.' Jacob glanced back at the piece of paper. 'You should call the police.'

He was ashamed to admit that he was afraid. That he wanted the old man out of his gallery – fast – before anything happened. To either of them.

'It all comes down to the motive,' Lowe pushed on, feeling Jacob Levens out, trying to see if he was hiding anything.

'No one ever discovered what it was,' Jacob replied, changing the subject. 'What are you going to do about that note? Was it hand-delivered?'

'Yes.'

'So they know where you live!'

'They do,' Lowe agreed. 'But then again, so do a lot of people here and abroad. I've had plenty of visitors to my home over the years. I like entertaining, listening, watching. It's just tough to think that one of my guests might well turn out to be my murderer.'

'You can't go back to your house.'

'It's my bloody home!' Lowe replied shortly. 'I've got staff to look out for me. They're well paid.'

'*It's serious!*' Jacob snapped, the drink flushing his cheeks. 'You wouldn't be joking if it had been your sister murdered.

Or if you'd found the Weir twins.' He took a long drink of whisky. 'Call the police.'

'The only person I want to see is Gil Eckhart.' Lowe stood up, clutching his oxygen tank. 'Get him to call, will you?' He smiled slyly. 'And stop worrying about me. I've got an alarm system that could stop Mossad agents. The bloody place is lit up like a brothel at night. Besides, I'm no fool. I won't be opening my doors to any strangers.'

'Alma did,' Jacob said sadly. 'But then again, maybe it wasn't a stranger.'

Twenty-Four

4.00 p.m.

After picking up his messages, Gil returned the call from Bernard Lowe, but no one picked up. Surprised, he phoned Dr Dunning. The pathologist's message had sounded unusually animated.

'I found an injection mark,' Dunning said as soon as he heard Gil's voice. 'It was hidden under Sebastian Weir's hair, in his scalp, at the base of his skull. Easy to miss.'

'What about Benjamin?'

'Same,' Dunning replied. 'You were right, Mr Eckhart: the Weir brothers were sedated. With a muscle relaxant. Perhaps we should check out the Huber victims.'

'We can't. They were cremated,' Gil replied. 'Have you told Inspector Simmons about the drug?'

'I've left him a message, but you got back to me first.'

'This muscle relaxant – why didn't you find it before?'

'Because this drug's effects wear off very quickly, about

an hour after the injection's been administered. It didn't show up in their blood tests.'

Gil frowned. 'So how d'you know it was there?'

'I took *two* sets of bloods,' Dunning replied. 'When I arrived at the gallery, I took blood from both brothers. But one of the police officers there accidentally touched the syringes before I'd bagged them—'

'So the tests would have been contaminated?'

At the other end of the phone, Dr Dunning nodded. 'And I only found out *after* I'd finished examining the bodies – which was over an hour later. So then I had to repeat the blood tests.'

'And by that time all trace of the drug would have gone?'

'Exactly,' Dunning agreed. He glanced at the notes in his hand. 'But there was a particular test I could do, which would show traces. And it did. I've just got the results back, and they confirm it. The Weir brothers *were* drugged. Their systems were paralysed. Completely helpless. They knew what was happening to them, but they couldn't move.'

'The scalping?'

'Was done while they were still alive,' Dunning continued. 'Likewise the injuries to their genitals. Strangulation eventually killed them.'

'With this drug inside them, could they talk?'

Dunning paused, thinking for an instant. 'No. Their vocal cords would have been paralysed too. They might have been able to grunt, but they couldn't have made understandable speech.'

'That means one of two things – that the Weirs had already told their killer what he wanted to know, so communication no longer mattered and the added torture was just a bonus. Or they *didn't* tell him – maybe they didn't even know – and he tortured them out of spite. He would have been angry that they didn't come up with the goods, didn't give him what he wanted. In his mind, they deserved to be tortured. As a punishment.'

He could sense the pathologist's shock over the phone line.

'But surely he knew how much they'd suffer?'

'Of course he knew,' Gil said wearily. 'That's why he did it.'

Twenty-Five

After double-locking the gallery door, Jacob drew the heavy black blind down over the window and then walked into his office at the back of the building. He was afraid to stay and afraid to leave. Outside, the street looked menacing and empty, the surrounding galleries closed, few tourists around on a sodden January night. And only fifty yards away blue and white police tape cordoned off The Weir Gallery, the window emptied.

There had been so much blood, Jacob remembered, swallowing hard. His first reaction had been disbelief when he had found the bodies, and then revulsion, his gaze fixing on the blue lips, the flecks of spittle on Sebastian's chin. Even though the temperature had been over a hundred, the bodies had lost their flesh tones and were turning into grisaille, a monochrome engraving of torture. Details imprinted themselves on Jacob's mind: the pool of urine under Benjamin Weir, the scuffing of the carpet where Sebastian had struggled frantically, kicking his feet, and the nail gun left between his legs. Details roared at him.

The blood from the Benjamin's left ear, the tongue half bitten off, the snot from Sebastian's nose, his bound hands clawed up behind him.

Reaching for the bottle of whisky, Jacob then shook his head. No, he thought, as he pushed it to one side and moved over to the safe instead. His girth made bending down difficult but he knelt on one knee and entered the security code. When he heard the reassuring click, he opened the safe door and reached in.

He hadn't looked inside the envelope for many years, but found himself suddenly compelled to shake out its contents onto his desk. There were photographs, notes, letters – and a small plastic bag in which there was something wrapped up in tissue paper.

You take it, Jacob, his sister had said to him. *You look after it and make sure Greta never finds out. I don't want her to know, and I don't want her in danger. Hide it and I'll come over to London in the spring to take it back.*

But Alma had never made it. To London, or the spring. She had been murdered instead.

He was so angry, Alma had told her
brother over the phone. *I've never seen*
anyone so angry. I thought the
shock would kill him.

Her voice had been panicked, the fear in it unnerving. Terror, genuine and raw.

I could see that he didn't believe me, but I swore I didn't know.

You should never *have told me, Jacob! You should never have told me. I have a family, a daughter to protect.*

He reached for the whisky again, then threw the bottle across the room. It smashed against the far wall.

You dragged me into this. It's your duty to get me out of it. We're being watched, did I tell you that?

Alma had been beside herself, desperate.

Last night someone was hanging around outside the gallery. I've sent Greta away, but for how long? This is her home.

His hands shaking, Jacob picked up the plastic bag again.

If anything happens to me – or to my family – it will be your doing. Yours alone.

Jacob stared at the bag. Its contents were hidden, but he knew what they were. And then he remembered how he had lied to the Berlin police. How he had said that he had no idea why anyone would kill his sister and brother-in-law. They had no enemies, they were popular, well liked.

Did they have any criminal connections?

Jacob had stared at the policeman, incredulous. *Criminal connections? My sister? Terrill? No, they were hard-working people, good people. They had a successful gallery, but never overreached themselves. And they had scrupulous reputations as dealers. Everything they did was respectable. Ask anyone who knew them.* He had gone on emphatically. *No one had a reason to kill them. No one.*

The words resounded in Jacob's head. Mocked him, sneered at him for the liar he was. And in his hand he held the little plastic bag which contained the secret Alma was desperate to protect. The secret she had promised to come back for. The secret he had used as a weapon against her. Just a piece of official paper, but capable of ruining lives. He hadn't wanted to use it, but his hand had been forced.

It was a secret which would set in motion events that would destroy them both.

Twenty-Six

Departure Lounge, Berlin Tegal Airport

The one person Luca Meriss didn't expect to contact him was Gil Eckhart. But while he waited for his plane to New York the call came through. Luca picked up nervously.

'Hello?'

'Luca Meriss, can I talk to you? I'm an investigator.'

'Police?'

'No, I've been hired privately.'

Luca struggled to control his thoughts. 'What d'you want with me?'

'I need to talk to you about your website.'

'You didn't send me that photograph, did you?'

'What photograph?' Gil replied, hearing the background noise of a tannoy. 'Where are you? An airport? You said you were based in Berlin. Are you leaving the country–'

'*Why d'you want to know?*' Luca replied, out of his depth and floundering. 'Have you spoken to Ms Hoyt?'

Gil took a stab in the dark.

'You're going to see her in New York?'

'It was her idea. I had to get out of Berlin,' Luca continued, looking around him.

He was spooked, jumpy. Unsure as to whether he was doing the right thing. It had been a long shot, but it had worked. Pretending that he had been attacked had forced the dealer's hand and brought forth the invitation to New York. Temporarily out of Berlin, and danger, all Luca had to do was to make sure no one discovered his deception.

'*Who* did you say you were?'

'Gil Eckhart. It's OK, you can trust me.'

'I doubt that! I don't think I can trust anyone.' Luca hurried on, sticking to his story. 'How do I know who you are? You might be the man who attacked me.'

'I didn't attack you, Mr Meriss,' Gil said, surprised. 'I'm in London, but I think that the person who attacked you might have something to do with the case I'm working on.' He could sense that the Italian was starting to relax. 'Did all this happen after you put up your website?'

'Yes.'

'You said you were sent a photograph. Of what?'

Luca was torn. Should he trust Gil? Or was it was just a ploy to get him to open up? But then again, he needed help. He hadn't imagined the photograph, or the fact that someone was after him. Luca looked round at the people in the Departure Lounge, many of them checking the board overhead. No one was looking at him. He was on his way to New York, but how well did he know Catrina Hoyt? He was trusting her – but why? He didn't know her. He might simply be jumping from one danger into another.

'Mr Meriss, are you still there?'

'What's the case you're working on?'

'There's been a double murder in London,' Gil replied. 'I think it might be connected to another double murder in Berlin seven years ago.'

'*What have I got to do with that?*'

'You might have nothing to do with it. I only wanted to talk to you about the Caravaggio paintings. But after what you've just told me, I've got to warn you.'

'Warn me?'

'You don't know what you've got yourself into. You're setting yourself up, Mr Meriss. You publicly announced that you know the whereabouts of two valuable paintings – and now you've been attacked.' Luca was silent, listening as Gil continued. 'You should have gone through a dealer.'

'I've nothing to hide!'

'It's not a question of hiding anything, it's going through the proper channels,' Gil continued, thinking of Bernard Lowe. 'Dealers will be glad to deal with you—'

'*And cheat me!*' Luca snapped. 'Don't you think I don't know what the reaction will be? That people will sneer at what I've got to say? Of course they will! That's why I wanted to do it right, but no one would listen.' He thought back. 'I talked to Naresh Joshi a long time ago, but he thought I was a crank.'

Surprised, Gil thought of the historian.

'You went to Joshi?'

'I wanted him to believe me. I *am* a descendant of Caravaggio and I *do* know where the paintings are. *I have proof.* Naresh Joshi's respected. If he'd believed me other people would have done. *I wanted to do it right!*' Luca said, his tone plaintive. 'I didn't want to go public on the internet and bring all this down on my head.'

'Drop your voice—'

'You think someone's listening?'

'Someone attacked you, so yes, I think someone might well be listening.' Gil's first instincts about the Italian were mixed. 'What d'you want out of all this? Fame? Notoriety?'

'*Respect!*' Meriss hissed. 'I want respect!'

'Well, you went the wrong way about it. The *Nativity* was allegedly stolen by the Mafia – you want them after you?'

'They didn't take it!'

'You know that?' Gil pushed him. 'And the Fillide Melandroni portrait that was supposedly burned – you think you can just declare that you know where it is and *not* expect a reaction? What's the angle? You want to push up the price? Work up a frenzy before you sell the paintings?'

There was a pause on the other end before Luca replied.

'*Sell them?* They're not my property.'

'I thought you said you knew where they were.'

'I do, but *they're not my property*! They belong to everyone!' His voice plummeted. 'That's why I went to Naresh Joshi, to put them in his hands, to make sure that they would be safe, protected.'

Gil sighed. Luca Meriss was either stupid or naive.

'But you can't have believed that no one would come after you. Those paintings are worth a fortune. People would do anything to get hold of them. I'm not talking about recognised dealers, I'm talking about the runners, the thugs that get hold of works of art for collectors. They use any means, Mr Meriss. Didn't you know that?'

'I never thought . . .'

'You say you're a descendant of Caravaggio.'

'I *am!* I have proof.'

Gil cut across him.

'Don't go online again. Stay away from the internet. Don't answer your calls. Stay quiet. You've set yourself up, Mr Meriss, so now do what I'm telling you. It's good advice. Call me when you get to New York. I know the art world, I can help you—'

'But I don't know *you*.'

'You don't know who sent you that photograph either. Or who attacked you.'

'No.'

Gil thought for a moment. 'Go to Catrina Hoyt if you want, but be careful.'

'Can I trust her?'

'I don't know,' Gil answered frankly. 'But you can trust me.'

The Italian was unnerved, wavering. 'I just wanted to tell people who I was.'

It was suddenly clear to Gil.

'That all that matters, isn't it? Not so much the paintings

Twenty-Seven

London
6.00 p.m.

Tipping back his chauffeur's hat, Gary Rimmer stared at the approaching woman. He had tried his luck a couple of times with the nurse, but she had played hard to get, treating him like a nobody. He wondered unkindly if she was after her patient, if she had designs on the old bugger Lowe, but knew she would be out of luck there.

Frieda knew she had Gary's full slavering attention and surprised him by walking over to the car.

'Hello.'

'Hi.'

He loved the German accent, shit hot. 'How you doing?'

'OK,' she said, leaning against the door and running her finger along the top of the half-opened window. 'I just thought I'd say hello, seeing as how we're both working here.'

His luck had changed.

'Yeah, well, it's nice to chat. How's the old man doing?'

'Mr Lowe's fine. I'm just coming to relieve the night nurse. She'll kill me if I'm late.'

'You tell me if she gives you any trouble, OK?'

She smiled at him warmly, looking at the Rolls. 'Lovely car. But then Mr Lowe's got a lot of money, hasn't he? All those antiques and paintings in the house. I'm so scared of knocking into something. I walk around with my arms by my side all day, just in case.'

Enchanted, Gary smiled. 'You're tiny. You couldn't knock anything over.'

She peered in through the car window. 'God, it's a beautiful car. And he's got a car phone.'

'Yeah,' Gary replied, bigging himself up. 'And I get to hear some pretty interesting things, I can tell you.'

'About what?'

'His business.'

'Oh.' She looked unimpressed, and Gary was eager to hold her interest. 'He talks to some important people.'

'He's pretty important himself, isn't he?' Frieda replied, her attention wavering. 'But business talk is always dull.'

'Not Bernard Lowe's business. I heard something interesting yesterday – and this morning . . .' Gary continued. 'He's onto some famous paintings. Caravaggio.'

Her expression was blank.

'One of them might have been stolen by the Mafia.'

'*Mafia?*'

'But now it's turned up. At least that's what I think's

going on.' He could see that she still wasn't impressed and upped the stakes. 'I looked up the artist on the net. His work's worth millions, rising every day.'

She was listening now.

'Millions?'

Gary nodded. 'Made me think, I can tell you. I mean, what's the old man going to do with millions? He's damn near dead – can't take his money with him, can he? It's all wrong. Why waste it on him?' Confident that he now had her interest, Gary dropped his voice. 'And he was also talking about the Weir murders yesterday. The victims were tortured, you know. Blood everywhere.'

Her eyebrows rose.

'I heard about that. Who killed them?'

'I dunno. No one does. But – I mean I'm just guessing – maybe it's connected with this Caravaggio business?'

She was listening, taking it all in, ready to pass every word on to Oscar Schultz.

'Did you know the men who were killed?'

Gary whistled between his teeth.

'Been to that gallery many times. They looked like a couple of ponces, but they say not.' His voice dropped again. 'Not a word to anyone—'

'I promise.'

'—but I did overhear one thing that made me think.'

'What?'

'It was just a chance remark, a throwaway line really. Old man Lowe had been to see another dealer, Jacob Levens, and when he got back to the car he made a call. I don't know who he was talking to, but he was rattled, I could see that.'

'What did he say?'

Behind them, her name was suddenly called out. On the top of the front steps stood the night nurse, irritated and eager to leave.

'You better get going,' Gary said, jerking his head towards the irate woman. 'We can talk again later.'

Frieda didn't want to wait. 'But what was it?'

'What was *what*?'

'What did Mr Lowe say?'

'Oh, that.' Gary dropped his voice again. 'He said that it had just been a matter of time. And that he knew it would catch up with them one day.'

Twenty-Eight

Berlin

Walking in at the back entrance of the gallery on the Friedrichstrasse, Greta Huber froze, a queasy feeling in her stomach. Seven years earlier she had walked through the same doorway at nine thirty on the evening of 14 March. She had been out with friends and was tired, but had promised to call in to see her mother, and had dropped by on her way home.

The back door of the gallery had been locked. Greta remembered opening it with her key, and had been surprised that the lights had been turned off. Earlier her mother had made a point about how she would be working on the gallery accounts, saying she would be at there until at least ten p.m. So the darkness that greeted Greta had been unexpected as she made her way to the desk and flicked on the lamp.

As her mother had said, she *had* been working on the accounts. The ledgers were open, the safe door yawning wide. A cold mug of coffee was still sitting by the phone and Alma's jacket was draped over the back of her chair. Looking around, Greta had expected her mother to walk in at any moment, but when Alma didn't appear, she called out.

'*Mutter? Mutter?*'

She had checked the private lavatory off the office, only to find it empty. Likewise the staff kitchen. Growing anxious, Greta had then moved into the gallery itself, opening the door to find her mother facing her, slumped on the floor. Naked, bound, covered in blood, her breasts mutilated. Obviously dead.

Rigid, unable to understand what she was seeing, Greta had stared at the grisly image, shaking uncontrollably. Then she had run – run as fast as she could, screaming into the street.

The police had interviewed her soon after, but by then she had hardly been able to speak. Words had fluttered out of the back of her mind. Nothing lodged, only the image of her dead mother. The police called an ambulance. The hospital called in a doctor. The doctor called a psychiatrist, and Greta Huber stopped talking. For eighteen months she had remained mute, eating what was given her, doing what she was told.

You walk, you sit, you eat, you watch the television.

But you don't, Greta had thought to herself. You don't watch anything. Because there is only one image in your mind – the murder.

You think and see and hear and smell everything about

that. Nothing *now*, nothing of this time, only that evening of the 14th of March, on the Friedrichstrasse. I can still smell blood, feel the cold handle of the gallery door as I wrenched it open. I can hear my running footsteps and taste that burnt, acrid odour of terror.

You think I'm recovering? I'm suspended, eternally hanging from the killer's rope. And I'll stay here for as long as he wants me to.

The shock had been so intense that the news of her father's death was withheld from Greta. The doctors never realised that she knew. That she had guessed. Because if Terrill Huber had been alive he would have been with her. Another door closed. Months passed, a year, then another. Greta had had no siblings to confide in, there had been no sharing of grief. The load had been hers and hers alone. Sometimes people visited her – the staff from the gallery, an old friend of her mother's. But finding her uncommunicative, they stopped calling. Another door closed.

To Greta's relief she found herself beached in her own mind, with the sound of the sea in her ears and the cawing of gulls, which, at night, had sometimes sounded like children. Slowly she recovered and the murder scene was no longer her only thought. Occasionally Greta found herself thinking back to her time teaching English in Berlin, and her mind could – if she pushed it – go back home. For a little while.

A door opened.

In the time it took Greta to return to sanity the only person who came to see her more than once was Gil

Eckhart. He was a big man, very still, composed, breathing slowly. He had asked her questions and when she didn't answer, he hadn't even seemed surprised. But he *had* come back and asked her again, and on the third occasion she had answered him. Hardly making words, but turning in his direction when he said the name Jacob.

Her uncle, in London. Her mother's brother, Jacob Levens. *Would you like to see him?* Gil Eckhart had asked. Her head had remained turned in his direction, but she had said nothing. Because she hadn't been close to her uncle. And any chance of a closeness in childhood had been destroyed by their later distance apart.

Then Greta remembered the last time she had seen Gil Eckhart, noted the change and known he was suddenly *like her*. Suffering some incredible, unbreachable loss. She had never known what had caused his grief, and had never seen him again. One year and five months later, Greta left the institution. She abandoned Berlin and went to live in Munich, where she taught German to students. Later she went to India to teach. She made no close relationships and developed anorexia, but she kept teaching, grubbing out some sense in words.

And now she was back in Berlin, opening the same door, walking into the same gallery that she had entered seven years earlier. The legal arrangements had been finalised only that afternoon, the premises Greta had inherited sold on after years of being leased out. The lawyers had wanted to tell her everything about the purchaser, but she had not been interested in any personal details. The money for the sale would be invested, but not in the art world. The gallery held nothing for her. The place was little more than a catacomb for her parents. She had only returned to hand over the final set of keys.

If you bring them around yourself about five o'clock, the solicitor had said earlier, *I can introduce you to the new owner.*

Greta had made her own plans instead. She would leave the keys on the office desk early, with a note, then pull the door closed as she left. That way she would never have to see the new owner, offer good wishes she didn't feel, or pretend interest for someone who had just obtained premises she believed cursed.

But her plan had failed, Greta realised as she walked into the gallery. The place wasn't empty.

Slowly she moved into the main viewing area and looked around. A Persian rug lay over the place on the floor where her mother had been slaughtered, and she could smell turpentine, not blood. But what surprised her the most was the presence of someone sitting at the desk where her mother had once worked. A man Greta knew. A handsome man, who turned as he heard her walk in.

'Greta!' Oscar Schultz stood up and walked over to her, smiling. 'How good to see you.'

She was openly hostile. 'What are you doing here?'

Despite her animosity, he was friendly to a fault.

'My dear, your lawyer tried to tell you the news, but you didn't want to know . . . I'm so sorry if it's come as a shock to you . . .' he shrugged, '. . . but I'm the owner now.'

Twenty-Nine

London

Surprised that he had been unable to contact Bernard Lowe, Gil made his way to Eaton Square to find Gary Rimmer in the car, waiting beside the kerb with the engine running.

Knocking on the window, Gil watched Rimmer let down the glass. 'Yeah?'

'You're Bernard Lowe's chauffeur, aren't you?'

'So what?'

'I've been trying to reach him for a couple of hours, with no luck. Are his phones off?'

'Mr Lowe,' Rimmer managed to instil a potent dislike into the name, 'never answers his phone. And if he tells the staff not to, they won't either. He uses the one in the car.'

'But you're expecting him?'

'No. Why d'you ask?'

Gil gave him a slow look. 'Your engine's running.'

'I was told to bring the car round and wait for him.'

Rimmer checked his watch. 'That was three quarters of an hour ago.'

'And that didn't strike you as odd? Keeping you waiting that long? Why not turn the engine off?'

'Mr Lowe said, 'Keep the engine running,' so I've kept the engine running,' Rimmer replied, his tone curt. 'You do what Mr Lowe says. *Everything* he says. You don't question it.'

Gil glanced over at the house, then walked up to the front door. On his third ring, a Filipino maid answered, recognised him from the morning, and let him in.

'I came to see Mr Lowe. He's expecting me.'

'Just a moment, sir,' the woman replied, walking off.

The house was very quiet, no sounds of phones or any other activity, although Gil knew that Bernard Lowe had offices in the lower ground floor. Earlier in the day Gil had heard footsteps from below and from overhead, together with the muted murmur of frenetic staff and the ringing of the doorbell. But now the house seemed emptied out, office hours over, the evening activities in abeyance.

Glancing at his watch, Gil remembered what Lowe had said earlier:

I know what the motive is. The motive in return for the paintings. Fair swap, I'd say.

Fair swap indeed, Gil thought, as he looked through the hall window. Outside, he could see the sullen Gary Rimmer sitting in the car, the engine still running.

Then the maid reappeared from the back of the house, flustered. 'Sorry, sir, I thought Mr Lowe was upstairs,' she said, letting Gil into the drawing room, 'but he must be in here.'

Half expecting Lowe to be where he had been sitting that morning, Gil moved over to the sofa. He was right: the old man was exactly where he had been before, the oxygen mask over his face.

'Mr Lowe, I came back like you asked me to,' Gil began. 'You wanted to tell me something.'

Frowning, he glanced at Lowe, but the old man's eyes were closed. He was asleep. Uncertain of what to do next, Gil hesitated. Thought about leaving. About waking Lowe up. Then he leaned closer towards him.

'Mr Lowe? Mr Lowe?'

He touched the old man's shoulder. And then slowly, very slowly, Bernard Lowe slid over onto his side, the mask still attached to his face. Quickly bending down, Gil felt at the side of the old man's neck, but could get no pulse and took the mask away.

Bernard Lowe was dead.

Thirty

London
8.15 p.m.

'We should get a post-mortem—'

'Why?' Simmons snapped, looking over at Gil. 'Lowe was old, he was sick. That's why I took him off the list of suspects. So why do we need to do a post-mortem?'

Gil knew he was treading on thin ice. He wasn't going to tell the police that Lowe had been about to confide the motive for the murders. It was information he wanted to keep to himself. Information that convinced him that Bernard Lowe hadn't died of natural causes. The timing was just too convenient.

If only Lowe had confided in him that morning, instead of waiting until the end of the day, Gil thought, frustrated. Or had he been bluffing? The old man had said that he had some jobs to do. What jobs had been so important? Gil wondered. What errands, what visits, what tying up of loose ends had commanded his attention? Bernard Lowe had been astute and cunning. But perhaps old age had age dulled his instincts, and he had talked to someone else about what he knew.

Or had someone *overheard* the conversation Gil had had with him and reacted by killing the old man to keep him quiet?

He would have been easy to kill. Bernard Lowe had been frail, unsteady on his feet, breathless. A child could have overpowered him and no one would suspect anything, because he had been ill for years, surviving on an oxygen machine, grasping at the fag end of his life.

Gil was certain he was right.

'Please get a post-mortem done.'

'OK, OK, but it'll be a waste of time. He was old. He died. End of,' Simmons said brusquely. 'After all, who the hell would *need* to kill Bernard Lowe?'

Thirty-One

Jerkingawake,LucaMerisslookedaroundhim.Intheaeroplane seats across the aisle, two men were talking and drinking. The seat in front of him was empty, but the one next to it held an overweight woman doing a crossword puzzle. At regular intervals she paused and tapped her pen against her front teeth as though loosening words from her brain.

Luca glanced behind him. A family – two warring parents and a couple of fractious kids – were arguing, but there was nothing suspicious or threatening about any of the passengers.

Breathing out, Luca leaned back in his seat. He was safe, he could go back to sleep again. But sleep wasn't about to make another appearance and instead he got up and walked down the aisle to the toilet. It was occupied. Leaning against the wall, Luca looked around – and suddenly caught the gaze of a solitary man at the back of the plane.

He swallowed.

The man stared at him.

Luca glanced away.

Then looked back.

The man was still staring at him.

Unnerved, Luca heard the toilet door open and pushed past the woman leaving. Inside, he locked the door and looked in the mirror. His forehead was shiny, his cheeks mould-coloured under the unflattering light. His hands shook as he washed them and then splashed cold water on his face.

His actions seemed suddenly ridiculous. Childish, stupid. To blurt out what he knew on the internet! God, was he mad? Luca thought of the conversation he had had with Gil Eckhart. The warning. He was an investigator, possibly an ally. He needed one, Luca thought, and he didn't know if Catrina Hoyt was the right person to trust. Maybe neither of them were. Maybe he shouldn't go to New York at all, should go home instead, to Palermo, to his father. Hide away for a while, until everyone forgot what he had said.

Then Luca remembered what Gil Eckhart had told him about a double murder. *Two* double murders. Trembling, he sat on the toilet seat and thought about the danger he had put himself into. Could he risk endangering his father by going home? No. He had committed himself to Catrina Hoyt. But she was a dealer, she might only be interested in the paintings. Would he better off with Gil Eckhart? He was an investigator, he knew the art world – but what did *he* want?

Luca bowed his head, confused. No one seemed interested in his lineage. All they wanted were the paintings. And he realised that, unless he was very careful, he might turn out to be a dispensable nonentity.

Unlocking the toilet door, Luca walked out and moved down the aisle. The man seated at the back of the plane was no longer looking in his direction as Luca approached his seat. Then he stopped dead. A folded piece of paper was lying there, waiting for him. Several moments passed before he had the courage to read it:

NEW YORK IS NO SAFER THAN BERLIN.
WAIT TO BE CONTACTED.

His legs gave way and he sat down in his seat, struggling to control his breathing. He was thirty thousand miles above the Atlantic, on a plane, being watched. Among the crying children, laughing men and sleeping executives was the person who had written him the note.

His blood fizzing in his brain and his heartbeat echoing in his ears, Luca slowly got to his feet and moved to the back of the plane, heading for the man who had been watching him earlier.

'Did you write this?'

The passenger looked up, blank-faced, taking off his headphones. '*What?*'

'This note,' Luca said, waving it in front of him. 'I left my seat and when I got back this was waiting for me. What d'you want?'

The man was surprised, but also unexpectedly amused.

'You've got the wrong person, mate. I broke my leg yesterday – I can't get anywhere without help.' He pointed to the plaster cast on his thigh. 'I don't know who left you the note, but it certainly wasn't me.'

Thirty-Two

St Bartholomew's Hospital, London

After she had left a message on Gil's mobile phone, Bette leaned back against the pillows of her hospital bed. Outside, sleet was slapping the pavements and making the roads greasy. Gil had visited her around eight, and although he had insisted everything was fine, Bette hadn't been convinced.

'How's the case going?'

'Fine. It'll blow over soon.'

'You said that yesterday,' she had teased him. 'It's going to take a while, isn't it?'

'No, not long. Not long.'

It wasn't like Gil to lie, Bette thought, but then again she was heavily pregnant and he wasn't going to do, or say, anything to worry her. She didn't want to worry him either, so she wasn't going to mention the fact that Jacob Levens had visited her late the previous night, looking for Gil.

Closing her eyes, Bette thought about the coming baby.

She had convinced herself that when the case was over, the child born, life would settle. Gil would step back, he would solve the investigation and close the porthole on the past which had caused such a bitter draught. Then he would walk away.

But that was before Jacob Levens had come to visit her.

He had been looking for Gil, hoping to find him visiting his wife. An old employer, an old friend. And although he smelt of peppermint and cologne, the odour of whisky had still lingered faintly underneath.

'Sorry to disturb you, my dear, I just thought Gil might be here.' He had pulled up a seat but not taken it, hovering around the bed instead. 'How are you?'

'I'm fine.'

'Good, good,' Jacob had replied.

Bette watched him carefully.

'Can I pass on a message? Gil's bound to call me later.'

'It's about . . . Oh, it doesn't matter,' Jacob had said, stout in his bespoke suit, flushed around the jowls. 'It's probably not important.'

Bette hadn't been convinced. 'Come on, Jacob, you look like it's very important.'

'Gil doesn't answer his mobile.'

'I know,' she said. 'But he always picks up his messages eventually.'

'I don't know why people have mobile phones and don't answer them.'

His unease had unsettled her.

'What is it?'

'Nothing.'

'God, Jacob, who are you trying to kid? I used to work for you, remember? I know you inside out. Just tell me what's bothering you.'

Reassured, he had turned to her, blurting it out. 'It's Holly.'

The name slammed into the room, leaving Bette stunned.

'*Holly?*'

'She left some computer disks with me and . . . well, you see, someone's just broken into my gallery and stolen them.' Then Jacob had suddenly altered, panic turning to composure, as though he had realised he was talking to a pregnant woman in a hospital bed and had badly overstepped the mark. 'I'm sorry, Bette. I shouldn't have troubled you. Forget what I said, just forget it.'

That was the last thing she would do.

'*Holly left some disks with you?*'

'Forget I said anything! I'll talk to Gil myself. You just look after yourself, you hear? That's all you should be thinking about.' Jacob had then kissed her on the forehead and scurried out.

For a long time Bette had stared at the door, thinking. And she decided that she wasn't going to pass the message on. The news wasn't going through her. She touched her stomach protectively, feeling the baby inside. Whatever was coming – whatever threat from the past – it wouldn't be *her* letting Holly Eckhart back in.

Thirty-Three

St. Thomas's

As he walked into the morgue, Gil could see Dr Dunning standing next to a dissecting table. In silence, he watched as the pathologist paused to dictate into a recording machine suspended from the ceiling by a cable, his gloved hands held waist-high, palms upwards.

When he had finished speaking, Gil moved closer. 'Simmons told me what you'd found.'

Dunning turned, nodding a welcome. 'So you heard that Bernard Lowe didn't die of natural causes?'

'Murdered?'

'He certainly was,' Dunning replied, taking off his gloves and moving over to a side table where he had the file notes. 'Bernard Lowe fell into a state of unconsciousness, coma, then death.'

'Because?'

'Because someone tampered with his oxygen cylinder. It wasn't oxygen – Bernard Lowe was breathing pure nitrogen.'

Gil frowned. 'I thought we breathed in nitrogen every day?'

'We do – mixed with oxygen. With the two combined, nitrogen is harmless. But on its own, it's lethal. With an old man like Bernard Lowe, in poor health, with compromised lung function, it was a quick and certain killing.'

'Would switching the cylinders be difficult to do?'

'Not if you disguised the colour of the bottle. Under some freshly applied paint the cylinder Bernard Lowe was using was green. It should have been black. Someone painted it to look like an oxygen cylinder. Mr Lowe wouldn't have realised what was happening to him.'

'Well, that's something. At least it was a painless death – not like the Weir brothers'.' Gil thought for a moment. 'Could a layman organise something like that?'

'Yes, if they had access to the cylinders. And, let's face it, someone could easily have stolen the nitrogen, or even obtained it illegally. Or legally – for commercial or laboratory purposes. It's not a banned substance.' He took off his surgical cap. His hair looked like his mother had cut it. 'Bernard Lowe had rabbit skin glue in his mouth. Only a tiny amount, but it was there.'

Silent, Gil let him continue.

'I wanted to ask you something. It was something you said – or rather you *didn't* say – before. The wounds on the Weir brothers: there were eight of them.'

Gil was giving nothing away. 'So?'

'You reacted when you heard me say that. I wondered if

it was important. If it had anything to do with the Berlin murders. You said they were similar killings, the same scalping, similar injuries. Did Alma and Terrill Huber have eight wounds?'

'Yes.'

'D'you know why there were eight wounds?'

Gil paused. 'Why are you asking?'

'Because Bernard Lowe had been stabbed. Tiny stab wounds–'

'Where?'

'In his scrotum. They were little more than nicks at the skin. But they were deliberate.' Gil said nothing, forcing the pathologist to continue. 'I counted them. There were eight marks, Mr Eckhart. Eight. Just like there were eight stab wounds on Benjamin and Sebastian Weir and the Hubers. It's no coincidence, is it?'

He dodged the question. 'Bernard Lowe wasn't scalped.'

'He was.'

Gil flinched.

'He wore a wig, so it wasn't obvious at first. It was a bad wig, but glued down firmly. Thing is, the killer scalped him, then put the wig back afterwards.'

'*What?*'

'He scalped him, then re-glued the toupee in place.'

'With all the blood?'

'It was done after Bernard Lowe was dead, so there wasn't as much blood because his heart had stopped pumping.

Besides, someone had taken their time. He'd been well cleaned up. That's why you didn't notice it.'

Gil stared at the pathologist.

'So whoever did it was prepared. They knew about the oxygen and the wig. A stranger couldn't have done that. It had to be someone with easy access to Lowe.'

As he said the words the double doors to the morgue opened and Phil Simmons walked in. The detective was red-faced, the rash raw from where he had scratched it, his collar undone. Rain had splattered the shoulders of his coat and dampened his hair.

'OK,' he said, ignoring the pathologist and talking to Gil. 'So how did you know Bernard Lowe was murdered?'

'I thought it was possible.'

'Why?'

'He was an importer and collector, well known in the art world–'

'So are hundreds of others. Should I be expecting a massacre?' Simmons stared at Gil. 'You think this killing is related to the other three murders?'

'It could be.'

'But the Hubers and the Weirs were tortured, Bernard Lowe put to sleep. What connection did Lowe have with the Hubers or the Weirs?'

'They were all dealers. They traded.'

'So they could have been rivals?' Simmons asked, scratching the skin on his neck. 'If I find out that you know something I don't, and you've held it back, I'll–'

Gil stalled. 'I don't know anything.'

He wasn't going to tell him about Luca Meriss. Gil had been hired by Jacob Levens, not by the Metropolitan Police Force. Levens was paying his fee, and deserved his loyalty. But there was something else that kept Gil silent. Bernard Lowe might now be off the list of suspects, but Jacob Levens wasn't. Gil wondered if Lowe had spoken to Jacob about the motive. After all, if the old man had been prepared to confide in him, Lowe might well have confided in a friend. Especially as that friend's sister had been one of the first victims.

Unless Bernard Lowe had suspected Jacob Levens of some involvement.

Gil thought back. Lowe had been desperate to get the paintings and Jacob would want them too. He dealt in Italian Baroque. And yet he hadn't shown any interest in the Caravaggios. The thought made Gil uneasy, and suspicious.

Simmons was watching him steadily. 'I've been thinking. You used to work for the art world, *solely* for the art world. You knew all their dirty tricks. So why would Jacob Levens call you in unless it was for something art-related?'

Gil shrugged. 'We're friends – of course he would call me. It doesn't mean it was about the business.'

'Oh, come on! You've been out of the art world for years,' Simmons persisted. 'So why bring you back, unless Jacob Levens thought there was a connection?'

'We've already been through this. There *was* a connection – the Weirs were murdered like the Hubers–'

'And now Bernard Lowe's dead. And he'd dealt with all the victims, and he also knew Jacob Levens.'

'Everyone knows everyone in the art world,' Gil said simply. 'It's very enclosed. Few people manage to infiltrate it–'

'A killer did. Which make you wonder how. Unless, of course, he was already *in* the art world. A dealer, or a collector.'

Gil smiled.

'Oh, come on, a dealer or a collector? Hardly. How could a violent killer do business and act normally for *over seven years*?'

'Maybe he's been out of the business for a while. Maybe he comes and goes – like you.'

'Yeah? Well, I didn't kill them,' Gil replied. 'And I still say that no one who could torture like that could behave normally. They'd give off some signs, some warnings.'

'You know that for a fact, do you?'

Gil bridled.

'Actually, I do. I've been on other murder cases and killers aren't stable. They can act normally for a while, but it doesn't last.'

'Doctors have been serial killers.'

'They usually drug their patients and the victims don't know what's happening to them. It's once removed. Not like stripping a person, torturing them, and then strangling them slowly. That takes time and effort. It's concentrated cruelty. And it's personal. Why don't you look at the chauffeur?'

'I already have. Gary Rimmer has an alibi.'

'He can't have. He was parked outside the door with the car engine running when I found Bernard Lowe.'

'Rimmer was talking on his mobile for over fifteen minutes. We checked it out. He wasn't killing Bernard Lowe, he was arguing about child maintenance with his ex-wife.'

'What about Lowe's nurses? Have you talked to them yet?'

'Only the night nurse, who was with her husband. The day nurse is a different matter. She was here earlier, left to pick up something from the pharmacy, and didn't come back. She's not answering her mobile, and no one's at her flat. We're checking her out.'

'Good idea,' Gil said sarcastically.

'Why?'

'Because she'd just started working for Bernard Lowe.'

'How d'you know that?'

'The chauffeur fancies her, chats to her. He said that he saw her this morning when she came on shift. He also said that Frieda Meyer had an accent and that she told him that she came from abroad.' Gil paused, then added, 'Berlin, of all places.'

Thirty-Four

Meatpacking District, Manhattan, New York

Catrina Hoyt was talking on the phone when she spotted a stranger through the glass wall of her office that looked out onto Reception. The man was handsome in an overblown way, but he looked spooked, unshaven, and was clinging onto a cheap canvas holdall.

Beckoning her secretary to come in, Catrina ended her phone call. 'Who's that?'

'He says you're expecting him. Mr Luca Meriss.' She glanced over. 'You want me to get rid of him?'

'Nah! Show him in,' Catrina replied, getting to her feet and walking to the door.

Holding it open, she watched as the Italian moved past her into the office. She was taller than him, and as he passed she caught a brief whiff of supermarket cologne. His ears were pierced but he wore no jewellery, just a digital watch on his right hand.

'Mr Meriss,' she said, waving for him to take a seat. He was nervous, taking the nearest chair and putting the holdall by his feet. 'I'm glad you got here.'

He nodded, dry-mouthed. Catrina poured him a glass of water. He took it gratefully, drinking it off in one go, then wiping his mouth with the back of his hand.

'Thank you.'

'For what?'

'For helping me.'

She flicked away the words, pointing to the bag at his feet. 'Is that the proof?'

'Someone was on the plane, watching me,' Luca said, ignoring the question and handing Catrina the note.

NEW YORK IS NO SAFER THAN BERLIN.
WAIT TO BE CONTACTED.

In silence, he studied her as she read it; the long, muscled legs in high heels, the strong arms. Impressively Amazonian, her hands as large as a man's. Catrina Hoyt was not what he had expected, and neither was the gallery, open-plan, its walls red brickwork, steel girders supporting the vaulted ceiling. And the paintings confused him too: a cacophony of abstracts and graphic eroticism, with only the occasional Baroque picture thrown in like an afterthought.

She tossed the note back to him. 'Who gave it to you?'

'I didn't see. I went to the toilet and it was there when I

got back. On my seat. There had been a man watching me, but it wasn't him.'

Folding her arms, Catrina leaned back against the glass desk. 'But it had to be someone on the plane?'

He nodded. 'It could have been anyone.'

'And no one's contacted you?'

'What?'

'The note said *wait to be contacted*. Have you been?'

'No, no one's approached me – and I threw away my mobile phone. I thought it was the right thing to do,' Luca replied, resting his left foot against the holdall.

'What's in the bag?'

He ignored her again, looking around the gallery. 'It's all modern art.'

'On this floor, yes,' she agreed. 'Upstairs we have Italian Baroque.'

'I read that you admired Caravaggio. That you knew everything about him and his works.'

'Are you cross-examining me?'

'No . . .' Luca stammered. 'I just wanted to know that you were serious.'

'You wanted to know if *I'm* serious!' she snapped. 'You son of a bitch!'

And then, in one quick movement, she snatched up the holdall and emptied the contents out onto her desk. Luca was on his feet in an instant, watching her in horror as she picked through his belongings. Finally she flung the clothes onto the floor and threw the empty bag to one side.

'OK, joke over. I paid for your fucking flight. We had a deal. I help you, you help me. You said you had proof of who you were–'

'I do!'

'–and that you knew the whereabouts of two Caravaggio paintings–'

'I do!'

'So where's the proof?' she demanded, grabbing his arm.

'I'll tell you! I'll tell you in a little while!' He wriggled in her grip, panicking, realising that he was way out of his depth and desperately trying to stall. 'Can't we talk a little? We need to talk and I need to think–'

'Your time for thinking has long gone.' She towered over him. 'I want the truth. Now. Or I'll call the police and tell them it was *you* that broke in here the other night. Oh, I know that you were in Berlin, but how long d'you think it'll take them to find that out? D'you know how long you can get for breaking and entering in New York?'

'It wasn't me!'

'But it *was*, Mr Meriss,' she said, her tone chilling. 'I saw you. You pulled a knife on me, threatened me, and then you took my jewellery.'

His eyes were fixed on her, his mind reeling, his hand reaching for the holdall she had thrown on the floor.

'It wasn't me! That's a lie! I wasn't even here! It wasn't me–'

'I bet whoever's after you will find it really easy to get to you in jail,' she said bleakly. 'You're stupid. A stupid amateur.

You should learn to keep your mouth shut. Blabbing all over the internet!' She looked at the cowed man trembling in front of her, his arms wrapped around the empty holdall. 'You're a long way from home, Mr Meriss, remember that. But we don't have to make this unpleasant, you know. All I want is the proof. What you promised me. That's all. It's simple. Just give me what I expected.'

The one thing Catrina Hoyt didn't expect was the sudden and violent punch to her stomach. Caught unawares, she fell backwards, grabbing for Meriss but catching hold of his bag instead. Winded, gasping for air, she doubled over and slid to the floor. And as she did so, Luca Meriss smashed the nearest window and made for the fire escape.

Wednesday

Naples, Italy
1610

It was dawn, a cock crowing, a little bleak sun making its hesitant way into life. Rising to his feet, Caravaggio moved to the door, passed the sleeping woman and the two men. He could smell the urine on his pants, the sweat making his shirt stiffen, along with the dried blood. Wiping his sweating hands on his trousers, he moved on, glancing in a broken mirror by the door.

The reflected image confused him and he turned, wondering who had come behind him. Then, slowly, he looked back at his own reflection. His left eye was drawn down at the outer corner, the dark knife wound running down to his neck and distorting his cheek. Disbelieving, Caravaggio touched the ruin of his face. His attacker had been thorough, severing the nerve on his left side so that his mouth drooped like an old man's in sleep.

Rumours of the assault would spread – perhaps his attacker might believe he had killed him. Certainly the people who had seen him the previous night would doubt he could have survived. When they woke and found him gone rumours would follow. That Caravaggio – his throat cut – had slunk away to die.

Carefully he drew his collar upwards. Then, realising it would not cover the mutilation, he hung his cloak over his shoulder and drew it partially across his ruined face. Opening the door, Caravaggio looked out into the early day. His disguise would aid him, as would his disfigurement, perhaps long enough to escape the city.

Hope rising, the artist stepped out into the alleyway and moved swiftly towards the docks. He would board a boat, hide himself until he left the Bay of Naples behind, then return to Rome and await his pardon.

It wasn't the end. Michelangelo Merisi da Caravaggio wasn't dead. No man could kill him . . . He hurried along, his face ripped with pain, the left eye drooping, the right eye fixed on the street ahead of him. It took him every ounce of will to keep upright and walk on. Zigzagging along cobbles, intermittently resting against walls, he moved towards his escape. Towards his pardon. Towards his freedom.

And just a little way behind him, a man followed.

Thirty-Five

London
10.45 a.m.

'What did you tell Bette?' Gil asked, staring at Jacob incredulously. 'That Holly left some disks with you? Why would she do that? And why didn't you tell me before now?'

'She just asked me to look after them for her. She said she'd come back, but she never did – she was killed in that car accident. I kept them and forgot all about them until now.'

'And now they've been stolen?' Gil said, his suspicion obvious. 'Are you really expecting me to believe that you forgot about these disks?'

'But I did!' Jacob insisted. 'I didn't know they meant anything.'

'What did Holly say they were?'

'Work. Computer stuff.'

'And she gave them to you? An art dealer?'

'She'd been in Berlin with you, and called by to see how

I was after Alma's death. She was my friend, and she was being kind. She was worried about me,' Jacob went on. 'I asked about her work, just making conversation, and she told me she was working on some computer analysis, and that she had some disks she wanted to copy. Her own computer was broken – she couldn't burn copies on it.'

'But you could?' Gil was incredulous. 'Oh, give me a break, Jacob! You wouldn't know how to burn a copy of a disk. You wouldn't know how to burn paper—'

'*I didn't say I did!* I just told Holly that she could use my equipment. You called her back to Berlin and she asked if I'd look after the disks for her until she got back.'

'Did you look at them?'

He was stunned.

'I can't work a computer. My secretary does all that. No, I didn't look at them. I just let Holly put them in the safe and I forgot about them.'

'For seven years?'

'It's a big safe – they were right at the back with some old ledgers,' Jacob said coldly. 'What's the matter? You still don't believe me?'

'Why would someone steal the disks now? After seven years?'

Jacob shook his head. 'I don't know.'

'But you missed them. You'd forgotten about them for years, but you realised they'd gone.'

'I've just had a break-in at the gallery! Someone opened the safe. I had to check what was missing, and go through everything – and that's when I remembered them. And knew they'd gone.'

'What else was taken?'

'Some money. Ten thousand pounds.'

'You've been very unlucky lately. A burglary at your flat, and now a break-in at the office.' Gil paused, holding the dealer's gaze. 'D'you want to tell me what's really going on?'

Jacob shook his head again, his breath whisky-sour. 'You don't want to know.'

Tell me.

'You won't like it, Gil.'

'Let me be the judge of that.'

'I can't–'

'*Tell me.*'

'Holly was working with Bernard Lowe.'

Gil blinked, like someone caught in the headlights. '*What?*'

'You know Holly, she was always up for a challenge and she took on a job for Bernard Lowe. Don't look at me like that!' Jacob said, shamefaced. 'It was just a lark for her at first. She asked me not to tell you; she said you wouldn't understand. You were investigating those fakes that had come in from Rome and you'd just exposed David Rapport. Then he'd had you charged with assault–'

'What's that got to do with Holly?'

'Where was she when you were working on that case?'

Gil thought for a moment. 'New York, setting up a computer programme for a gallery over there.'

'It was a good cover, wasn't it? Even you didn't suspect it.' Jacob paused, putting his head on one side. 'Come on, you knew what Holly was like.'

Gil could feel his head buzzing. Jacob Levens was talking about Holly, his wife. The woman he had loved. And trusted.

'Bernard Lowe was bringing in pieces from the Far East. Transporting them in through his own shipping company. Holly smuggled some artefacts for him.' Jacob paused, walked round his desk and reached for the whisky bottle in his drawer. He refilled his glass and pushed one over to Gil. 'Have a drink. You look like you need it.'

'I don't want a fucking drink!' Gil exploded. 'My wife was smuggling while I was investigating David Rapport? *And you knew?*'

He was desperately trying to make sense of what he was hearing. This was his friend, Jacob Levens, the man who had been so understanding after Holly was killed, the man who had introduced him to Bette. This was the person with whom he had empathised in those terrible days in Berlin, and he was now telling him about his late wife's illegal dealings. About treachery.

Gil stared at the dealer, who couldn't return his look, remembering all the niggling doubts which had begun to plague him. Like why Jacob hadn't mentioned the Caravaggios. Why he had been the one who found the Weir twins. And now there was another question he had to answer. Why he had kept quiet about Holly for so many years?

Holly, his wife, smuggling for Bernard Lowe. And Jacob

had known and hidden it from him. Gil had thought him open-hearted, only a fool when drunk, but he had been blindsided by affection. Jacob Levens was treacherous.

'I don't believe any of this.'

Jacob shrugged. 'It's true. All of it. Holly was always keeping secrets. That was how she was. She played people off against each other. Had a different face for everyone. She led Bernard Lowe by the nose, and me.' He finished his drink and poured another. 'She swore me to secrecy. She was afraid it would reflect badly on you if it got out what she'd been up to.'

'Reflect badly on me?' Gil repeated disbelievingly. 'It would have ruined me!'

'That's why she begged me to keep quiet. She didn't want to lose you. She was afraid of your temper—'

'What are you talking about?' Gil retorted. 'I loved my wife. I never raised a hand to her, and she knew I never would. You're lying, Jacob. Don't take me for a fool.'

'I'm telling you the truth.'

'How much?'

Jacob blinked. 'What?'

'How much did you get out of this?' Gil repeated, leaning over the desk towards the dealer. 'There must have been money in it. It wouldn't have been worthwhile otherwise. Did you force her into it? Or was it Bernard Lowe? Who made her do it?'

Sighing, Jacob looked at Gil.

'How well did you know Holly? I mean, how much of her

life did she tell you about? I was surprised when you two married. Lovers, yes, that was on the cards, but marriage? No, I never thought it would come to that. I'm sorry, but she wasn't what you thought she was.' Jacob could see the anger in Gil's face and put up his hands. 'Don't take it out on me – I'm just telling you the truth. If you'd asked me before you married her, I'd have told you then. Holly liked excitement, danger. She got bored. If she hadn't died, she would never have stayed with you. Don't you know that?'

Gil was breathing rapidly, staring at the dealer. 'You bastard.'

'She was leaving you,' Jacob went on. 'Sorry, but that's the way it is. She was tired of London, wanted to get to California, but she wanted to live well there. She couldn't do that working in computers. Even as a freelance consultant it would have taken too long. And you didn't have the kind of money she needed. Holly had two choices – get money from another man, or steal it.' Jacob downed his whisky. 'She did both.'

'Who was he?'

'I don't know,' Jacob said. 'But it wasn't me.'

For a long, silent moment Gil stared at him. Every cell in his body wanted to strike out, to throw a punch at the dealer who had fooled him for so long. It would have been so easy, Gil thought, to knock him senseless. His hands itched, his heart pumped, adrenalin coursed through every nerve. But he controlled himself. He suspected that Jacob Levens *wanted* some form of beating for what he had done. Or what he was doing.

'It's a pity I can't check your story out with Bernard Lowe. You know he's dead?'

'I just heard.'

'He was murdered.'

Jacob's head shot up. '*Murdered . . .*' His spite evaporated, fear taking over. 'Oh, Christ.'

'Looks like it's your turn to be surprised,' Gil said coldly. 'Surely it can't be that much of a shock, can it?'

'I warned him when he showed me the note.'

Gil wasn't sure if the dealer was play-acting or not. 'What note?'

'Someone sent Bernard Lowe a message. Said they were going to call and see him – something like that. I told him not to go back to his house, but he wouldn't listen. Made light of it, said that he had staff around, that he was safe. But he wasn't, was he?' Jacob paused, his voice faltering. 'Five dealers killed. Jesus, what's all this about?'

Gil ignored the question and asked one of his own.

'Why haven't you mentioned the missing Caravaggio paintings? The ones that everyone's talking about?'

The words caught Jacob off guard. His face was expressionless but his eyes flickered. 'Paintings are not my chief concern at the moment. What the hell d'you take me for?'

'An art dealer, because that's what you are. And no dealer could resist wanting to know about the Caravaggios.'

'Five dealers have now been killed!' Jacob wailed. 'I could be next!'

'Why? What d'you know?' Gil asked him. 'Maybe you're

not in danger at all. Maybe you're the killer. After all, you knew all the dealers, Jacob – they would all have let you close. Especially Bernard Lowe.'

Jacob was blustering.

'Don't be ridiculous! My own sister was killed—'

'Yes, I know. I worked on the case. You hired me, remember? And I think that Alma was murdered by someone close to her—'

'I couldn't have killed her!' he snapped, panicking. 'I've never hurt anyone. Are you crazy?'

Gil was deliberately provoking him, trying to shake out what he knew. Shocking him into a response.

'Bernard Lowe wanted me to act as his go-between and get him the Caravaggio paintings—'

'*What are you talking about?*' Jacob roared.

Bernard Lowe had said nothing about a deal to him. For all the old man's posturings about honesty, he had kept quiet about the Caravaggios. And how much more? Jacob wondered, maddened. Had Bernard Lowe been working alone or with the others? Was Jacob Levens the only member of *Der Kreis der Acht not* to know about the Caravaggios? Were they plotting against him, cutting him out? Or setting him up as a scapegoat?

Jacob struggled to think clearly, the booze inhibiting his focus. If he told Gil about *Der Kreis der Acht* he would be exposing his own crimes, but if he stayed silent he could turn out to be the next victim. In that instant Jacob Levens realised what a fool he had been in making an enemy out of Gil Eckhart.

'I can't believe–'

Gil interrupted him. 'Bernard Lowe did a deal with me.'

'A deal?'

Slowly, Gil drew him in. 'I promised to get the paintings for him. In return, he told me the motive for the murders.'

'He told you?'

Unwavering, Gil lied. 'Yes, he told me.'

The words resonated around the office as Gil tried to read Jacob's expression. Was he shocked or did he already know the motive? Or worse, if he was the murderer, was he now feeling threatened? As the two men faced each other Gil studied Jacob Levens. He was stocky, physically strong. Not big enough to overpower a man, but certainly capable of knocking someone out and injecting them. And clever enough – when sober – to plan murder.

But was he ruthless enough to kill his own sister?

'Look, I said too much . . .' Jacob began, desperate to repair the damage he had done. 'Sorry, Gil, sorry. I drink, I talk nonsense.'

Gil shook his head. 'Forget it. You're on your own now.'

'But you have to help me! You have to!'

'I don't have to do anything.'

'But they could kill me!' Jacob shouted, grasping Gil's arm.

'Saves me the problem,' Gil replied, shaking him off and walking out.

Betrayed by his closest friend, cuckolded by his dead wife, Gil left the gallery a changed man. He had lied. He *didn't* have the motive for the killings – but Jacob Levens didn't know that. It had been an unsuccessful bluff to try to force a confession from the dealer, but now the lie would now find its own nasty hole. Would worm itself into Jacob Levens' guilt, or call out someone far worse.

Gil had claimed a knowledge he didn't have. And it might well kill him.

Thirty-Six

New York

Luca thought back. He had gone down into the subway and jumped on the first train, slumping into his seat. His left leg had been heavily bruised from his frantic jump onto Catrina Hoyt's fire escape, his breathing rapid. He had lost everything that had been in the holdall: a change of clothes, a razor, toiletries. But nothing important. He had had more sense than that.

Reaching into his inside jacket pocket Luca had taken out a notebook, and felt into the inner, concealed pocket, relieved that his passport and money had still been there. Likewise the plane ticket back to Berlin. Wary, he had looked around, but no one had been paying him any attention, so he had turned back to the notebook and a list of names he had made:

Bernard Lowe
Jacob Levens

Catrina Hoyt
Harvey Crammer
Oscar Schultz
Naresh Joshi
Gil Eckhart

The names *Bernard Lowe* and *Catrina Hoyt* he had scored out, knowing he had made a dangerous enemy of the latter. But that hadn't been his only problem: his most pressing concern had been who to contact next.

On edge, Luca had leaned back in his seat. A group of teenage boys had been sitting across the aisle talking, a solitary woman reading a magazine. Above her head had been an advertisement for toothpaste, an all-American beauty displaying a set of impressive veneers. The train had come to a jerky halt at Harlem station, a name which had meant little to Luca, but he had decided he would stay down in the subway until he worked out what to do next. Maybe wait until dark before he risked the streets again. At the next station a few people had got on the train and Luca had studied each of them, but no one had even looked in his direction. Thoughtful, Luca had remembered the shock on Catrina Hoyt's face, the sheer disbelief when he had hit her.

The train had continued, juddering through a tunnel. As the lights had gone out then come on again, Luca had clung on to his notepad. He had realised Catrina Hoyt would come after him. Not in person – she would send someone – but he knew he could never have worked with her, couldn't have shared his treasure with a philistine. Luca knew he had been too trusting, too quick to throw in his lot with the dealer. And as a result he had been forced to run. Again.

He had thought then of the note on the plane. Of the gory photograph which had been sent to scare him. Within three days Luca Meriss had managed, single-handedly, to catapult himself from obscurity into notoriety and danger, making the biggest blunder of all when he had put his own image onto his website.

It had been an act of hubris. Placing his likeness against that of Caravaggio and saying, *See for yourself. See the characteristics from the fifteenth century repeated in the twenty-first.* But, in reality, it had ended up being little more than a WANTED poster.

Panic had set in fast, as Luca realised he had to disguise himself. Buy a baseball cap to cover the thick dark hair, get some glasses and another jacket, anything to make himself less conspicuous. Then what? He had paused, glancing back at the list of names. Who to go to? He hadn't known them and wouldn't have recognised any of them.

At that moment Luca hadn't known who to trust. His little list had seemed pathetic, simply the names of Caravaggio devotees – something anyone could have drawn up. It hadn't been surprising that they had all contacted him after he went public. Of course they would have done, hoping that he was an amateur, easy to manipulate. But besides the dealers, Luca had wondered how many other people had seen his website? How many others had seen his image? Read his declaration that he, Luca Meriss, knew the whereabouts of two Caravaggio paintings?

That he had had proof.

The train had stopped suddenly, ticking over in a tunnel as Luca looked around nervously. The teenage boys had got off, the woman had still been reading, but Luca had noticed a man standing at the far end of the compartment. His arms had been folded and he had stood immobile, then turned.

And had begun walking towards Luca Meriss.

Thirty-Seven

Campolfelice, Nr Palermo, Sicily

'*Ciao, vecchio mio. Come stai oggi?*' A man called out to his friend.

'*Più giovane di te!*' he replied, laughing and shaking his fist in mock anger.

There had been rain that morning, but the village had dried out and the square was busy again. The ever-present tables and chairs had been caught in the unexpected downpour and now steamed weakly in the cool sunshine, pigeons coming down low from the church overhead.

Having lived his whole life in Sicily, Carlo Ranuccio had no desire to travel, no interest in other countries. He had resigned himself to his existence, and when his wife died had accepted the role of widower as though born to it. His emotional freedom resulted in longstanding friendships and flirtations with women who knew not to take him seriously. Card games and heated discussions about wine and politics quickened the passing of the hours.

At fifty he had been working, harassed, married. At seventy he was retired, relaxed and widowed. His children – three girls and one boy – had all left Palermo, his daughters often visiting with their latest men or offspring. They came, they went, they caused no anguish to the old man. Except for one. His son, Luca.

I don't know where he is, Carlo had said when questioned the previous night. *We don't talk.*

A lifetime's lack of curiosity hadn't failed him. Carlo had no interest in his son, or anyone who might be looking for him. Luca's life was off limits to his father, his activities unknown. A few years earlier there had been postcards, sent from various addresses abroad, while Luca travelled. Doing what, his father never asked. He didn't know, simply remembered – with regret – his only son being a sickly child, prone to moods. Later there had been other rumours. Luca didn't have a girlfriend. Was he homosexual? In a place like Sicily such leanings were hazardous.

Luca's artistic ability had further estranged his father. When he developed a fascination for Caravaggio his intensity made him a laughing stock. But then something changed – Luca changed, became focused. Soon he was researching the family history on his mother's side, pressing his father for details, visiting local churches. He discovered libraries, records, later the internet. His mother died and he moved away from Sicily. He kept reading. And then silence. For four years nothing was heard from Luca. Until the previous day.

A man had asked Carlo where Luca was. A man no one

had ever seen before. A man in a city suit, with a Roman accent. Smiling confidently, like a judge.

'Are you sure you don't know where Luca is?'

Carlo had shrugged. 'I told you, I haven't seen him for years.'

'He's becoming famous,' the man continued.

Carlo was reluctantly curious. 'Famous? Luca Ranuccio?'

'Luca *Meriss*.' The man corrected him. 'He's claimed his ancestor's name.'

'*Il suo antenato?* What are you talking about?'

'Your son has announced that he's a descendant of Michelangelo Merisi da Caravaggio.'

'Who told you this?'

'Your son did. He told the world, put it up on the internet. You do get the internet here, don't you? Look him up – www.meriss.icon.com. And he's also declaring that he knows the whereabouts of two of the artist's missing paintings. One of them taken from Sicily in 1969.'

'From Palermo?' Carlo asked, knowing the story full well. At the thought of the Mafia, he began to sweat. Dear God, he thought, what is Luca involved in?

Uninvited, the stranger sat down, drumming his fingers on the marble table top.

'Your son assaulted a dealer in New York–'

'Luca? You're wrong. My son never fought any man.'

'He struck a *woman*. Robbed her too, they say.'

Carlo couldn't take it in. His son a thief, a thug. His son a liar, a fool.

'Was it you?'

The old man blinked. '*What?*'

'Was it you that put these stories in his head, about Caravaggio?'

'I'm a trader!' Carlo snapped. 'Done manual work all my life. I don't know about artists. He never heard this rubbish from me. He's mad – *è pazzo*.' Carlo didn't want to hear any more. He wanted to slip back into his life, into where he had been only minutes before. 'I can't help you. I don't know where he is–'

'You have a phone number for him?'

'No!'

'I find that hard to believe.'

Belligerent, Carlo jutted out his chin. 'It's the truth. I don't have an address or a number. *Lasciatemi in pace!*'

The man shrugged, seeming almost regretful.

'I'd like to leave you alone, Mr Ranuccio, but I can't. So I want you to think very carefully about where your son might be. Because I have to find him. It's important, for me and for you. Perhaps you remember some place he used to visit? Some person he knew? Somewhere he might hide?' The words hung in the drying air. 'And when you remember, tell Luca Meriss to contact me.' He slid a number across the table. 'Remind him that five people have died already – nobody wants to make it six.'

Shaken, Carlo could barely speak. 'You want me to help you? *So you can kill my son?*'

'You misunderstand, Mr Ranuccio,' the man replied. 'Unless Luca contacts me the next death will be yours.'

Thirty-Eight

Peckham, London

It had been a bad day for Gary Rimmer. Not only had he lost the best-paid job he had ever had, he had been questioned by the police and had then fallen out with his ex-wife. Smoking a cigarette on the landing outside his council flat, he leaned on the railings and thought of Frieda Meyer. Thought of what he had told the police about seeing her leave the Eaton Square house, heading for the pharmacy two streets away.

He had just brought the car round to the front entrance, and called out to her:

'Hey, where are you going?'

She had jumped, turned. 'Oh, I'm just off to get a prescription.'

'Fancy a coffee later?'

'A coffee?' She had nodded. 'Yes, yes, that would be good.'

Then she had walked off and he had watched her and fantasised about having sex with her – then wondered why she was carrying the holdall. It had looked heavy. She had been struggling a little. Why would anyone take a holdall to the chemist? he had thought, then forgotten about it. Until an hour later, when Gil Eckhart had found Bernard Lowe dead.

For a while Gary had wanted to tell the police, but he had stopped himself, even when Frieda didn't come back and a rumour started about Bernard Lowe having been murdered. A rumour that had built up a head of steam, connections being made with the other dealers who had been killed. Maybe, Gary thought, he had been a bit reckless with Frieda, giving her a key to his flat so that she had been able to let herself in the other night, after her landlord had locked her out. His generosity – fuelled by his sex drive – didn't seem too clever in the cold light of day.

Tossing his cigarette butt over the railings, Gary picked at the skin around his thumbnail. Maybe he'd been a bit stupid, showing off like that. But he had wanted to impress Frieda and she'd been interested. What was the harm?

What was the harm? His fucking employer had been murdered and the nurse had gone missing. And he – stupid bastard he was – had told her about Caravaggio. And worse, he'd talked about Harvey Crammer and exaggerated about how well he knew Jacob Levens, and then he'd topped it all off with a stupid boast.

She had let him kiss her and was promising a lot more – it was just a lie. A way to impress her.

'I know where they are.'

'What?'

'Those paintings I was telling you about.' He'd nuzzled her neck and slid one hand up her skirt. 'They're worth a fortune. Quick way to make money.'

He had seen how excited she'd become. 'You can get them?'

What was one more lie after so many?

'Yeah, I reckon I can,' Gary had boasted. 'If I knew where to go, I could sell them on. Set me up for life, it would. Me – and anyone else I fancied having around.'

'We could go on holiday,' she had said, kissing him, her hand moving to the bulge in his trousers. 'We could have some real fun.'

'Oh yeah, a good time.'

'So where are the paintings?'

'I'll tell you tomorrow.'

'Why not now?'

'Tomorrow,' Gary had repeated, grabbing hold of her. 'Have a bit of patience, hey?'

Still picking at the skin around his thumb, Gary thought of Bernard Lowe and shivered. He had been in the car outside, talking on the phone, while the old man had been topped only yards away. Alive one minute, dead the next. And it wasn't hard to guess why. Bernard Lowe had been talking about the Caravaggios. He had been spooked, visiting other dealers, talking to the likes of Harvey Crammer.

Old age hadn't done the old man in: Caravaggio had killed Bernard Lowe.

Gary shuddered, sweating with fear, glancing up the

empty landing. He had been afraid of being alone, but not selfish enough to go to his ex-wife's house. Instead he had gone to the pub and stayed there, then moved on to the betting shop. Anywhere busy, anywhere he was surrounded by people. And all the time he thought about the murders, about the torture of the Weir twins and the old man being killed right under his nose.

He had told the police he'd seen no one suspicious, nothing unusual. But he didn't tell them about a good-looking nurse carrying a holdall. He kept quiet because he was afraid – afraid that Frieda Meyer was involved with the old guy's murder. Not on her own, but with someone else. Someone else who might just come after him if he didn't keep quiet. He just had to keep quiet, Gary thought helplessly, and he'd be all right.

Unnerved, he jumped as he heard the lift stop at his floor, and stepped back as a woman passed with a toddler. The kid reminded him of his own daughter, reminded him of how much he had to lose. God, why had he been so stupid? Made up such a lie to impress some tart? Frieda Meyer couldn't really have believed him, could she? Couldn't really think he knew where the paintings were? Gary gripped the railings with both hands to steady his nerves, then scurried back into his flat, slamming the door closed and locking it.

He didn't realise he was locking someone *in*, not out.

Thirty-Nine

New York
6.45 a.m.

To Luca's surprise, the man simply walked past him and got off the train at the next station. Breathing out, he tried to relax and to calm his nerves. He had hidden out in the subway all night, then jumped on one of the earliest trains, travelling with the cleaners and early shift workers. He felt safe underground: no one had bothered him and he had even managed to sleep a little, although he hadn't decided what to do next.

So he was anxious when a heavy man suddenly sat down in the seat next to his. Furtively, Luca stole a glance at the stranger, and was surprised by the expensive overcoat and classic leather brogues. Maybe he was just a passenger, he thought. Or some freak trying to pick him up. Luca glanced at the man again. He had large, ugly features, but his skin had the expensive look of treatments and his hands were manicured.

Uncomfortable, Luca changed seats.

The man followed him.

Then he smiled and put out his hand.

'Harvey Crammer,' he said, shaking Luca's unresponsive hand. 'I think we should talk.'

'*Harvey Crammer?*' Luca stared at him, taken aback. 'I . . . I wanted to talk to you. You're on my list.'

'Am I in good company?' Crammer put his large head on one side. 'Mr Meriss, you don't have to be afraid of me. I'm trying to help you.'

'How did you know I was in New York?'

'I spend a lot of time here, and your presence was noted and reported to me. You have quite a following since you went online.' Crammer smiled, crossing his legs as the train passed through a deserted station without stopping. The compartment was empty apart from them. 'I know you've been talking to Catrina Hoyt. How did it go?'

Silent, Luca stared at the floor, at the crusty deposits of gum trodden into the metal plating.

'You can refuse to tell me, of course, but I don't see why. You're in a strange city, and you're on your own, and people are looking for you. You need an ally, and frankly I'm the best you're going to get.'

'Gil Eckhart said the same.'

'Oh, Eckhart.' Crammer smiled at the name. 'What does he want?'

'He has a buyer for the paintings.'

'Who?'

'He didn't say, and I didn't ask.' Luca turned to Crammer. 'The paintings aren't for sale. I never set out to sell them–'

'But you have them?'

Luca hesitated, then got to his feet and walked over to the door. Sighing, Crammer followed him.

'Let me spell this out for you. You've told the world that you're Caravaggio's descendant and that you know where two of his missing paintings are. Am I right?'

'Yes.'

'You have proof?'

'Yes.'

'Did you show Catrina Hoyt the proof?'

'No,' Luca replied, turning away. The train was moving fast, picking up speed.

Thoughtful, Crammer regarded the Italian. He was jumpy. Pushing too hard might spook him, make him run again. Perhaps a softer approach would work.

'Where did you stay last night?'

'In the subway. I hid – it seemed safer here than anywhere else,' Luca replied. 'I was in a hotel, but I'm not going back. Catrina Hoyt will look for me there.'

'Did you tell her anything about the whereabouts of the paintings?'

'No.'

'You can stay with me. I have an apartment in New York. Don't worry, I'm not gay. I'm after the paintings, not your body.'

'I can manage–'

'No, you can't. If you stay out here on your own you'll get picked off, Mr Meriss. Have you heard about the murders in London?' He paused. 'I can see from your face that you have. You know that Bernard Lowe has been killed?'

'*What?*'

'Was he one of the names on your list? I imagine he was – Bernard would have been frantic to get hold of the Caravaggios.' He tapped Luca on the shoulder. 'Let me help you.'

'You just want the paintings.'

'Of course I do. I make no bones about that. But I'd also like to live, and three dealers being killed within days is worrying. The only thing they had in common was their interest in Caravaggio. It can't be a coincidence that your announcement coincided with their deaths.'

'I had nothing to do with it!'

'Not directly, no. But indirectly, I think you did.' Crammer gazed out of the window as they flashed through a closed station. 'How did you find out about the paintings?'

'I'm not telling you that! I don't know who I can trust. You just want to get hold of the Caravaggios and then leave me to fend for myself.'

Crammer sighed. 'All right, let's try a different tack. How long have you known about the paintings?'

'Over seven years.'

'Seven years,' Crammer repeated, thoughtful. 'Seven years ago two art dealers – a husband and wife – were killed in Berlin. In exactly the same way as the recent killings in London. No one knew why. Jacob Levens found the bodies,

Gil Eckhart worked on the case, and I was in Berlin when it happened. And now all of us are reunited because of the new murders. Seven years ago did you talk to anyone about the paintings?'

Luca thought of Naresh Joshi. 'I talked to someone, yes.'

'You showed them the proof?'

'No. We spoke, but it never led anywhere. I didn't tell them anything important. Certainly I said nothing about proof.'

'But there must have been someone you confided in,' Crammer continued. '*Did* you talk to anyone else about the paintings all those years ago?'

Luca closed his eyes and gripped the handrail, trying to hold onto himself, fighting panic.

'I only told one other person. I'd found out about my family history, traced it back. I'd been working on it for years. Kept it a secret until I was sure that I was related to Caravaggio. When I knew, it wasn't that difficult to work out where the paintings were. I told one person only and he didn't even believe me. He just shrugged it off. But it was important. It was family.'

'Who did you tell?'

Luca looked at him, desperate. 'My father. I told my father.'

Forty

Peckham, London
2.30 p.m.

She caught him unawares, coming into the shaded hallway and making him jump.

'Jesus Christ!' Gary snapped, staring at the woman incredulously. '*Frieda?* Is that you?'

She was standing with her back against the light, her face indiscernible.

'Are you OK?'

Moving over to her, he touched her arm and she suddenly dropped to the floor. Flicking on the light switch, Gary knelt down. Blood was seeping out from under her body, bubbles coming from the corners of her mouth. Her face and head had been beaten, her features swollen, pulped. He thought for a moment that she had been knocked down by a car, then realised that she could never have made it from the street up to his flat.

'Christ, what happened to you?'

She tried to speak but couldn't, gripping his arm instead.

'Hang on! I'll get an ambulance.'

But she wouldn't let go of his arm. Gary tried to loosen her grip.

'Let me go – you need help.'

Blood was pumping from her body and spreading across the hallway, and then her eyes went blank, the bubbles stopped coming from her mouth, and she let go of his arm.

Frieda Meyer was dead.

'Jesus!' Gary sobbed as he jerked away from her and fell back against the wall.

Someone had come to his flat and killed Frieda Meyer. Had they been looking for him and found her instead? Or had she come to his place to hide and been cornered there?

Wiping his hands on his jeans to get rid of the blood, Gary scrambled to his feet. He could hear music coming from the flat next door and flicked off the light. His heart thumping, he stepped over the corpse and grabbed his jacket and mobile phone, making for the door.

Peering out into the landing, Gary could see a man letting himself into another flat and a teenage girl smoking by the lift.

Should he call the police or make a run for it?

He might have deceived Bernard Lowe, but the police would find out about his conviction soon enough. Two years earlier his ex-wife had reported him for assault. It had been an act of malice and she had dropped the charges, but it was on his record and there it stayed, ready to be found by the police. And then how would Gary Rimmer explain away a dead woman in his flat?

Suddenly he realised that whoever had killed Frieda Meyer had known his history. Known that Gary Rimmer would serve as the ideal scapegoat. He could sense the body behind him, his flesh crawling, the smell of blood turning his stomach. He had never seen anyone dead before, never seen a person die. And he was afraid, terribly afraid. He pressed himself against the wall, uncertain if he should risk the outside world, but he knew he couldn't stay with a bloodied corpse leaking fluids onto his floor.

Staggering out of his flat, Gary Rimmer headed for the stairs, running down six flights towards the street below.

Forty-One

Campolfelice, Nr Palermo, Sicily

He had no appetite for food any more. Instead Carlo moved out of the sun and walked home, keeping to the shade of the houses. Several times he glanced behind him to see if he was being followed by the man who had threatened him, but there was no one there. Not even a shadow falling on the heated cobbles. Only his shadow, smaller now, walking like a phantom.

When he reached his house he fumbled with the lock, then entered. It was cool, inviting, but he didn't see it, instead remembering the man who had stopped at his table and overturned his life. And all because of his idiot son! Moving over to a side table, he scrabbled around inside the drawer, overturning it in his temper. Finally he discovered the note he had been searching for – a note with a phone number on it.

He had despised his son for years, thought him an embarrassment, forgotten him as much as he could. But he was damned if he was going to be threatened, or put his son in danger.

Reaching for the phone, Carlo punched in Luca's number and waited. But there was no answer. His son was out there somewhere. Carlo hadn't cared to know where, hadn't asked, hadn't wanted to know about Luca or his life, certainly hadn't wanted to talk to his son.

But he wanted to speak to him now.

Above his head a clock read four thirty, and outside a sick dog scratched itself helplessly in the last dying rays of a late sun.

Forty-Two

London

Gil was visiting Bette when his mobile rang, and he walked out into the hospital corridor to take the call. The line was bad, the worried voice familiar.

'Mr Eckhart, it's Luca Meriss.'

'Where are you?'

'Berlin,' the Italian replied. 'I was in New York, but I came back home. I've been talking to Harvey Crammer.'

'He found you?' Gil said, glancing out of the hospital window into the car park below. 'I expected him to get in touch with you.'

'I saw Catrina Hoyt too.'

'And?'

'It went badly,' Luca confessed, dodging into a shop doorway. He had bought a new mobile and his first call was to Gil. 'Look, you were right, this is all getting out of hand. My father needs help.'

'What's your father got to do with any of this?'

'I told him about the Caravaggio paintings. I told him about the proof,' Luca replied. 'He didn't believe me, but I told him. I've put him in danger.'

'I don't understand.'

'Harvey Crammer was talking about the dealers being murdered and how it was strange it had all happened when I came on the scene. Then he told me about the earlier killings in Germany. Said you were involved, and Jacob Levens, and that he was there too.'

'Yes. So?'

'Crammer asked me when I first knew about the Caravaggio paintings. And I told him it was seven years ago.' Gil took in a breath as Luca continued. 'Then he asked me who I'd confided in and given the details to – and I said no one. Except my father.'

'*You told your father where the paintings were?*'

'Not exactly. I told him I knew where they were. But I left something with him – some proof. It's in his house, hidden. At least it was seven years ago. I don't know if it's still there.'

Gil kept his voice steady. 'Did you tell Harvey Crammer?'

'No. I just told him that my father knew about the paintings. Nothing about the proof or what it was.' Luca looked around him. 'I've tried ringing my father, but there's no reply. And he can't get hold of me because I dumped my old phone. I've still got my passport, but only a bit of money left.' He was talking in jerky sentences, short of breath. 'You're the only person I've called, the only person with this number. I won't give it to anyone else.'

'You shouldn't have made an enemy of Catrina Hoyt.'

'I know, and I know she'll be after me. And Harvey Crammer's trying to get me to trust him but I don't.' He snatched a breath. 'I can't stay in Berlin either. I'm going back to Palermo.'

'Don't do that. You could be walking into a trap. You don't know that what Crammer said was true. Your father might not be in any danger–'

Luca cut him short.

'I confided in him! Of course he's in danger!' he retorted, slinking back into the doorway and watching the passers-by outside the airport. 'He's an old man. If they get to him they might hurt him. Jesus, they tortured those dealers – what's to stop them doing that to my father?'

Finally Gil had a connection between the Berlin murders and the London killings seven years apart. The news about Caravaggio had leaked out from Palermo. But from Luca? Or his father? Another thought occurred to him. Why were the Hubers the first victims? They dealt in Baroque paintings and admired Caravaggio, but so did many other dealers. So what was the link? Who, or what, sent the killer to the Friedrichstrasse that March night?

'You've lived in Berlin for a while,' Gil said. 'Did you know the Hubers?'

'No.'

'And you're sure you didn't tell anyone else about Caravaggio?'

'No!' Luca snapped.

'But if you had the information over seven years ago why didn't you go public then? Why wait?'

Luca paused.

'Are you still there?'

'I have to help my father,' the Italian replied, but his tone had altered, a chilling distance about it. 'I have to get home.'

'Why did you wait for so long?' Gil persisted. 'Why?'

'I couldn't speak out then.'

'Why not?'

'I was ill.'

I was ill.

'Hospitalised?'

'Yes.'

Gil was feeling his way along. 'What was wrong with you?'

Silence.

'Luca? What was wrong with you?'

'I had a breakdown,' he said finally. 'That's why I couldn't speak out. I was committed to a mental institution.'

Gil paused, remembering the conversation he had had with Bette days earlier:

But if it was the same man, where's he's been for seven years?

Abroad. In prison. Hospitalised. Who knows?

'Seven years is a long time.'

'I was very ill. I had a lot of treatment: drugs and therapy.' The Italian went on. 'I'm not crazy, Mr Eckhart – I recovered. It was a good hospital, outside Berlin. They had all the latest equipment, the best doctors, psychiatrists. It took a long time to get better, but I did.'

The confession was troubling, raising more questions than answers.

'When were you admitted?'

'March 29th 2007.'

Gingerly, Gil felt his way along. 'What was wrong with you?'

'You mean am I mad?' Luca countered. 'No, I was suffering from depression, hearing things – the world scared me so much I withdrew, shut myself off. I might still be cut off if it hadn't been for the hospital. They brought me back to life.'

'With medication?'

'At first, yes.'

'You had a therapist?'

'We all did.'

'Did you talk to him?'

'Not about Caravaggio. I'd learnt to keep that quiet because they thought it was a symptom – that I was delusional when I said I was related to him.'

'So you did tell someone?'

'When I was first admitted.' Luca hurried on. 'But I never mentioned it again.'

Someone had heard it, Gil thought. Someone in that hospital had heard about Caravaggio and the paintings. Luca might have forgotten it, but while he recovered the news spread into the wider world and set everything in motion. It might not have been his father who had talked; Luca could have given himself away.

'You stayed in hospital for seven years?'

'Yeah, it took a while but they got me better. In time I learnt how to cope in the real world. How to function, so that I could a get a job when I left. You could learn a lot of things in the hospital: Bookkeeping, gardening . . .'

'You learnt to garden?'

'No, I learnt how to work a computer.'

Gil felt a chill run down his spine. He didn't know what was coming, just that it was.

'Did you have a teacher?'

'We had a few. But my favourite was an Englishwoman. She was the best. Only came in part-time – all the patients adored her.' Luca paused. 'I think she was some kind of high-flier in her career. She said that she travelled a lot, but she used to volunteer at the hospital when she was in Berlin.'

'D'you know her name?'

Because I do, Gil thought. I know her name. I know who was in Berlin seven years ago. I know who charmed you, who found out about Caravaggio. Because she will have done. You might not remember, Luca, you might not recall what you said or how you said it, but she will have found out.

'Luca, what was her name?'

I know before you tell me, but I want to hear just the same.

'She was called Holly. I didn't know her last name, but I'll never forget her.' Luca changed the subject suddenly. 'What about my father? I have to go home.'

It took Gil a moment to rally. 'No, that's the last thing you should do. Make for the nearest hospital, Luca. Go to the psychiatric department and say you're sick, you're having a relapse. Tell them your history, say you want to get checked out. They'll admit you, and you'll be safe there.'

'I don't want to go back into hospital.'

'You've no choice. There's nowhere else you'll be safe.'

'What about my father?'

'Leave it to me,' Gil replied. 'Your father's my concern now.'

Forty-Three

She had heard him say the name, *Holly*. A simple name, almost childlike. Unsuitable for the woman who had owned it, Bette thought, watching her husband as Gil flipped off his mobile and stood by the corridor window. His shoulders were slumped, his head bowed, and she knew something terrible had happened, just hearing the name Holly and seeing the way his body had reacted, how every part of him was suddenly under threat.

'Are you OK?'

He walked back to her and guided her into her room, sitting beside her on the bed.

She said it for him. 'You're going away, aren't you?'

'Not for long.'

'What did she do?' Bette asked. 'I heard your conversation, I heard you say her name. And you wouldn't tell me what Jacob said this morning about Holly and the disks. So I know it's bad. It *is* bad, isn't it?'

He stared at her, mute.

'Yes,' she said, answering herself, 'it's bad. And you can't go to the police?'

'No.'

Gil thought of his late wife's involvement with Bernard Lowe and Luca Meriss. No, he couldn't go to the police and tell them what he knew. No one would ever believe that he hadn't been in league with Holly. Five dealers were dead, and he was sitting right in the middle of the maelstrom, as he had been in Berlin.

The police would look at him and see the obvious. Not the truth, but what would pass for the truth. Seven years ago Gil had worked in the art world and been called in on the Huber murder case. He had known all the dealers, had had easy access to them. And he had a history of violence. The treacherous Jacob could say that Holly had been afraid of her husband and jealous that he had been duped for another man. And besides, Gil Eckhart knew all about Caravaggio. The police would believe that Holly had told him about it at first, then Luca Meriss had confided the rest.

Gil knew he didn't have a leg to stand on, and the last place he could go for help was the police.

'What did she do?' Bette repeated, resting her head on her husband's shoulder. 'Talk to me, Gil. I love you and I'm the only person you can trust.'

He took her hand. 'I didn't know her at all. I didn't know the woman I was married to. Jacob told me what she was like this morning, and I didn't have any idea. She fooled me completely.'

Bette tightened her grip on his hand. 'What about the disks?'

'They were stolen. Or so Jacob Levens said. Conveniently taken – after he'd had them for seven years.'

'What was on them?'

'I don't know.'

'What d'you think?'

'I think they were something damning. Obviously something Jacob's worried about.' His voice hardened. 'Levens is guilty. I'm not saying he's the killer, but he's guilty of something. He was like another man this morning – he was a bastard.'

Her voice dropped to a whisper. 'Are you in trouble?'

'Yeah.'

'Can you get out of it?' she asked, gripping his hand even harder. 'Can you?'

'I don't know.'

'But you have to go away?'

He nodded. 'I have to go back to the beginning, to where it all started. It's the only chance I've got.' His lips rested against her forehead, his breath cool. 'You were right to hate Holly.'

'I never said I did.'

'You didn't have to. I knew you hated her, I just didn't know why.' He put his arms around his wife, resting his head against hers. Like her, he was whispering. Like children do in the dark. 'I have to clear up this mess. No one else can. I have to do it . . . You understand, don't you?'

She nodded. 'Promise me one thing?'

'What?'

'When you've solved the case, walk away. Don't look back. And get rid of her. Bury her. Get Holly out of our lives – once and for all.'

Forty-Four

New York

Harvey Crammer bent down and wiped the rain off his shoes with a handkerchief. It amused him that his fastidiousness surprised people, but even an ugly man wants to look good. Stretching up, he checked his mail then his mobile, irritated that there had been no message from Luca Meriss. He had been sure that the Italian would turn to him for help, especially after Crammer had intimated that his father might be in danger.

A buzz on the intercom of Crammer's flat disturbed his thoughts and a strident female voice answering his greeting.

'I need to talk to you.'

He buzzed her up. Watched as Catrina Hoyt walked into his apartment in jeans and a thick quilted jacket. Sighing, she slumped into a chair, pulling off her knitted hat and gloves. Her nails were painted dark red and she wore a ring on each thumb.

Crammer had known Catrina for several years and had always disliked her. 'What can I do for you?'

'Luca Meriss,' she said without preamble. 'And don't pretend you don't know who I'm talking about. I know you've been in touch with him – he told me.'

'So?'

'He's in New York. I paid for him to come over and the little bastard turned on me.' She rubbed her hands together. 'It's freezing in here. Why don't you put some heating on?'

He ignored the comment. 'What d'you want from me?'

'I want to know where Meriss is.'

'I don't know.'

'Are you sure?'

'What d'you want him for?'

'The same fucking reason you want him: to get to the Caravaggios.' She folded her arms, face pinched with cold. 'Of course he could just be jerking us all around with that crap on the internet. It could all be rubbish. I bet the son of a bitch doesn't know anything, he's just some deluded nutter.' She glanced around at the immaculate apartment, her gaze resting on the stuffed deer head. 'Kill it yourself?'

'Actually I did,' Crammer replied deftly. 'In Canada.'

'You must be a good shot.'

'I always hit my target.'

She laughed loudly. 'So, what d'you think about Meriss? You think he's genuine? Did he show you any proof about these paintings?'

'No. And I know he didn't show you anything either.'

'I *knew* you'd talked to him!' she snapped. 'He's been in touch with Bernard Lowe too.'

'You haven't heard then?'

'Heard what?'

'Bernard Lowe died yesterday. He was murdered.'

Her face was incredulous. 'You're joking!'

'He was the third dealer to be killed in three days,' Crammer replied. 'We appear to be dropping like ducks in a shooting gallery. That's five now. Perhaps we should consider a change of career.'

'Five?' Catrina echoed. 'I've only heard about three.'

'There were two others, seven years ago. In Berlin.' Her astonishment amused him. It felt good to get one over on the abrasive Ms Hoyt. 'You didn't know about the Hubers?'

'No . . . How are they connected to the London murders?'

'I wouldn't know,' Crammer said enigmatically. 'I'm not a detective, but I believe that one's been called in. Gil Eckhart. Oddly enough he worked on the Berlin case. Jacob Levens hired him then, and again now.'

She was trying to follow but couldn't join up the dots. Not too much, Crammer thought. Just give her enough to keep her interest. To keep her close.

'Jacob Levens? He's in on this too?' She frowned. 'Of course he is. He'd want those paintings as much as we do. What about that German?'

'Oscar Schultz?'

She nodded. 'He'll be aching to get in on this.'

'I don't doubt it,' Crammer replied elusively.

'Have either of them talked to Luca Meriss?'

'Who can tell?'

She was trying to piece it all together, and failing.

'I don't know why I'm surprised. There'll be plenty of others interested. We won't have been the only ones who saw Meriss's website. There could be hundreds out there, all looking for him. Cretin! Why did he go and expose himself publicly? He was attacked in Berlin, you know . . .' She paused, but Crammer said nothing. 'Made him pretty keen to leave Germany. Said someone left a note on the plane for him on the way over here. Some kind of warning.' She rubbed the side of her nose. 'Meriss was scared shitless when he came to the gallery. Desperate for help. I never thought he'd do a runner–'

'Why did he?'

'We didn't get on!' she snapped. 'He was pissing me about. I was beginning to think he had made the whole thing up. He said he had proof, but not with him.'

'Maybe he didn't trust you.'

'He didn't trust you either, did he?' she countered. 'I don't see Luca Meriss here.'

Thoughtful, Crammer moved over to his laptop, entering Luca Meriss's website. It came up at once and seemed unchanged, until he noticed that a clock had been added in the bottom left-hand corner, the hands ticking by the seconds as he watched.

'That's new.'

Catrina looked over his shoulder.

'Meriss told me that no one else had access to the site.' She pointed to the ticking clock. 'So how did *that* get on the website?'

'Good question. I think Mr Meriss has a hacker.'

As they watched the ticking clock, a series of images suddenly came up. The first was of the Weir twins, bloodied and tortured. Not dead, but dying. The second was of Bernard Lowe, the oxygen mask over his face. And the third was the photograph that had spooked Luca Meriss, that of the two scalps laid out on a tabletop.

The dealers watched the screen, transfixed. But it was the last photograph that shocked them the most. It was an image shot through an apartment window and it showed two people talking, an ugly middle-aged man and an athletic young woman.

Harvey Crammer stared at the image.

Catrina Hoyt stared at it.

They were looking at themselves as they had been only seconds before.

Forty-five

Campolfelice, Nr Palermo, Sicily
11.30 p.m.

Checking the address he had been given, Gil made his way across the small, scruffy square towards Carlo's home. There was only a little moon and the air was surprisingly cold as he hurried along. Unfamiliar streets were empty in the darkness, lights shining out from upper floors and the occasional car passing but otherwise quiet. Eerie.

The rain had kept people indoors, but it wasn't just the weather that was casting such gloom. It was the place itself. The house was set back from the row, a pair of rusting, buckled iron gates pulled open at the entrance. A poor man's house needing attention, money made to stretch to necessities, no more. Above the bell was a note with a name on it, too faint to read. Gil stepped into the porch and knocked loudly.

He could hear a dog barking inside, but no footsteps. A moment later he knocked again, then glanced at the upstairs windows. They were unlit, but he had the distinct feeling the place was occupied. That someone was inside, hiding. Cautious, he moved round to the back of the house and a woman's silhouette appeared in the window next door. She paused, looked out, then moved away.

The air was clogged with water; but not refreshing, too cold to be pleasant and too quiet to be comfortable. He tried the back door. Locked. Then he moved to the kitchen window, slid it open, and clambered in.

The blow hit Gil on the back of his head. The force was enough to knock him out, his knees buckling as he hit the stone floor.

Forty-Six

When Gil came round he was tied to a kitchen chair and three men were watching him. Two were young and the third was an elderly man wearing glasses. Shaking his head to clear his thoughts, Gil stared at the older man.

'Carlo Meriss?'

The young men looked at each other. '*Che cosa ha detto?*'

'Me, Carlo Ranuccio,' the older man said, pointing to himself. 'Not Meriss. Carlo *Ranuccio.*'

Gil nodded, wincing as the pain shot through his head. 'Are you Luca's father?'

There was a momentary pause as the old man struggled with his English. 'Who are you?'

'I want to help,' Gil began. '*Aiuto.*'

'*Aiuto?*' one of the younger men questioned. '*Perche?*' He gestured towards a back room as a stout woman entered and shuffled over to them.

'I speak English,' she said to Gil. 'Carlo wants to know who you are. Why you broke in.'

'My name's Gil Eckhart. I came to help Carlo. Luca sent

me.' He could see the old man react to his son's name as the woman translated for him.

Taking off his glasses, Carlo rubbed his eyes, speaking angrily in Italian.

'He doesn't know where his son is,' the woman translated.

'I know he doesn't, but I've seen Luca.'

She translated again and Carlo interrupted her. 'Is he OK?'

'Yes, but he's worried about you.' Gil looked back at the woman. 'Tell him that I know about the Caravaggios. Luca told me that he confided in his father seven years ago and gave him something . . .'

She translated. Carlo nodded, his eyes never leaving Gil's face as he continued.

'And now Luca's put himself in danger. People are after him because he's saying that he knows where two Caravaggio paintings are hidden. He says he's a descendant of the artist and that he has proof of this.'

She translated, the younger men listening, Carlo blowing out his cheeks.

'Crazy!' He slapped the tabletop with the flat of his hand. 'Crazy!'

'Do you know where the paintings are?'

'No!' He said something else and the woman hesitated to translate.

'What did he say?' Gil prompted her.

'He said why should he tell you? Even if he knew, why would he tell you? You might be lying. You might be working for the man who came here this morning.'

'Who came this morning?' Gil asked, glancing at Carlo and then back at the woman. 'Was he threatened by someone?'

There was a long pause, Carlo defiant, his arms crossed, the other men watching Gil.

He turned to the woman.

'Can you get my phone out of my pocket?' She hesitated then did so, laying it on the table in front of him. 'You want to untie me?' Prompted by the younger men, she shook her head. 'OK,' Gil said wearily, 'I'll give you a number to call.' He watched her punch out the digits and the phone rang on the table between all of them.

Luca answered, his voice little more than a whisper.

'Hello?'

'*Luca!*' his father said, snatching up the phone and talking into it hurriedly in Italian. After another few moments he gestured for Gil to be untied, then passed the mobile back to him.

'Are you OK?' Luca asked Gil. 'They thought you were after my father. You see, I told you he was in danger.'

'I know–'

'Some man threatened him, asked him to contact me. But he couldn't, he didn't have my number. They said that unless he gave me up, they'd kill him.'

Gil turned to the woman. 'Ask Carlo about the man who threatened him. What did he look like?'

She translated, but the old man shrugged.

'He wasn't wearing his glasses,' she explained. 'He couldn't see clearly. But the man was tall and spoke with a Roman accent.'

'Did you hear that?' Gil asked Luca down the phone. 'Does that sound like anyone you know?'

'No.' Luca dropped his voice so low Gil had to strain to hear him. 'I did what you said. I had myself admitted to hospital. They don't know I've got a phone. They don't allow them but I smuggled it in. And I used another name, Zerafa. Luca Zerafa.'

'Good.'

'I can't stay here long.'

'You have to stay there – you're safe there.' Gil paused, knowing everyone was watching him. 'I need to know where the proof is. That's what the man wanted from you and that's what I need now to help your father.' When Luca said nothing, Gil pressed him. 'Where did you hide the proof? And don't lie to me – I've kept my side of the bargain. Where is it?'

'Ask for a torch and a spade and go into the garden.'

Gil spoke to the woman. She was surprised, but walked away and returned a few moments later with both items. Taking them from her, Gil walked out into the garden.

'Now,' he said down the phone, 'where do I go?'

'There's a cypress tree at the far end. Can you see it?'

Gil walked towards it. 'OK, I'm here.'

'Move round the back, and there's an old pond. It's been filled in with soil.'

Propping the torch up to illuminate the spot, Gil felt the earth, covered with weeds. 'Now what? Do I dig?'

'No. Feel round the back of the pond and there are two loose bricks. Got them?'

'Got them.'

'You'll have to knock them out. They won't just come out – they've been there for years. You might have to kick them loose,' Luca went on, listening down the phone as he heard Gil trying to loosen the stones. It seemed to take a long time, until finally the bricks fell backwards onto the path behind.

'OK, stones are out.'

'Now dig about a foot down.'

Putting aside the phone, Gil began to dig. Six inches, a foot, eighteen inches . . . Finally, exasperated, he snatched up the phone again.

'There's nothing here!'

'There must be!'

'If you've lied to me—'

'I put it there! I put it there years ago!' Luca said desperately. 'I buried it – I know I did. It's there! It has to be!'

'There's nothing here,' Gil repeated. 'Nothing.'

'But I buried it—'

'What did you bury, Luca? What was it?'

'A plastic bag.'

'What was in it?'

'Disks,' Luca said brokenly. 'Two computer disks with the proof of where the paintings are. With everything on them: names, dates – everything. All the proof anyone would ever need.'

Gil felt light-headed as the breath was sucked out of him. He knew where the disks had gone. He knew who had taken them all those years ago. The same person who had befriended Luca Meriss and taught him how to use a computer.

His ex-wife. The late lamented Mrs Eckhart.

Thursday

Naples, Italy
1610

Seeking protection from the powerful Colonna family, Caravaggio waited for his pardon from Rome. Having thrown himself on their mercy, he was given a place to work and a guard to stand watch over him. His injuries were slow to heal and his face was disfigured, the wound drawing down his left eyelid, his mouth irregular.

Skirting mirrors, Caravaggio kept to the dark. His hired bodyguard might stand at his door, but there were windows – other means of entry to his studio. Belligerent and nervous by turns, he recovered, then ventured back into the Neapolitan streets. His appearance did not go unnoticed, the news spreading to his enemies, whispered in taverns, and skimming over the water towards the redoubtable Simon de Wignacourt, the Governor of the Knights of St John, in Malta.

De Wignacourt had been one of the artist's greatest admirers. He had posed for his portrait and rewarded him with a suite of rooms, a slave, a gold chain. Finally he had made him an honorary member of the Order. The painter had revelled in his status, until a skirmish with one of the Knights had resulted in his being jailed. News travelled to Rome, tales of Caravaggio's notorious temper fuelling the rumours. There was to be a trial, he was to be exiled from the Order 'like a rotten and fetid limb'.

Overnight Simon de Wignacourt had become an implacable enemy, and Caravaggio knew it. Desperate, he escaped from Malta and returned to Naples. But he had been followed.

Old enemies had traced him. Some said de Wignacourt had sent a man to kill the artist and redeem the reputation of the Order. Others whispered about Sicily, where Caravaggio had been pursued by relatives of the murdered Ranuccio Tomassoni. Every place, every city, was pitted with rivals and men eager for the painter's scalp.

Time passed. Cornered, Caravaggio hid, waiting for the pardon to be granted. And he worked. Summoning his favourite model from Rome, Fillide Melandroni, he began his painting of Salome with the Head of John the Baptist. Indolently beautiful, Fillide became surly and lazy, falling asleep as Caravaggio painted her, provoking him, mocking his disfigured face. But she slept in the crook of his arm, and listened to the footsteps of the guard outside the door. And she watched the canvas cradle her image in among the all-devouring shadows of the background.

When the picture was finished Caravaggio sent it to Simon de Wignacourt, with a note explaining that the severed head of John the Baptist was his own self-portrait. An offering, a token to apologise, to beg a painterly sacrifice. Here is my head on a plate. I give you something all Italy would prize: valuable, admired, another for the collection of the Order.

Take the image of my skull, but leave me whole.

Word finally came, first from Malta. The painting had been rejected. The Knights wanted Caravaggio's real head, not a painted image. Caravaggio painted another sacrificial picture, of David and Goliath, and this time the giant's severed head was his.

He rushed the painting, irritable, nervy, the pain in his face flaring as the nerves tugged under the tightening wound. Soon the magnificent image was on its way to the notorious cardinal Scipione Borghese, a long-time admirer of Caravaggio and a man powerful enough to grant pardons.

Spring turned over, summer coming early, hot and Fillide Melandroni returned to Rome. In his rooms, Caravaggio received news that his longed-for pardon was finally about to be granted. But was also informed that de Wignacourt resented his painterly attempt at an apology. On Malta, the Knights of the Order took the painting as an insult, a trumped-up attempt to placate them. Caravaggio might have escaped Malta, but he hadn't escaped them.

Disturbed, haunted, hunted, Caravaggio slept with a knife under his pillow, roaring at anyone who approached him. At the slightest criticism of his work he ripped up the canvas he was working on, lapsing into rages, unstable. Summer came hot. Summer came quick. He slept, sweating in his armour plate, and waited for his pardon.

And he listened to the footsteps of his guard outside the door, wondering if – or when – they would become the steps of his murderer instead.

Forty-Seven

Campolfelice, Nr Palermo, Sicily
12.30 a.m.

'What was on the disks?' Gil asked, sitting down on the mouldering brick wall, too far away from the house to be overheard – although he knew he was being watched from the kitchen window. His head was aching from the assault, his patience exhausted. '*What was on the bloody disks?*'

On the other end of the phone, the Italian snapped to attention. 'The whereabouts of the paintings.'

'Where are they?'

'*The Nativity* is still in Palermo . . .'

'Still here?'

'It never left the island.'

'Not stolen by the Mafia?'

'That's what everyone was supposed to think.'

Gil could hear noises over the line, Luca's voice dropping. 'I think someone's coming!'

He hurried on. 'What about the portrait of Fillide Melandroni? Where's that?'

Luca's voice very faint, barely more than a whisper. 'It's in Berlin.'

'*Where* in Berlin?'

'It's on the disks.'

'For God's sake, just tell me!'

'*The Nativity* is—'

The line went dead.

'Luca? Luca!' Exasperated, Gil tried to redial the number. But all he got was voicemail.

He wondered if Luca been caught by the medical staff, his phone confiscated, forbidden by the hospital rules. At this moment Luca Meriss might well be on his way back to bed, chastened like a child. Gil hoped so. But then again, there might well be some more sinister reason for the sudden cut-off.

Uneasy, Gil turned to the woman. 'Ask Mr Ranuccio exactly what his son told him about Caravaggio and the paintings, will you?'

She spoke to the old man, listened to his reply, and turned back to Gil.

'Luca said their family was related to Caravaggio, and that he knew where the missing paintings were.'

'Nothing else? Nothing more specific?'

He waited for her to interpret. 'No, Mr Ranuccio says there was nothing more.'

Gil stared at the old man. His hands were thrust defiantly

into his pockets, his glasses smudged with fingerprints. His expression was combative, without fear. He had realised he was in danger, but his first thought was not for himself. Speaking to the woman, she nodded and turned to Gil.

'Mr Ranuccio says for you not to worry about him, but to help his son.'

'I should–'

She waved his interruption aside. 'He says that he has good friends here.' She gestured to the two young men, one pointing to a shotgun leaning up against the wall. 'He says he will be all right. He wants you to help Luca.' She listened as the old man spoke again, then translated. 'Mr Ranuccio asks if you will save his son.'

Gil paused for an instant. 'If I can.'

She stared at him intently. 'Where are you going now?'

'Back to London. But not before I visit the church where *The Nativity* was stolen.'

'The Oratory of San Lorenzo?'

He nodded, then scribbled down his mobile number. 'You can call me any time. If you hear anything, or think of anything, call me. I mean it – keep in touch.'

'You won't find anything at the church,' the woman told him. 'There's nothing there.'

'No reason not to look.'

She said something to Carlo and he nodded.

'Mr Ranuccio says that you must stay here tonight, and go in the morning. The church will be locked until then anyway.' She guided him back into the house, towards the kitchen table. 'Eat some food, then rest.'

In silence Carlo took a seat next to him, watching as Gil was given some bread and cheese. When he had finished eating the woman showed him into the sitting room beyond, dusty and cool, handing him a blanket and gesturing to an old sofa.

'Sleep,' she told him. 'Nothing will happen tonight.'

'How d'you know?'

'Because you are with us,' she teased him. 'Now, rest.'

The following morning Gil rose before six, walked into the yard and washed himself at an old pump. The sun was curling upwards, promising day, a cockerel marking its vocal territory in the waiting stillness. No one else was about and he woke no one. Instead he helped himself to some more bread and cheese, drank some milk, and left.

It was only when Gil reached the gate that he realised Carlo Ranuccio had followed him. Glancing behind him, the old man checked that no one was watching, and then handed Gil a faded suede pouch, closing his fingers over it.

His expression was intense. '*Dio sia con te* . . . God go with you.'

Nodding, Gil tightened his grip around the pouch then walked off, closing the rusty gates behind him.

Forty-Eight

The Oratory of San Lorenzo, Palermo
9.00 a.m.

Dusting off his clothes, Gil entered the church. It was smaller than he had expected – hardly more than a large room. The opulence of the interior surprised Gil, frosted statues and soaring figures materialising like ectoplasm from the icing-sugar walls. Around the ceiling, ghost limbs, white-marbled, hung like elegant sides of meat, and a chandelier was frosted with unlit candles. Pews inlaid with mother-of-pearl and ivory rested on the blood-red marble of the floor, the gold on the statues prickling in the early sunlight.

Gil looked around him at the pristine interior, almost shocking in its lack of colour. Every statue, every pillar, every niche, was locked in crystallised perfection. Every white face, white hand, white limb was transfixed. Time had not entered the Oratorio. Nothing had faded or dimmed. Nothing had aged. No sun, no wind, no rain had effected any changes over the centuries. It was, he thought, a deeply unsettling place.

As quietly as he could, Gil moved towards the altar and paused, staring at the huge painting facing him. Although only a copy of *The Nativity with St Lawrence and St Francis*, it had the power to thrill, its bravura composition and colouring profoundly moving. Gil could understand why the painting had meant so much, and had been so desired. What a coup for Palermo to own such a masterpiece! And then, one October night in 1969, the original had been cut from its frame and bundled out. It was never seen again.

His gaze moved over the replica Caravaggio, the power of which was intensified by the elegant frippery of its surroundings. And then he tensed. To his right, a door closed. Gil turned, but no one was there. Another noise alerted him and he turned again, only to see a man enter, cross himself, and begin to pray in a pew behind him. The woman had been right: there was nothing to see at the Oratorio of San Lorenzo.

Gil heard a cough behind him.

'You like the painting?' Startled, he turned to find the worshipper watching him. 'You like the painting?'

Gil nodded, waiting to see if the man would say more, but to his surprise he just shrugged and returned to his prayers.

Sliding into a pew at the back, Gil took out the pouch from Carlo Ranuccio. It was aged, greasy with fingerprints, the cord fraying as he eased it open and shook out a small, narrow piece of wood. Gil frowned, staring at it and turning it over in his hands. But it wasn't simply wood. On closer inspection he could see that it was the top of a paintbrush, the ferrule holding the remains of sable hairs, the handle broken, only two inches long.

Hurriedly, Gil felt into the pouch, drawing out a slip of paper on which was scrawled *Pennello di Caravaggio Michelangelo Merisi da, Palermo 1608*.

Stunned, he took in a breath. So the old man *had* known something, perhaps proof of his family's link to the painter. A link that Carlo Ranuccio had decided to suppress – especially as it concerned a painting stolen by the Sicilian Mafia. He had tried to secure his family's safety by denial.

And failed.

The broken brush might prove to be a fake. But if it didn't – if it *was* confirmation of Luca Meriss's claims – it meant that the Italian was telling the truth about everything else.

Gil stared at the piece of wood. He could imagine how coveted such a prize would be. How the likes of Crammer, Schultz, Hoyt and Jacob Levens would slaver to own it. Jesus, Gil thought, the Italian was lucky to be alive. No wonder his father had been threatened. *And whoever had threatened Carlo Ranuccio would now be watching him.*

Gil sat immobile in the pew, knowing that his visit to the old man would not have gone unnoticed. Perhaps they would guess that he had been given something and would want it. Gil might have got Luca Meriss to a safe house, but he was hanging in the wind. In his hand he was holding history – and his own noose.

If proved authentic it would be the brush used by Michelangelo Merisi da Caravaggio, dating from Palermo in 1608, the year the artist was exiled, moving from country to country, running for his life.

Just as Luca Meriss had been.

Just as Gil was now.

Forty-Nine

London
11.00 a.m.

'I told you, I had nothing to do with it!' Gary Rimmer repeated, staring at Phil Simmons. 'She turned up at my flat and died there–'

'Just like that?' he replied, his expression weary. 'She was Bernard Lowe's nurse. She had access to him, she was the one person who could tamper with the cylinders. And you knew her. I spoke to the housekeeper – she said you two talked a lot.'

'We worked at the same place!' Gary spluttered. 'I fancied her, that was all. I just chatted her up, I didn't kill her.'

'But Frieda Meyer's body is, nevertheless, in your flat,' Simmons replied, 'and her employer's been murdered. And that looks very much as though she was involved – and you were too. Did you plan it together? To kill off the old man and–'

'I never wanted to kill him!'

'Someone did.'

'All right,' Gary said, raking his hands through his hair. '*Why* would I want to kill Bernard Lowe?'

'His house is full of valuables.'

'Was anything taken?'

'Not that I know of,' Simmons replied, 'but then again, you might have had something particular in mind that no one else knew about. Lowe was a very wealthy man. Perhaps you saw something you fancied? Or heard about something he was after?'

Gary swallowed, thinking of the Caravaggios.

'I didn't steal anything from Mr Lowe.'

'You've got a record for assault.'

'Oh, fuck.'

'Yeah, it doesn't look good.'

'My ex-wife made that complaint. She dropped it later.'

Simmons' expression was flat. 'Did you make her drop it?'

'No! She was after me for child maintenance, so she made the complaint to the police to throw a scare into me.' He paused. 'I paid the fucking maintenance. She was lying about the assault. Ask her.'

Simmons sat down facing Gary. The rash on the detective's face had begun to die down, the redness slowly fading.

'Why did you kill Frieda Meyer?'

'I didn't kill her!'

'All right, why would she come to your flat and then die there?'

'*I don't know!*' Gary said pleadingly. 'She came in the back door, I said her name and she dropped down – just like that, onto the floor. There was blood everywhere.'

'And you ran away?'

'Whoever killed her could have been after me–' Gary stopped short, realising that he had said too much.

'Why would they be after you?'

'I dunno . . .' He was floundering. 'We both worked for Mr Lowe.'

'And that was a death sentence, was it?'

Shut up, Gary told himself. Stop talking now. You're only making it worse.

'I want a lawyer. I'm not saying another word until I talk to a lawyer.' Gary's face set. 'And I want to talk to Gil Eckhart too.'

Fifty

London
12.00 noon

Walking down Cork Street, Greta crossed the road and made her way to The Levens Gallery. The window was displaying a series of sixteenth century Italian drawings, similar to the ones her parents had once dealt in. It reminded her of her childhood, nostalgia for days past catching her unexpectedly.

Peering in, she rang the doorbell and waited until a young woman of about her age appeared and let her in.

'Can I help you?'

'I want to see Mr Levens,' Greta replied, 'He's not expecting me, but I'm his niece.'

Once inside she stood by the wall, her tiny frame hardly taking up any space, and a moment later Jacob appeared.

'Greta, how good to see you!' He kissed her cheek but she didn't respond, following meekly into his office at the back of the gallery.

'I didn't even know you were in London,' he said, caught off guard. 'Are you on holiday?'

'No, not really. I just thought I'd drop by because I wanted to talk to you. I know it's been a long time and we haven't been in contact. I should have replied to your letters but I was . . .' She drifted off, both of them uncomfortable, thinking of the past.

'Are you working?'

'Yes.'

'Still teaching English?'

'Yes, but not in India any more.'

Surprised, Jacob looked at his niece. 'You went to India? Why so far away?'

'I wanted to get away from Germany, as far away as I could. Mr Joshi was very good to me. He arranged everything.'

'*Joshi?*' He thought of the historian. 'You mean Naresh Joshi?'

Greta nodded. 'When I got better, he offered me a holiday, then a job, and I stayed on. He looked out for me. Nothing romantic, nothing like that – he was just very kind.' She glanced around the office. 'I like the drawings in your window.'

'They're by Guercino,' Jacob said, then returned to his previous subject. 'I should have been in touch.'

'You weren't really interested though, were you?'

Her bluntness took him by surprise.

'There should be no bad feeling between us, dear. Your parents and I lived in different countries. We met when we could–'

'My mother said that you weren't family minded,' Greta went on, her voice expressionless. 'It doesn't matter – I didn't expect anything from you, even after my parents were killed. You sent flowers to the funeral, which was thoughtful, although I imagine my mother would have liked you to be there.' Her voice trailed off, the rebuke hanging in the air. 'I heard about the murders that happened here. They're the same, aren't they?'

'I . . . I think so, yes.' Jacob was nonplussed by the frail young woman facing him. She seemed calm, but there was an anger about her that was palpable.

'D'you think it's the same killer?'

'It looks that way.'

'You said "looks that way" – did you know what happened to the victims?'

'I found them.'

She didn't seem surprised. 'I found my mother . . . Stays with you, doesn't it?' For a moment she held his gaze, then changed the subject. 'I sold the gallery in the end. After seven years.'

'Yes, I heard,' Jacob said, clearing his throat. 'Is that what you wanted to talk to me about?'

'In a way. I wanted to ask you if you knew who had bought it. I know I didn't involve you with the sale. Well, it had nothing to do with you really, did it? But I wondered if you know who turned out to be the new owner?'

He had a feeling that he wasn't going to like the answer.

'Oscar Schultz.'

'*Oscar!*' Jacob said, alarmed. The very man who had chosen the name of *Der Kreis der Acht*; the man who had not seen fit to mention his purchase of the Huber Gallery. Jesus, Jacob thought, was else was the German hiding?

'You didn't know?'

'No,' Jacob said, trying to cover his unease. 'Well, it makes sense: Oscar's based in Berlin and he has one gallery in the city already.'

'My mother hated him.'

'He's all right. A bit oily, but—'

'She would *never* have sold the gallery to Oscar Schultz.'

'But you did,' Jacob countered, with an edge to his voice.

'That's the point – I didn't,' Greta replied. 'I sold it to a company called Lexington Limited. A shipping company. There was no mention of Oscar Schultz. I admit I didn't get very involved, but I do remembering asking who owned the company. The Managing Director was listed as a Mr Bernard Lowe.' She let the words settle before continuing. 'The name meant nothing to me then. But now . . . Bernard Lowe was a collector, wasn't he? And he's one of the people who have just been killed. Now, Uncle, I ask you – doesn't that seem a bit strange?'

Without answering, Jacob reached for a drink. His jowls coloured up as the alcohol hit his system, his left hand gripping the glass. Clever little bitch, he thought. So she was trying to work it all out, was she? After seven years Alma's little girl was going to uncover *Der Kreis der Acht*. And when she did, what else? The way he had involved her mother? What else was this tiny little demon going to find?

'What's this got to do with me?'

'I don't know yet,' Greta replied flatly, 'but I'll find out. Just like I'll find out what my mother was afraid of. Because she *was* afraid. She wouldn't tell me why, but in the months before her death every time your name was mentioned, she flinched.'

He laughed off the comment.

'*What are you talking about?*'

She was defiant, resolute. 'What did you do to my mother?'

'Nothing!'

'After the murders I was so ill I never thought about it. But I've been thinking about it now. About the time before my parents were killed. About who was around then. There was a group of dealers my people knew and traded with – including The London Galleries Limited . . .' Jacob was watching her silently. 'Did you know they were owned by Sebastian and Benjamin Weir? Odd coincidence, isn't it? Like the fact that Lexington Limited was owned by the late Bernard Lowe, and is now managed by Oscar Schultz.'

'Look, I–'

'There was someone else around my parents at that time: Harvey Crammer. But then he had always been a constant, probably because he was still fond of my mother. He was married to her once, after all, and they liked each other. But we mustn't forget the one other person who was around. Who hadn't been around for a while, and seemed to suddenly pop up – *you*.'

'She was my sister!'

'All you dealers knew each other, didn't you?'

'So what, my dear?' Jacob said lightly. 'The art world is like that. Tight. Everyone knows everyone else.'

'But doesn't it seem strange that within that tight little group *five* of you are now dead?' Greta stood up, fastened her coat, and then looked back at him. 'What did you do to my mother?'

Jacob stared at his niece. And as he stared he remembered. Remembered being envious of Terrill Huber's clients and making a deal with Alma to try to benefit from their contacts. Pressurising her into joining *Der Kreis der Acht*. Blackmailing her into agreeing. Making it impossible for her to refuse. She had despised him for it. Later Jacob had felt remorse, but brushed it aside. He was giving his sister a business opportunity, he told her. She should thank him.

In the years that followed, everyone had made money. But Alma Huber never forgot the means by which her brother had forced her hand and it drove a wedge between them. Ignorant of the circumstances, Terrill didn't understand her animosity, and even when she hinted at illicit trading he brushed it off. Terrill Huber had been a greedy man, like Jacob, unwilling to break ranks with the likes of Oscar Schultz and Harvey Crammer.

But for Alma, no amount of money or prestige could excuse her brother's actions, and in early 2007 she tried to leave *Der Kreis der Acht* again. Jacob had prevented it by giving her something for safe keeping, something he knew was damning, and dangerous.

'What did you do to my mother?' Greta repeated.

'Nothing.'

'I don't believe you. I think you were all involved in something, something you had to keep hidden. Was it important? Big enough to kill for?'

'*I've never killed anyone in my life!*'

'I never said you did.'

'I loved your mother,' Jacob said, trying to smile. 'I care for you too, my dear.'

'I'm not a fool, Uncle,' she replied, staring at him coldly. 'I don't know if you're the killer. But if you aren't I certainly hope you're the next victim.'

Fifty-One

Heathrow Airport, London
2.00 p.m.

Arriving back from Sicily, Gil left the airport, sliding into a cab and calling Luca's number again. Having tried repeatedly to contact the Italian, he was relieved when the phone was finally picked up.

'Hallo?'

'Luca!'

'*Wer anruft?*'

'What?'

'Who's calling?' The voice slid from German into English effortlessly. 'Can I help you?'

Gil was praying that Luca's phone had been confiscated; that it was just hospital rules that meant his mobile was out of his hands.

'I'm sorry, I was just talking to a friend on this line.'

'Mr Zerafa. Yes, this is his phone,' the voice went on. 'But we don't allow phones in the ward, so we had to confiscate it. It's hospital policy.'

'I understand . . . How is he?'

'Are you a relative?'

'A friend. I'm coming to see him and he asked me to bring some things for him. To the hospital. Things he needed.'

'Really?' the nurse replied. 'I find that strange.'

'He just wanted some clean clothes.'

'No, I don't find that strange. It's just that Mr Zerafa left us yesterday.'

The words were chilling. 'He discharged himself?'

'No, his doctor came for him.'

'*His doctor?*'

'Dr Lieberman,' the nurse continued. 'That is, Dr Lieberman sent an ambulance for Mr Zerafa and a nurse to accompany him. We were given very precise instructions. Mr Zerafa was to be sedated as he was a bad traveller and liable to panic when moved.'

Gil tried to keep his voice steady. 'Where did he go?'

'The Gruber Institute,' the nurse replied. 'All the papers were in order. The Gruber Institute is world famous, their psychiatrists the best. Rest assured, Mr Zerafa couldn't be in better hands.'

Fifty-Two

Gil's phone call to the Gruber Institute was short and clear. No, they had not admitted a patient from Berlin called Mr Luca Zerafa. No, Dr Gruber had not sent an ambulance for anyone. They were emphatic. No patient had been admitted and besides, Dr Gruber was in Egypt lecturing for the entire month.

It was exactly what Gil had feared. The papers given to the psychiatric hospital would have been in perfect order. He could imagine how precisely they would have been forged, so that no one would question them. He could also imagine the panic Luca would have felt on being sedated and taken against his will, to God only knows where. Events were escalating, spiralling out of control, Gil thought when he called in to see Bette at the hospital before returning to their flat.

The place seemed bleak without her, the nursery uninviting. Unsettled, Gil turned on the central heating, but the atmosphere was blighted, somehow changed. On his office phone he found several messages. As expected, an inebriated, panicked apology from Jacob Levens, plus a call from the gas company and one from Phil Simmons, asking him to phone back.

But it was the last message that surprised Gil. Glancing at his watch, he then called the number, and Naresh Joshi picked up almost immediately in South Delhi.

He sounded relieved.

'Forgive my contacting you, Mr Eckhart, but I have an important matter to discuss. A delicate matter. I know you're investigating the Weir murders and I need to talk to you.'

'How can I help?'

'This conversation must be in the strictest confidence.'

'Goes without saying,' Gil replied, sitting down in his office chair and touching the radiator. Stone cold.

'I've heard that you were hired by Jacob Levens.' When Gil said nothing, he continued. 'I've known Mr Levens for many years, not as a friend but as a colleague. However, I've been very disturbed by something I heard today.'

Puzzled, Gil leant down and turned up the thermostat on the radiator.

'Go on.'

'Mr Levens called me.'

'*He called you?*'

'About the Caravaggio affair.'

'Which you already know about,' Gil replied deftly.

'Luca Meriss told you that?'

'Yes. He told me that you'd talked a long time ago, when

he first approached you in Italy. But that you weren't interested in what he had to say.'

'I was stupid and dismissed him,' Naresh replied, irritated with himself. 'The man was genuine: he wanted the best for the paintings and I took him for a lunatic. More fool me.'

Gil smiled. 'So what did Jacob Levens tell you?'

'He rambled on for a while about the murders, seemed very afraid. Then he said that he was going to fire you and hire someone else to investigate the killings and Luca Meriss's claims.'

Gil kept his voice even. 'When did he say all this?'

'Only an hour ago.'

'But why would he tell you?' Gil asked, suspicious. 'Like you said, you weren't friends.'

'Jacob wants my help. He said that we should work together.' Naresh paused, patently embarrassed. 'Mr Levens seems to think that my reputation would assist him.'

'Have you worked with him before?'

'Never. But I am an authority on Caravaggio, and I do have a following.'

'So has a muck cart,' Gil said shortly.

'I don't mean to annoy you, Mr Eckhart. I only wanted to warn you. Mr Levens is behaving badly towards you, and I doubt his motives with regard to the Caravaggios. I would not like them to fall into his hands.'

'But you wouldn't mind them falling into yours?'

There was a long pause on the line before Naresh Joshi spoke again.

'I understand your suspicion. After all, why should you trust me? I ring you out of the blue and tell you this – why should you believe me? You've known and worked with Jacob Levens for years.'

'How d'you know that?'

'I'm based in Delhi but I travel the world, Mr Eckhart. As you know, the art business is very incestuous. Everyone is attached to everyone else in some way and gossip is the marinade. Please do not be angry, but I had you checked out. Surely the fact that I'm calling you proves that I am on your side?'

'I didn't know we were taking sides.'

'I think it might be wise to do so,' Naresh continued. 'When Jacob Levens phoned me he was drunk, barely making sense. As you know, back in the nineties he had a severe drink problem and suffered blackouts. I believe he was also hospitalised?'

'Dried out,' Gil agreed. 'And warned that if he didn't stop drinking, it'd kill him.'

'When he sobered up we all forgot about it. About how aggressive he could be. Jacob Levens made a violent drunk.' Naresh paused. 'He was a good person when he was off the alcohol, but now he's back on it and he's changed. Jacob Levens is not the man he was.'

Amen to that, Gil thought. 'So?'

'I'm just warning you to watch yourself, Mr Eckhart. Jacob Levens is deceiving you. I will be very honest: I regret the lost opportunity I had with the Caravaggio paintings and Luca Meriss–'

'But throwing suspicion on Jacob Levens and pretending to be my ally would jump you to the front of the queue again, wouldn't it?'

'*What gives you the right to talk to me in this way?*' snapped Joshi, uncharacteristically ruffled. 'I knew the Hubers and the Weirs. I liked them. I'm not a dealer. I didn't have business with them. I knew them socially. It's a small community and recent events have shaken us all. Despite what you may suspect, I care for works of art, and for the understanding of them. I have no interest in accumulating vast wealth or becoming a connoisseur. I am an academic, not an avaricious man.'

'I'm sorry,' Gil said, remembering the historian's reputation. 'I didn't mean to insult you, but people are seldom what they seem.'

'I understand your doubts. But I am exactly what I seem. Please accept my offer of support and any financial help you may need. I know Mr Levens hired you, but in light of this conversation you may soon find yourself replaced. I do not wish to see that. I want you to stay on this case, Mr Eckhart. So if you need funding to continue, allow me to provide that.'

Gil paused, weighing the historian's words. Finally he spoke again. 'Do you think you're in danger?'

'No!' Naresh almost laughed. 'that isn't what worries me–'

'So what does?'

'Death, Mr Eckhart, but not my own. You see, I did Mr

Luca Meriss a disservice and I regret it. I know he's in danger now and I feel partially responsible. I should have helped him years ago. Maybe then none of these murders would have happened.'

'You can't know that for sure.'

'I think we both know that somehow the Caravaggios and the murders are related,' he said reprovingly. 'Your job is to find out how.'

'And the paintings?' Gil asked. 'What about them?'

'Find them. But not for me – for the world.'

Fifty-Three

Belgravia, London
3.00 p.m.

'I need to ask a favour,' Gil said, walking in at the back door of The Van der Las Gallery. He had picked his time, waiting until the owner had left when he knew he would have private access to the best researcher in London. In fact, Gil could smell him before he saw Stuart Lindsay, body odour catching at his throat in the narrow confines of the passageway that led to the laboratory.

'Busy. Go away. Hate you, Eckhart.' A smiling head popped over a dividing screen. Eyes tiny under bushy brows, a pen stuck behind his right ear. 'What d'you want?'

'I need your help,' Gil replied, moving closer. 'You stink.'

'Do I?' Stuart replied, sniffing his left armpit. Unconcerned, he shrugged. 'No sense of smell myself.'

'Take it from me, you smell.'

'Keeps the flies away,' Stuart said, leaning against his

workbench. 'And people. Anything that keeps people away is all right with me.'

Gil smiled.

'Look, I need a favour – and don't make me have to remind you *why* you owe me this favour.' He reached into his pocket and pulled out the pouch. 'Are you still bloody amazing?'

'Even more so,' Stuart replied as Gil dropped the pouch into his open hand.

Carefully Stuart shook out the broken brush, then looked at the note. His expression didn't alter, his attention fixed. For over twenty years Stuart Lindsay had worked at The Van der Las Gallery, his equipment state-of-the-art, a bank of computer screens surrounding him, chemicals loaded onto shelves above a double sink, an expensive microscope training its eye on a lens below. By the barred window was a table on which was an easel supporting a Hogarth painting, cleaning tools lying alongside in regimented rows.

The gallery had invested over a million pounds in equipment, and continued to invest – in the equipment and the researcher. Once an academic in Cambridge, Stuart had developed agoraphobia, and gradually his world had narrowed until finally his whole existence had become contained within the impressive laboratory of The Van der Las Gallery. And knowing that he had the most gifted chemical researcher in London, Johann Van der Las allowed Stuart to live at the gallery, rent free. In return, he was not to work for anyone else.

But Gil Eckhart was an exception.

Stuart glanced over at him curiously. 'You're working on the Weir murders, aren't you?' He didn't wait for a reply. 'Everyone's scared stiff. I got myself a dog as a guard.'

Gil looked round. 'Where is it?'

Staring at the broken brush, Stuart gestured to a far corner where a poodle was fast asleep. 'I know he's only small, but poodles are supposed to yap. I thought he'd be a warning system. Got him from the rescue. But it turns out he's deaf, and I didn't have the heart to return him.' He waved the broken brush in his hand. 'You think it's genuine?'

'Maybe.'

He shrugged. 'What d'you want me to do with it?'

'Carbon-date it.'

'Date the note too?'

Gil nodded. 'Yeah. Can you check out the pigments?'

Stuart reached for a magnifying glass and studied the ferrule. 'Might be something left here . . . Yeah, I'll check it. And before you ask, I'll run a check on the ink on the note too.' He put down the glass. 'That *was* what you were going to ask, wasn't it?'

Gil smiled. 'Exactly. How soon can you do it?'

'A week.'

'Too long. Three people have been killed since Monday. It's Thursday now – I haven't time to waste.'

Stuart put up his hands.

'OK, two days. Come back Saturday afternoon, late as you can, after the gallery's closed. I'll leave the basement gate open for you, but not the door. Just knock and I'll let you in.'

'Thanks. Be careful.'

Stuart's burly eyebrows rose. 'Is it dangerous?'

'Just keep your doors locked. Don't let any strangers in.' Gil paused, frowning. 'Look, you can say no. You can refuse to do this—'

'Fuck off!' Stuart said lightly. 'You saved my career, remember? Anyway, I don't let anyone in.'

'You let me in.'

'I saw you on the monitor.' He gestured to a screen over his head. 'You think I'd have released the door if I hadn't known it was you? Look, Gil, I can take care of myself. I don't talk to anyone and I don't go out. Your secret's safe with me.'

'Keep it that way,' Gil insisted. 'I mean it. Don't tell *anyone.*'

Stuart crossed his heart with his index finger, watching as Gil walked to the door.

'There's a lot of nervy dealers out there,' he said. 'All worried about themselves, wondering who's going to be next. Who the killer is. Can't you feel it?'

'Feel what?'

'The atmosphere,' Stuart said. 'I can even feel it down here – everything's different. You can see dealers watching from the windows, like they think they'll see the murderer coming. They want him caught, want it to be over. You're the cat set to catch their pigeon, Gil. And they want that pigeon dead.'

'I'll catch him.'

'Yeah, I think you will. But remember one thing – no one gives a fuck about the cat.'

Fifty-Four

Berlin
4.00 p.m.

He had never been a brave man. Opportunistic, yes. But brave? Never. Oscar Schultz moved around his newly acquired Huber gallery. He had paid over the odds, but what did that matter? He had the gallery and now he could search it room by room, inch by inch. In his own time.

Oscar wasn't used to manual labour, but for once he was going to force himself. Fear was changing him, and the death of Frieda Meyer had sent him scurrying from London before anyone connected him to the nurse. He thought of what Frieda had told him. For a while he had even been excited, believed he was onto something. Bernard Lowe was talking to Harvey Crammer about the Caravaggios and both of them were talking to Luca Meriss.

Neither of them had told Oscar what was going on. So much for a collaboration, he thought bitterly, conveniently forgetting the times he had cut them out of deals. They couldn't have believed he wouldn't get to hear about Meriss and his claims, or think they could steal a march on him. How could they think that a dealer of Oscar Schultz's cunning wouldn't find out information that was readily available all over the bloody internet?

Surely they didn't take him for a fool? Oscar pulled himself together and looked around the gallery. Frieda Meyer should have been a good plant with Bernard Lowe, but Oscar had only gleaned a little information that way. The London police would be puzzled by Frieda Meyer, he thought contemptuously. Perhaps they would connect her to the death of Bernard Lowe. Certainly it would keep them busy for a while, thinking she had killed the old man – but he knew differently. Bernard Lowe's death was deliberate and Frieda Meyer was just unlucky.

As for the bastard Eckhart . . . Oscar fumed. So free with his accusations, so quick to speak his mind! He should be careful – now was hardly the time to act like a hero. And he was running around in circles. Call himself a detective! Oscar thought. The man couldn't detect water in a well.

Checking all the gallery doors were locked, Oscar moved into the main viewing area, thinking of *Der Kreis der Acht*, the group he himself had named but not formed. It had been Harvey Crammer's idea. The Canadian had been the one to suggest that they collaborate, bringing in Jacob Levens and the Hubers. Bernard Lowe had been the last member to join, his shipping company a useful asset. Did they smuggle? Of course they did, but Oscar doubted that anyone knew how much. The dealers might pretend affiliation, but they were all devious, out for themselves. Which, in a way, made it easier.

He thought of the Canadian, Harvey Crammer's ugly features imprinted on his memory. Once seen, never forgotten. A dealer and collector known around the world, a traveller to the bone, Crammer had contacts and money and he was the cleverest of all of them.

But Oscar had the Huber gallery.

Fifty-Five

New York
12.00 a.m.

Concentrating hard, Catrina Hoyt thought back to Luca Meriss as she reached into a bottom drawer and pulled out his holdall. Emptying the contents on the floor, she sieved through them carefully, but, as before, there was nothing to find. Her visit to Harvey Crammer had infuriated her and now she was too angry to be afraid. Someone was watching her and the Canadian. Someone was filming them and then putting it up on the internet, on Meriss's website.

Someone was laughing at them.

Catrina didn't like to be mocked, didn't like to be outsmarted. She flicked on her laptop. But this time there was no image of her or Harvey Crammer. Only the clock was the same, ticking over, minute by minute . . . Catrina clenched her fists. To have been so close to getting the Caravaggios, and Harvey Crammer didn't fool her in the least. He was testing her, trying to find out what she knew. Feeding her titbits so she would let something slip.

As if . . . Carefully she jotted down what he had told her: Gil Eckhart, the Huber murders in Berlin. Typed in the words Huber and Berlin art dealers murdered and waited for the results to come up. Seconds later she was looking at the beautiful face of Alma Huber, and next to her, an image of her husband, Terrill. Hurriedly she read the account of the murder, then came across the name Gil Eckhart.

Typing it into Google, Catrina read that, as Crammer had said, Eckhart had investigated the Huber murders seven years earlier. She read his profile, and then remembered that Gil Eckhart had been hired by Jacob Levens on *both* occasions. Coincidence? She doubted it. In fact, she was beginning to think that there might well be a tie to Luca Meriss and the murders. All the murders.

The news report on the Huber killings mentioned torture and UNUSUAL AND BIZARRE PRACTICES. Torture had been used in the Weir killings too. And Bernard Lowe had been murdered. No details forthcoming yet. Then she thought of her conversations with Luca Meriss over the phone, when he had read out the names of the people who had contacted him.

Harvey Crammer, Bernard Lowe and the London Galleries Limited. *The London Galleries Ltd*. Catrina struggled to remember what she had heard about them, then turned back to her computer, entering the company name. After reading about them she continued searching, finally uncovering the names of the directors – Sebastian and Benjamin Weir.

Her eyebrows rose. Of all the dealers who had contacted Luca Meriss about the Caravaggios, three were now dead . . . Leaning back in her seat, Catrina stared at the screen. She had been talking to Meriss. Was she next? Spooked, she thought back. Someone had broken into her apartment. Someone had threatened her on the phone, and in person. It hadn't been Luca Meriss – even disguised she had known the voices were different. So who had it been? And if it was the same person who had murdered the other dealers, why hadn't he killed her?

Picking up the handgun from her drawer, Catrina put it in her pocket. Suddenly, getting hold of the Caravaggios seemed secondary to staying alive.

Fifty-Six

London

4.30 p.m.

Simmons was sitting in his office, watching as Gil walked in. The detective looked tired and the rash around his neck had flared up painfully. Gesturing for Gil to sit down, Simmons sighed.

'Gary Rimmer wants to talk to you, and as I can't get anything out of the stupid bastard, I'm willing to let you have a try.' He picked at his neck. 'Go on, I've cleared it with the officer in charge – he'll take you to the holding cell.'

As soon as Gil walked in Gary Rimmer jumped to his feet, his voice shrill. 'I didn't kill her!' He looked totally different out of his chauffeur's uniform: younger, thinner, with a buzz cut and wearing a cheap T-shirt.

'I don't think you did.'

'The police do!'

'Why would you kill her?' Gil countered. 'They're just checking it out, don't worry.'

'Don't worry?' Gary replied. 'You didn't see her. She just walked into the hall and dropped down dead. Fucking hell, there was blood everywhere. I didn't kill her.'

'I know,' Gil repeated, leaning towards him. 'You were friends?'

'Yeah.'

'You said she came from Berlin. What else did she tell you?'

'Only that she'd been in London for a month or so.'

'And what did you tell her?' He could see Gary flush and knew he had struck a nerve. 'Was she pumping you for information?'

'No, not really . . .' He paused, thinking back. Had Frieda asked him about Bernard Lowe? No. But then again, she had been interested. Pretended not to be, but she had asked *some* questions. Christ, he thought, had he told her something dangerous? Was her death his fault? 'It was just talk, bigging myself up.'

'What did you tell her?'

'That Lowe had been all het up about some Caravaggio paintings, excited about them. They were worth a lot of money.'

'Money you could have used, hey?' Gil asked. 'I know you didn't kill Frieda Meyer, but I bet you tried to impress her, didn't you? Talked about getting hold of the paintings? Talked about some great heist?'

Gary flushed. 'It was just talk!'

'I know, I know. Men brag to get women into bed.' Gil paused. 'Did you mention which paintings they were?'

'I only knew about one. That religious picture that the Mafia were supposed to have nicked.' He shook his head. 'I didn't know it would be bad for Frieda – it was just a story, just bullshit. I didn't know it would harm her! I was just bragging, just trying to look big–'

'Did she have any friends in London? Any family?'

'Nah, she was on her own.'

'You never saw her with anyone?'

'Only the guy that dropped her off the first morning.'

'What guy?'

'I was working on the car and I'd been for petrol and I was just coming round into Eaton Square and there was this taxi pulled up. Right on the corner, stupid bastard! I had to stop to avoid hitting him. I tooted the driver and he gave me the finger.'

'Who was Frieda with?'

'Because I'd had to stop I could see right into the cab. He was a well-dressed guy,' Gary said with a touch of bitterness. 'I thought he was her boyfriend, but when I looked in my rear-view mirror as I pulled off she got out of the cab without kissing him or anything. I can't tell you how surprised I was to see her arrive at Lowe's place only minutes later–'

'What did the man look like?'

'Well dressed.' Gary thought back. 'Handsome. To be honest, he looked like a bloody film star.'

'Fair or dark-haired?'

'Fair.'

Gil reached for his mobile, found a photograph of the dealer, and showed it to Gary.

'Yeah, that's him! Who is he?'

'Oscar Schultz,' Gil replied, flicking off his phone. 'Did you see him again?'

'Nah.'

'Did Frieda mention him to you?'

'Nah.'

Gil stood up to leave.

'Where are you going?' Gary asked, panicked.

'I'll come back. Don't worry, you didn't murder Frieda Meyer and I'll prove it.'

'Did he do it?' Gary asked desperately. 'This Oscar Schultz? Was it him? She was really beaten up. I mean her face was all smashed in. If it was that bastard, you do the same to him. Just promise me the same will happen to him.'

Fifty-Seven

5.00 p.m.

Phil Simmons was standing in the corridor as Gil walked out of the holding cell. 'Did you beat a confession out of him?'

'Gary Rimmer didn't kill Frieda Meyer. I think he was set up.'

'I think so too,' agreed Simmons. 'But my bosses want results. And the press want answers. And the galleries are hassling me twenty-four hours a day. This *is* about the art business, isn't it? That crafty bag of snakes who keep everyone out until they need help.'

Gil had no loyalty to Jacob Levens any more, but he wasn't about to divulge what he knew to Simmons.

'I'll keep you posted on what I find out.'

Simmons folded his arms, staring at Gil. 'The killer's not finished, has he? No one kills repeatedly, using the same methods over and over again, without wanting to send a message. Frieda Meyer wasn't one of his victims, because she wasn't killed in the same way.'

Gil sidestepped him. 'How *was* she killed?'

'Someone used a hammer on her head and face, then stabbed her. Last wound punctured her lung.'

'Was she killed in Rimmer's place?'

'No,' Simmons replied. 'She was murdered somewhere else and dumped outside Rimmer's flat. Whoever did it must have thought she was dead, but she wasn't. She managed to get to her feet and then collapsed. That's when Gary Rimmer found her.'

'Premeditated.'

Simmons nodded. 'Exactly. Rimmer's just the scapegoat, someone to capture our attention for a bit and take the blame.' He sighed, shook the empty ointment bottle he was holding and then tossed it into a nearby bin. 'Seven years – that's how long the killer had to plan all this.'

Gil said nothing, just let Simmons continue. 'Since the murders in Berlin there was nothing, but now he's off again. And all you have to do is find out why.'

Gil raised his eyebrows. 'Don't you mean *we*?'

'Not any more. You won't tell me what's going on, you want to keep control. I get it – you didn't catch the killer seven years ago and he's making you look like an idiot.' The detective shrugged. 'But I want to find him too. We could have worked together, but you're shutting me out. So I'll go after him my way, and you go after him yours. Sorry, Gil, but I can't play with half a pack of cards.'

Fifty-Eight

6.00 p.m.

Making coffee in his kitchen, Gil heard a sudden noise from the empty flat below: the sound of glass breaking. He knew that the builders had finished for the day and that no one else was living there. Cautiously he moved to the front door of the apartment and listened. There were footsteps coming up the stairs.

He tensed.

The footsteps stopped.

He looked through the spyhole in the door.

Nothing.

But there *had* been someone there, Gil knew, even if they had now gone. A soft noise behind him, a gentle tinkling sound, made him jump as the computer screen flashed up the image of an envelope. Gil walked into the sitting room and then stopped in his tracks. If he stood by the computer table he could be seen from across the garden at the back of the houses. Someone using a zoom lens could follow his every move.

Ducking down, Gil closed the shutters. In virtual darkness, he felt his way back to the front door and listened. There was no sound from below, from the unoccupied flat. The house was still. Checking the locks, he moved back to the computer and opened the message. It was the image of a foetus.

The threat had found its mark.

Fifty-Nine

St Bartholomew's Hospital
7.00 p.m.

Sitting next to her hospital bed, Gil put his hand on Bette's stomach and bowed his head to kiss the back of her hand. After receiving the email he had phoned Simmons.

'It's just a threat, Gil.'

'Just a threat!'

'We can't trace where it's from, or who sent it. We can't do anything. It's just a threat. Someone's throwing a scare into you.'

He was right, and Gil knew it.

The killer was getting close. Too close. This time it wasn't just Gil; this time it was his wife, his child. Everything that he had built up out of the ruins of his life seven years earlier. Every piece of security was now threatened. The killer's focus had shifted – onto Gil.

His time away from the art world had limited him. Rumours and gossip he would have been privy to seven years ago had eluded him and now he was struggling to regain an advantage he had lost, to re-enter a world that had once been his by right.

Suddenly he felt the baby moving under his palm.

'We're OK,' Bette reassured him.

He hadn't told her about the image he had received. He wouldn't. Instead he had spoken to the doctor. The medic had been anxious, but had reassured Gil that the hospital was safe.

Gil had shaken his head. 'I want to move her–'

'You can't. Your wife's condition isn't stable. If you moved her it could be serious for her and the baby. She needs bed rest until the baby's born.'

'Until he's born?'

'That won't be long,' the doctor had replied. 'This baby won't go full term. I think your wife will go into labour within the next few days, which is another reason why she has to stay here.'

Here. Where the killer knew she was. Gil had realised that the moment he saw the image on his computer. The murderer knew everything about them because he was watching.

Gil tried to reassure himself by checking out Bette's exact location at the hospital. She was on the seventh floor, in a private room midway along a corridor. No one could access her room via the window, or the corridor, without being seen. And apparently only staff were permitted on the seventh floor. *It was safe*.

Bette was watching him anxiously. 'You look tired. How's the case?'

'Coming along.'

'Liar.'

He slid onto the narrow bed next to her, his left leg hanging over the edge, his foot on the floor and in silence rested his head on her shoulder. The scent of her talcum powder mingled with the scent of the night air on his clothes, one smell comforting, the other desolate. The thought of losing her and the baby worked like a maggot into his brain. His eyes closed, lulled by the warmth of Bette's body against his. He needed a stroke of luck, some insight, some detail that would unpick the case for him. In Berlin, and now in London, the murderer was mocking him. Six people were dead, four within a few days, and as the number of victims had risen, the number of suspects had dwindled.

Gil thought of those who were left: Harvey Crammer, Catrina Hoyt, Oscar Schultz and Jacob Levens. Even Luca Meriss. Maybe the Italian was duping everyone? He opened his eyes and looked at the ceiling, at the spotlights recessed in the plasterwork. Lights similar to those used in galleries. Lights with dimmer switches. Lights he had seen in dozens of galleries here and abroad.

Suddenly alert, he jerked upright on the bed.

'What is it?' Bette asked.

'I have to go back.'

'*What?*'

He scrambled to his feet. 'I have to go back to Germany.

I'm going to finish this once and for all. The answer's seven years old. It's in the Huber Galley on the Friedrichstrasse. That's where it all began. That's where he made his first strike, his first killing.' Gil stared at his wife intently. 'I've been looking in the wrong place. I won't find him here because it didn't begin in London, it began in Berlin.'

Sixty

London
7.00 p.m.

His tie loosened, flushed, Jacob Levens lumbered around his office, slumping onto a leather Chesterfield and refilling his glass. The alcohol was raising his blood pressure and his colour was high, his eyes bloodshot. Too drunk to be coherent, he had locked himself into his office that morning, refusing to let anyone enter and leaving his phone unanswered. Outside was the threatening world. Outside was a killer. Outside was the man who had tortured and murdered his sister and four others. He might well be next – and it was his own fault that he had no allies.

His own stupidity had alienated Gil Eckhart and left him unprotected. So he stuck to his confines and drank, and kept on drinking. Urgent phone calls to Harvey Crammer and Oscar Schultz had not been returned, and Greta's hatred had cowed him. She didn't know the whole story, but what she had guessed was enough. Someone would piece it all together soon.

Jacob's decision to hire Gil Eckhart had been a devious one. True, Eckhart had been involved in the Berlin case, but he had been out of the business for years and Jacob relied on the art world's notorious insularity to make life difficult for him. If Eckhart *did* inveigle his way back in it would take time, and besides, his attention would be fixed on the killer, not on the peripheries.

Jacob knew that Gil Eckhart would be unable to refuse the challenge of catching the killer who had eluded him before. The old murders and the eerie echo of Berlin would reel him in . . . he drank his whisky, sodden with guilt and terror. Who would find out what he had done? His gaze moved over to the safe, which was now empty, the disks gone. Jacob couldn't imagine how they had been stolen. After all, who knew about them? Who but Holly? And Holly was dead.

He thought of the late Mrs Eckhart, mercurial, fascinating and manipulative. Bernard Lowe had introduced her to *Der Kreis der Acht*, explaining to the others how she had connections in the Far East. She could get them some valuable artefacts, Holly had said. And Bernard Lowe had nodded, like the wizened old ape he was. They had all known that his shipping company would be pressed into service. After all, it had been used before to transport paintings and *objets d'art* from Europe and further afield.

Never fully accepted into the dealers' hierarchy, Holly

joined *Der Kreis der Acht* as an honorary member. She had always travelled in her work, so her many journeys attracted little attention, even from Gil. And what a cover her marriage to him had turned out to be! Eckhart never suspected his wife and Holly had played along perfectly, even tipping off the members of *Der Kreis der Acht* when her husband's investigative work threatened any of them.

Jacob knew that her reason for treachery was twofold. Emotionally demanding, she resented Gil's independence, his time away from her. Holly might be free to come and go as she pleased, but she wanted Gil under the cosh. A year after they married, she found out that he wasn't that kind of man and turned to others she could manipulate more easily. She had always flirted with Jacob, but they had never had an affair. Instead he had always wondered which one of the circle was her lover.

Certainly not Bernard Lowe. Oscar Schultz? Harvey Crammer? Terrill Huber? It could have been any one of them. Or all of them . . . Jacob drained his glass and refilled it immediately. In the gallery beyond he could hear the door being locked and the low hum of the alarm being set. The business premises were safe, leaving just the back door off the system, so that Jacob could come and go from his private quarters as he pleased.

But he didn't please. Instead he chose to stay inside, the doors of his rooms bolted. He should never have got his sister involved, but he had and he was going to pay for it just as she had. Jesus! Jacob thought, remembering the Weir twins, the bound bodies back to back, the bloodied genitals. He didn't want to die. He didn't mean for it all to get out of hand. But the tables had turned since Berlin. In seven years all his scheming and double-dealing had backfired. The gun he had pointed at others was now turned on him.

His hand reached out. I can't die, Jacob panicked. I can't.

Blearily he squinted at his phone and punched a number in, listening to the eerie tone as it rang, unheard and unanswered, far far away.

Sixty-One

Berlin

8.00 p.m.

Oscar Schultz leant against the office desk. His sleeves were rolled up, his hair sweaty and dishevelled. So far his search had yielded nothing, but he wasn't overly worried. The Huber gallery was a large city property on three floors, with a cellar below. It would take days, maybe even a week, to search everywhere.

If he could have hired someone to do the dirty work, he would have done, but Oscar didn't want anyone around. If he found what he was looking for, he wanted it kept secret. And people talked. People always talked. Flicking on the main light, he looked around him. The top floor had been thoroughly searched. Nothing could have been hidden there. So next it was time to search the offices.

The enormity of the task didn't faze him, his attention only distracted by the phone ringing in the room beyond. It rang out several times and Oscar cursed himself for forgetting to put it on voicemail. When it stopped, he relaxed and headed for the back offices where the gallery staff had once worked. But once in there, the phone began ringing again. Leaning over the desk, he diverted it to voicemail. No one was going to disturb him.

Resuming his search, he began with the filing cabinets, emptying each drawer and going through the contents, then feeling round the back. He did the same with each desk, but found nothing. Going into the staff toilet, he climbed up and lifted the top off the cistern, grimacing as he felt inside. Water, no more. Climbing down, he rinsed his hands and checked the broom closet, pulling out brushes and buckets, tugging down shelves and tapping walls. Again, he found nothing.

As he searched he thought of his colleagues, of their slyness at never mentioning Luca Meriss or the Caravaggios, those missing paintings worth a fortune. And there was more. Meriss had proof of their whereabouts and his claims of lineage. As everyone knew, proof was everything. Provenance dictated the sale of a work, the price, just as it dictated the validity of a story.

Oscar didn't give a toss if Meriss was a descendent of Caravaggio or not. Who cared if he could prove that a hundred times over? The paintings were all that concerned him. The paintings that none of his mendacious colleagues had even mentioned.

Well, Oscar thought, he might not be the best educated, but he was the most sly. When it came to deceit he was a master of the art. Concentrating, he walked out of the bathroom and crossed the corridor into the accountant's old office. It smelt vaguely of damp and there was a crack in one of the upper windows. On the wall were three spaces where paintings had once hung, Oscar moving over to a stack of pictures leaning up against the wall.

His hands were shaking with excitement. It couldn't be that easy, could it? Surely it couldn't? Pulling off the covering sheet, he stared at the old hunting prints. Then, one by one, he ripped off the backing boards, pulling them free to expose what was there. The first was only a print, as was the second. And the third. Infuriated, Oscar kicked out at the frame, hearing the wood splinter. All right, he told himself, it wasn't going to be that easy. He would just have to keep looking.

After all, he had all the time in the world.

Sixty-Two

Berlin

Regaining consciousness, Luca opened his eyes, panicking when he remembered what had happened to him. He had been cornered in his hospital room and then injected before he had even had time to struggle. The last thing he remembered before he passed out was the white orb of the light hanging over his head and the pressure of someone's hand covering his mouth.

And now he was in an ambulance, travelling at speed, but without its siren switched on. There was no one sitting with him in the back, but he could hear the voices of two men coming from the front cabin of the vehicle and tried to sit up. He couldn't move. He tried again, but his arms were bound and a broad leather strap ran across his chest, holding him down.

He panicked. His heart was pumping erratically, his pulse thumping in his ears, sweat making his skin slimy. Calm down, he told himself. Calm down. . . . Finally he composed himself.

Then, silently, he began to wriggle his body downwards. He was agile, thin from days of barely eating. He drew his knees upwards as he inched his body under the strap.

It was no use. Sweating, he paused, breathed in, then exhaled, his chest falling as he squeezed himself down, the tight leather binding cutting into his flesh as he squirmed under it. Finally, with one last effort, he managed to slide out his left arm. Frantically he tugged off the strap, throwing it aside, then paused, listening, checking that no one had heard him move. No one had. The men were still talking in the front of the ambulance. Sitting up on the bench, Luca peered out of the back window.

They were on the outskirts of the city, but he didn't recognise the location and could only see from the road signs that they had been travelling for about half an hour away from the centre of Berlin. He looked around feverishly, then spotted a paramedic jacket and pulled it over his white hospital T-shirt and trousers. Next he found a pair of rubber boots and put them on. Bare feet wouldn't get him far and were a certain giveaway.

He had no plan and no weapon, no idea where he was or where he was going.

The ambulance was travelling fast, too fast, then suddenly it began to slow down. Luca looked out of the window again. It was taking the feeder lane which led onto the autobahn. He knew that once they hit the motorway it was all over. They could travel for hours without stopping. Going God knows where.

He didn't think twice. As the ambulance was forced to slow down for oncoming motorway traffic, he wrenched open the back doors and jumped.

The car following screamed to a halt, just missing Luca as he made for the hard shoulder, scrambling up the dark bank without looking back.

Friday

Naples, Italy
1610

His wound wasn't healing. The knife had sliced through his cheek and into his mouth, nicking the jawbone. He had rinsed his mouth with wine, spitting out gobs of pus as the infected wound burst. His temperature spiked, sweat curdling on his skin, his hands gripping the brush as he continued to paint.

Word had come that his pardon was imminent. All he had to do was wait . . . Outside, the man he had hired as his personal guard squatted on his haunches as the sun rose, and two passing women pointed out the house and began to gossip. Notorious as much for his temper as his talent, Caravaggio kept to the shaded cool of his studio and worked on a portrait of David and Goliath; the face of the fallen giant, his own. Like himself, Goliath had once been all powerful, defeated by an unexpected danger. The victorious David bringing down the giant as Rome had toppled Caravaggio. That worm of innocence in the sling that had felled the ogre.

He was rushing the painting, irritable, nervy, the pain in his face flaring as the nerves tugged under the tightening wound. Then suddenly, he heard voices and a knock at the door.

Automatically he felt for the knife in his belt. He had paid the guard well, but someone else might have paid him better for the scalp of Caravaggio. He watched as an old priest walked in, and relaxed. The man blinked for a few seconds after coming out of the sunshine, then stared at the artist. The shock of Caravaggio's appearance rendered him mute and the painter jerked his thumb towards a table.

'Wine.'

The priest shook his head, skirting the painter as he approached the easel. He could see the puckering wound on his face and smell his sour sweat. Small wonder rumours had come to Rome that Caravaggio was dead. He was obviously injured, wasted, his left eye cloudy.

'You're hurt.'

Caravaggio nodded, smiling bitterly. 'I am hurt.' His voice was impatient. 'You have a message for me? What?'

'I come from Cardinal Scipione Borghese . . .'

Caravaggio paused, his brush halted in mid-stroke. Borghese was the very man for whom he was creating the picture – a bribe, a plea for help from a long-time admirer and sponsor. Cardinal Scipione Borghese, infamous and powerful enough to grant pardons.

'Go on.'

The old priest stepped back against the wall. He was afraid of the artist, of his reputation as a killer. Police files on Michelangelo Merisi da Caravaggio were copious, his brawls common knowledge, his aggression unpredictable and quick to provoke.

'Cardinal Borghese wishes you to know that he is working to obtain your pardon. He feels that it will be granted soon.'

Turning away, the painter slumped into a chair. 'How soon?'

'Quickly.'

Caravaggio stared at the old priest. 'Would you lie to me?'

The man paled. 'No, no!'

'How old are you?'

'Seventy-nine,' the priest said, reaching for his rosary and running the beads through his fingers.

Caravaggio's face was half in light, half in darkness, like his paintings. But it was his mutilated side that was revealed, his rheumy eye fixed on the old man. 'Would you lie to me?' he repeated, leaning towards him over the arm of the chair, his black hair matted.

'No, on my honour, I do not lie.'

Tapping his lips with his fingertips, Caravaggio leaned back, his whole face now shadowed, his voice hoarse.

'Come closer.' He beckoned to the priest. 'Come. Come. Are you afraid of me?' When the old man didn't reply he continued, 'I should be the one afraid. They are trying to murder me. Wanting the reward for killing Caravaggio. Men I wronged, men with none of my talent, trying for my scalp . . . Do I frighten you?'

'A little,' the old man admitted.

The painter made a grunting sound in his throat. 'Come a little closer. Come!' Irritated, he lumbered to his feet, taking the priest's hand and pulling him over to the easel. 'I have a message for the Cardinal.' He turned the old man's head towards the painting and the priest stared at the image of the sorrowful David and the severed head of Goliath. Blood oozed from the neck of the fallen giant, his mouth hanging open, his eyes vacant.

'This is you,' the priest murmured.

Caravaggio nodded, then pushed the old man away. 'Go back to Rome. Tell the Cardinal to hurry. I am ill. If someone doesn't kill me I will die anyway if I am left here to rot. I need the pardon.' He pointed to the easel. 'Tell Cardinal Borghese I have a masterpiece for him. Tell the old goat I offer a bribe—'

'Signore!'

'Phrase it how you will,' Caravaggio urged, 'but tell him the painting is his. I ask nothing for a fee. Only the pardon.'

The priest moved to the door. 'I'll tell the Cardinal.'

'Seventy-nine . . .'

'What?'

'You said you were seventy-nine?'

The priest nodded, confused. 'Yes.'

'Is it good to be old?'

'I . . . I don't know what to tell you, Signore. Why d'you ask?'

'I want to know about something I will never experience.' He waved the priest away. 'Tell the Cardinal what I offer – a painting for a pardon.'

Sixty-Three

Taubenstrasse, Berlin
10.00 a.m.

She was surprised, but pleased to hear from him, turning up at the cafe for their meeting dead on the hour. The tiny figure of Greta Huber slid into the seat opposite Gil and smiled when he ordered hot chocolate.

'You remembered.'

'You always liked it,' Gil said, 'and it's freezing outside. The perfect morning for drinking chocolate. Jesus, it is colder than London.'

Pulling off her gloves, Greta cupped her hands around the mug then took a cautious sip.

'It's good to see you again.'

'And you. I heard you were doing OK.'

'You're the only one who ever bothered to check up on me. Apart from Naresh.'

'Naresh?' Gil asked. 'D'you mean Naresh Joshi?'

She nodded, her hair white-blond, eyes dark grey, the

whites bluish. 'He was very kind to me after my parents died. I stayed with him in India.' She smiled, raising pale brows. 'Nothing like that! He's like a big brother. Always very respectful. Very proper.'

'He seems like that,' Gil agreed.

'So you know him?'

'By reputation, for years. But I spoke to him for the first time the other day.'

She smiled, hardly moving the corners of her mouth.

'I thought you'd been hired by my uncle.'

'I un-hired myself.'

'Good.' Her eyes fixed on him, her hands pink now that the flesh had warmed up. 'Why did you want to see me?'

'I need to talk to you about the murders seven years ago,' Gil said. 'I know I'm asking a lot, but I need help. You're the only person I can ask.'

'I wasn't very helpful at the time, was I?' she asked, embarrassed.

'You had a breakdown. And you were very young.'

She nodded. 'Tell me what you want to know.'

'Can you tell me about that night?'

Her gaze moved over Gil's shoulder and fixed on a distant point. It was almost as though she was stepping back to remember. 'It was March the fourteenth 2007. I'd been out with friends. My mother said she'd be working late so I went into the gallery by the back entrance and looked for her. She wasn't in the office. She was dead. In the gallery, on the floor.'

The recount was chilling in its sparsity.

'When I spoke to you back then you said there had been a man hanging around the gallery in the days before the murders.'

Greta thought for a moment. 'Oh, yes, I remember . . . He looked like a tramp. My mother saw him too.'

'D'you remember anything about him?'

'Beard, hair dark.' She shrugged. 'Nothing stood out. He was very dirty. I can't tell you any more.'

'And before the murders, were your parents acting differently?'

She paused, changed tack abruptly. 'D'you think my uncle might be murdered?'

Taken aback, Gil hesitated. 'Why do you ask?'

'Because he was one of them, wasn't he? One of their group. I've been thinking. I even asked Jacob about it, but he wouldn't tell me the truth. He lies, always has done – that's why my mother mistrusted him.'

'You said he was one of a group,' Gil prompted her. 'What group?'

'The dealers. The Weir brothers, Harvey Crammer, Oscar Schultz, Jacob and Bernard Lowe. They all traded.'

'So? That's the business.'

Greta was still staring over his shoulder, avoiding eye contact. 'My parents traded with all of them. My uncle said that the art world's like that, very cliquey. But I think there's more to it – and now five of them are dead I'm sure of it.' This time she looked straight at him. 'When my parents were killed, I kept some of their belongings. I wasn't thinking straight, I just piled a load of papers into a bag. I wanted their handwriting – something they'd held and written.' She paused, placing her palm over the top of the mug. 'I never read them until a week ago, just after I'd sold the gallery. I should have read them earlier.'

'Why? What was in them?'

'Have you heard of The London Galleries Limited?'

Gil nodded. 'Very small concern, low profile. But I don't know much else – they were set up after I left the art world.'

'So you didn't know that they were owned by Sebastian and Benjamin Weir?' Gil shook his head as Greta continued. 'Did you know that Bernard Lowe owned a company called Lexington Limited?'

Jacob's voice came back to him:

Bernard Lowe was bringing in pieces from the Far East. Transporting them in through his own shipping company. Holly smuggled some artefacts for him.

'I knew that Lowe had a shipping company.'

'Did you know that it was managed by Oscar Schultz?' Greta paused, watching Gil's face. 'The same Oscar Schultz who now owns my parents' gallery.'

The news shook Gil.

'*What?* When did that happen?'

'The other day. I should have looked into the sale more carefully, but once I'd decided to get rid of the gallery I just wanted it over and done with. Lexington Limited made their offer and I accepted. If I'd known Oscar Schultz was involved I'd never have sold it to him. My mother hated Schultz.'

'She wasn't alone.'

Greta dropped her voice so that Gil had to strain to hear her. 'I'm so sorry about your wife. I know what happened. It must have been terrible for you. The accident, I mean.'

Gil paused, staring out of the window into the Taubenstrasse. The weather was squally, a man walking past head down against the wind, sleet making itself felt as the temperature plummeted. He was thinking of Oscar Schultz and of what Jacob Levens had told him. Had Jacob been lying about Holly wanting to leave him? *Had* there been another man? The thoughts Gil had suppressed since Jacob's outburst overwhelmed him suddenly, along with the swelling suspicion about his late wife.

'Who else knows about all of this?' he asked, turning his attention back to Greta.

'I don't know. I suppose someone could put two and two together if they were in the trade.' She lifted her hand from the mug and steam rose like a feather. 'It was my uncle who introduced my parents to Oscar Schultz and Bernard Lowe. Harvey Crammer had always been around. I'd known him most of my life. He was always helping out, giving advice.'

Gil chose his next words carefully. 'He was in Berlin when your parents were murdered.'

'You think he's the killer?' She sighed, looking away. 'He loved my mother.'

'How did he get on with your father?'

'They weren't friends.'

Greta took several sips of her drink, like a white bird at a water fountain. Timid, ready to fly off.

'She was afraid of my uncle.'

'Did she say why?'

'No. But when I was little Jacob came to Berlin and stayed with us. He took the flat over the gallery. And then one evening there was a terrible argument between him and my mother. My father wasn't there, and in the morning Jacob had gone. They hardly spoke after that. But a year before she was killed Jacob was back in touch with my mother and they were trading again.' She blew out her cheeks, unexpectedly emotional. 'I told her to cut him off, but she wouldn't hear of it. Said she couldn't. That there were things I didn't understand.'

'You have no idea what she was afraid of?'

'No,' Greta said firmly. 'But she was tied to Jacob somehow. It was almost as though he had a hold over her.' Her voice faltered. 'I think he killed her.'

'He can't have done. I checked your uncle out seven years ago. He was in London when Alma was murdered.'

'I don't mean that. He didn't lay a finger on her but he frightened her to death. He told her something. Shared something he shouldn't have done. My mother was keeping a secret from me and my father. I don't know why she couldn't tell us, but she didn't. It was the secret that killed her. The secret her brother gave her.' Greta's eyes were blurry, tears barely held back. 'One of those bastards – or *all* of those bastards – killed my parents. My mother was hounded to death and I want you to find out who did that to her.' Greta picked up the mug, her hands shaking. 'I ran away before – I couldn't face it, but I can now. I have to. I've come back to live in Berlin again.'

Gil was surprised. 'You think that's wise?'

'It's not home but it's where I have to be, close to my parents.' She nodded as though making a promise to herself. 'You'll find the murderer, I know you will. Finish it, Gil. Then we can all move on.'

Sixty-Four

The Royal Academy, London
12.00 noon

Naresh Joshi had come to London to give a lecture on the Italian Baroque Painters and he was heartened by the turnout – a full house. Students who had followed his research pressed him for information and news of the next book he was preparing to write, but when he left the exhilarating confines of the Academy and walked out into Burlington Gardens, Naresh paused.

There was a definite charge in the atmosphere; it was static, fizzing with unease. As he stood outside The Weir Gallery, Naresh touched the police tape, glancing at the empty window behind the metal grille. He remembered the Weir twins and turned to find himself being watched by a dealer across the road. When he realised that he had been seen, the man turned away and Naresh moved on into Cork Street.

The terror was palpable. Fear was in the air. The murderer

had struck and disappeared. No one had any clues as to his identity and where, or when, he would come again . . . For some reason the old London fable of Spring Heeled Jack came to Naresh's mind. The killer, who, in folklore, jumped into places, killed, and jumped out again.

Spring-heeled Jack . . . He glanced up at the banner outside Jacob Levens' gallery. The wind had caught it and wrapped it around the suspending pole, bunching it up like a chrysalis that would never hatch. The tourists were still on the street, but no dealers. No little groups of men muttering over catalogues, or brandishing glossy inventories from Sotheby's. Where once cafes sported dealers drinking coffee and talking on their mobiles, now there were only empty seats.

The art world had closed in on itself.

Naresh glanced at the door of The Levens Gallery, then rang the bell. A young woman answered, smiled as she recognised him and let him in.

'I'm so sorry, but Mr Levens is busy.'

'I see,' Naresh said pleasantly, dropping his voice. 'Busy or drunk?'

'Drunk,' she replied, relieved. 'He hasn't come out of his office for over twenty-four hours. Won't answer his phone or the door. I don't know what to do about the customers.'

'Tell them he's travelling,' Naresh replied. 'Can you let me into Jacob's office?'

'I'm not supposed to.'

'I'll take full responsibility,' he reassured her. 'Someone should check on him, to see he's all right.'

Sixty-Five

Taubenstrasse, Berlin

Gil was just saying goodbye to Greta when his phone rang.

'*Sie akzeptieren ein R-Gespräch kostenlos?*' A voice asked Gil. Frowning, he beckoned to Greta, passing her the phone. She listened, then translated.

'The operator wants to know if you'll accept a collect charge call.' She spoke quickly in German. '*Wer ist es?*' Greta turned back to Gil. 'It's someone called Luca Meriss.'

He nodded, taking the phone from her. 'Luca, are you all right?'

The voice was shaky, barely decipherable. 'You have to come and get me–'

'Where are you?'

'They came for me, they were going to kill me!' Luca shouted, then dropped his voice. 'I had to hide. I had to hide!'

'Where?'

'In a garage. The lock was broken on the men's room

door. I've been there all night, until now. I had to sneak out to get to a phone.'

'Are you out in the open?'

Luca shivered down the line. 'You have to get me! You said I'd be safe in hospital! *You promised me!*'

'Luca!' Gil snapped as Greta looked at him curiously. 'Calm down. Where are you?'

'I'm in Neukölln, near the Stadion Britz-Süd.'

'Neukölln?'

Greta's eyebrows rose as she listened to the one-sided conversation.

'Don't hang about in the open, Luca,' Gil advised him. Neukölln was a rough area, hardly the place for someone on the run. 'You said you were in a garage nearby?'

'It's derelict, near the Stadion entrance. Have you got a car?'

'Hire car, Audi,' Gil told him, hurrying on. 'Why didn't you call me last night—'

'*I couldn't find a public phone!*' he almost screamed. 'I'm freezing and I'm scared. They wanted to kill me—'

Gil interrupted him.

'Go back to the garage, Luca. Go back to the garage and wait for me. I'll find you.'

The Italian was shivering so badly that he could barely talk. 'Hurry! Please, hurry.'

Sixty-Sixe

London

'*What the fuck!*' Jacob exclaimed, waking up and pushing Naresh away. His face was flushed, his eyes bloodshot. 'What the hell are you doing here?'

Naresh was taken aback. 'I thought . . . I thought you were dead.'

Glaring, Jacob wiped his mouth with the back of his hand, then walked into the bathroom. Naresh could hear him urinating, then the tap running. Finally he came out, drinking a glass of water. His expression was hostile as he stared at the historian.

'I haven't see you for a while.' He struggled to put his shoes back on, still inebriated. 'First Greta, now you. All hoping I'm dead, are you? You very close to my little niece, Naresh? I bet you are. Bet you've got your eyes on the money she made selling the gallery.'

'I didn't know she had,' Naresh said honestly. 'I've been travelling. I haven't spoken to Greta for over a week.'

'You want to catch up. Little Greta's in the money now.' Jacob belched, his breath sour as he tried to compose himself. 'I told my secretary that she wasn't to let anyone in–'

'She was worried about you. I said I'd take full responsibility.'

'Good. You can be the one to tell her she's fired,' Jacob replied, flopping back onto the couch.

'Dear God, what happened to you?' Naresh asked, glancing around the room. 'Why are you drinking again?'

'Why d'you care?' Jacob replied. 'You and I aren't friends, so why the concern? Why are you even here? . . . It's the murders, isn't it? Or is it the Caravaggios you're after?' He could see he had hit the mark and pursued it. 'I thought so! You despise us dealers, but you're the same as we are underneath. You don't want the paintings to sell, you want to "talk about them" and puff up your own reputation at the same time. You're fooling no one, Joshi, with all this holier-than-thou crap. You're as keen on making a reputation as the rest of us, it's just that you don't like getting your hands dirty. "I want to protect and preserve culture." He mimicked Naresh's cultured voice. 'Bloody outsider. Why don't you go back to India and worship your bloody elephants or whatever it is you people idolise?'

Naresh flinched. 'I was educated in this country!'

'Doesn't make you any less of a foreigner,' Jacob replied. 'You're Asian, Naresh. You'll never get accepted by the art world. Not really. They pay you lip service, but they despise you behind your back.'

'You should stop drinking. It's making a monster out of you.'

'Maybe I was always a monster, it just came out with the alcohol,' Jacob replied, finishing the glass of water and rubbing his forehead. His bile was dissipating, his self-pity suddenly overriding it. 'I found the bodies of the Weir twins. It was like Alma, all over again . . .'

The words had no effect on Naresh.

'I should tell you that I've been talking to Gil Eckhart. He's no longer working for you.' Naresh paused, but when Jacob didn't reply, he went on. 'So I've hired him myself to find the killer.'

'Good luck. He's not doing too well so far.'

'Why did you hire him then?' Naresh asked, smiling coldly. 'You're pitiful, Jacob. All your scheming is so transparent. You hired Gil Eckhart because he'd been out of the art world for a while, that's why. Perhaps you knew it would make his job that much harder. Perhaps you *wanted* that.'

'The killer could be after me!'

'The killer could *be* you,' Naresh retorted.

'Don't be ridiculous! Do I look like a murderer?'

'You look like a drunk,' Naresh replied curtly. 'I've been talking to your niece–'

'Who hates me.'

'Be that as it may, she's uncovered some interesting facts.' He could see Jacob was listening. 'Why did Oscar Schultz buy the Huber Gallery?'

'How the hell would I know? Ask him.'

'Why didn't you buy it?'

'My sister was murdered there. I didn't want the place.' Jacob picked up the whisky bottle from the floor and jiggled its contents.

'It'll kill you.'

'Have you never got drunk, Naresh? Never lost control? Nah, I doubt it.' He sneered at his visitor. 'Come on, man to man, let's be honest for once – what d'you know about the Caravaggios? You must have seen Luca Meriss's website.'

'Actually, I met him years ago and I didn't believe his claims.' Naresh could see the surprise on Jacob's face. 'Yes, I was wrong. I made a mistake. I dismissed him and lost one of the biggest stories ever to hit the art world. I could have believed him and furthered my own career, but I was foolish.' He leaned towards Jacob, his tone calm. 'But you know something? I'm glad. Too many people have died because of those paintings and I don't want to be among their number.'

'*You spoke to Meriss years ago?*' Jacob was finding it hard to breathe. 'Where did you meet him? What did he tell you about the Caravaggios?' He pushed aside the whisky bottle, sobering up. 'His website said he had proof.'

'Of his lineage and of the whereabouts of the paintings.'

'Did he?' Jacob asked, his voice barely audible. '*Did he?*' Naresh smiled and turned away as Jacob's voice rose. '*Did Luca Meriss have proof?*'

'Have you seen the clock on Meriss's website?' Naresh asked, moving his index finger from side to side. 'It's up there, ticking away. Someone put that on his site. Can't have been Meriss himself – he's running for his life. So who did it? And *why*?'

'What are you talking about?'

'I think it's the killer. The same person who tried to find the proof in Berlin seven years ago and failed. And now he's back, trying again. Three London dealers dead in only a few days. How very quick our murderer is. Just strikes and disappears. He would need to be an insider to move around so easily. Someone all the dealers trusted. Someone Luca Meriss would have trusted.'

'In that case it could be you!' Jacob hissed, slopping some whisky into his glass.

'No, as you just reminded me, I don't have the art world's ear,' Naresh said bitterly. 'The inner sanctum is closed to me. I don't have their confidence, never did. But Gil Eckhart does. He might have been out of the sphere for a while, but he was in Berlin working on the first murders – and he's a very clever man with something to prove, which is the best of incentives. He knows how the business ticks. Like that clock on the website, Jacob. Tick, ticking away.'

'*Get out of here!*'

Naresh ignored him. 'Is it you? Or one of your associates? You know that Meriss is running for his life now, but you want that proof. You *have* to get the proof or it's all hearsay. The proof is the only way to the paintings. Poor Luca Meriss, being run to ground like a cornered animal. And when the proof's been wrenched away from him, then what?'

'You're rambling!'

'I'm not the drunk here. You know what I'm saying is the truth. Think of it, Jacob. Imagine if it was *you* who found *The Nativity with St Lawrence and St Francis*, and the portrait of Fillide Melandroni. Who cares that Meriss might be a descendant of Caravaggio? He's dispensable to you. What's a man's life in comparison to those paintings? What are two lives? Five lives?'

'Why are you hounding me?'

'Because you were in Berlin when it started,' Naresh countered.

'So were Oscar Schultz and Harvey Crammer!'

'I know you're involved, Jacob. *All* of you might be involved. I just don't know how.' Naresh moved to the door and paused, struggling to keep his temper. 'Gil Eckhart will find out the truth – I can't. But he'll discover what you've done. What *all* of you have done. Your business might have shut me out, but wait and see what the world will do to you.'

Sixty-Seven

Stadion Britz-Süd, Neukölln, Berlin
1.30 p.m.

Gil drove up to the garage, parked at the kerb and looked around. A group of teenagers was gathered together, some sitting on the wall, the others kicking a ball against the shuttered windows of the garage showroom. None of them even glanced in his direction. Gil started as the passenger door was wrenched open and Luca clambered in.

His face was drawn with cold and he was shivering uncontrollably. The jacket he had taken from the ambulance was several sizes too big for him, the rubber boots loose around his calves.

Handing him a sandwich and turning up the heater, Gil watched as Luca ate it hungrily, his hands trembling.

'What happened to you?'

'They took me from the hospital,' Luca explained, looking round repeatedly. 'They injected me and next thing I knew I was coming round in an ambulance. I jumped out when it slowed down.' He yanked up his left sleeve to reveal a bruise like a side of beef running the length of his arm. 'I thought they were going to kill me.'

'What did they look like?'

'I don't know! They were dressed as male nurses. They just came into my room and overpowered me.' He began to sob, raking noises in his throat, the sandwich dropping onto his lap. 'I'm finished, aren't I?'

'No.'

'I'm am! I know it!' Luca's voice fell. 'Who is it? Who's after me?'

Gil didn't like to say that it could be one of a number of people.

'I'll get you somewhere safe.'

'I can't go back to my flat!'

'You won't have to,' Gil reassured him.

It was obvious the Italian couldn't go back to his old apartment. He had to be hidden somewhere no one would think of looking, somewhere safe. A block of apartments with a porter on duty twenty-four hours a day. A secure apartment many floors above ground level. An apartment with someone Gil could trust.

He glanced at Luca. 'A friend of mine, Greta Huber, is willing to let you stay with her.'

He hadn't wanted to get her involved, but he had had little option. Greta had known from the phone call that someone was in trouble so Gil filled her in about Luca Meriss and his connection to the murders. Her response had been immediate. Luca had no identification papers so going to any hotel or a rented room was out of the question. With no clothes and no papers, there had been no choice. And besides, Greta had wanted to help.

'Why would a stranger help me?' Luca asked, surprised.

'Her parents were the first murder victims. Seven years ago, in Berlin.' Gil paused, his tone warning when he spoke again. 'I'll take you to Greta's place. But when you get there, you stay there, you hear me? You don't talk to anyone, you don't let yourself be seen or heard. You don't endanger yourself, or her. Just stay put.' Gil started the car, turning to Luca before he pulled out into the road. 'Greta's as much of a victim as you are. Remember that.'

Luca paused, then began talking in bursts.

'It's all my fault. I should never have talked about the Caravaggios. My ancestry – bragging about it. Going on the internet. Jesus, it's all my fault.' He glanced over anxiously. 'My father – is he all right?'

Gil nodded, thinking of the pouch he had been given. The object which had been passed from hand to hand, in a relay across centuries.

'Your father's safe now. And none of this is your fault, You never realised what could happen.' He paused, staring at the group of teenagers. It was cold, rain beginning to fall, the boys still kicking the football against the showroom wall. 'Your father gave me something when I was in Sicily. Proof. I took it to a friend in London and I'm having it carbon dated.' He looked at Luca. 'Where's the rest?'

'The brush and the note is all I had. Apart from the disks. Have you found those?'

Gil shook his head. 'No.'

'The brush and the paper are genuine. It's all his.'

'Caravaggio wrote the note?'

'*I'm sure of it.*'

Gil stared at him. 'You have to tell me where the paintings are. You *do* know, don't you?'

Luca nodded, picking up the sandwich again and biting into it. He chewed slowly and Gil waited until he spoke again. '*The Nativity*'s in Palermo.'

'So you said, but where?'

'I'll take you to it.'

'You still don't trust me!'

'I'm protecting you!' Luca replied, his tone agonised. 'You're in danger because of me.'

'No, because of the *paintings*,' Gil corrected him. 'Because of the people who are after them. Because of them, not you.'

He thought of the image of the foetus he had been sent: without words, but chilling enough to turn his stomach. Then he thought of Bette and the baby, as vulnerable as a bubble between thorns. And he knew how much he would fight to keep them. Because they were good. Because they were a million miles away from Holly and the art world.

His late wife's image came unbidden and unwelcome. To be betrayed by the person closest to him – to be manipulated and used as a decoy – was almost unbearable. Luca wasn't the cause of the trouble, and neither were Caravaggio's paintings. It all began with a woman – the woman Gil had loved but never truly known, Holly Eckhart.

'We have to go back to Palermo.'

Gil turned to him. 'If this turns out to be a wild goose chase . . .'

'Why would it?' Luca replied. 'My life's in danger here.'

'Not just yours. My family have been threatened too. If you show me where the paintings are, then what? Will that take me to the murderer?'

Luca looked away. 'I don't know.'

'Are *The Nativity* and the Fillide Melandroni painting in the same place?'

Luca shook his head. 'No. The portrait's in Berlin.'

'How d'you know?'

'It was supposedly burnt in 1945 in the flak tower, Berlin – along with other paintings taken there from the Kaiser Wilhelm Collection for safety.' Luca swallowed. 'But the Fillide Melandroni painting was saved, cut out of its frame and smuggled out.'

'By who?'

'A German doctor.'

'Why would he take it?'

'He knew its value. Remember, there were thousands of Berliners hiding in the flak tower at the end of the war. They stayed until their supplies ran out and then they had to leave.'

'And this doctor just happened to leave with the portrait?'

'When the fire broke out he was in the area where the

paintings were stored. He cut the portrait out of its frame, rolled it up and took it with him. It was small, remember? He could carry it.'

'And how did you find this out?'

Luca hesitated. 'I heard the story when I was in the psychiatric hospital seven years ago. It was when I talked about Caravaggio and said I was related to him – before I realised they thought it was just one more symptom of my craziness and shut up.'

'But someone told you the story of the painting?'

'A nurse did. She was old, coming up for retirement, but she told me the gossip. Said it was a rumour that one of the doctors had taken the painting. She had worked for him after the war and knew about it . . . She swore me to secrecy. Said it would mean her job if anyone found out that she'd talked.'

Gil looked at him, his voice wary. 'I don't suppose she gave you a name, did she?'

'The doctor's name was Crammer,' Luca said quietly. 'Bertholt Crammer.'

Sixty-Eight

Piccadilly, London

Still smarting from his argument with Jacob Levens, Naresh crossed the road at the traffic lights and headed towards Hyde Park. The insults had gone deep, the drunk dealer reminding Naresh of the bigotry he had encountered many times in his life, but never as openly. Usually muttered behind hands, or implied in faux smiles. The sheer brutality of Jacob Levens' attack had been shocking.

Naresh reached for his mobile and called Gil. He answered quickly, recognising the number.

'Luca Meriss is safe.'

'Thank God. You found him then?'

'He's fine,' Gil replied.

'Where is he?'

'I'd rather not say. Not over the phone,' Gil replied, overtly cautious but unwilling to risk Luca. He had him safe, in Greta's secure apartment, and he had paid the porter extra to ensure his vigilance.

'Is he in Berlin?'

Gil ignored the question. 'I'm staying here a little longer–'

'Are you on to something?'

'I don't know,' Gil said honestly. 'I'll keep you posted.'

'I saw Jacob Levens.'

'And?'

'That man is capable of anything. He's so drunk I doubt he's been sober for days now.'

'The Weirs were killed on Monday . . .' Gil thought back. 'Jacob was drinking then. I remember smelling booze on his breath.'

'He's a different person now. He was never this bad before. You think he began drinking before or after the Weir murders?'

Naresh let the inference hang for a moment. Gil was surprised. 'Are you asking me if I think Jacob Levens is capable of murder?'

'Yes.'

'He could be. If you'd asked me that question a month ago I'd have laughed in your face. But now . . . it's possible, yes. He's certainly hiding something.'

'Greta thinks so.'

'You two have talked?'

'Not lately. I've been travelling and we seem to have missed each other. I was surprised that she sold the gallery. It seemed so sudden.'

'I think she just made her mind up and wanted to get rid

of it,' Gil said, without mentioning what else Greta had said about who had bought it.

'She intimated that she had discovered something that worried her,' Naresh went on. 'She said she had told you about it.'

Gil hesitated. He liked and admired Naresh Joshi, but no one could be trusted entirely, even the man who hired you.

'There was nothing to it,' Gil lied, 'nothing important.'

Naresh sighed. 'You will keep me informed? If Greta needs any help, any financial support, you must come to me.'

'You're a good friend to her.'

'She was alone after her parents were killed. At eighteen to be left alone is hard, particularly on a girl. Her uncle was no help.'

'Was it your idea that she went to India?'

'It was a holiday that turned into a new life. Greta settled down in Delhi, took a job teaching, found some peace.'

'What about boyfriends?'

Naresh laughed.

'Was I her boyfriend? No, Mr Eckhart, I was not. Greta is like family to me. I love her, but not as a man – as a brother, a friend.' Naresh turned into Hyde Park, walking along the winding pathway through lawns where the short grass buckled in the winter cold. 'I'm the wrong race and religion. I would not fit.'

The words surprised Gil. They sounded oddly vulnerable. Unexpected, from such a cultured man.

'Did Luca Meriss mention the paintings?' Naresh continued.

'I might have some news about that soon,' Gil replied. 'Some proof.'

'*Proof?*'

'I should have the whole story on Monday.'

Naresh took a breath, obviously surprised. 'Monday? That's only three days away. Why Monday?'

'Because I think I'll know everything then.'

'How are you so sure?'

Gil wasn't – he was just setting out a marker, giving himself three days' grace. He was prepared to do anything, follow any hunch, but only for a little longer. Bette was in danger, their baby due to be born. He wanted out of the mire, and fast. On Monday it would be a week since the Weir brothers had been murdered. One week in which Bernard Lowe and Frieda Meyer had also met their ends. Seven days in which Jacob Levens had shown his hand, Oscar Schultz had bought the Huber Gallery, and Luca Meriss had been terrorised.

He had to move fast. The dealers were watching him, just like the killer. Gil didn't know which one of them it was, but he knew he had to force their hand, compel them to show themselves. The murderer would be impatient by now. He had waited a long time, been cheated out of his prize for seven years. Killed for it, plotted for it, and *still* it eluded him. That would burn. He would want it to end, he would want a conclusion as much as Gil did. The murderer would be tiring of the bloodshed, getting older, getting wearier, slower. But he would keep coming because he wanted what he had always wanted: the paintings. And Gil would take him to them. Offer them up, like Salome offered up the Baptist's head.

And then he would finally catch the killer. Yes, Gil thought, three days would be enough.

Seventy-two hours and counting.

Sixty-Nine

New York

It was very early morning, but Catrina Hoyt was already up and about, sitting with her feet up on her desk, her skirt riding high on her thighs. Something was bothering her, the same something which had been niggling at her for days. Whoever had broken into the gallery had not come back. Neither had they contacted her, posted any shocking images, or in any way suggested they were still watching her. Which meant only one thing – she had been discounted. But why? The answer was obvious; she no longer had access to Luca Meriss, was no longer dealing with him. Catrina Hoyt was now irrelevant.

Snatching up the phone, she put in a call to Harvey Crammer's mobile.

'Hello?' the Canadian answered.

'Has anyone contacted you? Or threatened you?'

'Good Lord, Catrina, is that you?' he replied, amused. 'Still not over being secretly filmed?'

'The pictures are off the website but the clock's still on,' she replied. 'Still ticking. Made me wonder why.'

'Clocks do tick, dear. That's what they do.'

'Cut the crap!' she countered. 'The clock means something. Unless you put it up on the website.'

'I was with you when we saw it, remember?'

'You could have pre-recorded it and preset the computer.'

'For the clock, yes. But how could I photograph myself with you?'

'You could have hired someone to do that.'

He was genuinely amused. Excellent, Crammer thought. He really had rattled her cage. 'Why would I hire someone to do something so pointless?'

'To scare me,' Catrina replied, 'make me feel threatened, off balance. After all, I'd had a break-in at the gallery and I was jumpy. You could have arranged that too.'

'I can't imagine you being jumpy, Catrina. You're hardly the nervy type.'

'Dealers are being murdered – that would make anyone nervous.'

'Only in London. I don't think the killer's reached New York yet.'

Stung, she retaliated.

'Well, he's certainly been to fucking Berlin.' There was silence on the line. 'You still there, Crammer? I've been looking into something, totting up all the little crumbs you left me. You've mixed with some very unlucky types: the Hubers, the Weir brothers, Bernard Lowe – all murdered.

All dealers who traded with you, Jacob Levens, and that smarmy bastard Oscar Schultz.' She could sense she had irritated him and pushed on. 'Was it some kind of secret society you lot had going? Did you do all that trouser-leg rolling up and wearing aprons?'

'That's the Masons,' Crammer replied coolly. 'Our association was just business—'

'But you're dropping like flies. I mean, that can't be a coincidence, can it? And then I had another thought – I dealt with your lot too. Not for a while, but in the past. Was that why I was involved?'

'You're imagining things. We had no collaboration,' Crammer replied, but he was needled, knowing that the redoubtable Catrina Hoyt wouldn't let it rest. 'You and I have only one thing in common – Luca Meriss. And that hardly makes us unique.' His tone calmed. 'Just think about it, Catrina: how many other people have seen Meriss's website?'

'Yeah, that's a point.'

'It's a very good point,' Crammer replied. 'We aren't the only dealers who are interested in the missing Caravaggios. There must be hundreds.'

'You're right. Many people probably *have* seen the website . . .'

'That what I mean.'

'. . . and know about Luca Meriss . . .'

'Exactly.'

'. . . and many of them will want to get hold of the Caravaggios too . . .'

'Precisely,' Crammer replied, his tone persuasive. 'We're talking about many, many people.'

She smiled grimly down the line. 'But how many of them were in Berlin seven years ago?'

Clicking off her mobile, Catrina swung her legs off the desk and walked into the storeroom. When she found the holdall she returned to her office and sat down, staring at it. Luca Meriss had reacted very violently, the last thing she would have expected from a timid man. So what had triggered it?

She remembered Luca on the floor, trying to grab the holdall. And he would still have it had she not snatched it off him. Catrina stared at the bag, her instinct alerted. Carefully she turned it inside out, feeling along the seams, then inside the pockets and lining. As before, she found nothing. Finally she tipped the bag over and stared at the underside.

Nothing remarkable, but something prompted her. Grabbing a paperknife, she slashed open the bottom of the holdall and stopped dead. Something glinted, catching the light. Carefully, she drew out a capsule and held it up to the window. The liquid was clear, with no smell.

Catrina Hoyt had little problem getting the substance checked out, and that afternoon her local pharmacist explained what it was. A muscle relaxant, he said, but only to be used in moderation.

'Why? Is it dangerous?'

'In excess it sure is,' he replied, pointing to the vial. 'In small doses, it relaxes muscle spasm. But that much could stop a man in his tracks. His muscles would be paralysed. He wouldn't be able to move or speak.'

She stared at the pharmacist. 'But he wouldn't be dead?'

'No,' the man replied, 'he'd recover when the drugs finally left his system. It wouldn't kill him—'

'Just keep him paralysed until they finished him off.'

Seventy

Huber Gallery, Berlin
3.30 p.m.

Gil had thought about entering by the main door, but decided against it and instead climbed over the high back gate. He remembered the building well, skirting the stone steps to the first floor and aiming for the basement. Having been unoccupied for years, the Huber Gallery was showing signs of neglect and the windows were blackened from Berlin traffic fumes.

He was making for a little-used window which opened on to the unused part of the cellar. As luck would have it, the glass was already cracked. Wrapping his jacket around his arm, Gil smashed it open. Pausing to check that he hadn't been heard, he then climbed in and silently moved to the door which led to the rest of the basement.

The gallery was silent above him. There had been no cars in the parking spaces outside and no street lights nearby. Even though it was only mid-afternoon, rain had made the day prematurely dark. Gil hoped that the gallery was empty as he made for the cellar steps, then waited. No sounds from above. Would the alarm still be working? he wondered. He hoped not. After all, the Hubers' collection of paintings had been sold or put into storage many years before and there was nothing of value left to steal.

Pausing at the top of the basement steps, he slid out into the entrance hallway. The windows were covered with metal grilles, some shuttered, and light was at a premium as he moved into the main gallery. A memory of the crime-scene photographs came back to him: Alma Huber naked and mutilated on the floor, blood seeping from her wounds, her eyes open, watching . . .

Hurrying on, Gil moved past the desk and into the main gallery space. The walls were blank apart from old posters of past exhibitions and a couple of catalogues lay on the floor. Outside, the rain intensified and hissed against the barred windows as he headed for the staircase to the offices above.

Hearing footsteps, he stopped and looked up the stair-well. But there were no lights on, nothing to indicate there was anyone up there. Gil thought back. He had checked that Oscar Schultz was in London, out of the way. So who was in the gallery? Obviously someone who was looking for something. Perhaps the same thing they had been looking for seven years earlier.

The hairs stood up on the back of his neck as Gil felt into his pocket, his hand closing round the stun gun he had brought with him. He wasn't going to be the next victim . . . Carefully he edged his way towards the back of the gallery, moving into the offices. What he found there surprised him. Books, files, ledgers, papers had all been thrown haphazardly onto the floor, filing cabinets turned over, desk drawers pulled out. Someone had been searching avidly, desperately. Even in the toilets the tops of the cisterns had been taken off.

Gil paused, listening. Silence. No more footsteps.

Maybe he had been mistaken.

Imagining things.

Was he alone?

Or was there someone waiting.

Listening, just as he was?

His mouth dry, Gil crossed the room, making his way towards the Huber safe. It was large as a potting shed, made of steel. Used to store papers and, if needed, paintings. It was also locked. Remembering the combination Greta had given him, Gil entered the numbers, listening as each clicked into place. Finally he turned the handle and the enormous metal door swung open, the darkness inside unfathomable.

Seventy-One

New York

Returning to her apartment, Catrina Hoyt rang Harvey Crammer again and asked for Gil Eckhart's mobile number. If the Canadian was surprised he didn't sound it – simply passed the number on hurriedly and rang off. He had obviously been in an airport; Catrina could hear a tannoy and the familiar sounds of a busy terminal in the background.

She glanced at the vial on her desk. Her suspicions had been right: there *had* been something strange about Luca Meriss, and she had found it. He had been carrying a drug strong enough to paralyse a man. The Weir twins had been paralysed and tortured . . . The little bastard, Catrina thought, remembering Meriss. The snivelling little fucker, posing as a victim.

Infuriated, she dialled Gil Eckhart's number. She had to warn him about the Italian. He was chasing the wrong person. And looking in the wrong place.

Seventy-Two

Huber Gallery, Berlin
4.00 p.m.

The mobile went off in Gil's pocket, ringing out twice before he could turn it off. Cursing himself for not putting it on mute, he froze, knowing that whoever was in the building would have heard it. Gil's instinct fired up. He couldn't hear anything, but he could *feel* it. Someone was there.

His heart pumping, Gil moved from the safe, ducking into the shadows. Just as he had suspected, someone *had* heard. Footsteps came down the stairs, paused, then continued into the room where he was hiding. After another second he could see a figure in the doorway and heard the click of the light switch.

The room was abruptly illuminated as a man walked in and looked around. Then he spotted the open safe and moved towards it, pulling back the door as Gil came up behind him.

Seventy-Three

'I thought you were in London, Oscar.'

Schultz spun round, startled. 'Eckhart! I knew I heard something. You should turn off your phone while you're breaking and entering.' He glanced at to the safe. 'Thanks for opening it. I didn't have the combination. How did you get it?'

Gil ignored the question. 'Why aren't you in London?'

'I'm going tomorrow. And I don't have to answer to you, you have to answer to *me*. This is my property and you're trespassing.' He moved over to the safe, looked in and shrugged. 'Empty.'

'What are you looking for?'

'Just clearing out.'

'No, you bought this gallery for a reason. You're searching for something. What is it, Oscar?' He moved closer him. 'The same thing you were looking for seven years ago? A painting? A Caravaggio? Did someone tip you off about it? Someone you knew back then?'

Leaning against a desk, Oscar folded his arms. 'What are you talking about?'

'You don't have to pretend with me – I know what's it all about. You found out about the paintings via my wife.'

Oscar rubbed the side of his nose, smiling. 'Your wife? I don't even know her.'

'My *late* wife, Holly.'

'Ah, Holly . . .' Oscar said. 'Clever woman, that. Very bright indeed.'

'She was working for Bernard Lowe, smuggling for him, using Lexington Limited to bring in the stuff from the Far East and Europe,' Gil said coldly. 'Yes, I know. Did she work for you too?'

'This is all rubbish!'

'Did she work for the Weir twins? Or were they just part of your group? I mean, there *is* a group of dealers, isn't there? Some little association you've got going?' Gil watched him. 'It would make sense, explain a lot. Holly heard about the missing Caravaggio paintings from Luca Meriss when he was hospitalised seven years ago.' He could see Oscar pale and pushed on. 'She got it out of him and told you – all of you. I imagine the Hubers were part of your group. Jacob would have brought them in.'

'Bullshit.'

'No,' Gil said calmly, 'Greta said her mother was afraid of Jacob. I guess it was because he involved her in something she didn't like, which makes me wonder what he had on his sister. By all accounts Alma was a decent woman – she must have been blackmailed into helping him.'

'You're floundering in the dark.'

'I was, but it's getting lighter all the time,' Gil replied. 'The Weirs had a company – The London Galleries Limited – which Bernard Lowe owned and which you now run.'

'So what? People set up companies all the time.'

Gil nodded. 'They do. But it's strange that the Hubers, the Weirs, and Bernard Lowe are now dead. As is Holly.'

'Holly's death was an accident!' Oscar snapped.

'I never believed that, and now – no way. Holly told you about Luca Meriss and the Caravaggios. They would make a fortune, make you rich, make your name. Not so much the second-hand car dealer with those finds, hey, Oscar?'

'Fuck you,' he said dismissively, 'I'm not a killer. You're looking in the wrong place.'

'I'm looking in exactly the right place, and you know it,' Gil continued. 'Where are the disks?'

'*What?*'

'The disks Luca Meriss made, the disks my late wife helped him create. The proof.' He was surprised by Oscar's blank expression.

'What bloody disks?'

'Luca Meriss made disks with the proof of his claims. He hid them in Palermo, but they were stolen from there. Holly knew about them – she gave copies to Jacob Levens for safe keeping. Copies that were stolen a few days ago in London.' He paused. 'You really *don't* know about them, do you?'

'No. Looks like you're on the wrong track again.'

Infuriated, Gil moved towards him and Oscar leant back

with his hands raised. A coward, unnerved. 'I swear I don't know about any disks–'

'Who brought Holly into the group?'

'What group?'

'*Your fucking group!*' Gil shouted, catching Oscar by the collar. '*Tell me!*'

'She *wanted* in,' Oscar replied, blundering on. 'She liked the excitement, liked the thrill of smuggling. Holly wanted to join us all–' He stopped short, knowing he had said too much.

Gil gripped his collar and twisted it. 'Join you all in what?'

'*Der Kreis der Acht* – The Circle of Eight,' Oscar blurted out, trying to free himself from Gil's grip. 'It was a collaboration between dealers. We would club together, bid for each other at sales, sometimes join forces and raise funds for works we couldn't have bought independently. The smuggling was a sideline. Using Lowe's shipping company, it meant we could get stuff out of the Far East ourselves.'

'No one ever found out?'

'No. It worked like a dream. We were all greedy – the Weirs were bastards, out for what they could get, and Lowe would do anything to get hold of a piece he wanted. Holly became our go-between. She'd charm people, she was always travelling for her work, and she could speak several languages.'

'What happened seven years ago?'

'What?'

'Berlin, seven years ago!' Gil repeated. 'Take me back.

Holly came to your group and told you about Luca Meriss. Then what?'

Oscar tried to knock away Gil's hands, but he held onto him. 'Let go of me! I can't breathe!'

'You're lucky I've let you breathe this long. Tell me what happened.'

'Holly was excited, said we could make a killing.'

'Did she tell all of you?'

'I don't know! She told me and said it was in confidence, but she was a liar–'

'That's my wife you're talking about!'

'She was a whore!'

Gil's fist smashed into the dealer's nose. He felt the bone crunch and a second later watched as blood started coursing down Schultz's white shirt. Reeling, the German staggered back, flopping into an office chair and holding a handkerchief to his face.

'You're mad.'

'Tell me what happened,' Gil said, standing over him. 'I want the truth.'

'Holly said she'd only told me, but I could tell that Harvey Crammer knew, and Alma Huber. The atmosphere in the group had changed – everything was awkward, strained. I heard Alma arguing with her brother when Jacob came over to Berlin.'

'When?'

'Just before the Hubers were killed.'

'So your group knew there were two Caravaggio paintings up for grabs seven years ago? Why didn't you go after Luca Meriss then?'

'He was in hospital. No one could get to him—'

'Where was Holly in all of this?'

'She was the only one who *could* get to Meriss. She encouraged him to confide—'

'And make the disks?'

'*I don't know about any fucking disks!*' he snapped, touching his face and wincing. 'You've broken my nose, you bastard.'

Gil ignored him.

'*Why* did you buy this gallery? What were you searching for? Did you think the paintings were hidden here? That they've been here all along? What did Holly tell you?' Gil paused, firing into the dark. 'Or what *didn't* she tell you?' He could see he had struck a nerve. 'You thought it was just you and her, didn't you? Just the two of you in on the secret? But she told the others . . .'

'She was playing us off against each other! She denied it, but I knew she told Jacob Levens. And Harvey Crammer. Thought she could get her hands on the paintings and then sell them on to each of us, without the others knowing. Rip us all off.'

'How? You had a collaboration, you'd talk to each other.'

'Christ, you're stupid, aren't you? We all thought we were on to something that would make us a fortune. You think we'd share that?' He paused, dabbing at his nose. 'It used to make me laugh to watch the others and know that I had one over on them. I never realised that all the time they were laughing at me, and at each other. Holly took us all in.

She was sure we'd keep silent because she knew our natures so well. Knew how greedy we were.'

'So how did the group find out that you *all* knew about the Caravaggios?'

'Alma.'

Gil frowned. 'What about Alma?'

'She told us the night before she was murdered. She called a meeting of *Der Kreis der Acht* and revealed what Holly had done. Jacob was there and they had a row, which left Alma in tears. Terrill intervened and tried to smooth things over, but it was no good. Then Jacob left for London.'

'And the following day the Hubers were killed,' Gil said, thinking back. 'I was called to Berlin to work on the case. Holly was already here – she said she'd been hired for a computing development programme. Harvey Crammer left the day after I arrived. You were here, hiding in your gallery, scared to death. The story of the murders was big news, all over the TV.' He glanced at Oscar. 'Why were the Hubers killed? Why them, seven years ago? If you *all* knew about the paintings, why were they the only ones who died?'

'How would I know?'

Gil stared at the dealer. 'You think the paintings are hidden here, don't you? That's why the killer murdered the Hubers. That why he didn't go after the rest of you seven years ago. The Hubers couldn't – or *wouldn't* – give him what he wanted. He tortured and killed them, but it was all for nothing.'

Oscar Schultz stayed silent.

'And then, seven years later, Luca Meriss blabbed all over the internet and the game was on again. He was out of hospital, vulnerable, advertising what he knew. An easy target, which everyone went after.'

'Not me.'

'Yes, you,' Gil corrected him. 'You hired a nurse, Frieda Meyer, to look after Bernard Lowe. Don't bother denying it. She was feeding you information about her employer. But Bernard Lowe was killed, and then she was murdered.'

'I didn't kill them! The police arrested Lowe's driver.'

'Who's now been released,' Gil said. 'Which is a relief, seeing that he didn't kill the nurse or Lowe.'

'I don't know who killed Frieda Meyer. Look at the others in *Der Kreis der Acht*.'

'But there aren't many of you left. Only you, Jacob Levens and Harvey Crammer. And my money's on you, Oscar.'

'I've just explained what happened.'

'It could all be a lie. Maybe the others didn't know about the Caravaggios until last week. Or maybe Holly only told you *part* of the truth. Maybe she kept the rest to herself. She knew the Hubers well, had access to this gallery. What was to stop her hiding something here?' He stared at the dealer, who had looked away. 'You know, don't you? That's why she's dead. Holly told you, thinking that you could work together, that you loved her. Jacob said she had another man. It was you, wasn't it? And when Holly told you everything you wanted to know, you killed her. It wasn't an accident, you just had to get her out of the way. Silence her.'

Slowly, Oscar Schultz rose to his feet. His nose had stopped bleeding, his arrogance returned.

'Get out of my gallery or I'll call the police.'

'Call them. I'd like to talk to them.'

'And say what, Eckhart? You've no proof of anything. It's all hearsay. Millions could have seen what Luca Meriss put up on the internet. There could be hundreds out there chasing him.'

Gil nodded. 'True, but the police will only be interested in the people who were involved seven years ago.'

'*And what happened seven years ago?* A wealthy couple got murdered by a lunatic that no one ever caught. And a young woman got killed in a traffic accident.'

'Holly was my wife–'

'Holly was my lover,' Oscar replied. 'Seems we both lost out.'

Gil was watching him, keeping his temper controlled as Oscar shrugged. 'You've nothing. The people who were involved are either dead, beyond reproach – like Harvey Crammer – or washed up, like Jacob Levens. Where are the paintings that prove all this? The proof that Luca Meriss is who he says he is? It could all be a scam, Eckhart, and the joke's on you.' He moved to the door, opening it for Gil to leave.

'You won't get away with it. I'll stop you if it's the last thing I do,' Gil said quietly. 'And I'll ruin you into the bargain.'

'Didn't you once say you'd kill me? Or doesn't that threat still hold, now that you've found out what your wife was really like?'

To his surprise, Gil smiled.

'You're dead, Oscar. Today, tomorrow, next week – who knows? But you're dead already.' He walked to the door, then turned back. 'You want to know why? Because if I don't get you, the killer will.'

Seventy-Four

When Gil got out onto the street, he checked his phone. The message from Catrina Hoyt was short and not too sweet. Phone me. Fast.

She picked up at once. 'Where are you?'

'Berlin,' he said. 'What did you want to talk to me about?'

'That fucking Italian, Luca Meriss. He's a fake.'

Gil stopped walking. 'What?'

'I found something in his bag and had it checked out. It's a muscle relaxant. In large doses it can paralyse a man.' She paused before adding, 'Sound familiar? Why would Meriss have that unless he was intending to use it? And why would he even know about it, unless he'd used it before? On the Weirs.'

Jesus, Gil thought. *Greta* . . . Clicking off the phone, he began to run across the traffic, cars blaring their horns for him to get out of the way as he raced between a coach and a bus to get to the other side of the street. He knew it would take him at least five minutes to reach Greta's apartment. Five minutes in which anything could happen.

Still running, he dialled Greta's number, hearing it ring out. Finally it was answered.

'Greta?'

'Gil?' she asked, surprised. 'Are you OK?'

'Where's Meriss?'

'In the spare bedroom, asleep.'

'Check on him.'

He could hear her moving down the corridor, opening the door and then calling out his name. A moment later, she came back on the line.

'He's gone.'

'What?'

'Down the fire escape.' She paused, moving back into the sitting room and looking round. 'And he's taken my money.'

Seventy-Five

Sitting on a bench in the Albrechtshof railway station, Luca shuffled around in his new clothes. The jeans and jacket he had bought were nondescript, the baseball cap disguising his colouring and making him look like any of the hundreds of other tourists or students. Above his head a tannoy announced the train arrivals and departures, a guard blowing a whistle as a freight train pulled out of the station.

He watched everyone: men, women, even children. Waited for someone to approach him. But no one did. An hour passed, then another, the day giving in to evening, the station lights coming on. Restless, Luca walked down the length of the platform, keeping away from the edge. Sweet wrappers and the early evening paper were blowing down the tracks towards the sidings. He glanced at his watch, stared at the second hand, counted the moments out, then returned to his seat.

He was cold. Alone. And scared. Jiggling the money in his pocket, Luca thought of Greta. She had been very kind, had made him food and offered him a bed. The sheets had smelt of washing powder, the duvet yielding softly under him as he lay on it. But he hadn't slept – he wouldn't risk that. He could hear her singing along to the radio in the kitchen and had wanted to join in, but instead he just moved his lips in time to the words. Singing in silence, lying on a duvet covered in printed roses.

'Luca.'

He jumped at the sound of his name, then slid along the bench to allow room for someone to sit down next to him.

'It's not your fault,' Gil reassured Greta, looking out of the window and down the fire escape. 'I don't get it. Did he say anything to you?'

She shook her head. 'No, nothing. He seemed to relax. I gave him something to eat and he just said he wanted to rest. So I left him to it.'

'How long d'you think he's been gone?'

Greta glanced at the clock. 'It's six now, and I last saw him about an hour ago. We talked a little about the dealers, but that was it.' She frowned, moving over to her handbag and searching through it. 'He's taken my mobile too! And my keys—'

'We'll get your locks changed.'

'Not the keys for here, the keys for the gallery,' Greta said, staring at Gil anxiously. 'I had a spare set and forgot to hand them over when we exchanged contracts. They were labelled – Luca would have known they were the gallery keys. But why would he take them?'

Gil thought back, remembered that Luca had told him the Fillide Melandroni portrait was in Berlin. As he had suspected all along, it was hidden in the Huber gallery. Oscar Schultz knew it, and Luca Meriss knew it ... Gil thought of the phone call from Catrina Hoyt, of the drug found in Meriss's bag. Could he be the killer, clever enough to fool everyone as he played the victim? Gil toyed with the idea. Someone had threatened Carlo Rannucio in Sicily – that couldn't have been Luca. Unless he had paid someone to do it.

Uneasy, Gil turned back to Greta. 'Go and stay in a hotel tonight.'

'What?'

'Don't stay here, in case he comes back.'

Her eyes were wide with shock. 'You think he's dangerous?'

'I'm not sure, but he could be and I don't want to put you at risk.' He paused, thinking back. 'Did your mother ever tell you about any disks?'

She shook her head. 'No.'

'Did she ever say that there was something hidden in the gallery?'

'No.'

'You said that there was an argument between your mother and Jacob Levens just before your parents were killed. D'you know what it was about?'

She looked away. 'They were always arguing when they met up. That's why I hated my parents working with him, especially when my father got ill. My uncle disrespected them.'

So Jacob Levens wasn't just a mean drunk, he was vile with his family too.

'Harvey Crammer hated the way he talked to my mother—'

'Crammer?' Gil said. 'Was he involved in family arguments?'

'No, but my mother used to talk to him, and when he was in Berlin he would help her out. She used to ask for his advice. He knew Berlin, knew tradespeople, contacts. My father was never very practical.'

She stopped talking suddenly, watching Gil. Intrigued, she followed his gaze until both of them were staring at a photograph on a shelf of books. It was of Greta and Harvey Crammer smiling into the camera.

'*That's* what spooked Luca,' Gil said, picking up the photograph and realising that although only Greta and Crammer had been visible, Alma and Terrill Huber were also in the photograph but had been hidden behind a book. 'He saw that and thought you were working with Crammer.'

'Working with Harvey Crammer?' Greta shook her head. 'I haven't seen him for years.'

'But he visited your parents' gallery?'

'Yes, but so did the other dealers, Jacob most of all.' She paused, thinking back. 'It was always difficult, always an argument. My father and my uncle even came to blows once. I don't know what it was about, I just came downstairs when I heard all the noise and saw them fighting. He was very strong, very aggressive.'

'Jacob?'

'No,' she said, surprised. 'My father. I'd never seen him like that before, and I never saw him like that again. Whatever my uncle said to him tipped him over the edge. He looked like he was going to kill Jacob, then my mother intervened and stopped the fight.'

'You never knew what it was about?'

She shook her head. 'No. When I asked, my mother said it was a secret. Something priceless. Beyond money.'

Something priceless, beyond money ... The Fillide Melandroni portrait? Gil wondered. The painting supposedly hidden in the Huber gallery? The gallery now owned by Oscar Schultz. The gallery to which Meriss had stolen the keys. The place where *Der Kreis der Acht* was formed, where eight dealers had met and plotted. The gallery where Alma Huber was murdered on 14th March, 2007. The place where it had all begun.

And where Luca Meriss was now headed.

Saturday

Naples
1610

The night was a long one. Caravaggio woke, then walked to the door. He nodded to the guard, tossed him some fruit, and closed the door again. Locked it. Lying back on the bed he rested his hand against his heart. Beating, always beating. And then against his face, on the crinkled skin, the buckling of nerves and sinew.

They would be waiting for him. He knew that. Knew they would never give up. He tried to keep ahead of them, change his guards often to make sure none fell into the pay of his enemies. Made no friends, had no friends, only the old priest calling by as the months passed. What news? The pardon is coming. The pardon is coming.

They are coming for me.

He is waiting.

Listening.

Wonders how the knife will feel as it goes into his body. Cold or hot? Maybe hot, like the sun, like hell. Like the pigments he had left on the windowsill the previous day. They dried, but not entirely. He could still press the soft centre of the paint and see the yellow ochre burst like a boil under his hand.

He had left his brushes in the sun too. He knew they would be ruined, but wanted them dry and brittle so that he could run his thumb across the hairs and watch as they bent under the pressure and broke, only a few snapping back.

He snapped back. Whatever he did, whatever was done to him, he snapped back. His mind returned to his childhood and the hills, which were black when the sun went down, rounded like the belly of a whore. He had come to Rome no more than a boy, promiscuous and dark-browed, knowing what he needed to make himself a name. Painting in corners, in the backs of inns, then palaces, where the cardinals moaned over his lascivious cupids and his corrupting angels.

Caravaggio turned on the narrow bed, the sheet sticky under him, and listened to the guard pissing against the wall outside. Tomorrow it may come, he told himself. Tomorrow the pardon would arrive. With the pardon he could return to Rome, batten his enemies, desert the sweating dens in which he had been forced to hide – going against his nature, taking advice to save his life. Hide they said, create no trouble, hide and the pardon will come to you.

He opened his eyes suddenly. Outside the door he could hear a horse whinnying, then footsteps approaching.

He held his breath.

Was it the priest? Or the pardon? Or the end?

Seventy-Six

Van der Las Gallery, London
11.30 a.m.

Rain, rain and more rain. Rain that came hard and relentless, the sky louring, bad-tempered with cloud. Flicking on the passageway light, Stuart Lindsay came out of the back lavatory to find a man standing in his laboratory. He was silhouetted against the top half of the door, outlined against the glass, as Stuart squinted into the dimness to try to make him out.

'Hello? Mr Van de Las?'

The figure didn't respond and Stuart hovered nervously by his bench, then he realised that the man was carrying something in his hand. Without thinking, he moved towards him.

'What have you got there?'

He could see his report and the small pouch that held the paintbrush and note he had been testing.

Stuart Lindsay may have been timid and agoraphobic,

but his laboratory was sacrosanct. It was his territory, the only place on earth in which he was master. Reaching out, he tried to snatch the items back.

'Those are mine!'

The man responded by grabbing Stuart, twisting him round and getting him in a headlock. As he struggled Stuart could feel himself being lifted up, his feet leaving the floor. Surprised, and fighting for breath, he kicked back at his attacker, who held on and tightened his grip till Stuart was about to pass out. Frantically he scrabbled at the bench behind him, his fingers closing over a glass container. With a last, frantic effort, he flung the contents into his attacker's face.

The man screamed and let go, running for the door and stumbling up the basement steps towards the street. In shock, Stuart stood rubbing his throat, sweating, panting. Then he collected together the papers and the pouch which had dropped to the floor, slammed the back door closed and locked it.

The rain was falling more and more heavily, the sky tipping out its contents onto the street below as the intruder lifted his face to the downpour. The acid had missed his eyes, mostly striking his hat and his clothes, chewing its way through the material. Enraged, he felt the pain a moment later and touched his neck, moving his fingers carefully.

He hadn't escaped injury after all, he realised, feeling the skin as it puckered from the chemical burn. The bastard had got him, and worse, he'd left the proof behind. But he had been lucky. He had feared that the acid would mark his face and brand him. Point him out as surely as a sign above his head. But fortune had been with him again. Turning to look into the reflection of a shop window, the man pulled up his collar to cover the injury, moving his head from side to side to check that it couldn't be seen.

Satisfied, he walked on. He hadn't got what he wanted, but he knew where it was. All he had to do was keep his patience. Follow his plan. Wait. Plan. Wait. Plan. Soon he would have what he wanted.

After seven years, what were a few more days?

Seventy-Seven

St Bartholomew's Hospital, London

Bette was asleep, lying with her left hand on her stomach, her breathing slow and regular. Her condition was worrying, both to her and the doctors, but she didn't tell Gil. What he had started he had to finish, for all their sakes. Instead Bette tried to calm herself, feeling the baby moving under her hand.

Everything was waiting its time. She whispered to the baby in her womb, reassuring it, asking it to stay still, keep growing, wait. Wait a little long, baby, wait a little longer. Soon Gil would be home and then the child could be born. Born to a safe world, its father returned.

In her sleep, Bette moved, disturbed, dreaming of her husband and of Holly, the first Mrs Eckhart. Holly, brilliant as a comet, sly as a stoat. Holly. In her dream Holly was talking to Gil, taking his arm and pulling him towards her. They were on a street Bette didn't know, among buildings that were unfamiliar to her, and it was raining. In the distance she heard someone call a name, but couldn't make it out.

But Holly heard it. Turned, alarmed, and then grabbed Gil's arm tighter, clinging like bladderwrack to a sinking boat. She was white-faced, dressed in a red coat, and then she was gone. Relieved, Bette looked for Gil, but he was gone too.

Restless, disturbed, she shifted in the hospital bed. And from between her legs blood, red as cadmium, seeped into the sheet below her.

Seventy-Eight

Huber Gallery, Berlin
1.00 p.m.

If Oscar Schultz had been telling the truth, he was out of Berlin, visiting London. But as Gil arrived at the gallery he could see lights on in the first-floor windows. Luca Meriss? Could be – he had stolen the keys, after all. Access wouldn't have been a problem. But then again, would Schultz have left the gallery before he had found what he was looking for? Gil paused, looking up at the lighted windows. Oscar Schultz owned the Huber Gallery now, he had all the time in the world to search it, so why hurry? Perhaps he had had more pressing business in London.

Walking round to the back entrance, Gil saw that the window he had used the previous day had been boarded up. Pushing against it, he felt the wood bend, but it took a few more attempts for it to give way. Finally it did so and Gil pausing, listening. A moment later he climbed the basement steps into the hallway, looking up the stairwell to the floor above. The light was on, shining half-heartedly, the sound of movement clear in the empty building.

When he reached the first landing Gil paused, looking through an open door into the office beyond. The safe was still wide open, empty, but a chair had been pulled up to it. Curious, Gil moved towards it. There were dirty footsteps on the seat. Someone had stood on it. But why? He looked at the top of the safe. The dust which had accumulated was now disturbed, streaked. Someone had used the chair to get high enough to reach not into the safe, but *behind* it.

Gil peered down the back, into the narrow space between the steel safe and the wall. The light shone through it. If there had been something there, it was gone now. Had Oscar Schultz found something? Or had Luca Meriss? As quietly as he could Gil knelt down, feeling the wall in case something had been pasted onto it. But his fingers touched wallpaper, nothing else. There was nothing there.

Standing up, he crossed the room and pressed his foot down on the floorboards. A safe as heavy as the one in the Huber Gallery needed a strong floor to hold it. Slowly, Gil walked the length of the room. A few boards groaned, but none were loose. Next he tried the wood panelling, catching sight of the outlines of fingerprints and palm prints on the wood. He paused, trying his own hand against one of the prints. It was much smaller than his, almost feminine. Puzzled, Gil left the room and glanced down into the stairwell below.

To his surprise he could detect heavy footsteps stomping

around, hardly bothering if they were heard. Moving quickly downstairs Gil followed the footsteps. Surely Meriss would be more circumspect? Gil paused outside the door which he knew led out into the storage room.

Carefully, slowly, he pushed it open, and a man spun round as he did so.

'*Was machst du hier!*'

Gil baulked, looking at the old man: a caretaker in overalls, his expression combative.

'Quiet!' Gil whispered, putting his finger to his lips to try and silence him.

But the old man wasn't having any of it. '*Wer sind Sie?*'

Gil frowned. 'I'm English—'

'I don't care! You have no right here! I'll call the police!'

Above them, a door creaked. Gil looked up, the old man following his gaze. Again Gil put his finger to his lips then moved out into the hallway. The floorboards groaned again above, the old building giving away the intruder as Gil began to climb the stairs. He was halfway up when there was a sudden resounding crash from below, the caretaker dropping the bucket he had been carrying and staring, mouth open, at the cellar door.

Seventy-Nine

The noise had alerted the intruder and by the time Gil reached the upper floor, whoever had been there had gone. Exasperated, he retraced his steps downstairs and found the caretaker still staring at the open cellar door.

The body was lying halfway up the stone steps, naked, spread-eagled. The man's genitals were punctured by wounds, blood soaking his thighs and buttocks. It was obvious that he had been dead for hours, the murder having taken place the previous night in the deserted gallery. Leaning down to reach the body, Gil touched the head, the loose scalp moving under his fingers. Then, skirting the corpse, he made his way into the cellar below. An old worktable that had once been used for packing and unpacking paintings was smeared with blood, knife marks scored into the surface, a discarded nail gun left covered in gore.

Der Kreis der Acht had lost another member.

Behind him the cellar door slammed shut, the caretaker bolting it on the outside.

'*What the hell are you doing?*' Gil shouted. 'I can explain—'

'Tell the police,' the caretaker replied, 'explain it to them. I'm not letting you out!'

Gil could hear the old man removing the key and then the sound of his footsteps scurrying to the front door. A moment later it closed behind him.

Silence fell. Just Gil in the cellar, with a dead man. Trying repeatedly to break down the cellar door, Gil paused to look at the corpse on the steps behind him. The smell of blood was overwhelming, along with the odour of excrement and urine. In the semi-darkness the body glowed like a starfish, the lips drawn back in pain, the teeth bared. Despite the injuries, the man was still beautiful. Even though his nose was bruised from an earlier injury and his eyes were bloodshot from a beating, Oscar Schultz remained handsome. Scalped, tortured and helpless, he had been dragged to the steps and left there to bleed out, and was now lying, milk-white, like a fallen idol.

Sitting down opposite the body, Gil looked at his dead rival. His prediction had turned out to be even more accurate than he could have hoped.

. . . if I don't get you, the killer will.

Well, the killer had got to Oscar Schultz, but he was going to make sure that Gil Eckhart took the credit.

Eighty

3.00 p.m.

The last person Gil expected to see was Harvey Crammer, standing in the reception area of the Berlin police station. His expression was one of amusement as he watched Gil being led out of the cells.

'I was having dinner with the police chief superintendent, which turned out to be very lucky for you.' Crammer pulled on his leather gloves. 'I'm afraid they had you down for Oscar's murder, you two being enemies.'

Gil picked up his belongings, pocketing them and putting on his watch. 'I had an alibi for last night.'

'I know. They spoke to the hotel staff and that cleared you,' Crammer replied. 'You don't have to thank me.'

Ignoring the comment, Gil walked out of the station, Crammer following. The rain had turned to sleet and the roads were greasy, slick puddles filling up the gutters. Crammer turned up the collar of his cashmere coat, his large head turned in Gil's direction.

'Aren't you going to ask how I heard what happened?'

'No, and I don't expect you'd tell me the truth if I did,' Gil retorted, changing the subject. 'Is your father still alive?'

'*My father . . .* ? No, he died many years ago. Why do you ask about him?'

'He was a doctor in Berlin, wasn't he? Like his father before him. Strange you never mentioned it.'

'Why would I?' Crammer replied. 'It never came up in our conversations.'

'But it should have done. After all, your grandfather had a very interesting story to tell, one he passed on to his son Bertholt. Your father must have mentioned it to you.'

Crammer's intelligent eyes remained steady. 'What story would that be?'

'About how your grandfather smuggled Caravaggio's portrait of Fillide Melandroni out of the flak tower in 1945. How he cut it out of the frame and took it with him, hidden under his coat.'

'Really? And what did he do with it then?' Crammer replied, shaking his head. 'It was a joke!' He laughed. 'A tall tale he used to tell, because he was in the flak tower with his wife. Yes, they did shelter there for a while and I imagine he saw the works of art that were housed there – but steal a Caravaggio? Never! Anyway, my father and grandfather fell out in the 1950s. They never spoke again and I never saw Bertholt after that. We moved from Germany to Canada and the family split up.' He gave Gil a sidelong glance. 'Don't you think I'd have been on to it if I thought the story was true? You really think I'd have let a Caravaggio slip through my fingers?'

Gil smiled. 'Maybe you weren't on to it at first. Perhaps you didn't know the story when you were a child, but found out later. Maybe that's why you became involved with *Der Kreis der Acht.*'

Crammer shrugged, brushing the remark aside. 'That was just a business arrangement.' Rubbing his gloved hands together, he grimaced. 'It's cold. Snowing now, damn it!' He glanced at Gil. 'You want something to eat?'

'I want some answers.'

Without replying, Crammer walked off, Gil following him into a restaurant. On entry, the collector was greeted warmly and ushered to a table in a booth by the window, the waiter taking his coat and gloves and then turning to Gil. After a moment's hesitation, Gil gave up his jacket and slid into a seat opposite Crammer. Putting on his glasses, the collector began to read the menu, then leaned forward and tapped Gil's copy.

'I recommend *leber und zwiebeln,*' Crammer said, translating, 'liver and onions – delicious. You're not a vegetarian, are you? I'm always suspicious of people who won't eat meat.'

'No, I'm not a vegetarian,' Gil replied, watching as Crammer ordered. 'Did the police chief superintendent tell you about Oscar Schultz's murder?'

'How else would I have found out about it so soon? And

your being taken to the station?' Crammer queried, looking over the top of his glasses. 'Beer?'

Gil nodded.

Although it was early, the restaurant was filling rapidly, businessmen and tourists taking the tables, the windows beginning to steam up as the snow fell outside. Heavy German woodcuts plastered the walls, together with some over-ornate carvings of wildlife and a stuffed deer's head, its glass eyes staring bleakly at the corpulence below.

'Why were your grandparents in the flak tower?'

'It was the end of the war. They were hiding from the Russians who had just invaded Berlin,' Crammer replied, thanking the waiter as he delivered their beers. He raised his glass to Gil. 'Cheers.'

Silence.

'I'm not your enemy.'

'That's strange, Bernard Lowe used the same words to me just before he died,' Gil replied. 'Just after he warned me about you.'

'Bernard had a wonderful sense of humour.'

'Seems like everyone you know was a comedian,' Gil said drily. 'What about Oscar Schultz?'

'He had no sense of humour at all.'

'He certainly didn't die laughing,' Gil replied, leaning back as two plates of liver and onions arrived.

Crammer inhaled the aroma.

'Ah . . . Nothing like good food on a cold day.' He cut into the liver, the inside of the meat still pink. 'Did Oscar die like the others?'

'Don't you know?'

'I wasn't there. You were.'

'I was there *after* he died. Perhaps you were there *when* he died.'

Crammer paused. 'You think I killed him? I was having dinner with the police chief.'

'You *could* have killed him. The pathologist can usually only tell within a couple of hours when a victim died, so you could have managed it – murdered him and then gone on to dinner. You would only have had to cross Berlin. You could have done it.'

Amused, Crammer leant back in his seat. 'All right, let's play your game. *Why* would I kill Oscar?'

'Why would you kill any of them?'

'Oh, so now I'm responsible for all the murders, am I?' He chewed his food thoughtfully, then took a sip of beer, looking around him. 'I used to come here years ago, when I was married to Alma.'

The change of tone took Gil by surprise. 'How long were you two married?'

'Only five years. Alma was a sweet woman, but she wanted a proper home life and a family and I didn't. I like to travel – can't stay anywhere for too long.' He cut into the liver again, the knife severing the meat. 'She was happy with Terrill. And when Greta was born she was overjoyed. Her daughter was her life. She meant everything to Alma.'

'Why didn't you marry again?'

'With these good looks?' he asked, laughing loudly, then shaking his head. 'Oh, no, I'm not interested in commitment. I like the life I lead.'

'Free to come and go as you please.'

'Indeed,' he agreed, pointing to Gil's plate. 'Are you enjoying that?'

'It's not bad.'

'Better than prison food, which you could have been eating,' Crammer joked. 'Everyone knows why you hated Schultz so much.'

'You mean because he was my late wife's lover?'

Crammer's eyebrows shot up. 'You've found that out?'

'I told you, I know about *Der Kreis der Acht* and Holly's involvement with it. I know that she told you about Luca Meriss and the Caravaggios.'

'Holly never told me.'

'What?'

'Your late wife never told me about any of it,' Crammer said smoothly.

'So who did?'

'Jacob Levens,' Crammer replied. 'It was Jacob who filled me in.'

'But you were rivals, competitors. Why would he do that?'

Crammer let his knife and fork drop onto his plate, clattering noisily against the china. His expression was cold.

'I've told you, Mr Eckhart, you're looking in the wrong direction. I'm not your killer. You think I'd help you to get out of jail if I was guilty? I'd want you to stay there, wouldn't I? A man who had something to hide would want to keep an investigator *off* his tail.'

'Unless it was a double bluff to throw me off track,' Gil responded. 'A clever man might try that. An arrogant one certainly would.' Gil pushed his half-eaten meal aside. 'Travel's second nature to you. You speak God knows how many languages, you use planes like most people use buses. You could get from one country to another easily. You have no wife, no family. Your work is everything to you. You're respected, admired, almost revered. And you're thorough too.'

'In what way?'

'Your research. The way you track down artefacts, paintings. I've looked at your writings and they told me a lot about your character.' Gil leaned across the table towards Crammer. 'You're methodical, intelligent and, above all, patient.'

'So?'

'You can wait. You can plan, run down the item you want, even if it takes years. You have resilience, tenacity. Seven years' waiting would be easy for you.'

The collector held his gaze. 'A man cannot hide his true nature.'

'No,' Gil agreed, 'but a certain kind of man could *disguise* it. A man who travels constantly, who has no family, no fixed friends. A man who comes in and out of other people's lives, never spending more than a few hours anywhere. *He* could manage it.'

Leaning back in his seat, Crammer finished his beer, wiped his mouth with his napkin and tossed it onto the table as Gil continued. 'You took the keys off Oscar Schultz, didn't you?'

'Which keys?'

'The keys to the Huber Gallery. You wanted them so you could search there in your own time.'

'Oh, Mr Eckhart,' Crammer said wryly, 'you're mistaken, very mistaken. I wouldn't need to kill Oscar for a set of keys I already own.' He paused for effect. 'I've had keys to the Huber gallery for many years now. And you know why? Because Alma gave them to me.' He stood up, smoothing down his jacket. 'Why did she do that? Because she trusted me. And I suggest you start to do the same.'

Eighty-One

New York

'So, did you find the little bastard?' Catrina asked as soon as Gil picked up.

'No. Luca Meriss is on the run again.'

'*Shit!*' she snapped. 'How did you lose him?'

'Hey! I'm not working for you.'

'You're not working for Jacob Levens either. I heard you'd deserted him for Naresh Joshi.' She paused. 'Don't be fooled by the honourable historian; he's not snowy white. There are a few rumours clinging to the bottom of his shoes.'

'Like what?'

'Like his girlfriend.'

Gil was listening. 'Who is?'

'Who *was*.'

He took in a breath. Not Holly, please God, not Holly . . .

'You used the past tense. Is she dead?'

'No, but the affair is. Dead and buried.' Catrina paused, pleased to have Gil hanging on her words. 'They were very discreet, but it still got out. You *don't* know, do you? Let me fill you in – Naresh Joshi was sleeping with Greta Huber.'

Gil flinched as Catrina continued.

'She was only seventeen at the time. I guess her parents weren't too thrilled.'

'Are you sure of this?'

'Yeah. Not many knew but an old boyfriend told me. He knew because he'd been a dealer in Berlin at the time . . . Of course after Greta's parents were killed the lovers had a clear run. Something good comes out of every tragedy, hey?'

Gil thought back to Greta's breakdown, supposedly brought about by her parents' murder. She had been catatonic, removed from the real world, inconsolable. Had it been genuine? he wondered. Or had Greta Huber discovered something she couldn't face, something which led to her breakdown? The only other alternative was chilling. Greta was working *with* Naresh Joshi.

After all, when she finally left hospital she went to India and stayed there. She had spoken to Gil of Naresh's kindness when she found herself alone but denied all closeness, just as the historian had done. Gil thought back. He had assumed that Luca Meriss had run from Greta's apartment because he had spotted the photograph of her with Crammer. But maybe there had been another reason. Had Luca discovered that Greta was working with Joshi? Naresh Joshi. The one person Luca had longed to impress – the man who might turn out to be deceiving him.

'Are you saying that you think Naresh Joshi's the killer?'

'No,' Catrina replied shortly, 'I'm just saying watch him, he's not what he seems. But then you could say that about everyone.' Her tone shifted. 'I just heard that Oscar Schultz has been killed. Is that true?'

'Yes.'

'And Meriss is in Berlin.'

'Crammer's in Berlin too. *He* could have killed Oscar.'

He could hear her take a breath.

'I guess you thought it would easier with all the suspects dying off?' she mocked. 'But then again, others are popping up everywhere.'

Gil changed tack. 'Were you involved with *Der Kreis der Acht?*'

'I don't even know what that means.'

'The Circle of Eight – a group of eight dealers, of whom only Crammer and Jacob Levens remain. The others are all dead.'

'I didn't know anything about it.' She paused, thinking. 'They kept that fucking quiet.'

'But you dealt with the Weir twins, Schultz, Crammer, Bernard Lowe and Jacob Levens.'

'So?'

'They never mentioned their collaboration?'

'I'm in New York, they were based in Europe. Sure they traded worldwide, but I was an outsider to them. They wouldn't have liked some American broad in on their act.'

Hoping to guard her off guard, Gil changed the subject. 'How did you find the drug? The muscle relaxant?'

'It was hidden in the base of Meriss's bag – the holdall he left behind here.'

'Why didn't you go the police with what you found?'

'What the fuck! It's a muscle relaxant. It's not illegal to own it.'

'Unless you're a killer. And if you *really* think Luca Meriss is the killer surely you'd want to stop him before he kills again? Or comes for you.'

'Why would he come for me? He wanted to deal with me.'

'But he didn't, did he? He bolted instead,' Gil replied. 'You could have planted the drug on him. You could be lying, tipping me off to get me on your side and find out what's going on.'

'You think I'm involved with these killings!' she laughed. 'I'm in fucking New York. I can't time travel.'

'No, but you could be working with someone else.'

Her voice hardened.

'You're chasing your tail, Eckhart. Yeah, I wanted the Caravaggios and I was willing to do business with the Italian. But he's long gone, along with my opportunity. I'm trying to help because I'm pissed at being duped.' She glanced back at the screen on her laptop, at Luca Meriss's website. 'The clock's still ticking. Only now there's something new been added.' She paused, then read out loud.

'*. . . Mr Luca Meriss wishes it to be known that he is returning to his birthplace, Palermo . . .*'

'Palermo. Of course.' Gil sighed. 'That's where *The Nativity* was stolen.'

And where Meriss said it still was.

'*I don't get it!*' Catrina said impatiently. 'Meriss was running away from everyone and now he's advertising his whereabouts? How stupid is this man?'

'He's not stupid,' Gil replied. 'He's gambling, dragging everyone out. Forcing their hands.'

'So they can kill him?' she queried, then paused. 'Unless *he's* the killer—'

'And he's calling his victims to him.'

Eighty-Two

Naresh Joshi's voice held a tremor of reproof. 'You didn't return my messages. I was wondering what was happening. Why didn't you call back?'

Gil sighed down the phone. 'I couldn't. I was arrested.'

'Arrested? What for?'

'Oscar Schultz was murdered. The police seemed to think I'd done it. We were enemies, and we'd just had a fight at the Huber Gallery.'

'Why were you there?'

'I thought Schultz was looking for something.' Gil paused, setting a trap, inviting the historian to fall in. 'He told me that the paintings were hidden there.'

Naresh laughed down the phone. 'He told you that!'

'He did. So I looked for them,' Gil replied. 'I knew how big a liar Schultz was, but he might have been telling the truth for once.'

'Don't tell me you found them?'

'No. I just found Schultz's body. He'd been killed in

exactly the same way as the others. Stripped, tortured and scalped.'

If Naresh *had* seen the trap, he had dodged it.

'Then it can't have been Jacob,' he said thoughtfully down the line. 'Jacob Levens has been in London, locked in his gallery for days.'

'Has he? Someone locking themselves away, refusing to answer the door or the phone, might not actually be there. After all, who'd *really* know?'

'No one. Where's Harvey Crammer?'

'In Berlin,' Gil replied, adding swiftly, 'Where are you?'

There was a bristling pause.

'London. And I resent what you're implying. I'm hiring you to find the murderer, Mr Eckhart, not insult me.'

'But you've insulted me. Withheld information. Like your affair with Greta Huber.' When the historian didn't reply, Gil continued. 'I found out from a very unlikely source. Why didn't you tell me?'

'I was ashamed,' Naresh admitted. 'I loved Greta very much, but it was wrong to go behind her parents' back.'

'How did it start?'

'I was travelling, as usual, and I came to Berlin to give a speech. Alma and Terrill invited me to dinner. They were respected dealers, very accomplished. We all got on well.'

'Especially you and Greta,' Gil said drily. 'When did the affair begin?'

'Soon after. It was madness – even now I don't know what possessed me! But we were so attracted to each other, so alike, and I was flattered.' His regret was genuine. 'Looking back, it was a love affair, yes, but there was more to it. For Greta anyway. I think she saw me as some kind of father figure.'

'She already had a father.'

'I know. But Terrill Huber was very interested in the business, not so much in Greta. She wanted attention, affection. Terrill wasn't a very demonstrative man.'

'When did her parents find out?'

'Only a week before they died, which made it even more tragic. We had an terrible argument. Alma was shouting at me – I was too old, the wrong nationality, religion.'

'You must have borne her a grudge for that.'

'You mean, did I kill her? Are you insane?' Naresh said heatedly. 'Alma Huber was right; Greta and I had very little in common. So I agreed not to see their daughter any more. Later that night Greta came to my hotel and begged me not to end the relationship.' His voice petered out, then regained its strength. 'Can you imagine how I felt when the Hubers were killed? Greta was alone. Of course she came to India after her parents died. She had been so ill, she needed someone she could trust. Who else did she have but me?'

'Are you still lovers?'

'No. The physical part of our relationship is over,' Naresh explained. 'It's deeper now. We are both alone in this world, Mr Eckhart. I am all Greta has, and she is all I have.'

'So you'd do anything for her?'

'Of course.'

'Then isn't it strange that you didn't tell me all this when you hired me?' Gil said. 'You said that you wanted to find the killer and protect Luca Meriss because you felt responsible for him, but you never mentioned Greta.'

'I wanted to keep the real reason a secret.'

'*A secret*,' Gil repeated. 'Trouble is, I'm now wondering how many other secrets you're keeping.'

'You cannot suspect me!'

'Men have killed for less. The Hubers were in your way. They were stopping you being with Greta. I'd say that was a pretty good motive.'

'But they didn't stop us being together,' Naresh Joshi replied coolly. 'Greta and I married in secret seven years ago.'

Eighty-Three

Van der Las Gallery, London
4.00 p.m.

Stuart Lindsay was surprised that he hadn't heard back from Gil. After leaving a couple of messages on voicemail, he sent him a text. It was to the point.

> CARBON DATING CAME THROUGH
> BRUSH AND PAPER AUTHENTIC

He was tempted to add something about the man who had broken into the gallery and tried to steal the evidence, but resisted. That information Stuart would relate personally, not by text. He had already added two more bolts to the door and a security light over the back entrance. Whoever had attacked him had meant business. And they had been thwarted, leaving without the proof. Without the information which would validate Luca Meriss's claims, prove that he had not been lying.

The carbon dating of the brush and paper coincided with the period that Caravaggio was alive and active. The paints and ink were of the period. The pouch was stained and old, and again, of the period.

Stuart Lindsay was agoraphobic. Had been for years. But he was also a loyal friend and that was what had driven him out of the security of his laboratory and onto the London streets. Head down, arms folded tightly across his chest, he had clasped the small package in a grubby Jiffy bag. Weaving between tourists and businessmen, Stuart had scurried to the Piccadilly bank where The Van der Las Gallery always conducted their business, one of the few London banks open on a Saturday.

Inside, the marble floor echoed with footsteps, faint classical music pumped from unknown sources, and two potted plants the size of yew trees flanked the door. Heart thumping, dry-mouthed, Stuart didn't notice a couple of people quickly move away from his sweaty form. He simply handed over the package to the manager and bolted out.

It took Stuart Lindsay four minutes and fifteen seconds to get back to the laboratory, six seconds to lock the two connecting laboratory doors, three further seconds to slide the bolts.

And an hour and a half to stop shaking.

Eighty-Four

Levens Gallery
5.00 p.m.

Jacob woke up, rolled over, and then staggered to his feet. His lips were dry, his tongue sticking to the roof of his mouth as he walked into the bathroom. Avoiding the mirror, he urinated into the toilet bowl and then pulled off his clothes, dropping them onto the tiles. The floor felt cold under his feet, drawing the warmth out of him as he turned on the shower.

Time meant nothing to him any longer. He had some vague idea that it was coming into evening, but couldn't remember what he was supposed to be doing. Had it been less than a week since the murders of Sebastian and Benjamin Weir? Only days since the whole maggoty mess had burst open? Stepping under the water, Jacob put back his head and leaned his hands against the tiles in front of him for support. He felt peculiarly ill – not just queasy but muffled in the head. Intrigued, he moved his left hand under the water, watching as it turned in slow elongated movements, his fingers pink and curling inwards to the palm like grubs.

The booze was killing him.

He didn't care.

He *did* care.

He cared . . .

Jacob let the water pelt down on his head, thinking of Alma, his dead sister, and of his niece Greta. He even remembered his late wife, someone he didn't often think about. His past reared up at him like a drawbridge, leaving him walking into nothingness, only the drowning water below. And he thought of the Caravaggios. Of *Der Kreis der Acht*, of ambition and the sleek rise of fortune they had all shared. Until now.

Jacob turned off the shower and towelled himself dry. Still avoiding direct eye contact in the mirror, he shaved and dressed himself, walking back into his office and glancing at his diary. It was Saturday, usually a day he would reserve for private viewings, taking the client into a plush room at the back of the gallery where they could view an item undisturbed. Jacob knew such treatment made them feel special and all the more likely to buy. After all, he was a master at the art of the subtle sell.

He would imply that something valuable would suit a home, not that it might make it. His bronzes, engravings and oils were merely an accompaniment to the good taste of his client, an underscoring of their learning rather than a bought piece, an instant brag. His own demeanour and knowledge reassured them that the handing over of thousands of pounds was wisdom, not fecklessness.

Jacob smiled to himself, but without any humour. In fact, he couldn't remember the last time he had genuinely laughed. Not sardonically, but with real mirth. Then he realised that no man could have a guilty conscience and a clear heart.

For a moment he was tempted to open the curtains, but resisted. It would be dark already, so why bother looking for light? And anyway, why advertise that he was alone? Allow any passer-by look in through the window and see him?

Turning on his computer, Jacob entered Luca Meriss's website, reading the latest news. The clock was still ticking, and there was an announcement that the Italian was returning to his birthplace, Palermo in Sicily. He sighed, holding back the side of the curtain and looking out. Sobering up, he began to feel the full force of his situation and realised how he had isolated himself. No friends, no family, no Gil Eckhart. He was alone. Exactly as he deserved to be.

His hand shaking, Jacob continued to stare out into the dismal street. He thought of the murdered bodies of the Weir brothers and felt his skin crawl. So much blood spilt, so much mess. The smell strong, clinging to his clothes afterwards, the heat of The Weir Gallery keeping the corpses temporarily pink.

It had taken them a while to die. Jacob knew, because he had watched their last moments. Seen their torment, the mutilation inflicted while they were alive but paralysed. And he had done nothing, too scared to react or even try to help them. Instead he had watched their eyes milk over, shift into dead mode in less than a heartbeat. And all the time the central heating was pumping out. Too hot for comfort, too hot for the paintings, too hot for corpses.

Walking to the door, Jacob unlocked it and paused. He was still able to function, but for how long? The booze was befuddling him, and guilt was doing the rest. Fiddling with his cufflinks, Jacob Levens stepped out into the street.

And the world watched him go.

Eighty-Five

St Bartholomew's Hospital, London
7.30 p.m.

'Don't tell him anything,' Bette said firmly. 'Gil doesn't have to know what's going on. Not yet.'

Watching the doctor leave, she leant back against the pillows, her hands resting on her stomach. No emergency phone calls, no dramas, she had insisted. What could her husband do? He was abroad, he couldn't just rush to the hospital. Instead he would have to travel back, taking hours, worrying, wondering what would face him. It wasn't necessary, she said. It wasn't time.

When she talked to Gil on his mobile she was calm, reassuring. She was fine, she said, and so was the baby. Both of them would stay put, hang on, until it was time . . . Bette could see the impatience in the doctor's face, but trusted her instinct. It was going to end soon. Very soon. Not long now.

She would wait. And the baby would wait with her.

Sunday

Eighty-Six

Palermo, Sicily

A child that is bullied always finds somewhere to hide and Luca was no different. Having been raised in a village outside Palermo he had devised a honeycomb of secret lairs, some in derelict properties, others in the countryside itself. One in a local church, a crypt in the graveyard splitting open after a prolonged, torrential downpour. The ground had shifted, the door of the sarcophagus gaping wide enough for a slight boy to enter. After one wet spring and a hot summer vegetation had grown over the entrance and the inside was a comforting, cooling hiding place.

It was one of Luca's favourite dens. The other was in the city, away from the country, in the Via Cipressi. The Catacombs of Palermo. All his childhood Luca had visited, saving pocket money for the entrance fee to go from the heat of the Sicilian day into the musty shadowed interior of the catacombs. But he wasn't there now. Now he was watching his father's house from the road outside. He could see the familiar outlines of the windows lit from inside, the door badly painted, the handle thick with rust. And he thought of his father, of the workman hands, the rage at having a son who was different.

Later the rumours drove him to be cruel. A homosexual son was shameful, something that scored out love and made a parent remote. Carlo didn't ask where his son went, was only grateful that the child didn't hang around the house, or dream in corners. He was relieved that the village boys went somewhere else to taunt, that the old gates weren't slammed backward and forwards on their hinges as they cried Luca's name.

For a tough man, Carlo was a moral coward.

Sliding behind a building that had been long deserted, Luca Meriss moved towards a shed half hidden by trees. In the early morning it smelt of dew and earth, a white spider trailing its cobweb girders across the ceiling struts. In the corner was the seat Luca had dragged in when he was a child. Riddled with moth and mice, it sagged under the weight of weather and years as Luca sat on a metal stool next to it and gazed out of the broken window.

He knew it was all coming to an end. That within days, possibly hours, everything would be solved, like a puzzle broken by an awkward child. Luca knew they would all follow him to Palermo. They would read his announcement on the website and come to him. No one would be able to resist.

He shivered, chilled in the cool morning. The scene

through the window had changed little since he was a child, and, as he had done when he was a child, he hugged his arms around himself, crooning, rocking backwards and forwards on the little metal stool, waiting.

Eighty-Seven

Taking the last available seat on the earliest plane, Gil had flown back to Sicily. He had no idea how many people would have seen Luca Meriss's announcement, but knew he would not be the only person heading for Palermo. Finally, tired and edgy, he arrived at the airport. His senses were heightened, waiting at any moment for someone to tap him on the shoulder.

But no one did. Instead he made his way in a hire car back to Carlo Ranuccio's house outside Campolfelice, and found the old man sitting in the doorway, smoking. He nodded as he saw Gil. The same woman who had translated for him before was pegging up washing on a slack line, the morning too cold to dry anything.

Smiling remotely, she moved over to Gil. 'He was here. Luca. We saw him looking at the house.'

'You didn't invite him in?'

She shrugged. 'When we opened the door he moved off. If he wants us, he'll come back.' She glanced over at the old man who was knocking a stub of ash off the end of his cigarette. 'Carlo wanted to know if you were happy with your proof?'

Gil thought of the message Stuart Lindsay had left him.

'More than happy. It's authentic. Right dates. Can't swear that Caravaggio wrote the note though, as there are no surviving examples of his handwriting.'

She shrugged again. '*Chi sa qualcosa di certo?*' Then she translated for him. 'Who knows anything for certain?'

Who knows anything for certain? Gil mused on the words, glancing around him. All was still, waiting, the old man watching, the two younger men staring from a front window. What did they think was going to happen? Gil wondered. It was as though they had expected him, that his arrival was no surprise. A thrill shot through him, a mixture of anxiety and foreboding. He had expected to find the answer in Berlin, but he had been forced to go even further back. Not in the life of Luca Meriss or the dealers, but into the life of Caravaggio himself.

It had begun in Palermo, Gil realised. First Sicily, then Berlin, then London. He picked his way through what he knew as he shielded his eyes from a sudden dart of sunlight. Luca had said that *The Nativity with St Lawrence and St Francis* was still in Palermo, that the painting had never left the town.

He turned back to the woman. 'Did Luca leave a message for me?'

She nodded, reaching into her pocket. Then she drew out a note and handed it to him. 'He pushed this under the door, with your name on it.'

DEAR MR ECKHART

I AM SO SORRY FOR ALL THE TROUBLE I HAVE CAUSED YOU. I KNOW MANY OF MY ACTIONS WILL HAVE SEEMED STRANGE. FOR THAT I APOLOGISE, I DID WHAT I THOUGHT WAS RIGHT, AND SAFE, FOR ME. EVERYWHERE I LOOKED THERE WERE SECRETS. EVERY PERSON I THOUGHT I COULD TRUST TURNED OUT TO BE SUSPECT. EVERY ANSWER I FOUND ONLY TURNED INTO ANOTHER QUESTION.

THE NATIVITY IS IN PALERMO.

YOU WILL FIND THE PORTRAIT OF FILLIDE MELANDRONI LAST.

THE KILLER IS IN PALERMO.
I KNOW IT. YOU KNOW IT.
I'LL COME FOR YOU, MR ECKHART.

Luca Meriss

Surprised, Gil turned to the woman. But she had already walked back into the house and was watching, with the others, from the shaded window.

Eighty-Eight

Van der Las Gallery, London

Irritated that they had missed each other's calls, Stuart Lindsay suppressed his reluctance and finally left a message on Gil's voicemail.

'Look, I wanted to talk to you directly, but I've got to tell you something important. There was a man here who tried to steal the . . . *stuff* . . . you left with me.' He hurried on. 'I'm OK. The bastard wanted to hurt me, but I'm fine. Tougher than I look, hey?' His voice was firm, clear down the line. 'I threw some acid on him. I don't know if I got his face, but I must have got him somewhere because he screamed, so I must have hit him. Look, I don't know what you're involved with – and believe me, I didn't tell anyone about the carbon dating – but watch your back, Gil. And don't worry about the things you gave me. I put them in the bank, in the Van der Las security box.' He paused, his tone warning. 'The man who came after me will be scarred. You'll know him, Gil. If you come across someone with an acid burn, it's him.'

Eighty-Nine

Campolfelice, Nr Palermo, Sicily
9.00 a.m.

Moving back into his hire car, Gil turned on the heating. The weather was colder than expected, the early morning shivering on the horizon, the fields smoked with mist. He had parked a little way from Carlo Ranuccio's house and was reaching for his mobile when someone tapped on the window.

'Luca!' he said, opening the car door and getting out.

Meriss was even thinner than before, his clothes loose, his colour pasty. His hair curled indolently around his narrow face, his eyes black, fierce with intent. Wearing jeans and a dark polo-necked jumper, he seemed far removed from the timid man Gil had rescued in Berlin. His voice was challenging.

'I knew you'd come.'

'I had to,' Gil replied, looking around him. 'But how did you know I'd be in Campolfelice?'

'Where else would you go in Palermo? This is the only

place you know. And besides, I knew you'd visit my father again. How is he?'

'Why didn't you ask him?'

'He knows why,' Luca said enigmatically, then pushed his hands deep into his pockets. The area suited him; he seemed for once in the right place.

But he was edgy, Gil could see that. 'So now what?'

Luca put his head on one side. 'What d'you think?'

'I think I'm tired of running around. My wife's due to give birth very soon and I want to go home. I want all this crap to be over. I was hired to find a killer, and that's what I intend to do.'

'He might not be what you expect.'

'Who is?' Gil said wearily.

He was watching Luca, waiting for anything to tip him off as to the man's true state of mind. Was he armed? A knife was quick and quiet. Luca Meriss had been running for a while. He was overwrought, hyper. Was he afraid that someone was coming after him? Or was about to rid himself of the man hired to find the killer?

They were alone, in a remote spot, and Gil wondered about Luca Meriss's mental state. Wondered if he had suffered a breakdown, and if so, whether he had recovered. Or whether he was a dangerous fantasist backed into a corner. And Sicily was his corner, not Gil's.

'I've had the proof authenticated.'

'I told you it was genuine!' Luca snapped. 'Do you believe me now?'

'I will when you show me *The Nativity*—'

'Why? I thought you wanted to catch the killer. I thought the paintings were secondary.' He stared at Gil, walking closer towards him. 'Or are you working for another dealer? I know Bernard Lowe was after the pictures, but he's dead. So who's paying you now?' He was circling Gil, hands still in his pockets. Aggressive, feral. 'Still Jacob Levens? I wonder how long before he gets here? And we can't forget Naresh Joshi. He won't be able to dismiss me so easily when the proof's staring him in the face. I thought he was a decent man. I gave him the first chance at the story. Bastard!'

Gil breathed in sharply. He could see that Luca was sweating, his face flushed. Unpredictable, even dangerous.

'And then there's Harvey Crammer.' Luca glanced over at Gil slyly. 'I saw his photograph in Greta Huber's flat.'

'So what? She knew him. Crammer was once married to her mother.'

Luca wasn't listening. 'Of course Oscar Schultz won't be coming.'

How did he know that? Gil wondered. *Unless he'd killed him?*

'It was you in the Huber gallery, wasn't it, Luca? You stole the keys from Greta. You were searching. I saw the marks on top of the safe – someone had climbed up to look down the back.' He kept his gaze fixed on him, waiting for any reaction. 'When I looked there wasn't anything to find – unless you'd already taken it.'

'The portrait wasn't there,' Luca said, smiling indulgently. 'You're way off.'

Gil ignored the comment.

'Why kill Oscar Schultz? Did he come back unexpectedly and catch you? He was killed in exactly the same way as the others. Only the killer knew that, only the killer knew *exactly* which injuries to inflict.'

'That's not true. The injuries were reported on the internet. Anyone could look them up or copy them.' Luca was taunting him. 'You think I'm the killer?'

'You could be. It would be clever to make yourself out to be the victim in order to throw everyone off track.'

'I was attacked!'

'Were you?' Gil replied, watching the Italian as he leaned against the car door. 'I've only got your word for that. As for being abducted from the hospital, perhaps you were taken away for your own good. Perhaps because you were relapsing, hallucinating. Dangerous. Perhaps you weren't under threat, but under doctor's orders.'

He moved so fast Gil barely had time to duck as Luca pounded his fist into the car door and then spun round, face distorted with rage.

'I'm not mad!'

'Prove it!' Gil replied, watching Meriss warily. 'Why did you leave Greta Huber's flat?'

'I didn't trust her.'

The sun was rising higher, a little warmth dribbling through the shutter of clouds.

'But she wanted to help you.'

'Are you sure of that?' Luca countered, recovering his calm.

'Greta isn't in the business. The paintings would mean nothing to her,' Gil retorted, changing tack. 'Why did you have the drug on your bag?'

'*What?*'

'Catrina Hoyt found muscle relaxant hidden in the base of your bag–'

'*Liar!*' Luca roared. 'She's lying!'

'Why would she?'

'Someone put it in my bag!' He was shaking his head, baffled, confused. 'Someone's trying to frame me!'

'Who had access to your bag?'

Luca thought back, then remembered the plane. 'On the flight – someone could have done it then. I left my seat. They could have planted the drug then!' His voice accelerated. 'There *was* someone on the plane, someone who left me a note. *They* did it.'

'Where's the note?'

Luca paused. 'In my bag.'

'The bag that you left at Catrina Hoyt's?' Gil said quietly. 'It's always the same story, Luca. Nothing adds up with you.'

'*I'm not mad,*' he repeated frantically. 'It's not me. I'm not the killer. I'm not mad.' He was confused, lost, suddenly relapsing into the same terrified man Gil had rescued in Germany. His moods were changing, flickering in and out of logic as he suddenly reached out and grabbed Gil's arm. 'I want to show you something. I *have* to show you. Follow me.'

Gil shook him off. 'Turn out your pockets first.'

'What?'

'Turn out your pockets,' he repeated, watching as Luca emptied them. He had a few crumpled banknotes, some coins, a comb, and a key with a label attached. Nothing threatening. 'OK. Now where d'you want to go?'

Luca gestured towards a nearby wall. 'I've got a bike. You follow in the car.'

It was obvious he knew the route, cycling fast down the long country roads, weaving through villages and then pausing for Gil to catch up, his own route hampered by traffic or pedestrians. Once Luca waited by the side of the road, right foot on one pedal, left foot on the ground, sipping at a bottle of water. Dark hair wiry under the growing sunlight. When Gil drew level he nodded, then set off again, following the signposts towards Palermo.

Even early on a Sunday morning, off season, there were people about. Some came from church, the women's heads covered with lace like frosting on winter trees. Children, released from over-long sermons, chased each other, ducking into alleyways as Gil followed the bike. He was surprised at the traffic, the city roads badly marked, narrow and shadow-warped, leading into squares and unexpected shopping galleries.

Slowing down, Gil watched as Luca stopped, got off his bike, and walked over to him.

'I'll show you where to park. We can walk from here.'

Ten minutes later Gil finally managed to secure a space, Luca impatient, tapping his foot as he watched him.

'Come on, come on!' he urged, moving off quickly through the streets, weaving into the middle of Palermo. Barely able to keep up with him, Gil was relieved when Luca finally stopped, pointing to a sign on the wall.

'Via Cipressi,' he said, his tone satisfied. 'Follow me.'

The building to which Gil was led adjoined a church. It was painted a pale terracotta, the walls flat-faced, with a small entrance over which was a jaunty, weathered blind. Outside, a couple of old men were opening up. Luca spoke to them and gestured towards Gil. A moment later, they nodded.

'Come with me,' Luca said, beckoning to Gil. 'Come on!'

There were no other people waiting as Luca led Gil through the doorway. The difference in light from the brightness of outside to the gloomy interior disorientated Gil. Taking a moment for his sight to adjust, he followed Luca down a flight of steps into the basement area of a church. On either side of the stone passageway were grip rails, shiny from the passing of a thousand greasy hands.

The smell was not so much damp as dusty, a peculiar mixture of dry sunlight and old clothes with an underlying odour of wood. Surprised, Gil followed as Luca led him on, the narrow passageway widening suddenly. In front of them was an elevated walkway that straddled a subterranean area, the passageway on which they were standing hung either side with dried corpses.

Startled, Gil jerked back. The cadavers were only feet away from him. Mummified, they were dressed in the remnants of their clothes, their faces skulls, their jaws hanging open. Clumps of hair were still attached to some of the heads, the bodies of the glowering monks held back by barriers, their crumbling remains forced upright by the use of wires and steel.

'God Almighty!'

'Come on!' Luca urged him. 'Hurry.'

Following the Italian, he continued onwards. And then the space opened further, into a vaulted, church-like interior. The walls were old, lime-washed plaster, the bodies arranged in rows from the floor to the ceiling. Rotting cadavers with hooded heads were packed into narrow arches, and on either side brick piles supported skeletons, torsos, and some crumbling bones of children.

Staggered, Gil looked around him. The electric lights had been turned on, their illumination crawling up the walls to where more bodies stood to attention. All were clothed, some in monks' habits, others in finery, Sunday best clothes grown mouldy with age, whites yellowed and curling with dust. As he turned, Gil could see above him a withered hand reaching from beyond the wire cage, a cardinal's hat slipping over a skeleton face.

'What is this place?'

Luca turned to him. 'The catacombs. They buried the monks here at first, when it was just for the religious orders. But later people buried their own dead. They dressed them in their best clothes and came to visit, to talk to them.' He pointed down the passageway. 'There are infants in there. One is perfectly preserved, like she's asleep.' His voice was low, reverential. 'I've been coming here since I was a child. I used to sneak in, hide, and then wait until it was quiet. The Fathers knew.' His smile was oblique. 'They left me alone. They knew I needed to be here.'

'But why do *I* need to be here?'

Luca seemed surprised that he should ask. 'Why? To find the answers you're searching for.'

'The killer?'

'And the painting,' Luca replied, his face questioning. 'Which answer do you want the most, Mr Eckhart? To know who the murderer is or where the painting's hidden? *The Nativity with St Lawrence and St Francis*, missing for so long, looked for, longed for. All those dealers wanting it. Willing to do anything to get their hands on it. Willing to kill.'

'You said it never left Palermo. That it was hidden.' Gil looked about him. 'Is it here?'

Shrugging, Luca moved away, walking towards a bank of dead monks held back by a wire fence. His hand reached out, his fingers curling around the steel.

'No one really believed me. No one was really interested in what I had to say. It was irrelevant that I'm a descendant of Caravaggio. All people wanted was the paintings and the money they would bring. They were prepared to kill me to get to them, just like they wanted to kill Caravaggio.

Strange that, how we both ended up being hunted.' He took in a long, measured breath. 'Are they here yet?'

Gil frowned. 'Who?'

'The people I've called out. I told you in my note, Mr Eckhart, the killer's in Palermo.'

'*You're* in Palermo.'

'As are you.'

'But I have no reason to kill the dealers.'

Luca held his gaze. 'Oscar Schultz was your wife's lover. Your wife was involved with the dealers. They used her. She used them. She used you.' He paused, knowing he had scored a direct hit. 'Bernard Lowe employed your late wife to smuggle for him.'

Gil could hardly breathe. 'How d'you know all this?'

'I was there at the start, remember? Seven years ago, in Berlin. Your wife was very interested in what I had to tell her about my heritage, and what I knew about the paintings. She used to tell me things too. Thought I wasn't really listening, or that I wasn't really sane. Who knows? She could be very indiscreet sometimes.' He smiled winningly at Gil. 'I liked your wife – your late wife. She was the only person I really talked to – before I learned it was wiser to stay quiet.'

'Did Holly tell you about *Der Kreis der Acht*?'

'She told me half the story, but that was enough. I found out the rest. I'm a good researcher, Mr Eckhart. Like you, I follow the facts. That was how I discovered who my ancestor was – from gossip. From things my father said, and my grandmother. People talk in front of children. They never realise how much a child retains.'

'But you said you had proof.'

'You have the material proof! The rest is hearsay. My father could tell you a great deal, but when he realised how interested I was, he became scared. Sicily is not a big place, *The Nativity with St Lawrence and St Francis* was thought to have been stolen by the Mafia. My father didn't want to encourage any curiosity that might endanger his family.' Luca was eager to talk. 'I was in the hospital when I heard about the story of Bertholt Crammer smuggling the Fillide Melandroni painting out of the flak tower.'

Gil interrupted him. 'I checked up on that. Harvey Crammer said it was a joke. And he should know – it was his family.'

'All the more reason to deny it,' Luca replied. 'Do you trust Mr Crammer?'

'I don't trust anyone.'

'Not even your wife? I mean, your *present* wife.' Gil ignored him. 'It was Holly that taught me how to use a computer. She encouraged me, said it was good therapy to write things down. I took to it easily, but then again, she was a good teacher. People have so many faces. *Too* many faces.' He looked around at the moulding remains. 'They can't talk. All their tongues are dried up.' He paused, listened. 'Sssh! Can you hear something?'

'What?'

'I thought I heard footsteps.' Luca sighed, relaxing. 'No, not yet. They'll come soon. They'll come.'

'Who are you talking about?'

'You should know, Mr Eckhart. Think back, remember Berlin.' He sighed again, glancing around him. 'I've paid the men on the door to go away for an hour or two. We have the place to ourselves. We're the only two living bodies among a sea of dead ones.' He looked at Gil, expressionless. 'Who'd notice one more corpse among so many?'

Ninety

Palermo

Harvey Crammer dressed himself with his customary care. A clean white shirt, a double-breasted navy suit and a silk tie. To finish his outfit on such a cool morning, he arranged a fine wool scarf around his neck and pulled up the collar of his overcoat. Satisfied, he left the hotel and headed towards the centre of the city.

It was a place he knew well and had visited often, but this time the visit was not for pleasure or for business. It was simply a matter of resolution. Harvey Crammer had relied on his intellect to establish him, and his power to maintain his status in life. When he had finished collecting and dealing in art he had promised himself a dabble in politics. Not as a candidate, more as a puppet master. But before he could slink into his new role he wanted to make one final coup. One last triumph. To retire from the art world as a titan, with a flourish that would reverberate for decades.

If he was the man who found the missing Caravaggios his reputation would have a place among the greats. For a modest man, it was enticing. For an ambitious man, it was irresistible.

Ninety-One

Gil was watching Luca Meriss cautiously. The Italian was talking too much and too fast. He ran his hands along the steel grilles, tipping his head from one side to the other as though he was listening. Gil thought of Bette and swore he was not going to die in the catacombs of Palermo. Turning towards him, Luca stared at Gil as though he was reading his thoughts, then looked away. His fingers curled around the grille, then unfurled slowly, the cool dankness of the place eerie. Quiet.

'Where's the painting?'

Luca turned back. His eyes were black, densely black, without visible pupils, his full lips opening as he prepared to speak. But before he could a noise startled both of them. Gil glanced over his shoulder at the corridor. No one came.

Uneasy, he turned back to Luca. 'Who are you expecting?'

'They'll come.'

'Who?'

'You'll see.'

He stared at Luca impatiently. 'Where's the painting?'

'D'you think he would approve of you, Mr Eckhart? You think Caravaggio would like you?' He seemed to consider the question gravely. 'He was a violent man too. A killer . . .'

The hairs stood up on the back of Gil's neck.

'He stabbed a man out of jealousy. Killed him.' Luca paused. His feet moved, but made hardly a sound. 'How much do we inherit in our genes? Can you inherit a killing gene?'

Gil faced him, implacable. 'Is that a serious question?'

'Yes. Can you inherit traits?'

'If you can, you should be a genius,' Gil retorted. 'Have you got any artistic talent, Luca?'

He let the question go.

'Perhaps we only inherit certain traits—'

'Where's the bloody painting?' Gil asked again. 'I'm not going to stand here all day listening to you. I've finished with listening to you, Luca.'

The Italian moved, but not towards Gil. Instead he slipped around the corner which led to a separate cubicle.

'Come on, Mr Eckhart, keep up!' he called, his voice disembodied. 'You don't want to get lost in here.'

Hurrying on, Gil moved into an arched antechamber where Luca's shadow loomed up on the back wall. There were two stone racks behind him, on which a skull and various sundry bones lay, discarded, unnamed.

'You know how this place worked?' Luca asked. 'They brought the corpse here and dried it out on ceramic racks. Some bodies were later washed with vinegar. Slowly the body mummified. But some were better prepared than others.' He touched the edge of one of the racks listlessly. 'As I said before, families paid for their beloved to rest here. They provided the church with a stipend to look after them. Thing is,' Luca's eyes were densely, impenetrably black, 'if the family reneged on the fee, the body was moved. Demoted, if you like. Pushed onto a shelf in the background until they paid up.' He sighed. 'Even dead, there's a pecking order.'

The dry walls were mottled with crumbling plaster, the dim light making the bones glow. Gil kept his back to the wall, making sure he stayed close to the exit. If Luca Meriss rushed him, he wanted to give himself a chance to escape. Gil wouldn't allow himself to consider the obvious – that Meriss knew the catacombs intimately. That he could draw Gil further and further in, disorient him, and then strike. One more corpse in a charnel house of bodies.

Silent, Gil let the Italian talk.

'I should be famous. That was what I wanted. I think that's what *everyone* wants these days. But I had something to say. Caravaggio is my ancestor – I have something of interest to the world.' Luca's head tipped to one side. 'Seven years is a long time to wait, Mr Eckhart.'

He sighed, then darted past Gil into the corridor, only pausing when he reached a sign marked *Cardinali* over the entrance to another vault.

Pointing to it, Luca said, 'Behold, the holy men.'

Then he moved into their sanctum.

In rows along the walls stood the dead priests, cardinals and monks. Some of the oldest, poorest monks had slumped forward in their supports, the ropes they had worn as a penance in life now hanging pointlessly from their withered necks. The cardinals – interred with all their regalia – had grown brittle, fingers breaking off, faded birettas slipping forward over grinning skulls. All the pomp of the church's ceremonies and costumes had dried up, the vestments breaking apart, decaying lace yellow as pus.

A hundred empty eye sockets stared hellishly at Gil as he faced Luca. 'I'll ask you one more time – where's the painting?'

Gil thought for a moment that Luca would lunge at him, but instead he began climbing. His grip fastened on the grille as he shimmied up the wire, clambered over it, and nestled for a moment between the bodies of two dead monks. Then he reached behind one and drew out a long, weathered cylinder.

Gil held his breath. Was this the Caravaggio which had been missing for so long? Number 1 on the FBI's Most Wanted Missing list? Had it been hidden in the catacombs since 1969? Had the Mafia stolen it and abandoned it here? Or had it been taken by amateurs unable to offload such a notorious work? Incredulous, he stared at the unmarked cylinder. All the theories, all the searching, all the money and man hours had come to nothing. A thousand conspiracy theories were left unproven and a myriad dealers had failed. Because *The Nativity with St Lawrence and St Francis* had been here all along, hidden behind the corpse of a dead monk.

'Is that it?'

To his surprise, Luca tossed it over the wire to Gil. 'I told you all along I had the proof.'

Catching the cylinder, Gil was surprised by the weight of it, the faded cardboard container sealed at each end with a metal cap.

Luca clambered back over the grille and jumped to the floor, putting out his hands.

'Give it to me. It's mine. I've earned it.'

Gil handed him back the cylinder. 'Was it worth it?'

'The murders?' Luca asked. 'How would I know?' He walked around Gil slowly, tauntingly.

'You want to make a move?' Gil snapped. 'Then make it. I'm not scared of you. Come on, give it your best shot.'

He could see Luca's eyes flicker and his head tip back slightly.

Then he flinched.

There was the sound of approaching footsteps, then a shadow fell on to the passageway behind Gil. He tensed, hearing the sound of breathing behind him. Luca stared ahead, immobile, transfixed.

His heart pounding, Gil turned round.

Ninety-Two

Even though Harvey Crammer's Italian was perfect, it had still been no match for the two guards on the entrance to the catacombs. However much he had tried to persuade them to let him in, he had been rebuffed. Even the usual coercion of money left them unmoved, and he walked back to his parked car and called Gil on his mobile.

But instead of Gil answering, the call had clicked over to voicemail. Crammer threw the phone onto the passenger seat beside him. If Gil Eckhart was underground in the catacombs he wouldn't be able to get a signal. Enraged, he slammed his hands against the car steering wheel. He had to get into the catacombs. Nothing was going to stop him now.

Ninety-Three

Gil turned, struggling to make out the man's face as he stood with his back to the light. Then he moved, his features illuminated, his expression relieved. It was Naresh Joshi, flustered and out of breath.

'Harvey Crammer's in Palermo!' he said frantically. 'Are you all right?'

'How did you get here?' Luca asked. 'I told them not to let anyone in.'

'I said it was an emergency. And it is. I've just seen Harvey Crammer. He must have followed you.'

Gil raised his eyebrows. 'Just like you did.'

'I wanted to find out what was going on,' Naresh replied. 'I hired you, Gil. I'm entitled to know what you're doing. I guessed you'd come over to Palermo after Luca announced he was coming here. I was right. And so was Harvey Crammer.'

Luca interrupted him. 'Why are you worried about me all of a sudden?'

'It's not all of a sudden. I hired Gil to find you and protect you.' Naresh moved over to the Italian. 'I'm sorry, I was wrong about you. I should have listened, believed you when you first came to me. I dismissed you out of hand.'

'You thought I was crazy!'

'No! That wasn't it. It was just that your claims seemed so incredible.'

'Too late, Mr Joshi. You could have been there from the start.' Luca's tone was sneering. 'You could have shared the glory of finding the Caravaggios, but you missed out.'

'I can help you!' Naresh was almost pleading. 'I have a reputation – people will accept what I say. If we publicise the Caravaggios together, the art world will listen.'

'So you make me respectable and I make you famous?' Luca countered, leaning back again the wire grille, the cylinder suddenly visible. Behind him, the corpses stared out over his head, grey with mould, ash-coloured, dry mouths opening silently.

Naresh stared at the cylinder, his voice hoarse. '*Is that the painting?*'

'I told you all along that I knew where it was.'

'We have to sort this out before Crammer gets to you.'

Surprised, Gil turned to the historian. 'How d'you know what Crammer wants?'

'He's after Luca, it's obvious,' Naresh replied. 'He wants the paintings. Crammer's insane – he's killed six people. We have to get Luca and the painting safe.' His gaze moved back to the cylinder. '*Is* that it?'

'Of course it is. I wasn't lying,' Luca said solemnly.

Naresh put out his hands. 'Let me see.'

But before the historian could get hold of it, Gil grabbed the container and shouted for Luca to run. Then he swung the cylinder round, catching Naresh Joshi on his left temple with the metal seal. Stunned, he fell heavily, striking his head against the stone wall. As Luca's footsteps faded away down the corridor a cut opened beside Naresh's eye. His fingers went to it, his expression incredulous.

'What the hell are you doing?'

'It's you,' Gil said, still holding on to the cylinder and looking down at the historian.

'Are you insane? I've told you, Harvey Crammer's in Palermo. He's the killer–'

'No,' Gil replied. 'I wasn't sure who it was. I even thought for a moment that it might be Luca. Until you came in.'

'I came to help!'

Gil shook his head. 'No, you came to find Luca. And the painting. You *had* to get hold of Luca, or it would all be for nothing–'

'*What are you talking about?*'

'The murders.'

'I had nothing to do with them. It was Crammer.'

'No, it wasn't,' Gil replied. 'You gave yourself away just now. You said that Crammer had killed six people. But only five dealers were killed. The other person was a nurse. And Frieda Meyer was supposed to have been killed by Gary Rimmer.' He held the historian's gaze. 'You finally made a mistake. You didn't say Crammer killed five dealers, you said *six people*. Only the killer knew that.'

Silent, Naresh thought for a moment, then looked back at Gil and pointed to the cylinder in his hands.

'That painting's worth a fortune. We could come to some arrangement.'

'And then you could kill me?' Gil sighed. 'I don't think so. And besides, you threatened my family. I'm going to make sure you pay for that.'

'I only wanted to scare you!' Naresh replied, moving his legs as though he was about to stand up.

'Stay where you are!' Gil warned him.

He flopped back against the wall. 'You're wrong.'

'Why did you do it?'

'You've no proof I did anything.'

'Was it Greta?'

His eyes flickered. 'What about Greta?'

'Her parents had the Huber Gallery. You knew them – you married Greta, after all. But the marriage was a secret, wasn't it?' He stared at the fallen man. 'Did it start because they disapproved of your relationship with their daughter?'

'I'm saying nothing. I've an unblemished reputation, and a good lawyer could sort this out in a minute–'

'Only if you get out of here.'

The historian faltered, looking at Gil and remembering his reputation. In a fight, Naresh knew he had no chance. A physical coward, he resorted to his intellect.

'We can sort this out between us,' he began. 'No one need know.'

'*I'd* know, and that's more than enough. Face it, Naresh, it's over. You're not getting away with this.' He peered at the historian curiously. '*Did* it start with your animosity towards the Hubers?'

The historian touched his head again, staring wonderingly at the blood on his fingers.

'It started before Greta. That was just another reason to hate the Hubers. You should have worked it out before this,' he continued, almost admonishing Gil. 'You had the information, you just couldn't fit it together. *Der Kreis der Acht* was when it began.'

'The dealers' group. What was the matter, Naresh? They didn't invite you to join?'

'They were bigots, every one of them. I was an Indian to them, a joke. The lowest of the low. Especially Jacob Levens. He was a bastard, set up the dealer group. Didn't invite me to join although I'd known him for years. Greta didn't know about *Der Kreis der Acht*: she just hated Oscar Schultz and her uncle because of the way they treated me. But it *was* Greta who told me that Jacob Levens had given Caravaggio's portrait of Fillide Melandroni to Alma.'

'I thought Harvey Crammer's grandfather took it from the flak tower in Berlin.'

'He did,' Naresh agreed. 'But what Crammer *didn't* know was that his estranged grandfather sold it after the war. It was drifting around Europe for a while and then Jacob Levens got it. He bought it off a senile old man in Turin for virtually nothing. When the man's son found out, he threatened to go to the police. Levens bought him off, but recently the son had been blackmailing him, threatening to ruin him.'

Gil thought of Jacob Levens, drunk, blundering, cornered. 'Jacob hid the portrait in the Huber Gallery?'

'He couldn't keep it in London, so he went to Terrill Huber,' Naresh continued, touching his head. 'I feel ill. I'm hurt, really hurt.'

'Get on with it!'

'Terrill said he would hide it and in time would find a collector to sell it on, splitting the proceeds with Jacob. Alma didn't like the arrangement, she didn't want anything to do with it. But her brother blackmailed her into hiding the portrait.'

'How?'

'Greta wasn't Terrill's daughter – she was Harvey Crammer's child.'

Shaken, Gil stared at the historian. 'Does she know?'

'She found out when she overheard an argument between her mother and Jacob.'

'How did she take it?'

Naresh snorted derisively. 'It made Greta angry that her mother could be so judgemental about me when she'd acted like such a slut herself.'

'How did *you* feel about Alma Huber?' Gil asked, knowing the answer, remembering what he had felt about the murder victim: that her injuries had been inflicted by someone she knew, someone close.

'I despised her. So when Greta said the portrait was hidden in the Huber Gallery I thought it was fate.' He paused. 'I wanted the painting. And I wanted my own back on *Der Kreis der Acht*, the dealers, *and* Alma and Terrill Huber. They had all disrespected me. I thought of the portrait as recompense. I'd earned it.' He paused. 'Greta doesn't know. She never suspected anything. Her breakdown was genuine. She couldn't accept that Terrill wasn't her real father and that her mother had lied to her. After her parents' deaths, she forgot everything.'

Gil thought back to his conversation with Greta in the cafe. 'She's piecing it together now. She's remembering the past. She doesn't understand all of it, but she will in time.'

'She's innocent!'

'You married her.'

'*I loved her.*'

'And wives can't give evidence against their husbands, can they?' Gil said, gesturing at the historian. 'Empty your pockets.'

Naresh sighed, taking out a map, a pair of glasses and a handkerchief, together with an expensive wallet. His focus was blurring. 'I'm hurt, badly hurt. I could have concussion . . .' His head was humming, blood running down his cheek as he looked at Gil. 'I'm not armed, you know.'

'That was an oversight.'

'I didn't think I'd need to be,' he said, smiling wryly. 'I never thought you'd work it out. I thought I'd walk out of here with the painting. After all, I'd got away with it in

Berlin. You didn't catch me then. Why would you catch me now?' He paused, touching his temple. 'I need a doctor.'

'No doctor. Keep talking.'

'You realise that your late wife was involved with *Der Kreis der Acht*?'

Gil nodded. 'I know.'

'Oscar Schultz was her lover.'

'And her killer.'

'You think so?' Naresh could see Gil frown. 'You always suspected it, but there was talk of there being two men in Schultz's car that night. It was obvious that you and Schultz hated each other. I could see it, so could everyone else. I did you a favour getting rid of Schultz. You had to wait seven years, but he died in the end.'

'You killed him when you were looking for the painting in the Huber Gallery?'

Naresh nodded, returning to his previous theme.

'Years ago, Holly was in love with Oscar Schultz. She told him about Luca Meriss, the patient in the psychiatric hospital–'

'But Luca Meriss had come to you before and told you, in person, about the Caravaggios.'

'I know, I couldn't believe it! He wanted me to *help* him, work with him.' Naresh was breathing rapidly, blood oozing from the wound. 'I was so excited. But I didn't want to make him suspicious, so I pretended I had my reservations – and he took it as a rebuttal. Can you imagine? I had him in my hands and he escaped.'

'And you only heard about Luca Meriss again when Holly told the dealers about him.'

Naresh nodded. 'She told them one by one, apparently in confidence, never letting them know that they were all in on it. That was a very dangerous game to play, but she liked danger.'

Gil was struggling to keep his voice steady. 'How well did you know Holly?'

'Not well. What I knew of her I learnt from Greta. Holly Eckhart was just the trail of gunpowder that finally led to the whole keg blowing up.'

Gil paused, thinking over what he had just heard.

'Of course you couldn't get to Luca seven years ago, could you? He'd been admitted to hospital.'

'He was locked up. Out of reach,' Naresh said bitterly. 'And the painting was supposed to be in the Huber Gallery. That's what Greta told me. If you ask her now, she won't remember. She forgot everything when she had her breakdown.'

'So all you had to do was to find the picture.'

'Yes,' Naresh agreed. 'I confronted Terrill Huber. He blustered, then said he didn't know where the portrait was. I knew it was in the gallery!' Naresh was breathing heavily. 'But he wouldn't tell me where. I tried, I tried for a while, but he wouldn't tell me.' Naresh closed his eyes for a moment, then reopened them, staring fixedly at Gil. 'I was sick to my stomach, but it had to be done. I've no liking for violence – it's not my nature. I was forced into it.' He was convincing himself as he spoke. 'Alma was working at her desk when I went back to the Huber Gallery. She kept saying she didn't know where the portrait was, but I knew she was lying and I hit her. She fell. She died soon after. Heart attack, I think. It was quick, quicker than her husband–'

'You still tortured her.'

'Her killing had to look the same as her husband's!'

'But you couldn't bring yourself to mutilate her genitals, could you?'

He flushed, glancing away. 'I hated her, but she was a woman. There was only so much I could bring myself to do.'

Sighing, Gil shook his head. 'But you didn't find the painting?'

'No. It was all for nothing. Two deaths, all for nothing. I'd done it for revenge, but also for recompense. But I didn't get it. I never found the painting.' He shrugged. 'I had to put it all behind me, continue with my life.'

'How did you live with it?'

'I married Greta, I took care of her. I worked, built up my reputation.' He held Gil's stare. 'You had no idea, did you? Neither did the Berlin police. You thought they were just random killings – some lunatic. Which was what I wanted you all to think.'

Gil refused to be baited.

'And then Luca Meriss announced his claims on the internet,' he said, 'for you – and every other dealer in the world – to see.' He almost smiled. 'You'd thrown the salmon back in the water and suddenly everyone was on the bank fishing.'

'I'm a patient man.' Naresh continued, touching his temple lightly and then looking at his hand. 'You have to help me – I'm bleeding.'

'Good,' Gil said dismissively. 'Go on. What about the others? The Weirs? Bernard Lowe?'

'They were all members of the Berlin group. All cosy together, all after paintings which were mine by right.'

'Did the Weir brothers know where they were?'

'No! They had no idea!'

'Terrill Huber was a sick man, and Alma was a woman. You could overpower them easily enough. But the Weirs were young and fit. Was that why you used the drug?' Gil looked at Naresh with contempt. 'You're a coward. You wouldn't take them on, you *had* to make them helpless.'

'They deserved it!'

'*For slighting you?*'

'I had the finest reputation of all of them! I was the most learned, the most accomplished, and they treated me like a waiter!' He paused, regaining his composure. 'The Weirs were no good to me. It became apparent that only Luca Meriss had the information I wanted. Bernard Lowe didn't know either, but he was dying anyway. I feel no guilt for his death.'

'Jacob Levens was one of the group. Why didn't you go for him?'

Naresh took a moment to reply. 'I was saving him for the last. I wanted him to sweat, to know someone was coming for him. I wanted him to squirm. Jacob Levens is a bad man. He covers it well but he's guilty of many things.'

'Frieda Meyer was innocent–'

'She was working for Oscar Schultz! She was talking to everyone. I didn't know how much she knew, only that she was a liability. She was hard to kill . . . It had been getting easier, but she was difficult. Wouldn't die. I had trouble with her. Had to keep hitting her . . .' Naresh was smoothing the crease in his trousers, working at the material, concentrating. 'Only Meriss knows where the Berlin portrait is. Jacob Levens was lying – it was never in the Huber Gallery. We've all searched that place and there's no trace of the painting. The bastard was lying–'

'What about the disks?'

Naresh looked at Gil blankly. 'What disks?'

'The disks that Luca Meriss made. The proof.'

'I don't know about any disks.'

Gil changed tack. 'Why did you scalp the dealers?'

'Why d'you think? I was literally collecting their scalps, putting them on my belt. My own private collection of trophies.'

'Why swap them around?'

'A joke, nothing more.' He shrugged. 'I wanted to make it look like the killer was a madman.'

'He was,' Gil said curtly. 'How did you plant the drug in Luca's holdall?'

'Same way I arranged for his father to be threatened, and for a note to be delivered to Bernard Lowe. I paid someone.'

'But you did the torture yourself?'

'I wanted to do that,' Naresh replied, chillingly.

'Only because they were paralysed and couldn't fight back. You're a fucking coward. You only had the guts to kill when your victims were already half dead.'

'I'm a historian, not a thug,' Naresh replied, piqued. 'But I have to say that I thought the rabbit skin glue was an inspiration, a gesture that the dealers would have appreciated – at any other time. One of those little in-jokes they loved so much.' His bitterness rose. 'Pompous bastards. Arrogant, pretentious bastards—'

'What did it mean?'

'The German word is *Karnickel*.' Naresh smiled, pleased with himself. 'It means rabbit. And it also means *scapegoat*.' He glanced up at Gil. 'I thought someone would work that out. Someone who speaks several languages, like Harvey Crammer or Jacob Levens. All of the dealers were scapegoats in the end. *My* scapegoats.'

'Why eight wounds? It was always eight. Why?'

Naresh shrugged. 'I was born on the 8th of October. It seemed a lucky number.' He paused, looking steadily at Gil. 'You're a day early.'

'What?'

'You said you'd solve the case by Monday. Today's Sunday.' He took in a deep breath. 'How do you intend to get me out of here?'

'I'm going to walk you out, Naresh. You won't take me on, because you know you'd lose. And you want to live. You *really* want to live.' Gil shook his head. 'You're already plotting, aren't you? Working out your defence? I reckon insanity would be your best chance.'

'A mental fugue?'

'That might work for one killing, not six.'

Smiling, Naresh rested his head back against the wall, breathing slowly. Blood was sliding down his cheek and neck, his collar darkening as he gestured to the cylinder.

'Let me see it.'

'Why should I?'

'Why shouldn't you?' Naresh countered. 'I'm finished. Let me see what I did it all for.'

Gil lifted the cylinder, then took off the seal at the end, carefully sliding out a battered, discoloured canvas. He could sense Naresh Joshi holding his breath as he carefully unrolled the painting and held it up for the historian to see.

His hands went out towards it, his fingers scrabbling at the air, but before he could touch it the canvas began to crumble, paint flaking off, a long tear travelling from the top right-hand corner and spreading across the body of the work. In seconds *The Nativity with St Lawrence and St Francis* was destroyed, the faces of Mary and the saints crumbling, the masterpiece returning to dust under the dry, blind gaze of the long-dead monks.

Ninety-Four

Harvey Crammer was in the middle of packing when Gil knocked on his hotel door. Smiling, he let him in, moving back to his suitcase. On the bedside table was a selection of books, one opened, his reading glasses resting on top of an illustration of Caravaggio's *Penitent Magdalene*.

'Thanks.'

'Oh, you didn't really need me,' Harvey replied, smiling his frog's smile. 'After I called them you handed Naresh Joshi to the police on a plate. Luca was scared but he's OK now. Wanted me to thank you. I imagine he'll do that in person anyway.'

'And then I'll have to tell him about the painting.'

Crammer shrugged. 'Well, it's a tragedy, but in the end it's a picture, not a life.'

'A picture that cost six lives.'

'But no more,' Crammer said crisply. 'What a waste of effort for nothing. I don't suppose it could be restored?'

'Not unless you know a magician, no.'

'Dust to dust, like everything else.' Crammer looked away

for a moment, occupied by his own thoughts. Finally he turned back to Gil. 'Did you know it was Naresh all along?'

'No. He gave himself away, slipped up. To be honest, I suspected everyone at some time.'

'Even me, I recall.'

Gil smiled wryly. 'I knew it had to be someone with no family, someone who travelled a lot. Someone no one really got close to, because they wouldn't have been able to hide what they'd done. I didn't know you had a daughter then.'

Crammer folded a jacket into his suitcase and then sat on the side of the bed. 'Go on, ask me.'

'Did you know you were Greta's father?'

'Of course I did. That's why I was always so close to Alma. We kept our affair a secret. She fell out of love with Terrill and these things happen.' He was resigned. 'Alma wanted a secure home, a family. I could never give her that. I'm a wanderer – I couldn't settle. Her getting pregnant was an accident, but a blessing too. She had the child she longed for, and she knew I was always there for her.' He paused, taking a moment to continue. 'Only I wasn't always there for her. Not at the end.'

'Is that why you joined *Der Kreis der Acht* – to keep an eye on her?'

'I knew Alma wasn't keen on the idea of the collaboration. She mistrusted the dealers and she knew Terrill could be greedy. But she was forced into it by her brother and now I know why.' His tone was bitter. 'Alma never told me that Jacob was blackmailing her about Greta. So in answer to your question – yes, I joined the group to keep close to Alma and to keep an eye on the others.'

'But that's not really true, is it? You had other reasons to stay close,' Gil said, catching the surprise in Crammer's face. 'You were the first one to know about the Caravaggio portrait. It was a story that had been passed down in your family for generations. You say it was a joke, but it never was, was it?'

'I don't know what you mean.'

'Where is it?'

'Pardon?'

'The portrait of Fillide Melandroni. You're a dealer, and a collector – I know how your mind works. The only way you could be so relaxed about the ruined *Nativity* is because you have the other Caravaggio,' Gil continued as Crammer watched him silently. 'I know it left your family's hands and came to Jacob Levens. And I know that he had to hide it because he was being threatened with exposure. He gave it to Terrill in Berlin and he hid it in the Huber gallery.' Gil caught a fleeting expression in Crammer's eyes and back-tracked. 'It wasn't Terrill who hid it! That's why he couldn't tell Naresh Joshi where it was. Because he didn't know.'

Crammer's expression was lethal. 'Do go on.'

'Alma hid it. Of course – that's why she was so scared! She was worried for Terrill and her daughter and she knew the bloody painting would open up a can of worms. Which it did when my late wife found out about Luca Meriss and tried to play the dealers off against each other.' He paused, watching Crammer and remembering something he had been told by Greta. Something he had forgotten until that moment. 'Did you organise the installation of the safe at the Huber Gallery?'

'Yes, I did. I helped Alma with many things. Terrill wasn't a practical man,' Crammer said smoothly. 'So what?'

'That safe's a hell of a size.'

'It had to be, so it could hold paintings if necessary, as well as documents.'

Gil shook his head.

'Of course there's nothing in it now. And there was nothing hidden under it either. I know that – it was checked out by the police. And there was nothing hidden behind it.' He was thinking, remembering. 'But someone had been looking. I saw the dust on the top had been smudged. Was it Meriss? Or was it Oscar Schultz?'

Crammer shrugged. 'How would I know?'

'Oh, but you do,' Gil replied, walking round the room, Crammer's gaze following him. 'You called in the police this morning. You helped me. And you saved Luca Meriss. Why? You've always been looking out for him, haven't you? You were in New York when Luca fell out with Catrina Hoyt.'

'It's true. I've tried to help him as far as he'd let me,' Crammer admitted. 'I didn't want anything to happen to him.'

'Why?'

'Because of Alma!' His heavy features tightened. 'I'd failed her. I didn't want another death on my conscience if I could do something to prevent it. Meriss was an innocent, a fool that had got in over his head. You only had to look at him to know he was vulnerable.'

'Like Alma?'

He nodded curtly. 'Yes, like her. Luca wasn't kidnapped from the hospital where he was hiding out. I arranged to have him moved, for his own safety. I never expected him to jump out of the back of the bloody ambulance.'

'He thought he was going to be killed. Why didn't you explain to him what you were going to do?'

Crammer was impatient.

'Because he didn't trust me! We'd met in New York and Luca was panicking. Didn't trust anyone, even though I offered to help more than once. In the end all I could do was watch out for him.' He sighed. 'I could see the way it was going – the murders, everyone desperate for the Caravaggios and after Luca Meriss. It was becoming a bloodbath and he didn't see it until it was too late. He thought the pictures were his guarantee of safety. They weren't – they were his death warrant.'

'And you did all of this out of the kindness of your heart?'

'You've a bitter soul,' Crammer shot back. 'Or are you just sickened by the art world? I wouldn't blame you – it's a pit of deceit. But you must understand something. I didn't have to kill anyone to get to the portrait in Berlin. I always knew where it was.'

Gil stared at him. 'How?'

'Because I was the one who hid it.'

Ninety-Five

Van der Las Gallery, London

Stuart Lindsay was smoking a cigarette, flicking ash onto the ground outside the back door of the basement. When a shadow fell over him, he shielded his eyes and looked up.

'About bloody time,' he said, recognising Gil as he walked down the steps. 'You take a while to pick up your messages. I was worried–'

'You said that someone threatened you. I'm sorry,' Gil said. 'I never thought it would come to that. I didn't think anyone knew I'd even been here.'

Stuart pulled a face. 'I got him, you know. Well, I think I did . . . maybe I didn't. Maybe I just threw the acid on his clothes. After all, you'd have noticed someone with face or neck burns, wouldn't you?'

Gil shrugged. 'It doesn't matter.'

'Doesn't now. You got him.'

'I got him,' Gil agreed.

'Naresh Joshi. Who'd have thought it?' Stuart smiled. 'How's Bette?'

'Due to give birth any minute. Impatient, glad to have me back. Begging me never to take on another case.'

'You wouldn't, would you?'

'Christ, no,' Gil replied. 'Is the proof still in the bank?'

'Yes. Locked away in the Van der Las security box. What are you going to do with it?'

'Give it back to Luca Meriss. It was his originally, so he should decide what happens to it.'

'I hope he doesn't flog it on eBay.' Stuart ground out the stub of his cigarette with the heel of his boot. 'You're all done then?'

'No, not yet. I came back to see Bette, and Jacob Levens. But he's disappeared. Left the gallery without a note or anything. Same with his flat. The man's gone.'

'Dead?'

'If he is, Naresh Joshi didn't do it.'

'Perhaps he's committed suicide?'

'No, he was too sly for that.'

Gil remembered the disks that no one had ever found, or even appeared to know about – apart from Levens, Luca Meriss and Holly. He thought of his late wife: the woman he had grieved for, the woman Bette resented, the woman whose recklessness had detonated a maelstrom. Holly Eckhart, devious but outclassed by men more ruthless than herself. A victim.

Gil cringed at the thought. How she would have hated to

be viewed like that, as someone out-manoeuvred and outsmarted. And for all her deception and betrayal of him Gil felt oddly forgiving. Holly had died with nothing, murdered by a man she had loved. Whereas Gil had a new wife, and a child about to be born.

'What if Jacob Levens washes up on some beach somewhere?' Stuart asked. 'He might.'

'No, Jacob's clever. People like that keep ducking and diving – they don't give up.'

Stuart watched as Gil moved to the door. 'You going home now?'

'No, not yet. I've still got one loose end to tie up, then it's done. I'm going back to Berlin. I have to settle something. After that, it's finished. No more investigative work.'

'You sure about that?'

'Oh, I'm sure,' Gil replied firmly.

'Funny to think that Luca Meriss was kosher, after all. Think about it – the living descendant of Caravaggio.' Stuart looked at Gil, curious. 'What? You don't believe it?'

'I think Luca believes it. And who'd risk their life for a fantasy? But no one can prove it for certain.'

'No one can *disprove* it either,' Stuart replied smartly. 'It's a great story. Should get Luca Meriss some bookings on the chat-show circuit. Even money he writes a book.' He warmed to his theme. 'I mean, no one will dare to harm a hair on his head now, will they? He can make a nice living out of being a victim. Although, to be honest, he's not exactly what you'd expect.'

Gil frowned. 'How d'you mean?'

'Caravaggio was the hard man of painting. Like someone once said, he's "the resident thug of art history". But Luca Meriss is the polar opposite. People tried to kill Caravaggio, and he fought back. It was almost a blood sport around Italy then – killing Caravaggio. Strange that the same thing happened to Luca Meriss. Only difference is that Caravaggio toughed it out himself, whereas Meriss relied on others to protect him.' Stuart inhaled again, then exhaled, making smoke rings in the London air. 'It's just odd, that's all.'

'What's odd?'

'That Caravaggio was famous for his talent, whereas Luca Meriss is going to be famous just for having some of his genes.'

Monday

Ninety-Six

Huber Gallery, Berlin

Head lowered against the freezing temperature, Gil walked down the Friedrichstrasse. Across the street cars were queuing, waiting for the traffic lights at a busy junction to turn from red to green. His eyes fixed on the lights as his thoughts went back seven years. Alma and Terrill had been murdered and Jacob Levens was calling him in to investigate. Had it been Holly's idea? *Bring in Gil*, she might have said. *He's my husband. No one will suspect us of anything if he's working on the case.* It would have been like her to suggest it. Like the Holly he had grown to know. How she was in other people's eyes, not his. And all the time Gil had been duped, Holly had been plotting, and in the end it had all come to nothing.

He stared at the traffic lights on the corner and remembered her car smashed into a window nearby. The metal had caved in, pinning Holly inside, and rain had started to fall, chilling that late night. Her face had been covered in blood, her arm broken across the wheel, her left eye swollen, her right eye closed. The police said she had been caught out, sideswiped, by Oscar Schultz. An accident. A tragedy.

It certainly had been for her.

Sighing, Gil continued on his way to the Huber Gallery. Harvey Crammer was already waiting by the door and let him in.

'I saw you coming.'

'Let's make it quick, can we?' Gil asked. 'I need to get back to London.'

He followed the big man into the gallery, crossing the main floor and entering the office at the back. Inside, it was warm as Crammer offered him a whisky.

'Take it, it's not poisoned,' he joked. 'Remember, you've caught the killer.' He watched Gil take a sip and leaned back against the desk. 'The gallery's mine now.'

'Lucky you.'

A noise outside startled them both, a car's brakes screeching. Crammer went to the window and looked out into the street, towards the traffic lights. 'It's that bloody corner. Always been dangerous.' He turned back to Gil, returning to his previous subject. 'As I said, the gallery's mine. That was part of the arrangement with *Der Kreis der Acht*. The place was to stay in our possession. If anything happened to the other dealers, the last one inherited it.'

Gil looked at him curiously. 'Quite a motive. I don't suppose he meant to, but Naresh Joshi did you a favour.'

'I certainly wouldn't kill for this gallery.'

Hesitating, Gil stared at the whisky in his glass as Crammer downed his drink in one.

'Not for the gallery perhaps – but for what's in it.' He glanced at Crammer. 'Where's Jacob Levens? I mean, he was one of your group and he's not dead. So why isn't he claiming his stake? He isn't usually a man to miss out on anything.'

'I've no idea where Levens is. Mind you, he had money abroad, so he's probably heading for Switzerland as we speak.' Crammer gestured to the glass. 'Want a top-up?'

'No.'

'You're very edgy.'

'I want to finish this case and get home.'

'Your wife's due any time, isn't she?'

'Yes,' Gil replied cautiously. 'How did you know she was pregnant?'

'I heard,' Crammer said, changing the subject. 'Luca's quite the hero. Giving interviews already. I imagine he'll be very famous soon. Of course, his story would be more interesting if he could have presented the world with both the Caravaggios. But still, there are remnants from *The Nativity with St Lawrence and St Francis* to prove what he said. A few vignettes, which can be preserved and exhibited. Along with the lurid tale of the insane Naresh Joshi.' Crammer smiled his wide, reptile smile. 'He had a brilliant mind, but he was over-educated for a serial killer. I heard he left Greta well provided for. She'll be rich–'

'And infamous.'

Crammer shrugged. 'D'you think she knew that Naresh killed her parents?'

'No.'

'But she had a breakdown.'

'I still don't think she knew. She blocked everything out. But one day it might all come back, and then . . .' He shrugged. 'It'll be hard for her if it does. She trusted Naresh.'

'You trusted your late wife.'

Gil bristled. 'I don't have time for this! You said you hid the Caravaggio in this gallery. That's what I'm here for. To finish this bloody case. Did you hide the painting?'

'I did.'

'I want it.'

'I'm sure you do,' Crammer replied. 'Why?'

'Luca Meriss knew it was here. Prove him right. He wants to exhibit the portrait, show it off to the world. After all, he's claiming to be a descendant of Caravaggio and Fillide Melandroni. The portrait's special to him.'

'Apparently she was a great whore.'

Gil ignored the comment.

'Luca wants to be Caravaggio's mouthpiece for the twenty-first century,' he continued. 'And he's got proof of what he's claiming, the paintbrush and note. They're authentic. So let him have the painting. He'll give it back to the Italian people–'

'And where does that leave me?'

'The hero. You could say you'd hidden it for safe keeping. After all, you can't sell it, can you? It's too well known to broker–'

'I thought you knew the art world,' Crammer retorted slyly. 'I could sell it to a private dealer tomorrow. So what if the world never saw it? The owner would have it all to himself, and that's what people want – exclusivity.'

'It cost six lives!'

'On the contrary. Naresh Joshi killed for revenge. The paintings were secondary to him.'

Exasperated, Gil looked around. 'So what am I doing here?'

'Think of it as a reward,' Crammer replied, moving towards the stairs. 'Come on, follow me!'

Together they moved into the upper offices, Gil remembering how he had broken into the gallery the first time and been locked in the cellar with the dead Schultz on his next visit. But now the office was empty, the door of the massive safe hanging open.

Crammer gestured to it. 'Get in.'

'What!'

'Only joking!' he replied, laughing and walking towards the safe. Then he pointed behind it. 'The painting's here.'

'No, it isn't,' Gil replied, keeping his distance. 'I looked behind the safe. Others people did too and none of us found anything.'

'I tell you, it's here.'

'No, it can't be. We all looked.'

Sighing, Crammer knelt down, the fingers of his right hand picking at the base of the skirting board. Carefully, he lifted a corner of wallpaper and began, slowly, to pull it away. He had little room for manoeuvre, but inch by inch Gil could begin to see the corner of a canvas being uncovered.

He jumped forward, crouching down. 'Is that it?'

'You can see for yourself.' Crammer turned to look at Gil. 'Behold, Caravaggio's portrait of his lover and muse, Fillide Melandroni.'

Gil was leaning forward, looking down at the edge of the canvas, when he glanced towards Crammer – and froze. The collector was struggling, leaning at an odd angle, his head bent, revealing a part of his neck which would usually be covered. There was a small, angry burn on the skin. A recent acid burn.

Gil breathed in, watching as Crammer lifted more of the wallpaper. The outline of Fillide Melandroni's hand holding the jasmine cane into view – luminous, even in the shaded light behind the safe.

'That's all I can show you for now,' Crammer said, standing up and brushing the dust off his hands. 'But it's there, safe as houses. Has been for years. Hidden away.'

'You hid it when you got the safe.'

Crammer nodded. 'Alma had this office redecorated. I'm not usually very handy, but when the decorators left that night, I took the painting off its stretcher and laid the flat canvas on the wall. Then I put another piece of wallpaper over it – taking care only to plaster the sides down, I wouldn't have wanted to get common glue on a masterpiece.' He was bragging. 'In the morning the safe arrived and was put in place. No one could move it after that.' He smiled, pleased with himself. 'People always look for the obvious. That something will be hidden behind, on top, or under something. Never that it's in plain sight, disguised to look like something else.'

'Like people,' Gil said coolly.

Crammer nodded. 'The cleverest people consist of layers. They're not just one personality, one character, but different levels of temperament: glazes of moods, perceptions, attitudes. Intelligent people shift, alter.'

'Dupe.'

Crammer shook his head. 'No, they challenge.'

'They manipulate.'

'If you like,' Crammer agreed. 'But what's manipulation anyway? The exploiting of one person's weakness to another's advantage.'

'You say it like it's a good thing.'

'Some people need guiding.'

'Some people need putting away,' Gil replied.

'You don't seem impressed,' Crammer remarked. 'You've just seen a painting the art world lusts after.'

'I saw another Caravaggio yesterday – which fell apart. Seen one, seen them all.' Gil was being deliberately provocative and Crammer bristled.

'You're a smug bastard, Eckhart. But you predicted you'd have it all sewn up in a week. Well, today's Monday. Don't renege on your promise.'

'What are you talking about now?'

'You just need the last piece of the puzzle,' Crammer

replied, 'and I want to give it to you. Think of it as a bonus. You were very clever. A bit slow at times, but you certainly picked up towards the end.' Gil frowned, watching Crammer as he continued. 'It was complicated, I thought I'd fooled you, but you got there. Diligence is an admirable quality in a man.'

Gil faltered, taken aback. '*You can't be the killer*. Naresh Joshi confessed, he admitted what he'd done.'

'Yes. He admitted what he'd done . . .'

The moment shimmered between them.

'*But you planned it*,' Gil said at last. 'You plotted it out. Played them all, didn't you? Of course you did. You knew every one of your victims intimately.'

'Not victims. I didn't kill them.'

'No, you got Naresh Joshi to do the work for you.' Gil paused, studying the big man in front of him. 'How long did you plan this? Years? Decades? You knew Naresh was hypersensitive, prone to hysteria about his origins, terrified of being snubbed. For all his learning, the art world patronised him. You worked on that. You made sure that *Der Kreis der Acht* rejected him, cut him out. And of course his affair with Greta played into your hands perfectly. Naresh resented her parents' disapproval and that was one more rebuttal.' Gil stared at him. 'But he killed Alma. You loved her–'

'Which was the reason why I had to destroy Naresh Joshi,' Crammer said coldly. 'I never thought he'd hurt her. I knew he'd go for Terrill, but Alma? You don't kill women.'

'You goaded him into it.'

Crammer was genuinely surprised. 'It wasn't all my fault. Naresh had it in him, the violence, or he could never have done it.'

'You played him.'

'*I guided him.* I admit that after he killed Alma it was easy. I wanted to see him in hell then. I wanted him in so deep he could never get out.'

'And you knew how to drag him down further and further, didn't you? How to make him *keep* killing. You knew the dealers better than anyone. Knew that Oscar Schultz was sly, but a thorn in Naresh's side. He refused to work with him, I remember now. As for Jacob Levens, he'd insulted Naresh Joshi for years. I imagine the Weir brothers—'

'They were a vicious wolf pack, all of them,' Crammer interrupted. 'The Weirs were arrogant and corrupt, Bernard Lowe was smuggling – with your wife – and Oscar Schultz was scared witless. It was so easy to keep them in line because they all had so much to hide. Once the murders started, Schultz and Levens panicked. They didn't know where to turn. Dealers aren't cage fighters, you know.'

'But it took you *seven years.*'

Crammer sighed. 'Longer, actually. It took seven years from when I heard about Naresh's affair with Greta Huber. After that, it was easier, I could manipulate Naresh, prey on his weaknesses.'

'But if you knew where the portrait was all along—'

'I didn't know where *The Nativity* was though, did I?' Crammer countered, surprised that Gil hadn't already worked it out. 'I wanted the gallery and *both* paintings. That's when I had to wait for Luca Meriss. Had to be patient – for seven long years – until he came out of hospital. I was going to pay him to give me the information, but the bloody fool went public and it turned into a free-for-all.'

'And when the dealers were all running around after the Caravaggios you created a serial killer? Got close to Luca so you could get hold of *The Nativity* and goaded Naresh to kill the dealers off so you'd inherit this place – and the painting in it.'

'And it worked.'

'Now what?' Gil asked, keeping his distance. 'You've told me what you've done – you can't expect me to keep quiet.'

'You have no choice,' Crammer replied, looking around the office. 'All good generals have strategies. All of them know how to wait, to plan for the outcome they want. I thought of it as a war, a personal campaign. And I took my time.'

'Was it you who put the clock on Meriss's website?'

'No,' he smiled, 'that was Naresh. He liked to be dramatic sometimes. To ratchet up the tension. He knew it would make the dealers panic even more.'

'Did he attack Luca Meriss in his flat in Berlin?'

'I don't know about that. Perhaps it was a little fantasy on Meriss's part? A little leverage with Catrina Hoyt? But I know Naresh hired someone to break into Catrina's gallery.

He had to make sure that if anyone checked, he was in India at the time, so he'd have an alibi. He was meticulous: he enjoyed baiting his tormentors. Started adding little flourishes, like sending photographs that spooked Catrina Hoyt—'

'But Naresh didn't kill her.'

'No, of course not! She was only important when Luca Meriss went to her for help. She wasn't a member of *Der Kreis der Acht*. Naresh had no grudge against her.'

'Just one thing still puzzles me: why did Naresh Joshi give up so easily?' Gil asked. 'He didn't put up any fight.'

'Of course not. He's a physical coward and besides, the game was up. He knew he'd gone as far as he could. He missed getting to Jacob Levens, but when Luca returned to Palermo, Naresh had to follow. When you cornered him he had nothing left. If I'm honest, I think it probably came as a relief.'

Gil shook his head. 'You're responsible for six deaths.'

Crammer raised his eyebrows. 'I didn't do anything. I wasn't the killer.'

'You incited murder. You can't get away with it.'

'But I already have. Only you know, and you won't speak out. Soon you won't be able to say *anything*.' He put his great head on one side, taunting Gil. 'That whisky you drank, it was drugged. Same drug Naresh used on the others. Before long you'll find your muscles tightening. Then you'll become slowly paralysed. Without help, your lungs will close down and you'll suffocate. By the time I've left this place with the painting you'll be close to dying.' He was watching Gil impassively. 'By the time I catch my plane you'll be dead.'

The words jammed in mid-air as Crammer relished his moment of triumph.

'You had to boast, didn't you?' Gil said at last. 'People like you always need applause, need to explain what they've done. It's the criminal's Achilles heel – their arrogance. You *had* to tell someone, even an audience of one.'

'But you won't be able to tell anyone else, will you?' Crammer replied. 'Think of it as a kindness. I had to let you know how it was done. You'd worked so hard, you deserved it. I mean, you caught the killer and you solved the case. On Monday, just as you predicted. It's a shame you won't be able to enjoy your triumph, but I felt honour bound to let you have the whole story.'

'And let me know you were the puppet master?'

Crammer moved closer towards him. 'I'd sit down if I were you. It'll be easier when the drug kicks in.'

Gil slid into the chair beside the desk, his voice low. 'How long will it take?'

'Ten minutes, then a further half an hour to paralyse you completely.' Crammer paused, giving him a warning look. 'I intend to stay here until you're helpless. It would be silly to risk anything now.' He glanced around. 'My bag's already packed and my flight's booked. All I have to do now is to get the painting out.'

He turned away from Gil and moved back to the safe. Bending down, he began to carefully lift the wallpaper away from the wall. Working in a confined space, it was a struggle for him to loosen it and release the canvas, but after a little while he began to ease the painting out from behind the safe. Finally, after ten further minutes, he laid the image on the floor at Gil's feet. Fillide Melandroni had deserved her reputation; she had been beautiful, her face showing no sign of the aggressive street brawler. Instead she was placidly perfect, cupping jasmine in her hand.

'Jasmine is a sign of immortality, you know,' Crammer offered, glancing over at Gil. 'It was code, a way for Caravaggio to imply her true nature.' He stared at the painted face. 'This is worth a great deal of money and luckily I have a collector waiting to buy it. Seven years isn't that long to wait for such a fortune. Not when I have the rest of my life to enjoy the proceeds.'

'But you don't,' Gil said calmly.

'What?'

'You don't have the rest of your life. You have half an hour. Maybe longer, if I get help.'

He could see the colour leaving Crammer's face.

'Yes, that's right,' Gil said. 'The whisky you gave me – I didn't drink it. You did.'

Ninety-Seven

Crammer's heavy features flushed, his hand going to his throat, panic just under the surface.

'I saw you drink it!'

'You saw me pretend to take a sip.' Gil paused. 'Remember the car outside, braking and sounding its horn at the lights? You turned away for a moment and I swapped the glasses.' He nodded. 'Yes, you drank it.'

'Get an ambulance!'

'No need. The police are due any minute now.' He gazed at the historian, at the glowering man who was slumped on his knees on the floor, the portrait in front of him. 'Take a good look at the painting, Crammer. Remember Fillide Melandroni's face, because after today you won't see it again.' He pointed to the canvas. 'That's the painting you wanted so much. The one you planned for, the one that took seven years to get hold of and cost six lives.' He bent down towards the terrified man. 'What's to stop me calling off the police? I could tell them not to make a wasted journey. That I don't need them after all.'

Crammer was sweating, his legs twitching as the drug took effect.

'I could let you become slowly paralysed. I could even leave you alone here. You could die . . . I mean, that's what you were going to do to me, so why should I save you?' He stared at Crammer, his voice deadly. 'Give me one reason why I shouldn't just walk out of here now.'

Crammer was mumbling and Gil bent closer to hear him.

'What did you say?'

Crammer murmured something under his breath, his eyes wide open, staring.

'I can't hear you,' Gil said, stepping back and shrugging. 'Anyway, I'm going home now. As far away from this fucking place as I can get. I've heard enough about the dealers to last me a lifetime, and you know what? Most of it you bring on yourselves because you're greedy and immoral.' He could see Crammer crumple and fall over onto his side. 'Body packing up on you? Well, you told the truth about that, which means you've not long to go . . . You have no idea how pathetic you look, Crammer.' Gil towered over him. 'Who's the stupid one now?'

Then he walked out, moving downstairs and leaving by the back door. Just as the police and an ambulance arrived at the front.

Porte Ercole, Tuscany
1610

He was running. At noon, under the fearsome heat of the midday sun, the white light making a platinum haze around the buildings. The sea was molten, raw silver, no birds settling on the white glass surface. The pardon had been granted and was on its way. Within days, possibly even hours, Michelangelo Merisi da Caravaggio would be pardoned.

He had made his way to Porte Ercole the previous evening, ready to take the boat back to receive the pardon. His face, puckered from infection and old sores, he kept covered, a hat over his head so that no one could point out the painter Caravaggio. Say – 'there he goes, disfigured, mutilated, the sword used against him for once.' Mockery was not to be tolerated. No one mocked Caravaggio.

He moved along the shoreline. The fear he had denied for so long, which had punctuated his days and nights, was still there, in his bones, his muscles. Nerve memory. His legs were weak, his face flushed, but he had dressed himself in a doublet and black hose, his sword at his belt, his beard trimmed with a pair of rusty scissors. I am Caravaggio, he told his reflection in the mirror. No one can kill me. No one can take my blood.

I am alive.

Breathing with difficulty, he paused, shielding his eyes from the sun as he looked out to sea. And then he spotted it – the felucca. The boat on which he had booked his place. The boat which had been due to leave that afternoon. Caravaggio gasped, taking in the hot air, beginning to run. The felucca had all his possessions on board – his paintings, everything he owned – and it had left without him.

He ran. He ran so fast that his hat fell off, the sun burning his face and the wound, waving his arms frantically to try to catch the attention of someone on board. The heat smouldered on the sand, on the sea, on the blinding white sail of the departing ship.

And Caravaggio fell.

He fell, breathing hard, the heat and the fever taking him down. He fell on the shore, on the boiled white sand, under the midday sky, his arms flung out to his sides, his twisted face turned upwards to the wild Italian sun.

On 18 July 1610, the artist Michelangelo Merisi da Caravaggio died of fever at Porte Ercole, Tuscany. He left behind some of the greatest works of art ever created. He left behind his enemies and his assassins. He left behind a life of fame and violence. And he left behind the pardon that had finally come from Rome.

The order that had gone out for the killing of Caravaggio had failed.

But in its place, a legend had begun.

Epilogue

London
Nine months later

While Harvey Crammer hired a brace of lawyers to prove that he had no involvement in the six murders that Naresh Joshi had committed, Luca Meriss returned to his home in Palermo. But he didn't stay there. As Naresh Joshi was held at a secure mental facility, Meriss began to do interviews for the media. His rise to fame was rapid. People were thrilled at the thought of his being Caravaggio's descendant, and his escape from death made compelling reading. Touting the brush and note around Europe and later the USA, Luca assured everyone that the painting of his ancestor, Fillide Melandroni, would be exhibited worldwide, then donated to the Italian Government. All of which made him a local hero. A man of importance, a person of status.

He had done it.

And yet he seemed reluctant to keep in contact with the man who had saved him. For a while Gil had thought it was because of bad memories, reminders of the past that the newly fledged celebrity wished to shed. He was surprised nonetheless, and news that Jacob Levens had been spotted in Milan almost led him back to the case. But Gil resisted. He had a family: all memories of his first wife, and Berlin, had been severed. As Gil promised Bette, he would never look back.

Until one Tuesday morning in May when the past looked back at him.

'Just a minute!' he called out, hurrying to open the front door and taking a parcel. Thanking the postman, he moved back into the kitchen and undid the small package.

It contained two disks. Curious, Gil put the first into the DVD machine and sat down to watch.

He hadn't seen her for years and felt a jolt go through him as he saw his dead wife. Holly was looking into the screen, talking directly at it.

My name is Holly Eckhart . . .

He tensed, relieved that Bette was out with the baby.

. . . I'm doing this as a record. Along with a copy of another disk, which is enclosed . . .

Gil looked at the second unmarked disk.

. . . I'm recording this on the sixth of June, 2007. I'm in Berlin, working with a group of dealers called Der Kreis der Acht *– Terrill and Alma Huber, Sebastian and Benjamin Weir, Jacob Levens, Oscar Schultz and Bernard Lowe. I was brought in by Bernard Lowe to smuggle art works from the Far East . . .*

Gil paused, a clammy sensation overwhelming him. He

had an sudden impulse to stop the disk, destroy it. But he didn't. Instead he kept watching.

... it was fun at first. But when I wanted to leave they stopped me.

There were noises in the background and people laughing. Holly took a moment to continue.

I've just met someone called Luca Meriss. He's at the hospital and I've been teaching him how to use a computer. He was very ill, had some kind of a breakdown, and he's got no family. Well, not in Berlin. Anyway, he told me that he was a descendant of Caravaggio and that he knows where two missing paintings are hidden.

Gil paused the disk, waited for a moment, then pressed Play again.

... I thought he was crazy at first, but I think there's something in it. I've told Oscar and he seems very interested, and then I told the others in confidence ... but I'm not sure I should have involved Luca Meriss with the dealers ...

Gil flinched at the words.

... He's a sweet man, but confused, always wants to please. That was his problem in the hospital – the doctors said he would do anything for someone he admired. And Luca adores Jacob Levens.

Luca adores Jacob Levens ... Gil stared at the machine, waiting for what was to come next.

... Maybe I'm wrong, but everything's changed here. The atmosphere is charged, everyone's whispering behind each other's backs. Alma's terrified, and to be honest, I'm scared too.

She was still staring into the camera, calm, but remote.

... I just wanted to put this on record because I think I might

have bitten off more than I can chew. Whoever finds this, watch the second tape and take action. I made two copies, but one's disappeared. Make sure this one doesn't . . .

And that was it.

Shaken by what he had just seen, Gil put in the second DVD, transfixed when he saw Luca Meriss sitting alone in a comfortable room. He seemed uncertain, shy, his hands clasped together tightly.

'I'm Luca Meriss . . .'

There was the sound of the door closing, then a moment of silence before Luca began to talk again. His voice was low, almost muffled. Gil had the distinct impression that Luca didn't know he was being filmed and that the camera had been hidden in the room.

'. . . I'm Luca Meriss. I'm a descendant of Caravaggio, the painter.'

He paused, the words sounding stilted. Almost forced.

'. . . I've got proof that no one can doubt. A paint brush and a note he wrote. They're both in my possession . . .'

Another pause, then he carried on.

'. . . I know where the two missing Caravaggio paintings are hidden. One in Berlin and one in Sicily . . .'

He turned to someone in the room with him.

'Is that OK? Am I doing it right? About having the proof, I mean.'

'It's perfect, Luca. Really good.'

Gil recognised the voice immediately – Jacob Levens. Then the dealer came into view, his portly frame upright, his expression encouraging as he looked at Luca.

'Just carry on, and say what I taught you. We have to practise

until it's just right. You're a fast learner, Luca, and you'll get your reward.'

His voice was honeyed.

'. . . we must keep this as our secret. Just you and me. I mean, you can't be too careful, can you? You never know who you can trust.'

He touched Luca's shoulder, silkily kind.

'But you can trust me. I'll help you. I'll make people see how important you really are. Just do what I say and it will all work out perfectly. Now let's go over it again . . .'

On screen, Luca nodded, then Jacob asked him a question.

'What's the proof you're talking about?'

'A brush, handed down in my family.'

Gil took in a breath as Jacob interrupted Luca.

'You told your father what to say? That he must give the brush to Gil Eckhart when he comes looking for it?'

'I told him. He'll do it.'

'Your father was paid well. He should do it.'

Unaware that he was being filmed, Jacob smiled at the nervous man.

'And the note – he must give Eckhart the note too. The one in the pouch I gave you.'

Luca nodded earnestly.

'My father knows what to do. He won't let me down.'

Jacob patted him like an obedient animal.

'Good. Good boy . . . Now, let's go through it again. It's important that people believe you, Luca. Your story must be convincing. You want to be famous? Of course you do. You've earned it. You should be recognised as Caravaggio's descendant . . .

He leaned towards the Italian, paternal, kind.

'I can make your dreams come true, Luca. Just trust me and do as I say. I know the art world, I know what they want to hear, what they want to believe. What they need to believe . . . Only a little while longer, Luca. Only a little more practice and you'll be ready. It will all be worth it in the end, believe me.'

The filming stopped suddenly, the camera shut off. Only the disk was left spinning in the DVD machine as Gil stared at the blank screen. It was obvious what had happened. Holly had told Jacob Levens about the patient in the hospital and his claims about Caravaggio. Seeing a chance to make a killing, Levens had sought Luca out – a gullible man, mentally unstable, desperate to be important. A man who would follow anyone he admired. A man with a longing that could be moulded into reality.

All Jacob had to do was to make the story airtight. Luca already knew where the paintings were, but he had to be taken seriously. And for that, he needed proof of what he said. Proof Jacob Levens had provided him with.

The note and the paintbrush *were* old, from the time of Caravaggio, but that was all. The master had never used them, never written his name in his own hand. That had been Jacob Levens' doing. It would have been simple for a dealer in the Old Masters to obtain some paint, paper and a brush from the seventeenth century. Easy for someone in the business to fabricate the proof that the unstable Luca Meriss came to believe was his real history.

Because provenance always drove a sale. A sensational story to catch the attention of the press, a figurehead, the offspring of the painter himself – no one could resist that. Jacob Levens had known that he could secure global attention based on a simple bit of fakery. But what Levens *didn't* expect was Naresh Joshi. He didn't expect that murders would follow, that a lie to elaborate the provenance of the Caravaggio paintings would cost six lives, possibly even his own.

And Holly had secretly filmed Jacob coaching Luca Meriss, making sure she had a hold over the dealer. She probably even taunted him with it. Otherwise how would Jacob Levens know about the disks? Gil imagined the scenario: Holly giving Levens a copy of the damning film, so he could watch it and know she had the power to ruin him if he didn't do what she wanted. And she had wanted money – hadn't Jacob told Gil that himself? That Holly was greedy, longing for a rich lifestyle?

And so she tried to blackmail Jacob Levens to get it . . . Another thought came to Gil in that instant: Naresh Joshi commenting on Holly's death and his intimation that Gil had been wrong in suspecting Oscar Schultz. 'Some said there had been two men in the car . . .' Gil sat down, breathing rapidly, shaken by what he had just seen and heard. Jesus, he thought, he had always suspected Oscar Schultz – *but was it Jacob Levens who had killed his wife?* Knowing that he could get away with it? That Schultz would be the main suspect?

Gil stared at the blank screen. If the disk had ever been

released to the press Jacob Levens' career and reputation would have been destroyed overnight. No wonder he had been desperate to find the stolen disks, desperate to make sure that his deception was never exposed.

Gil thought of Naresh Joshi, of Harvey Crammer, of all the murdered dealers and of the only one left behind – Jacob Levens. Scared, certainly, but always cunning. He was out there somewhere, wondering what to do next. Wondering who had the disks and what they were going to do with them.

And Gil knew then that it wasn't over. That the story that had begun in Berlin seven years earlier wasn't at an end.

He studied the bag in which the disks had been delivered but could find no postmark or return address, nothing to indicate where it had come from or who had sent it. But Gil knew he would find out. Whether he wanted to or not, he would find out.

Turning back to the machine, he started the film again, watching the familiar face and listening to the same lost voice.

'. . . *I'm Luca Meriss, the living descendant of Caravaggio, the painter. And I have proof . . .*'

Bibliography

Works

'Caravaggio' *Wikipedia, The Free Encyclopedia*, Wikimedia Foundation, Inc.

Gash, John *Caravaggio*, London: Chaucer Press, 2004

Spike, John T *Caravaggio*, New York: Abbeville Press Inc., 2010

Collections

Lost Art Library Collection of Study Photographs and Clippings, ca. 1930–2000: Sterling and Francine Clark Art Institute Records, Williamstown, MA, *The Clark Digital Collections*, http://maca.contentdm.oclc.org

Websites

Roman Catholic Imperialist. http://www.romancatholicimperialist.org

ALSO BY ALEX CONNOR

ISLE OF THE DEAD

City of Splendour

In October 1555 the Italian master Titian painted the portrait of Angelico Vespucci – a Venetian merchant whose cruelty words could not capture.

City of Secrets

When Vespucci was revealed to be the elusive monster who had been flaying young women across the city, he vanished inexplicably, along with the painting. All that remained was a chilling warning: when the portrait emerges, so will the man.

City of The Skin Hunter

Now the lost Titian masterpiece has surfaced in modern-day London, and skinless corpses are amassing across the globe. And it will fall to an unlikely man from the fringes of the art world to unravel half a millennium of myth, mystery and murder.

ALSO BY ALEX CONNOR

MEMORY OF BONES

'Floating on the water at the edge of the canal,
hardly visible, was a bundle, wrapped tightly in
a soiled white blanket.

The beam illuminated the blood-spattered wrapping –
and the place where the parcel had come partially untied.

From which a disembodied hand,
fingers outstretched,
clawed its way to the light.'

IN THE FIGHT TO POSSESS THE SKULL OF ONE OF THE
GREATEST ARTISTS
THE WORLD HAS EVER KNOWN